The Kate Redman Mysteries

Books 1-3

Celina Grace

© Celina Grace 2013

The Kate Redman Mysteries Books 1-3
Copyright © 2013 by Celina Grace. All rights reserved.
First Print Edition: October 2014

No part of this book may be reproduced, scanned, or distributed in any printed or electronic form without permission. Please do not participate in or encourage piracy of copyrighted materials in violation of the author's rights. Thank you for respecting the hard work of this author.

This is a work of fiction. Names, characters, places, and incidents either are the product of the author's imagination or are used fictitiously, and any resemblance to locales, events, business establishments, or actual persons—living or dead—is entirely coincidental.

Table of Contents

Hushabye 5

Requiem 169

Imago 323

Hushabye

A Kate Redman Mystery: Book 1

Prologue

CASEY FULLMAN OPENED HER EYES and knew something was wrong.

It was too bright. She was used to waking to grey dimness, the before-sunrise hours of a winter morning. Dita would stand by the bed with Charlie in one arm, a warmed bottle in the other. Casey would struggle up to a sitting position, trying to avoid the jab of pain from her healing Caesarean scar, and take the baby and the bottle.

You're mad to get up so early when you don't have to, her mother had told her, more than once. *It's not like you're breastfeeding. Let Dita do it*. But Casey, smiling and shrugging, would never give up those first waking moments. She enjoyed the delicious warmth of the baby snuggled against her body, his dark eyes fixed upon hers as he sucked furiously at the bottle.

She didn't envy Dita, though, stumbling back to bed through the early morning dark to her bedroom next to the nursery. Casey would have got up herself to take Charlie from his cot when he cried for his food, but Nick needed his sleep, and it seemed to work out better all round for Dita, so close to the cot anyway, to bring him and the bottle into the bedroom instead. *That's what I pay her for*, Nick had said, when she'd suggested getting up herself.

But this morning there was no Dita, sleepy-eyed in rumpled pyjamas, standing by the bed. There was no Charlie. Casey sat up sharply, wincing as her stomach muscles pulled at the scar. She looked over at Nick, fast asleep next to her. Sleeping like a baby. But where was her baby, her Charlie?

She got up and padded across the soft, expensive, sound-muffling carpet, not bothering with her dressing gown, too anxious now to delay. It was almost full daylight; she could see clearly. The bedroom door was shut, and she opened it to a silent corridor outside.

The door to Dita's room was standing open, but the door to Charlie's nursery was closed. Casey looked in Dita's room. Her nanny's bed was empty, the room in its usual mess, clothes and toys all over the floor. She must have gone into Charlie's room. They must both be in there. Why hadn't Dita brought him through? *He must be ill*, thought Casey, and fear broke over her like a wave. Her palm slipped on the door handle to the nursery.

She pushed the door. It stuck, halfway open. Casey shoved harder and it moved, opening wide enough for her to see an out-flung arm on the carpet, a hand half-curled. Her throat closed up. Frantically, she pushed at the door, and it opened far enough to enable her to squeeze inside.

It was Dita she saw first, spread-eagled on the floor, face upwards. For a split second, Casey thought, crazily, that it was a model of her nanny, a waxwork, something that someone had left in the room for a joke. Dita's face was pale as colourless candle wax, but that wasn't the worst thing. There was something wrong with the structure of her face, her forehead dented, her nose pushed to one side. Her thick blonde hair was fanned out around her head like the stringy petals of a giant flower.

Casey felt her heartbeat falter as she looked down at the body. She was dimly aware that her lungs felt as if they'd seized up, frozen solid. She mouthed like a fish, gasping for air, but it wasn't until she moved her gaze from Dita to look at Charlie's cot that she began to scream.

Chapter One

Kate Redman stood in the tiny hallway of her flat and regarded herself in the full-length mirror that hung beside the front door. She never left the flat without giving herself a quick once-over—not for reasons of vanity, but to check that all was in place. She smoothed down her hair and tugged at her jacket, pulling the shoulders more firmly into shape. Her bag stood by the front door mat. She picked it up and checked her purse and mobile and warrant card were all there, zipped away in the inner pocket.

She was early, but then she was always early. Time for a quick coffee before the doorbell was expected to ring? She walked into the small, neat kitchen, her hand hovering over the kettle. She decided against it. She felt jittery enough already. *Calm down, Kate.*

It was awful being the new girl; it was like being back at school again. Although now at least, she was well-dressed, with clean hair and clean shoes. It was fairly unlikely that any of her new co-workers would tell her that she smelt and had nits.

Kate shook herself mentally. She was talking to herself again, the usual internal monologue, always a sign of stress. *It's just a new job. You can do it. They picked you, remember?*

She checked her watch. He was late, although not by much. The traffic at this time of day was always awful. She walked from the kitchen to the lounge – *living room, Kate, living room* – a matter of ten steps. She closed her bedroom door, and then opened it again to let the air flow in. She walked back to the hallway just as the doorbell finally rang. She took a deep breath and fixed her smile in place before she opened it.

"DS Redman?" asked the man on the doorstep. "I'm DS Olbeck. Otherwise known as Mark. Bloody awful parking around here. Sorry I'm late."

Kate noted a few things immediately: the fact that he'd said 'bloody,' whereas every other copper she'd ever known would have said 'fucking'; his slightly too long dark hair; that he had a nice, crinkle-eyed smile. She felt a bit better.

"No drama," she said breezily. "I'm ready. Call me Kate."

When they got to the car, she hesitated slightly for a moment, unsure of whether she should clear the passenger seat of all the assorted crap that was piled upon it or whether she should leave it to Mark. He muttered an apology and threw everything into the back.

"I'm actually quite neat," he said, swinging the door open for her, "but it doesn't seem to extend to the car, if you see what I mean."

Kate smiled politely. As he swung the car out into the road, she fixed her mind on the job ahead of them.

"Can you tell me–" she began, just as he began to ask her a question.

"You're from–"

"Oh, sorry–"

"I was going to say, you're up from Bournemouth, aren't you?" Olbeck asked.

"That's right. I grew up there."

"I thought that's where people went to retire."

Kate grinned. "Pretty much. There's wasn't a lot of, shall we say, *life* when I was growing up." She paused. "Still, we had the beach. Where are you from?"

"London," said DS Olbeck, briefly. There was a pause while

he waited to join the dual carriageway. "Nowhere glamorous. Just the outskirts, really. Ruislip, Middlesex. How are you finding the move to the West Country?"

"Fine so far."

"Have you got family around here?"

Kate was growing impatient with the small talk. "No, no one around here," she said. "Can I ask you about the case?"

"Of course."

"I know it's a murder and kidnap case–"

"Yes. The child – baby – belongs to the Fullmans. Nick Fullman is a very wealthy entrepreneur, made most of his cash in property development. He got married about a year ago – to one of those sort of famous people."

"How do you mean?" Kate asked.

"Oh you know, the sort of Z-list celebrity that keeps showing up in Heat magazine. Her name's Casey Bright. Well, Casey Fullman now. Appeared in Okay when they got married, showing you round their lovely home, you know the sort of thing."

Kate smiled. "I get the picture."

She wouldn't have pegged DS Olbeck for a gossip mag reader, but then people often weren't what they seemed.

"And the murder?"

"The nanny, Dita Olgweisch. Looks incidental to the kidnapping at this point, but you never know. What *is* known is that the baby is missing and as it – he's – only three months old, you can imagine the kind of thing we're dealing with here."

"Yes." Kate was silent for a moment. A three-month-old baby... memories threatened to surface and she pushed them away. "So on the face of it, we're looking at the baby was snatched, the nanny interrupted whoever it was, and she was killed?"

"Like you say, on the surface, that seems to be what's happened. We'll know more soon. We'll be there in," he glanced at the sat nav on the windscreen, "fifteen minutes or so."

They were off the motorway now and into the countryside.

Looking out of the window, Kate noted the ploughed fields, shorn of the autumn stubble, the skeletal shapes of the trees. It was a grey January day, the sky like a flat blanket the colour of nothing. *The worst time of year*, she thought, *everything dead, shut down for the winter, months until spring.*

The car slowed, turned into a driveway, and continued through formidable iron gates which were opened for them by a uniformed officer. After they drove through, Kate looked back to see the gates swung shut behind them. She noted the high wooden fence that ran alongside the road, the CCTV camera on the gatepost. The driveway wound though dripping trees and opened out into a courtyard at the front of the house.

"Looks like security is a priority," she said to her companion as he pulled the car up by the front door.

He raised his eyebrows. "Clearly not enough of a priority."

"Well, we'll see," said Kate.

They both got out of the car. There was another uniformed officer by the front door, a pale redhead whose nose had reddened in the raw air. He was stamping his feet and swinging his arms but stopped abruptly when Kate and Olbeck reached him.

"DCI Anderton here yet?" said Olbeck.

"Yes sir. He's inside, in the kitchen. Just go straight through the hallway."

They stepped inside. The hallway was cavernous, tiled in chilly white stone, scuffed and marked now with the imprint of shoes and boots. Kate looked around. A staircase split in two and flowed around the upper reaches of the hallway to the first floor of the house. There was an enormous light shade suspended from the ceiling, a tangled mass of glass tubing and metal filaments. It had probably cost more than her flat, but she thought it hideous all the same. The house was warm, too warm; the underfloor heating was obviously at full blast, but there was an atmosphere of frigidity nonetheless. Perhaps it was the glossy white floor, the high ceilings, the general air of too much space. A Philip Starke chair stood against the wall, looking as though it had been carved out of ice.

"Mark? That you? Through here."

They followed the shout through into the kitchen, big on an industrial scale. It opened out into a glass-walled conservatory, which overlooked a terrace leading down to a clipped and manicured lawn. Detective Chief Inspector Anderton stood by a cluster of leather sofas where a woman was sitting, crouching forward, her long blonde hair dipping towards the floor. Kate looked around her surreptitiously. The place stank of money, *new* money: wealth just about dripped from the ceilings. It *must* be a kidnapping. *Now, Kate,* she chided herself. *No jumping to conclusions.*

She had only met the Chief Inspector once before, at her interview. He was a grey man: steel grey hair, dark grey eyes, grey suit. Easy to dismiss, at first.

"Ah, DS Redman," he said as they both approached. "Welcome. Hoping to catch up with you later in my office, but we'll have to see how things go. You can see how things are here."

He gave her a firm handshake, holding her gaze for a moment. She was surprised at the sudden tug of her lower belly, a pulse that vanished almost as soon as she'd registered it. A little shaken, it took her a moment to collect herself. The other two officers had begun talking to the blonde woman on the sofa. Kate joined them.

Casey Fullman was a tiny woman, very childlike in spite of the bleached hair, the breast implants and the false nails. Kate noted the delicate bones of her wrist and ankles. Casey had bunchy cheeks, smooth and round like the curve of a peach, a tip-tilted nose and large blue eyes. These last were bloodshot, tears glistening along the edge of her reddened eyelids.

"I don't know," she was saying as Kate joined them. Her voice was high, and she spoke with a gasp that could have been tears but might be habitual. "I don't know. I didn't hear anything and when I woke up, Dita," she drew in her breath, "Dita wasn't there. She would normally be there with a bottle and Ch- and Ch-"

She broke down entirely, dropping her head down to her bare knees. There was a moment of silence while Kate watched the ends of Casey's long hair touch the floor.

Anderton began to utter some soothing words. Kate looked around, her eye attracted by a movement outside on the terrace. A man was walking up and down, talking into a mobile phone, his free hand gesticulating wildly. As Kate watched, he flipped the phone closed and turned towards the house. He was young, good-looking and, somewhat incongruously given the early hour, dressed in a suit.

"Sorry about that, I had to take it," said Nick Fullman as he entered the room. Kate mentally raised her eyebrows, wondering at a man who prioritised a phone call, presumably a business matter, over comforting his wife after their baby son had been kidnapped. *Not necessarily a kidnapping, Kate, stop jumping to conclusions.* She thought she saw an answering disapproval in Olbeck's face.

Anderton introduced his colleagues. Nick Fullman shook hands with them both, rather to Kate's surprise, and then finally sat down next to his sobbing wife.

"Come on, Case," he said, pulling her up and encircling her with one arm. "Try and keep it together. The police are here to help."

Casey put shaking fingers up to her mouth. She appeared to be trying to control her tears, taking in deep, shuddering breaths.

"Perhaps you'd like a cup of tea?" said Olbeck. He caught Kate's eye, and she immediately looked away. *Don't you bloody dare ask me to make it.* He looked around rather helplessly. "Is there anyone who could , er–"

"I'll make it."

They all looked around at the sound of the words. A woman had come into the kitchen. Or had she? Kate wondered whether she'd been there all along, unnoticed. There was something unmemorable about her, which was odd because she too was dressed in full business attire, her face heavily made-up, her hair straightened and twisted and pinned in an elaborate style on the top of her head.

"This is my PA, Gemma Phillips," said Fullman. There was just a shade of relief in his voice. "Gemma, thanks for coming so quickly."

"It's fine," she said with a brilliant smile, a smile that faded a little as she surveyed Casey, huddled and gasping. "It's terrible. I came as quickly as I could. I can't believe it."

"If you could make tea for us all, that would be wonderful, Miss Phillips," said Anderton.

"It's *Ms* Phillips, if you don't mind," she said, rather quickly. "Or you can call me Gemma. I don't mind."

Anderton inclined his head.

"Of course. We'd like to talk to you as well, once we've been able to sit with Mr and Mrs Fullman for a while."

He turned back to the Fullmans. Gemma shrugged and began to make tea, moving quickly about the room. Kate watched her. Clearly Gemma knew her way around the kitchen very well. What, exactly, was her relationship with her employers like? Had she worked for them long? Presumably she didn't live on the premises. Kate made mental notes to use in her interview with the girl later.

The tea was made and presented to them all. Casey took one sip of hers and choked.

"Oh, sorry," said Gemma. "I always forget you don't take sugar."

There was something in her voice that made Kate's internal sensor light up. Not mockery, not exactly. There was *something* though. Kate scribbled more mental notes.

Nick Fullman had been given coffee, rather than tea, in an elegant white china cup. He'd swallowed it in three gulps. Kate noted the dark shadows under his eyes and the faint jittery shudder of his fingers. A caffeine addict? An insomniac? Or something else?

"I heard nothing," he was saying in response to Anderton's question. "I was sleeping. I sleep pretty heavily, and the first I knew about anything was Casey screaming down the hallway. I ran down and saw, well, saw Dita on the floor."

"Do you have any theories as to who might have taken your son?"

Casey let out a small moan. Nick pulled her closer to him.

"None whatsoever. I can't believe anyone–" His voice faltered for a second. "I can't believe anyone would do such a thing."

"No one has made any threats against you or your family recently?"

"Of course not."

"Who has access to the house? Do you keep any staff?"

Fullman frowned. "What do you mean by access?"

"Well, keys specifically. But also anyone who is permitted to enter the house, particularly on a regular basis."

"I'll have to think." Fullman was silent for a moment. He looked at his personal assistant. "Gemma, you couldn't be a star and make another coffee, could you?"

"Of course." Gemma almost jumped from her chair to fulfil his request.

Fullman turned back to the police officers.

"Casey and I have keys, of course. Gemma has a set to the house, although not to the outbuildings, I don't think."

"That's right," called Gemma from the kitchen. "Just the house."

"What about Miss Olgweisch?"

Fullman dropped his eyes to the floor. "Yes, Dita had a full set."

"Anyone else?"

Casey raised her head from her husband's shoulder.

"My mum's got a front door key," she said, her voice hoarse. "She knows the key codes and all that."

"Ah, yes," said Anderton. "The security. Presumably all the people who have keys also have security codes and so forth?"

Fullman nodded. "That's right. There's an access code on the main gate and the alarm code for the house."

Kate and Olbeck exchanged glances. Whoever had taken the baby hadn't set off any of the alarms.

Casey pushed herself upright.

"What are you doing to find him?" she begged. "Why are we sat here answering all these questions when we should be out there looking for him?"

"Mrs Fullman," said Anderton in a steady tone. "I really do know how desperate you must be feeling. My officers are out there on your land combing every inch of it for clues to Charlie's whereabouts. We just have to try and ascertain a few basic facts so we can think of the best way to move forward as quickly as possible."

"It's just..." Casey's voice trailed away. Kate addressed her husband.

"Mr Fullman, is there anyone who could come and give your wife some support? Give you both some support? Her mother, perhaps?"

Fullman grimaced. "I suppose so. Case, shall I ring your mum?" His wife nodded, mutely, and he stood up. "I'll go and ring her then."

He headed back outside to the terrace, clearly relieved to be escaping the kitchen. Olbeck looked at Kate and raised his eyebrows very slightly. She nodded, just as subtly.

"You two look around," said Anderton. "DS Redman, I'd like you to talk to Ms Phillips once you're done. DS Olbeck, go and see how the search is progressing. I want the neighbours questioned before too long."

The house was newly built, probably less than ten years old. It was a sprawling low building, cedar-clad and white-rendered, technically built on several different levels but as the ground had been dug away and landscaped around it, the house looked like nothing so much as a very expensive bungalow. Or so Kate thought, walking around the perimeter with Olbeck. They had checked the layout of the bedrooms, noting the distance of the baby's nursery from the Fullman's bedroom.

"Why wasn't the baby in their room?" asked Kate.

Olbeck glanced at her. "Should he have been?"

"I think that's the standard advice. Everyone I know with tiny babies keeps them in their own bedrooms. Sometimes in their beds. Not stuck down the end of the corridor."

"I don't know," said Olbeck. "The nanny was right next door."

Dita Olgweisch's room and the nursery were still sealed off by the Scene of Crime team gathering evidence. Kate stood back for a second to let a SOCO past her, rustling along in white overalls.

"I'll ask Mrs Fullman when she's feeling up to it," she said. "Perhaps there was a simple explanation."

The view from the terrace was undeniably lovely. The ground dropped steeply away from the decking and the lawn ended in a semi-circle of woodland; beech, ash, and oak trees all stood as if on guard around the grass. Kate could see the movements of the uniformed officers as they carried out their fingertip search. Olbeck came up beside her and they both stood looking out on the scene. Kate wondered if he was thinking what she was thinking – that somewhere out in those peaceful looking woods was a tiny child's body. Her stomach clenched.

"I've never worked on a child case before," said Olbeck abruptly. Kate turned her head, surprised. "Murder, obviously. But never a child."

"We don't know that the baby's..." Kate didn't want to finish the sentence.

"I know." They were both silent for a moment. "I hope you're right. God, I hope you're right."

There didn't seem to be much else to say. They both had things to do, but for another moment, they stood quietly, side by side, looking out at the swaying, leafless branches of the trees.

Chapter Two

Kate found Gemma Phillips in what was clearly a home office, one of the smaller rooms off a corridor leading from the kitchen. There were two desks, filing cabinets, a printer and several swivel chairs. Gemma was typing busily on the keyboard of a laptop. As Kate got closer, though, she could see that all the girl was doing was updating her Facebook status. *What was she putting in her update?* Kate wondered. *Gemma Phillips...is about to be interviewed by the police.*

"Hi Gemma," she said, grabbing one of the swivel chairs and turning it to face Gemma's desk. "I'd like to have a chat, ask you a few questions, if I may?"

"No problem," said Gemma, but rather uneasily. Her long fingernails clicked on the edge of her laptop.

"You've worked for Mr Fullman for how long?"

"Um, seven years. Almost eight years."

"Quite a while then. What's he like to work for? Is he a good boss?"

Gemma looked even more uneasy. "He's okay. Bit of a slave driver, sometimes, but they all are, aren't they?"

Kate repressed her answer, which was something along the lines of no, she wouldn't know, having never been a secretary, thank God. That was mean and snobbish of her. What in God's name did she have to be snobbish about?

"Could you tell me more about him? I know he's in property development. What sort of thing does he do?"

"How do you mean?"

"Well, what sort of thing is he working on at the moment? Any particular project?"

Gemma frowned.

"Well, he's got a big residential building contract on the go. Newbuild flats over in Wallingham. Do you mean that sort of thing?"

"Yes, well–" Kate tried a different tack. "What sort of work do you do for him?"

Gemma looked at her laptop screen.

"I do all sorts. Deal with his diary, deal with his phone calls, arrange his travel. Type up the contracts and deal with the rental agencies."

"Do you do any work for Mrs Fullman?"

"A bit." Gemma sounded resentful. "Since she had the baby, she's been asking me to do more and more. That's always the way. You start off by doing someone a favour and then they take advantage."

She'd referred to the child as the baby, not Charlie. Was that significant?

"Have Mr and Mrs Fullman been married long?" Kate knew they hadn't, but she wanted to try and draw a bit more from Gemma on her employer's wife.

"Not really. Not even a year. She got pregnant before they got married."

"She was a TV star, wasn't she, before she got married?"

Gemma's lip curled. "Well, not really. She was in that reality show about the Mayfair hairdressers, that's all. She did a bit of modelling after that. She wasn't really *famous*. Not an A-lister, or anything." Kate looked her in the eye, and she flushed and dropped her head, obviously aware of the rising tone of her voice. "Anyway, she hasn't done much since the baby came."

"Charlie," said Kate. *He has a name.*

"Yes, Charlie."

Kate paused.

"How did you get on with Dita Olgweisch?"

Gemma looked stricken. Kate saw her throat ripple as she swallowed.

"I can't believe she's dead," she said, almost in a whisper. "I can't - it doesn't seem possible."

"You were close?"

"No, not really. Well, we were friendly. I mean, we'd chat and all that. I didn't really see that much of her. She was always out with the baby –with Charlie." The girl's hands were shaking. "I can't believe she's dead," she repeated.

Her distress seemed genuine. Kate observed her more closely, noting with a stab of pity that despite the carefully applied makeup, the ironed clothes, and the elaborate hairstyle, Gemma was undeniably plain. *Plain.* What a stupid, cruel word – but apt in this instance. There was something forgettable about the girl, something negligible. Was that the root of her resentment against Casey Fullman – the jealousy of the less attractive woman over the prettier one?

"Are you married, Gemma?" she asked suddenly.

Gemma flushed again. "No, I'm not. Why?"

Kate smiled, trying to put her at her ease. "Just being nosy. I'm permanently single myself."

Gemma half-smiled.

"I've got a fella," she said. "We're engaged. Practically engaged."

"Congratulations." Kate paused for a moment. "Anyway, let's talk a bit more about Dita, if it doesn't distress you too much. Are you happy to carry on?" She took the girl's shrug as assent. "How long had she been Charlie's nanny?"

Gemma thought for a moment. "Not long. Only a couple of months."

"Did Mrs Fullman need a lot of help with the baby? He's very young." In her mind's eye, Kate could see a small, crumpled face, eyes tight shut, black birth hair in a fluffy corona. She cleared her throat. "Did – did she have a difficult birth?"

"I don't know," said Gemma, looking offended. "She didn't talk about it with *me*. I don't think she even wanted a nanny, to be honest, Nick is the one who got Dita to come. It's what you do when you're rich, isn't it? Get help even if you don't need it." She clicked her fingernails on the edge of her laptop, an irritating, scuttering sound. "Nick's got money to burn. He just spends it for the sake of it."

Kate nodded. She eased forward and stood up, feeling that she'd got enough to be going on with for a while. Then she sat down again.

"What do you think happened last night, Gemma?" she asked.

"Me?" said Gemma. She looked startled, then frightened. "I don't know. How would I know?"

"Do you have any ideas at all?"

The mascara-laded eyelashes blinked rapidly. Then Gemma turned back to her laptop. Her shoulders were rigid. "Some paedo, wasn't it?" she said. She didn't look at Kate. "You hear about it all the time, paedophiles snatching kids."

"Very rarely babies, and very rarely are children taken from their own beds."

Gemma shrugged, still turned away.

"Well, you asked me what I thought," she said, with some hostility.

Kate stood up again. "And Dita?" she said.

Gemma shot her a hunted glance. Again, she looked frightened.

"I don't know," she said in a small voice. "She must have just got in – in his way."

Chapter Three

KATE AND OLBECK DROVE BACK to the station in Olbeck's car while Anderton followed them in his own vehicle. Kate stared unseeing out of the window at the bleak landscape, her mind running over her conversation with Gemma.

There was clearly no love lost between Gemma and her employer's wife, but was that significant? Probably not. So Casey hadn't wanted a nanny? Why had Nick employed one? Was it just, as Gemma suggested, that he could afford it? She dismissed the thoughts from her mind as they joined the ring road that encircled the town, knowing that they were nearly at the station.

Kate looked with interest at the buildings and people of Abbeyford. She'd taken a risk, taking a job here – she knew no one, she knew nothing about the town. Her flat was a good hour and a half's drive from the police station. Would that become a problem? She didn't want to leave her flat, she loved it, but if it was necessary for her career, then that was a step she was willing to take.

Abbeyford was a market town that had grown up around a tiny collection of medieval buildings, the last remnants of a vanished monastery that had once provided alms and charity to the poor of the county. Now the high street was lined with the usual coffee shops, charity shops, supermarkets and the odd, struggling independent store. There was a handsome Victorian town hall, a modern library, two secondary schools, and plenty of good and not-so-good pubs.

At the police station, a charmless, redbrick sixties building, Anderton assembled his team for a debriefing session. Kate, again feeling like the new girl at school, took a seat and fixed her eyes on the DCI. She was bothered again by that flash of attraction she'd had before, when he'd shaken her hand in the Fullmans' kitchen. She made an effort to concentrate on what he was saying.

"We're assuming the murder took place as incidental to the kidnapping," he said, gesturing to the crime scene photographs affixed to the whiteboard. "But should we assume that? Is it possible that the real motive for the crime was the murder of Dita Olgweisch and the kidnapping of Charlie Fullman is incidental to *that*?"

"It's possible," said Olbeck. "But where's the motive?"

"Exactly, Mark," said Anderton. "But I'm trying to make it clear that we can't take anything for granted here. It could be a kidnapping for money, although as yet there's been no ransom note or demand that we know of. It could be an abduction with a sexual motive, God forbid. It could be for another reason. Dita Olgweisch could have been killed accidentally. She could have been assisting the intruder. Or she could have been the primary target. How long had she worked for the Fullmans? DS Redman?"

Kate sat up straighter.

"Gemma Phillips says not long – two months. It seems to be Nick Fullman who employed her – I mean, it was at his request, rather than his wife's."

"Okay," said Anderton. "We'll need to talk to the Fullmans again, in much more detail. DS Olbeck, DS Redman, you'll accompany me on that trip. We'll go back this afternoon."

Kate watched. As Anderton talked, he had a habit of running his hands through his hair, tousling it roughly. For a man of fifty-plus, he had a good head of hair, grey as it was. He paced the confines of the crowded office and his team watched his every move. Kate was struck with the contrast of the last case in her previous job in Bournemouth, the murder of a middle-aged school teacher by her ex-husband. There, as the DCI had talked, her colleagues had surreptitiously checked their phones, whispered to one another, stared out of the window. Here, every eye was riveted on Anderton. Each officer sat alertly, even if leaning against their desks or straddling an office chair. *He has charisma*, she thought. *Damn.*

She dragged her attention back to what he was saying.

"Let's look into Olgweisch's background. Where did she come from, references, previous work history, does she have a boyfriend, etc, etc. Her parents have been informed and should be arriving from Poland in the next few days. They might be able to tell us more. What else?"

"The neighbours are being interviewed," said Olbeck. "As of yet, no one's seen anything of interest but it's early days."

"Fine. We'll need to collect statements from all the near neighbours, any other staff, the secretary and perhaps business associates of Nick Fullman." Anderton paused. "Do a bit of digging into his background, his business."

A DC with a head of vivid red curls raised her hand.

"Are the parents under suspicion, guv?" she asked.

There was no sound in the room, but Kate thought she could perceive a tightening of shoulders, a raised alertness in the people present. Anderton was silent for a moment. Then he spoke in a slow, deliberate tone.

"Everyone in that house – everyone with *access* to that house – is under suspicion. That goes without saying. But I don't want anyone thinking that it's an open and shut case. It's not. We have no idea, at this stage, as to what happened. But." He paused and looked around the room, looking everyone in the eye, one by one. "I can't emphasise enough how delicately we must approach this. I don't want anyone steaming in and upsetting anyone with clumsy innuendo or their own prejudices. We take it very carefully. Do you understand me?"

"Yes sir," murmured Kate, part of the chorus.

"Good." He took his hand down from above his ear, releasing his hair. "Now everyone go and get some lunch. Redman, Olbeck, meet me back here at two. Thank you all."

He didn't exactly sweep from the room, but there was a sense, when the door shut behind him, that some huge surge of energy had dissipated. Kate turned to her new desk, blowing out her cheeks. All of a sudden, she felt exhausted. An unsatisfactory night's sleep due to new job nerves combined with the early morning start, the emotional maelstrom of the case, having to present the best side of herself to all her new colleagues... she fought the urge to put her head down on the keyboard and sleep.

"Canteen?" said Olbeck, appearing at her shoulder and making her jump.

"Sorry?"

"Fancy the canteen for lunch?"

Kate grinned tiredly. "Only if you can show me where it is."

"Hasn't anyone given you the tour yet?"

"Nope. But it doesn't matter. I pick things up pretty quickly."

Olbeck looked at her appraisingly. "I'm sure you do."

They began to walk towards the door. Kate made a mental note to introduce herself to the rest of the team when they got back, as no one had yet done that either.

WHEN THEY ARRIVED BACK AT the Fullmans' house that afternoon, Gemma Phillips opened the door to them. Her elaborate hairstyle was still immaculate, her make-up still a powdery mask across her face. She showed them through to a different room, a more formal type of living room that led off the cavernous hallway.

"Casey's lying down," she said after showing them in. "She took a tranquilliser and crashed out. She's totally out of it, I'm afraid."

"We will need to talk to her," said Anderton. "But perhaps Mr Fullman could come and see us in the meantime."

"He's on a conference call at the moment." She saw the look on their faces and said hurriedly, "But I can go and get him."

"A conference call!" said Kate as soon as Gemma had left the room. "What's the matter with the guy? His baby son has been abducted, his wife's prostrated, and he still has time to take a conference call?"

"Clearly–" said Anderton but could say nothing more as footsteps were heard coming back towards them through the hallway.

When Nick Fullman entered the room, Kate was reminded of two things. One, that he was very good looking. He had the cheekbones of a male model, the tall, muscular body of a professional athlete. His height and slimness were emphasised by the excellent cut of the expensive suit he wore. Two, she disliked him. Always one to examine her feelings, she acknowledged the emotion, held it up for examination. Why? He was insensitive and work-obsessed, yes. Was that the real reason? She didn't think so.

He was a fake, that was why. Working class origins hidden under a put-on accent and middle-class trappings. She couldn't have said how she knew that, but she did. *You know that you think that because you're just the same.* Kate took a deep breath and turned her attention back to the matter at hand.

Fullman took a seat in front of the large picture window. With the light behind him, it was difficult to clearly make out his expression. Was that deliberate? Did he really have something to hide? *Everyone's got something to hide, Kate.*

Anderton asked him about the sequences of events of the previous evening, taking him back through the hours before Charlie's disappearance and Dita's body were discovered. Fullman's story was unremarkable. He'd worked until nine o'clock the previous evening, the majority of it spent at the new development's offices in Wallingham. He'd then had a drink in a nearby bar with a friend, "a business acquaintance" as he'd put it, before returning home at eleven thirty.

"We'll need to talk to your business acquaintance," said Anderton. "Can your wife or someone else confirm the time you arrived home?"

Fullman looked wary.

"Dita opened the door to me. Casey was giving Charlie a bottle or something but she came out after she'd settled him and said goodnight."

"You didn't go to bed yourself?"

"Not for another hour or so. I had some work to do."

"A long day," said Anderton in a neutral tone. As if coppers knew nothing about long days or nights of work.

Fullman half smiled. "That's the way you make money."

Anderton nodded. "I can see that you're a wealthy man, Mr Fullman. Do you think there's a possibility that your son has been kidnapped?"

"My God, I don't know."

"Has there been any ransom note? Any calls from people claiming to be holding your son?"

Fullman was shaking his head slowly. "No, no, nothing like that. Nothing at all." His phone rang suddenly, and he snatched at it, as if it were a reflexive action. After a second of staring at the screen, he pressed a button and the ringing stopped. "Sorry, what were you saying?"

"Have you received any suspicious calls? Any messages or notes or emails?"

"No. No, I don't think so." He went to the door and shouted. "Gemma! Come in here a second, would you?"

There was a quick tapping of high heels in the hallway outside, and Gemma Phillips put her head around the door. She looked flushed.

"Yes, Nick?"

"The police are asking if there's been any strange calls." He looked to Anderton as if for guidance. "About Charlie. Asking for a ransom."

Gemma's eyes widened.

"*Ransom* calls? Charlie's been *kidnapped*?"

"No, Miss Phillips," interjected Anderton quickly. "We're following up several lines of enquiry. Have there been any strange calls or messages that you're aware of?"

Gemma shook her head. She looked half appalled, half excited. "No, nothing."

Nick Fullman sat down on one of the sofas abruptly and put his head in his hands. Gemma hesitated and crossed the room to sit down next to him and put her arms around him.

"I'm so sorry, Nick," she said, rocking him. Kate watched her closely. There was something slightly unsettling about her expression, something slightly too much of the cat that got the cream.

Kate cleared her throat. "Can I get your wife, sir? Do you need a moment?"

Nick looked up and then got up, dislodging Gemma's arms. She sat back, clearly trying to appear unruffled.

"I'm all right," he said. "This is just such a nightmare. I can't believe it's happening."

Anderton nodded.

"We won't keep you much longer, sir. Could you just tell me whether Charlie has a passport?"

Nick stared. "I don't know. I don't think so. He's only three months old."

"Of course, it's not very likely, but we just have to ascertain the facts. Would your wife know?"

Nick nodded and shrugged at the same time. He sat back down on the edge of the sofa, some feet away from Gemma, staring at the floor.

"I'll check," said Olbeck.

"No, don't worry," said Kate, quickly. "I'll talk to her."

Kate found the bedroom, knocked gently at the door, and then entered the room without waiting for an answer. Given what Gemma had said, she expected to find the woman inside fast asleep, but Casey was awake and sitting up. Kate sat on the edge of the bed; it was enormous, an acre of white linen and silk coverlet and scattered pillows.

Casey Fullman sat against the padded headboard, the sheets bunched and crumpled around her raised knees. She still looked like a child, something of the pallid Victorian waif of old-fashioned Christmas cards. She was hunched forward, her shoulders rounded, her hair tucked messily behind her ears. Every so often, she took a breath that was deeper, one that was almost a groan, as if a sudden pain caught her unawares every few minutes.

Kate, keeping her face blank, was wrenched with pity for this bereft mother. Someone who'd only been a mother three months. Was that all the motherhood she'd ever know? Kate took a deep, shaken breath, suddenly stabbed with pain herself. *Get a grip.* She sat up straighter and pushed, for the umpteenth time, those memories away. She reminded herself that, despite Casey's genuine distress, there was the possibility that she was somehow involved in her son's disappearance.

"Casey," she said gently. "This must be very distressing for you so I'm sorry to have to ask you, but I have a couple of questions."

Casey hunched her shoulders even more, pulling the duvet cover closer. "Okay."

"Are you able to talk for a few minutes?"

Casey sniffed and nodded.

"Firstly, could you tell me whether Charlie–" \

At the sound of his name, Casey groaned again.

Kate hurriedly went on. "Whether Charlie has a passport?"

Casey shook her head, wiping her hand under her nose. "No. No he doesn't." She started to cry again. "Oh, Charlie..."

"Casey, I'm sorry–"

The room was filled with the sound of sobbing. A few minutes passed, and Casey seemed to struggle to pull herself together. She took a few shuddering breaths.

"Sorry," she said eventually. "I'm okay now. I know you have to ask me things."

"Thank you," said Kate. She glanced down at her notes. "Can you just take me through what happened this morning, again?"

Casey kept her eyes downcast. Her long nails picked at a loose thread on the bed throw. "I woke up about eight o'clock. The light woke me. I knew something was wrong because it was too bright. I got up and went to see where Dita was with Charlie. She normally wakes me up when he wants his first bottle." She stopped, cleared her throat. "I could see she wasn't in her room, so I went to Charlie's room and pushed open the door. I could see she was – she was – on the floor and her face was all – all wrong. And then I saw Charlie was missing."

"What happened then?"

Casey shot a quick look at her. "I screamed. I just kept screaming. I think Nick came running and he saw Dita – he shouted out something but I can't remember what – I just kept screaming for Charlie over and over again."

"What did you think had happened?"

"I don't know." Casey put a hand up to her eyes. "I wasn't thinking anything, I was just so upset, I couldn't stop screaming."

"Okay. What did Nick do?"

"Then?"

"Yes, immediately after he realised Charlie was missing – what did he do?"

"He got his phone and called the police, I think. He must have done."

"He did that straight away?"

"Yes. Yes, I think so."

Kate pulled her shoulders back, stretching out the ache in her neck. Casey's statement tallied with the one she'd given earlier. The time of the emergency call from the Fullman's house corresponded with the time Casey had given. It all seemed quite straightforward.

"You and Nick haven't been married long, have you?" asked Kate, changing tack.

Casey looked at her in surprise. "Almost a year. We got married last April."

"How did you meet?"

Casey almost smiled, her bunchy cheeks blossoming outwards. "At a party. I was in this TV show, and Nick came to the wrap party afterwards."

"That was the show about the hairdressers, wasn't it?"

"That's right. Did you see it?"

Kate would rather poke her own eyes out with a fork than watch any kind of reality TV show, but this was probably not the time to mention this. "Um, I think I may have seen it once or twice. I don't get time to watch much television, to be honest."

"Oh, right. Yeah, I guess so. Anyway, it was pretty big, lots of media attention, you know. I got quite a lot of work after it, modelling and that."

"Have you done much work lately? I don't suppose you've had time with Charlie being so young."

Casey's face clouded. "Not much. We did the *Okay* shoot after he was born. That was about the last thing." She pointed to the bedside cabinet. "There's a copy in there."

Kate retrieved the magazine. Casey took it from her and leafed through it, fairly pointlessly, as the magazine quickly fell open at the required page. Kate guessed that the article had been looked at many, many times already. Casey handed it to her.

"Very nice," said Kate. She folded it up again, not wanting to see Charlie's little pink face in the photographs. "May I keep this?"

"Sure. We've got several copies."

I bet you have, thought Kate.

She began to gently question Casey again about her relationship with Nick, their first meeting, the quick progression of their romance, their marriage. From Casey's rather hesitant answers, she gathered that neither Nick nor Casey had been exactly footloose and fancy-free when they'd got together. Still, what could you expect from these sort of people – a Z-list model and a social climber? She inwardly grimaced as soon as the thought had crossed her mind. What was the matter with her? What had Anderton said? *I don't want anyone steaming in and upsetting anyone with clumsy innuendo or their own prejudices.*

There was a knock at the door and Anderton poked his head into the room.

"Mrs Fullman, I hope you're feeling better."

"Yes," said Casey, unhappily.

"We'll be off now, but we'll be in touch very soon. There'll be a family liaison officer staying behind to support you and of course, if there are any problems, don't hesitate to get in touch. DS Redman, could you come with me?"

"Of course, sir." Kate got off the bed. Casey clutched at her arm suddenly.

"Will you find him, find Charlie? *Please.*"

Kate sat back down. "We're doing all we can, Mrs Fullman. I know it's hard to wait, but you must believe that we're doing absolutely everything we can."

Casey sagged back against the headboard. She was quiet for a moment and as Kate watched, her eyes filled with tears. She made no attempt to wipe them away and they trembled on the edge of her eyelids before sliding down her cheeks. She gasped. "Who could have taken him? I can't bear it. What if I never get him back?"

Kate leaned forward. She fought down the impulse to take Casey into her arms and rock her like the baby she was missing. "We'll get him back, Casey." She fixed the crying woman with her eyes. "We'll get him back for you."

I don't care what it takes, she added mentally.

It was nine thirty at night by the time Kate unlocked her front door. She kicked off her shoes and considered collapsing face down in the hallway before deciding to at least make it to the sofa. She sat back against the cushions, dropping her head against the back of the couch. She was so tired that if she sat there for more than a minute, she would fall asleep.

After thirty seconds, she got up, got undressed and into her pyjamas and stood by the fridge, contemplating what was inside it with little enthusiasm. *Another ready-meal heated up, then.* She made herself a hot chocolate and cradled the cup in both hands, feeling the steam gently heat her face. So comforting, like a memory of childhood, although not *her* childhood. She picked up the phone, glancing at the clock. A bit late to call, although there was always a fighting chance that her mum would still be fairly sober. She dialled.

"Hello?"

"Mum, it's Kate."

"Who?"

"It's *Kate*."

There was silence on the other end of the phone.

Kate sighed and gave in. "It's Kelly."

"Oh, hello love. What you doing calling me so late?" Her mum's voice had a trace of a slur, nothing too bad yet. Perhaps she'd even remember her conversation with her eldest daughter in the morning. Kate never knew whether her mum genuinely forgot that she'd changed her name when she was eighteen, or whether her refusal to remember was a way of signalling her disapproval.

"Coppers treating you well, are they?" Mary Redman always said that.

"Fine, thanks Mum."

"So, what's up? Why you calling me so late?"

Kate was silent for a moment. Why *was* she calling? All of a sudden, she felt like crying.

"Just wanted to make sure you were all right," she managed, after a moment.

"I'm all right, love."

In the background, Kate heard the clink of a bottle as it chimed on the edge of the glass. She sighed again, inwardly. She really needed to get some sleep. "Well, it *is* late," she said. "I'll let you go, Mum. Sorry if I disturbed you."

"Come'n see me soon."

"Will do. Night night."

After she hung up, Kate drank the rest of her cooling chocolate. She had her second shower of the day, dropped her clothes into the laundry basket, cleaned her teeth and her face, patted in moisturiser. She made the last round of the night, checking everything was neat and ordered and clean and tidy. She set her alarm for the morning. There was something to be said for going to bed dead on your feet – it stopped you thinking so much.

In her bed, clean and ironed duvet cover drawn up to her face, she remembered Casey, marooned on her giant white bed. Her last thought was of the photographs of Charlie in *Okay* magazine, his little face wrapped in sleep, tiny fists clenched. *I'll find you,* she murmured.

Unconsciousness broke over her in a grey and smothering wave.

Chapter Four

THE POST-MORTEM OF DITA OLGWEISCH took place the next morning. Kate attended with Anderton, minus Olbeck who had the unenviable task of gently questioning Dita's grieving parents. The Olgweischs had arrived on the first available flight from Warsaw that morning. Kate was heartily glad not to have that particular job – watching a corpse being dissected and examined would be the easier option.

The pathologist was a young woman of almost ethereal fairness; her white-blond hair was drawn back severely from a central parting, a hairstyle which emphasised her wide forehead and long, narrow nose. With her pallor, her colouring and her extreme thinness, she looked a suitably macabre doctor of the dead. But Doctor Telling, despite her bizarre appearance, was deft and gentle in her examination, explaining her findings in a quiet, measured tone. Her skilled fingers had repaired some of the damage to Dita's face, and Kate was glad, knowing her parents would soon be seeing the body.

"The blow to the head is what killed her, as you can probably see," said Doctor Telling. "Someone swung something hard into her right temple. I'm not sure what yet. Whatever it was fractured her skull and caused severe traumatic damage. It would have been instantaneous."

"I'm assuming that it was a deliberate blow?" said Anderton.

"You would assume correctly. Of course, we can't possibly

know that it was meant to kill. It could quite easily have been meant to disable. It's impossible to say."

Anderton raised his hand, hefting an invisible weapon.

"Kate, face me for a sec."

Kate hurried to comply, a little unnerved at how intimate it felt to be called by her first name. Anderton pretended to strike her across the face, quite slowly, stopping his hand about an inch from her face. He struck with one hand, then the other, forehand and backhand. Kate tried not to flinch and then tried not to smile. Doctor Telling watched them impassively, the shrouded body of Dita Olgweisch between her and the police officers.

"Hmm," said Anderton, eventually. He dropped his hand and nodded at Kate. "Thanks Kate. Well done, you'll live." Kate did smile at that. He looked at the pathologist. "Seems easy enough to do – to strike a hard blow, I mean, without trying hard."

"Easy enough for a strong man," said Doctor Telling.

"So a woman couldn't have done it?"

"No, either gender could do it, given enough force. It would just be easier for a man to – to overdo it accidentally, is what I meant."

"Right."

The traffic was heavy on the drive back to the station, and the car was stationary for minutes at a time. Kate found the silence between her and Anderton awkward, although she hoped that feeling wasn't mutual. She struggled to think of an appropriate topic of conversation, either case-related or small-talk line. She opened her mouth and shut it again. Anderton glanced over.

"We've thrown you in at the deep end with this one, DS Redman, haven't we?"

Kate smiled, a little uncomfortably. What happened to "Kate?"

"I've never worked a child abduction case before, sir, that's true."

"Always hard," said Anderton. "You never get used to the kid cases. Never." He indicated to turn right. "I've got three myself and you always find yourself thinking, well, what if it was one of mine?"

"Yes, I can see that."

"You don't have any kids yourself?"

Kate looked down at her hands folded in her lap. "No. No, I don't."

"Still hard," said Anderton, briefly. The police station car park gates were opening for them. Anderton swung the car into an empty bay.

Olbeck was shepherding a middle-aged couple through the foyer of the station as they came into the building. The couple looked bludgeoned, stunned into silence; the woman clutched her husband's arm as if it were the only thing keeping her from collapse. Kate and Anderton stood back, letting Olbeck steer the murdered girl's parents out towards his car, on their sad journey to view the mortal remains of their only daughter. Kate felt the first welcome surge of anger towards the perpetrator, the first real pulse of rage at whoever had done this; they had wrecked lives and shattered dreams for whatever selfish reason of their own.

They were approaching the front desk when Anderton was intercepted by a uniformed officer, who drew him aside and muttered something in his ear. Kate watched as Anderton raised his eyebrows. He looked over at her a second later and jerked his head to the right.

"Developments?" asked Kate, as they made their way down the corridor to the interview rooms.

"Certainly." Anderton stood back courteously, holding a door open for her. "We have a witness, apparently. Someone who saw something on the night of the abduction."

"Who is it?"

"A local wino, apparently. What makes it interesting, though," Anderton stood back again to let Kate go first and this time she felt a spasm of irritation. *Just get on with it.* "Our witness was once accused of sexual assault. No conviction, to be fair."

"And?" said Kate, stampeding ahead of him through the last doorway.

"The accusation was that he sexually assaulted an eighteen-month-old baby boy."

Kate stopped the door from swinging back into her superior's face. "Are you saying – what are you saying? Is he a suspect?"

"I don't know. All I'm saying is that we need to hear what he's got to say. It's probably nothing – but then again, it could be an extremely effective smokescreen."

They had reached the interview room. Kate reached out and lifted the flap that covered the peep-hole in the door. She could see the edge of the table, a leg clad in dirty denim, the edge of a filthy leather jacket.

"Why would someone like that draw attention to themselves?" she murmured, almost to herself.

"Good question."

Anderton put a hand on her arm and gently pushed her out of the way, opening the door. Kate felt herself beginning to blush. She forced the heat down by an extreme effort of will and entered the room with a face she felt was as blank as she could make it.

"For the tape, this is Detective Inspector Anderton interviewing Nicholas Draker, at two forty-nine pm, Monday sixteenth January 20—. Detective Sergeant Kate Redman is also present."

Nicholas Draker was younger than Kate had anticipated. He didn't look much more than forty-five, which, given his homelessness and general air of squalor, meant he was probably no more than thirty. He had a rounded face, long fair eyelashes and an upturned, piggish nose, all of which jarred with the greasy dark hair falling over his high forehead and the heavy stubble darkening his chin.

"So you admit to being on the grounds of Mr Fullman's estate on the night of Saturday the fourteenth of January, Mr Draker?"

"Yeah, I was there. I needed a place to kip."

"So in fact you were trespassing on Mr Fullman's land?"

Draker scoffed. "You can call it that if you want. Weren't doing any harm, was I?"

"Weren't you, Mr Draker? That remains to be seen." Anderton leant forward in his chair. "The Fullmans' baby son is missing, as well you know. A young woman has been killed. Did you have anything to do with these two events?"

"Course I fucking didn't."

"But you admit to being on the scene on the night of the crime?"

"I just said so, didn't I? Didn't mean that I had anything to do with it. I was there a week before all this happened and the night after it too. That's where I stay at the moment, or at least I did until you bastards moved me off. Where'm I going to go now?" No one answered him. "Look, I'm helping you out. I didn't need to say anything, did I? Fact is, I saw someone, like I told your man out there when they brought me in."

Anderton leant forward again.

"So what did you see, Mr Draker?"

"A man in a hood. Black hoody-type thing. He was walking towards the house."

"Did you see his face?"

"Nope. He was kind of side on, his back to me, you know."

"This was on Saturday night? What time exactly?"

"I dunno, exactly. Don't have a watch. But it was late, midnight or thereabouts." Draker put his hand up to his stubbled jaw and rubbed it. "He was moving kind of – dunno, kind of carefully. Watching where he put his feet, you know. That's kind of what drew my eye."

Anderton was silent for a moment and Kate took the opportunity. "It was dark, Mr Draker. How could you see this man?"

Draker gave her a look of outrage.

"You saying you don't believe me?"

"Not at all. I just wanted to get the full picture. How clearly could you see this man?"

"Clear enough," said Draker, sulkily. "Look, when you live rough, you get used to the dark. I can see in the dark much better'n you can, you know? I'm telling you, I saw a man, a bloke in a black hoody, that night. He was walking towards the house, looked like he knew exactly where he was going."

He blew out his cheeks. "Fucking coppers. Why am I doing your job for you?"

"Yes, thank you, Mr Draker," said Anderton, not sounding upset in the slightest. He looked down at the file on the table as if checking a fact. "You have a police record yourself, don't you? The fact is that you yourself have been accused of the sexual assault of a child."

If they had expected Draker to look ashamed, or shocked, they were disappointed. He scoffed, sitting back in his chair and rolling his eyes.

"That was the ex-missus, that was, stirring up shit for me. There weren't no conviction, was there? It was *nothing*. It was that bitch trying to make trouble for me. If you think I've got anything to do with what happened to the baby that night, you're dead wrong, right?"

"Charming character," said Kate afterwards, back in the office. "Do we believe him?"

Anderton was prowling before the whiteboards again. He stood before the picture of Dita Olgweisch spread-eagled out on the nursery carpet.

"Probably," he said. "I think his offence record is something of a red herring. Just because he was once accused of the abuse of a toddler doesn't mean he suddenly decided one day to bypass all the security, get past the CCTV, break into a stranger's house, kill the nanny and abduct a pretty much newborn baby. No, if there was an intruder, then it's someone who knew what they were doing, who knew the house."

Kate noted the emphasis. "*If*," she said, carefully.

Anderton glanced at her. "If," he confirmed.

Kate hesitated. "So, do we believe that Draker saw someone in the woods on the night of the crime?"

Anderton resumed his pacing. "Again, probably," he said. "He most probably did see someone. Was it someone intent on the crime, though? Could have been a poacher."

Kate raised her eyebrows. "Do we still get poachers, sir?"

Anderton shot her a quick glance.

"This *is* the country, DS Redman. Perhaps it was a dogger." Kate tried not to smile. Anderton went on. "Could have been another tramp. Perhaps Draker even imagined it or conjured it out of a meths bottle."

Kate swung her office chair back and forth, tapping a pen on the edge of the desk.

"Sir," she said eventually. "I'd like to interview Casey Fullman again. And Gemma Phillips as well. Particularly Gemma. I think there's something..." She hesitated, unsure of what to she was trying to say. "I'm not sure but I think there may be something she's not telling us."

"Good. Get onto it. We need to see them – the Fullmans – anyway. Always important to support the parents in a case like this until we – well, until we know more."

"I'll go first thing tomorrow."

Olbeck returned from his visit to the coroner's office looking tired. He stopped by Kate's desk and perched himself on the corner of it.

"You knocking off soon?" he asked.

Kate nodded her affirmative.

"Fancy a drink?"

Kate blinked. She considered refusing as politely as possible – it was late, she was tired and she barely knew him – but after a second's consideration decided that she may as well. The last thing she wanted to do was start to foster a reputation of being completely standoffish and unfriendly with her new colleagues.

They walked a few streets to the "coppers' pub." Kate knew there was one near every station – the quietest, least conspicuous place where you could sink copious amounts of alcohol was where you were going to find the off duty men and women trying to rejoin the real world after their shift. This pub – The Queen's Head, how anonymous – was exactly that: sticky carpet, a few old men at the bar, some battered leather booths and no background music.

"Good God, is that all you want?" said Olbeck, when she asked for an orange juice and lemonade.

Kate half smiled. She wasn't going to explain that after a lifetime of watching her mother hop on and off the wagon, the appeal of alcohol had long since receded.

"I'm thirsty," she said, which would do as a sort of half-truth. They took their drinks to one of the booths.

"God, what a day," said Olbeck. He slugged half his pint down in one go.

"How did it go with the Olgweischs?"

"About as well as you can imagine."

Kate grimaced.

"Dita did have a boyfriend," Olbeck continued. "He's been out of the country for the last couple of days. Bit of a shock for him when he came back, poor bastard. Anyway, he's coming in tomorrow."

His phone, which he'd left on the table next to his pint glass, started to vibrate. They both regarded it for a second.

"Don't you need to answer that?" said Kate, after a few moments.

Olbeck shook his head. "It'll keep. Anyway, how are you finding it? Everyone said hello yet?"

"Yes, not that I can remember any of their names, unfortunately."

"Theo is the handsome one, Jane's the redhead, Jerry's the old one and Rav is the whippersnapper." Olbeck grinned. "Does that help you?"

Kate pretended to write in her notebook. "Immensely, thanks."

She got them another drink. "What's Anderton like to work for?" she asked, sitting back down again.

Olbeck took a sip of his pint. She got the impression he was picking the words of his answer carefully. Was that because of loyalty – or something else?

"He's steady," he said eventually. "Once he's got your back, he's got it for life, so to speak. But he doesn't suffer fools gladly. He's got his own way of doing things, and it doesn't always go down too well with the high-ups." Kate nodded. Olbeck continued. "He can be...what's the right word? Hard. Ruthless, maybe. You don't want to get on the wrong side of him."

Olbeck's phone rang again. With a suppressed sigh, he picked it up. Kate got the impression that this was something of a recurring argument.

"No, I won't be late. It's just a quick drink." A pause. "With our new DS. Yes, I will. Yes. No, I won't." Kate caught his eye and he mimed a throat-cutting gesture with one hand. "No, I won't. Yes, all right. Sounds good. See you soon."

He cut off the call and placed the phone back on the table.

"Trouble?" said Kate.

"Just my other half." He didn't volunteer any more details.

"Do you need to go?"

"Yes, but I'm not going to. Have another drink?"

Kate didn't want to be the cause of any domestic strife. Besides, she had stuff to do and honour had been served with two drinks. She shook her head, trying to sound regretful.

"I'll pick you up in the morning," said Olbeck. "We're going back to the Fullmans' place with Anderton."

"Thanks for the drink."

"My pleasure."

Chapter Five

THERE WAS A SMALL CROWD outside the gates of the Fullmans' house when the officers arrived back the next morning. Kate thought they were curious onlookers until she spotted the cameras. Clearly the story had broken, and now the paparazzi were staking out the house, hoping to get a glimpse of the distraught parents.

"Vultures," said Olbeck, echoing Kate's thoughts. As they drove carefully through the gates, a fusillade of flashes went off. Kate turned her head away from the window. How anyone would want to be famous and actually *seek out* this kind of crap was a total and utter mystery. Inevitably, her thoughts turned to Casey. How was she coping?

As they drew up outside the house, she caught a glimpse of movement in one of the front rooms, the one they'd interviewed Nick Fullman in yesterday. She watched as Anderton parked the car. It was Nick with his arms wrapped around this wife, his dark head bent down to her blonde one. He seemed to be rocking her back and forth. Kate frowned. There was nothing more natural than a man in his situation comforting his wife but...well, she'd got the impression yesterday that he was not an affectionate man, not one to be patient and loving and kind. Perhaps she was wrong. She hoped she was.

Her first glimpse of Casey up close almost shocked her. The woman's skin was grey, her pupils huge and dilated. Her long hair hung in matted clumps. What was worse was her look of desperate hope.

"You've found him?" she gasped as the officers came into the hallway. She sagged as Anderton began to explain that they hadn't, that he was so sorry. Nick Fullman caught her and picked her up bodily.

"I'll take her into the bedroom," he said over his shoulder as he walked away with Casey sobbing in his arms. "Go into the kitchen and I'll be with you in a minute."

There was an older woman already in the kitchen, sat at the table with a steaming mug in front of her, flipping though a magazine. She was so like Casey, so much an older, more brittle copy of her daughter that Anderton didn't even bother to ask. He merely said, "You must be Casey's mother," and introduced himself and his team.

"Pleased to meet you," said Sheila Bright, shaking hands with them all with a vigour that belied her tiny frame. She wasn't as old as Kate had thought – either that, or she'd had plastic surgery. Probably the latter, thought Kate. The apple doesn't fall far from the tree. Then she castigated herself for being a bitch. What did it matter anyway?

Gemma Phillips was also there, typing furiously into a laptop at the other end of the table. She was fully made up, dressed today in a light grey suit. Plain or not, she had an excellent figure, and it was clearly on show in her tight pencil skirt and fitted jacket. Kate frowned. There was something inappropriate about her dress, given the circumstances. But perhaps it was the only kind of wardrobe she had.

Nick Fullman had come back into the kitchen. He took a kitchen chair and swung it backwards, straddling it. There was something about the gesture that was a little familiar, and it took Kate only a few moments to realise that she'd seen Anderton do the same in the staff room just yesterday. Fullman had the same quality of dynamism, a palpable energy that seemed to radiate from him. Gemma Phillips was watching him intently. *She fancies him*, thought Kate, and knew she was right. She must talk to her again; it could be important.

Anderton was talking.

"Mr Fullman, we're doing all we can to find your son. I know we've ascertained that Charlie didn't have a passport, but we've still alerted all of the airports and ports. We've interviewed the neighbours to see if they can give us any information that might be helpful."

"And have they?"

"We're still going through their statements at this time but I have to say that nothing has particularly stuck out as suspicious." Kate wondered whether he would mention Nicholas Draker and what he had or hadn't seen. Anderton didn't. "Is there anything else that you might be able to tell us that might be pertinent to this enquiry?"

Nick Fullman frowned. "No. I don't think so."

Anderton changed tack.

"The other thing we're coming up against, sir, is the fact that none of the alarms on your property were activated last night."

Fullman blinked, as if this had only just occurred to him.

"They weren't?" He seemed to recollect himself. "No, of course they weren't. My God, I hadn't realised, I didn't think of it."

"Do you change the codes for the alarms often? How many alarms are there?"

Nick got up from his chair.

"There's only two alarms. One for the garage, one for the house."

"Do you change the codes often?"

Fullman looked a bit sheepish. "No, I don't think I've ever changed them. It's the same code for both."

"Who would know the alarm codes?"

Fullman was pacing up and down, clutching his mobile phone like a talisman. He didn't appear to have heard the question.

Anderton prompted him.

"Mr Fullman?"

He came to with a start. "Sorry, I was – sorry. Um, Casey and I know them, Dita, Gemma..."

"I do, love," said Mrs Bright. Nick turned to stare at her.

"Yes, you do too," he said.

"Anyone else?"

"I don't know..." Fullman stared out of the window at the leafless trees and frosty lawn of the garden. "We've had cleaners and gardeners and so on. I guess they might have had them... I don't know."

Olbeck and Kate glanced at each other. Anderton said, with a touch of severity, "I'll need a list of everyone who might have had access to the alarm codes, sir. Especially if you've never changed them. Can you do that for us straightaway?"

Gemma sat up in her chair.

"I can do that for you, Nick, don't worry," she said. Nick glanced at her and nodded slightly. He went back to staring out of the window. Anderton's slight admonishment apparently barely registered.

DITA OLGWEISCH'S BOYFRIEND, TOM SPENCER, was a twenty-something young man with a pleasant freckled face and a thatch of thick brown hair. He worked as an IT consultant and had been working in Frankfurt when Dita died. Olbeck and Kate interviewed him in one of the more pleasant rooms on the first floor of the station.

"I can't believe it, I just can't," he kept saying. A cup of cooling tea sat untouched before him. "It just doesn't seem possible. Dita was the last person..."

Olbeck murmured something about being sorry for his loss and then asked whether Dita had enjoyed her job.

"She thought it was okay. I mean, it was just a stopgap. She was just doing it to earn some money. She'd done some work in a nursery back in Warsaw, while she was at university, and so I guess that's why they took her on. She had experience. But it wasn't her *career*. She wanted to go back to studying. She wants to be an architect. Wanted, I mean." His voice shook for a moment and he cleared his throat.

"Did she like her employers?"

Tom looked uneasy. "Well, I suppose so. They were okay."

"Only okay? Can you elaborate?"

"Well, I got the impression that the mother – that's Casey – didn't really want Dita there. So she could be a bit – a bit standoffish, I suppose. Dita always said she was really touchy about anyone else picking Charlie up while she – Casey, I mean – was in the room. If he cried."

"So, from what Dita said, Casey didn't really want a nanny? It was all Mr Fullman's idea?"

Tom nodded. "That's right. He had Dita start before the baby was even born, just helping out with housework and stuff."

Olbeck looked at Kate. She nodded very slightly.

"Do you know if Mr Fullman ever, well, looked after his child? Did he ever take over the care of Charlie when Dita or Casey wasn't there?"

Tom looked mystified. "I don't think so. I don't know."

Kate paused for a moment.

"Did Dita ever mention anyone who'd ever made any threats to the Fullmans? Any strange notes or incidents?"

"Threats?"

"Well, anything that might be construed as a threat. Anything out of the ordinary."

Tom looked down at the table. Kate didn't push him; she could see he was thinking deeply.

"There was one thing," he said eventually. Olbeck nodded encouragingly. "A guy came to the door one time. An Asian guy in a flash car. Dita knew because she'd opened the door to him.

Casey came out and took him into one of the rooms, and they had a huge argument. Shouting and screaming and all that."

"Really? What were they arguing about?"

"I'm not sure. Dita took Charlie away because he was getting upset because of the noise. It's just that afterwards, Casey asked her not to mention it to Nick."

"Mrs Fullman didn't want her husband to know about this?"

"That's right. That's what Dita said."

"When was this?"

"Not that long ago. Maybe a month? I remember because we actually saw the guy again, Dita and me." Tom brushed back a lock of hair that had fallen over his broad forehead. "We were out having dinner in Wallingham, and Dita saw him, pointed him out to me. She said, 'There's that man, the one that Casey had such a fight with. The secret one, the one I couldn't tell about.' I remember because he was getting out of his car, and it was a *nice* car, an Audi RS."

Kate tapped her fingers on the edge of the table.

"Did this man ever come to the house again?"

Tom shrugged. "If he did, Dita didn't see him."

They watched Tom walk away down the street from the window of the incident room on the second floor.

"Poor bugger," said Olbeck.

"Mmm." Kate put a hand up to her head, checking the neatness of her ponytail. She tucked in an errant wisp. "So who is the mystery man and is it important?"

"We'll have to ask Casey Fullman."

"But not in front of her husband."

"Good point," said Olbeck. "Not right now, anyway. How about a bit of lunch?"

Kate grinned. "Are you *always* hungry?"

For a moment, she wondered whether it was a bit too early on in their professional relationship for teasing. Luckily, Olbeck was smiling.

"You sound just like Joe," he said. "Always nagging me about my weight."

"I wasn't!"

"Teasing."

"Oh." Kate paused a moment, flustered. "Is Jo your partner?"

"That's right." There was a brief moment of silence. "Anyway, now we've established that I'm a greedy bugger, can we go and get some lunch?"

They were coming back from the canteen when they spotted Theo waving at them across the incident room.

"We've got something on the CCTV," he said. "The same car, seen in the vicinity of the house several times over the past two weeks. Pretty flashy car, it's an–"

"Audi RS?" said Olbeck.

Theo gasped. "That's right. You've seen the footage?"

"Not yet." Olbeck leaned over Theo's desk. "Let's see."

They all watched the grainy footage of the road outside the Fullmans' house, the flickering image of a powerful car moving slowly along, its headlights dimmed. Once, twice. Parked across from the gates for several minutes before moving off with a wheel spin. Driving past once more.

"It's definitely the same car," said Theo. His slim brown fingers manipulated the keyboard, bringing the image of the number plate up in close-up. "Whoever's driving it isn't making much of an effort to be discreet."

"What date was this?" said Kate. "Or dates?"

"I'll check. Give me five minutes."

"Run the plate number too, please."

Theo began to access the various databases needed for the information. Olbeck muttered something about getting hold of Anderton and walked off. Kate waited, holding each elbow in the opposite hand, tapping her foot. *Don't get too excited, Kate, it's probably nothing.*

"Here we go," said Theo after a few minutes. "Car's registered to an Ali Saheed, 15 Canterbury Mansion, London, SW7." He handed Kate the piece of paper he'd scribbled the details down on.

"Thanks." She looked down at the address. SW7 was Knightsbridge, wasn't it? Somewhere like that.

Olbeck had returned. Kate showed him their find.

"Anderton said we've got to talk to Casey and follow up this lead." He looked at the address. "South Ken. Hmm."

"I'll talk to Casey," said Kate.

There were even more photographers outside the Fullmans' gate this time. Kate had to edge forward carefully, tapping her horn once or twice as the gates slowly swung open. She was almost immune to the flashes of the cameras by now and kept her face neutral, not blinking or showing any kind of emotion.

Casey opened the door to her. She was wearing the same clothes she'd had on yesterday: expensive lounge wear marked with what looked to be splashes of tea, smudges of makeup, other unidentifiable stains. Her soft, rounded face seemed to be growing thinner by the day.

"Is Mr Fullman in?" asked Kate as they made their way through the house to the kitchen.

Casey shook her head. "He and Gemma had to go out, they had a meeting."

Kate inwardly chastised him, but she was also thankful. She wanted to talk to Casey alone.

Casey stood in the middle of the kitchen floor. She looked a little lost, awkward, as if it wasn't her kitchen after all. Kate thought back to Gemma Phillips making tea for them all on that first day, of how much more at home she had seemed.

"Do you want a drink or something?" said Casey.

"No, thank you." Kate watched without comment as Casey

poured herself a glass of wine. It was only three o'clock in the afternoon. But if anyone needed a drink, it was this poor girl. *Woman, Kate, woman.* It was hard to think of Casey as a woman; she was so tiny and somehow undeveloped, despite the artificial curves. It was hard to think of her as a mother.

"You might remember that we asked your husband whether anyone had made any threats against you, or whether there had been any strange occurrences or anything like that happening." Casey half nodded, her eyes cast down and her hands clasped around her wine glass. "Has anything come to mind?"

"No."

"Nothing at all?"

"No. Not that I can think of," said Casey.

Kate tapped her fingers on her leg. "It's just that we've been told that you had something of an – an altercation with a man recently. Someone came to the house and you had a – well, had a bit of a row?"

Casey looked up.

"No. I don't remember that."

"He was described as an Asian man." Kate persisted. Then, thinking of the name, "Perhaps Middle Eastern might be more accurate. Apparently this happened fairly recently." She didn't want to say the name aloud – she wanted Casey to say it. If it were true.

"Who told you that?" said Casey. She frowned. "I bet it was Gemma."

"I can't tell you that, Mrs Fullman, I'm sorry. Is it true?"

Casey didn't seem to have heard her. "She'd say anything to get me into trouble," she muttered, seemingly to herself. She was staring off into the middle distance.

"Was there a row with this man?" said Kate doggedly.

Casey appeared to come back to reality. She slid a sideways glance at Kate. "It wasn't really a row. Just a – a difference of opinion."

"Who is this man?"

Casey slugged back the remains of her wine.

"It was only Ali. That's all. No one – no one sinister."

"Who is Ali?"

"He's my agent. Former agent. We decided to go our separate ways. That's all. He was probably just a bit pissed off at something. It can't have anything to do with this." Her eyes filled. "He wouldn't have had anything to do with this. He *couldn't* have."

"Who can't have?"

Kate and Casey both jumped. Nick Fullman had come into the kitchen unnoticed by both of them. Kate was struck once again by his male-model looks and something she hadn't really grasped before, the sense of physical power he exuded. Casey seemed to shrink back into herself as he came closer.

"Nothing," she said, her voice shaking. "Nothing, Nick."

"What were you talking about?"

He was looming over both women, sat as they were on one of the sofas. Kate stood up quickly and stepped forward into his personal space, forcing him to take a step back.

"I was just questioning your wife about a car that had been seen in the vicinity recently," she said pleasantly. Nick raised his eyebrows.

"What car?"

Kate was silent for a moment, wondering whether to bring forward the subject of her conversation with Casey. Casey solved her dilemma.

"Just Ali's car, Nick, that's all," she said. She turned to put her empty glass down on the nearest side table and knocked it over, catching it before it rolled onto the floor. "You know, when he came to drop that stuff back. That's all."

Nick frowned.

"You think he's got something to do with this? That little shit?"

"We're following several lines of enquiry, sir," said Kate smoothly. Nick sat down at the table and put his head in his hands.

"This whole thing is just a nightmare," he said in a muffled voice. The two women watched him. He raised his head again and there were tears in his eyes.

"I keep thinking I'm going to wake up and it'll all be over," he said. He dropped his head back down. "It just keeps going on and on."

Casey jumped up and flung her arms around him. Kate stood for a moment, watching the embracing couple. I should feel sympathetic for him, she thought. But I don't. Why don't I? Is it because I think he's just saying something for the sake of it, that he doesn't really mean it after all? Am I getting that hard, that cynical – or is there something in what I'm thinking?

Chapter Six

Olbeck and Theo had driven to Ali Saheed's flat in South Kensington, fully expecting to find him away as it was the middle of a normal working day. Olbeck had queried whether they could have gotten a search warrant, but he knew that the process would involve several hours of form filling and sign offs. He was impatient to chase up this latest lead, even if it meant time wasted in trying to track down their latest suspect.

Saheed's flat was a basement one, in a street just off the Brompton Road. The elegant, white Georgian townhouses stood in serried rows, painted black railings separating them. The basement forecourt of the flat was empty, save for a solitary bay tree in a large stone pot standing like a sentinel by the front door. Olbeck rang the bell, not expecting an answer, but to their surprise, they heard footsteps approaching the door before it swung open.

The man regarding them with suspicion was short, although powerfully built, with carefully-tousled, thick black hair. He wore a suit that Olbeck's practised eye picked out as an Oswald Boteng and, rather jarringly, bare feet.

"Yeah?"

"Ali Saheed?" said Theo.

"Yeah," said Saheed, more warily. "What's this about?"

"Charlie Fullman, Mr Saheed," said Olbeck. "Mind if we come in?"

The flat was small but luxuriously furnished: granite-topped kitchen counters, black gloss units, black leather sofas and an enormous flat screen television. An empty espresso cup stood on the glass-topped coffee table, along with a packet of Silk Cut, a lighter and an ash-filled glass ashtray.

"I heard about the baby," said Saheed, who perched himself on the edge of one of the sofas, as if he was about to spring up at any time. "And that poor girl. It's terrible. I tried to give Casey a ring but–"

"Yes, Casey Fullman," said Olbeck. "I understand that you are her former agent?"

"Yeah."

"When did you – part company?"

Saheed reached for his cigarettes. "Not sure. Not long ago. Maybe a couple of months."

"So just after Charlie Fullman was born, really. Is that right?"

Saheed shrugged. "I guess so."

Olbeck leant forward. "Now we've been told that you and she had something of a fight recently, is that right?"

"A fight?" said Saheed. He looked uncomfortable. "No, not really, just a – well, a disagreement. That's all."

"What was the disagreement about?"

"Oh, nothing," said Saheed. He must have realised that that didn't satisfy them, as he went on, "I just thought she was making a mistake, that's all. About sacking me as her agent. I thought – I thought she was doing it for the wrong reasons, that's all. I just wanted to talk to her about it."

"What were her reasons?"

Saheed had smoked his cigarette down to the filter. He crushed it out in the ashtray with disproportionate violence.

"That's confidential."

"Nothing's confidential in a murder case, Mr Saheed."

Saheed looked startled. Olbeck wondered if he was unused

to being told no in any form. But as a theatrical agent, surely he heard it all the time? That was Joe's department, that sort of world. Olbeck resolved to try and get home at a normal sort of time, if he could, to try and talk to his partner about the industry.

"Her reasons, Mr Saheed?" he prompted.

Saheed shrugged.

"She – she just thought that I wasn't helping her enough. Wasn't getting her enough work. She'd just had a baby, for Christ's sake, she shouldn't have been thinking about work. She wasn't thinking straight."

Olbeck had been looking unobtrusively around the flat as they spoke. He didn't really think there would be any trace of anything belonging to Charlie Fullman, certainly not left in plain sight if Saheed had in fact taken him – and Olbeck was far from convinced that was the case – but you never knew. There was nothing to be seen, anyway, nothing but the usual detritus of a bachelor pad. His house had once looked something like this. No longer, since Joe had moved in. He sighed, inwardly.

"So this fight, my apologies, this disagreement you had with Mrs Fullman...was that the only time you'd been to their house in recent weeks?"

Saheed had lit another cigarette. Sheets of bluish smoke hung in the air, and Theo smothered a cough.

"That's right," said Saheed.

"That was the only time?"

"Yeah."

"You're quite sure about that, are you?" said Olbeck, holding his gaze. Saheed gazed back angrily.

"I said, *yes*. That's the only time."

Theo and Olbeck exchanged a glance.

"Well, Mr Saheed, I'm afraid that I don't quite believe you. Your very distinctive car has been seen on numerous occasions on the road outside the Fullmans' house, both driving past and parked on the verge. What were you doing there?"

The hand holding the cigarette was shaking.

"Nothing, I..." said Saheed. He dropped his eyes to the floor. "I wasn't doing any harm. Just parked on the road. That's not being at the house, is it?" He looked at them fearfully. "I had nothing to do with this, nothing, I'm telling you." The policemen regarded him with impassive faces. He swallowed. "Do I need a lawyer?"

He accompanied them back to the station with Theo sitting next to him in the back seat of the car. The traffic was heavy, and the journey took an hour longer than it had taken to get there. Olbeck thought of Kate and wondered how she was getting on at the Fullmans' house, questioning Casey.

Back at the station, they took Saheed into an interview room, accompanied by the duty solicitor.

"I'm telling you, I don't know anything about this," he kept saying. "All right, so I drove by a few times. I kept thinking that Casey would—" He was silent for a moment. "That Casey would change her mind."

"About employing you again as her agent?" said Theo.

Saheed nodded, after a moment.

"I'm assuming that she didn't, in fact, do this?"

Saheed's black brows drew down in a frown. "I'd been with her for five years," he said. "Five years. I got her that TV show, I got her into the papers. Five years and she just throws me away, bye-bye Ali, nice to have known you."

"That must have rankled," said Olbeck, non-committally.

"Yeah," said Saheed, a trifle uncertainly. Olbeck wondered whether he knew what rankled actually meant. "I was pretty pissed off."

"So pissed off that you thought you'd do something drastic? Something to get back at her?"

Saheed stared at him. "No. Nothing like that. I told you, I had nothing to do with Charlie going missing – and the nanny – nothing to do with it. You've got to believe me."

"So why were you driving up and down outside her house at all hours of the day and night?"

"I was – I was thinking." Olbeck looked sceptical. "All right, I was thinking about going back to see her. To try and persuade her to change her mind."

Olbeck sat back in his chair. Perhaps it was time to try another tack.

"What was your relationship with Mr Fullman like?"

Saheed stared again. "Like?"

"Did you get on well? How did he feel about your relationship with his wife?"

"Okay, I guess." There was a short silence. "He's a weird guy, you know. He's totally obsessed with his work, that's all he thinks about. Casey got fed up with it, sometimes."

"So Mrs Fullman would confide in you? You were close friends as well as business associates?"

Saheed half smiled. "I guess. You do get close, you know – when you both know the game..." He dropped his head. "She was lonely."

Theo and Olbeck exchanged a glance.

"So you're saying that, perhaps the Fullmans' marriage was in trouble? Under strain?"

Saheed shrugged.

"For the tape, please."

"What? Oh–" Saheed glanced over at the recorder. "I don't know what their marriage was like, we didn't really talk like *that*. Casey just used to say that Nick was always working and it pissed her off sometimes, particularly after she got pregnant. He didn't seem very excited about the baby. That's what I remember her saying, he didn't seem excited at all about the baby, and he was the one who'd suggested the whole thing to her."

Olbeck raised his eyebrows. "Nick Fullman suggested what to his wife?"

"That they have the baby, you know. Casey's still young, you know, she's not twenty seven yet. She's got loads of time to have a baby if she wanted one. Nick was the one who was keen to have one."

"Is that right? But Mrs Fullman took some persuading?"

"No, Casey wanted kids as well, it's just that – oh, I dunno – it was more that she would have waited…"

"Do you think the Fullmans are happily married?"

Saheed's eyebrows went up. "I don't know."

"What is your opinion?"

He looked uncomfortable. "I don't know. Maybe."

"You said Mr Fullman is a 'weird guy'. Can you explain any further?"

Saheed reached for his cigarettes and then realised that he wasn't going to be able to smoke. His foot was jiggling up and down on the floor and he put a hand on his knee, obviously to stop it.

"Don't know," he said. "All I know is that Nick does what he wants all the time. It's always about him. He gets his own way a lot of the time, seems to me. He always gets what he wants. One way or the other."

OLBECK GOT HOME LATER THAN he'd expected, and unfortunately, about two hours later than he'd promised. As he put the key in his front door, he braced himself. Joe was such a tempest, sometimes. There'd be storms of tears, shouting, even the odd plate thrown now and again. Then, just as quickly, calm again, all the energy dissipated. Olbeck knew he didn't deal with it very well. He'd tried being placatory and unruffled as he was berated for his wrongs, both real and imaginary. He'd tried shouting back. He hadn't thrown anything yet, but it was sometimes a near thing. It was *exhausting*, this relationship business, a constant battle between the compromises demanded by Joe and his own, selfish inclinations.

Joe was in the kitchen, clattering about with pots and pans.

A rich, garlicky smell hung in the air, reminding Olbeck of the length of time that had passed since he'd last eaten. Joe was a fantastic cook; it was one of the things Olbeck loved about him.

"You're late," said Joe, not looking around.

"I know." Olbeck hesitated and then wrapped his arms around his partner, kissing the back of his neck. "You know how it is when I'm on a case. I'm sorry."

"You're always on a case. You *are* a case. Headcase."

"Nutcase."

"That too." Sighing petulantly, Joe turned around and kissed him properly. Despite his hunger and his tiredness, Olbeck felt a stir of interest. His boyfriend really was very nice looking, after all...

Then Joe moved away from him, stomping to the fridge. Olbeck sighed. Play this wrong, and it wouldn't only be separate beds tonight, he'd been lucky not to be wearing his dinner. *Be nice, be calm, be interested...* Trouble is, he didn't *want* to be interested. What he wanted to do was have a quick and dirty shag, something to eat and then hit the sack without any more conversation whatsoever.

"Guess what?" said Joe, in a slightly-less-annoyed tone. He was stirring a bubbling pot on the stove, bringing the spoon to his lips to taste. "Ouch, hot. Anyway, guess what?"

"What?"

"Mandy and Sarah are getting married. Well, civil partnership, you know."

"Oh right," said Olbeck, scrolling frantically through his mental contact list to try and place Mandy and Sarah. He remembered – Mandy was an actress friend of Joe's and Sarah was her girlfriend. "That's nice."

"Isn't it? They're such a fabulous couple. I bet they'll do the big white wedding thing, that's Mandy's style at least."

"Right," said Olbeck, trying not to yawn.

Joe glanced sideways at him. "That's the kind of thing I'd like, as well."

"What is?"

"The big white wedding."

Olbeck's heart sank. "Okay," he said, not really sure where this was going but not liking the sound of it.

"Don't you want that?"

No, I don't. Olbeck knew he couldn't say that out loud. Instead he muttered something like "Of course, but it's not the right time at the moment..."

Joe was pouting. "You could at least sound a bit more enthusiastic."

"Do we have to talk about this now? I'm tired and it's been a long day."

"No," said Joe, ominously quietly. "We don't have to talk about this now. God forbid that you want to *talk* about making a commitment to your partner, God forbid that I might actually want to talk to you for a change instead of getting your voicemail all the fucking *time*." His voice began to rise. "God forbid that I've been here all day cooking for you and you promised to get home on time, promised and yet a-fucking-gain you don't!"

"Okay–" said Olbeck, trying to head off the inevitable, but it was too late.

"I'm fucking sick of it!"

The wooden spoon went flying across the kitchen, trailing drips of sauce. Seconds later, Joe slammed out of the kitchen and Olbeck heard his footsteps pound up the stairs and then the more distant slam of the bedroom door.

Olbeck remained standing for a moment with his eyes shut, breathing deeply. Then he got himself a plate from the cupboard and helped himself to the stew. He sat at the table, eating methodically, refusing to get upset. Joe would calm down. Merely a storm in a tea-cup. The stew was so good he had second helpings before he stacked the plate into the dishwasher – there, who could say he never did anything around the house? – and went through to the front room to watch television.

Chapter Seven

Kate parked the car in her usual spot, four doors down from her mother's house. She sat for a moment, ostensibly checking her handbag for various items but actually steadying herself with some deep breaths. Being here brought back so many memories.

She stared at the shabby grass verge, the litter piled in the gutter, the mean little front gardens that were either littered with garish plastic toys or paved over to become parking spaces. The houses were the usual charmless 1960s square boxes: windows slightly too small for the walls, concrete roof tiles, white plastic cladding.

Looking around, Kate realised the area had actually improved slightly – clearly, most of these houses were now privately owned including, incredibly, her mother's home. Kate had given her the deposit to enable her to take advantage of the Right to Buy scheme back in the mid nineties. Kate had delayed her own house purchase by a few years because she gave up that chunk of hard-earned savings. Now, looking at the peeling paint, the cracked window pane, the overgrown front garden, Kate thought she might as well have thrown that money down the toilet. *Loo, Kate, loo.* At least if her mum's property was still council-owned, it would be in better shape. She straightened her shoulders, locked the car and went up to the front door. She had timed this visit carefully. Too early, and her mum would be hungover and grumpy and unwelcoming, too late, and she'd be half-cut and sloppily sentimental. Now, at half past two in the afternoon, Mrs Redman would be as rational and as normal as she could be. So Kate hoped.

She was halfway to the front door when it opened violently and someone came stampeding out, her mother's screamed profanities following them. Kate flinched. The person running down the path was a teenage girl, hair teased up into a beehive, thick black eyeliner, stomping boots on the end of long legs. She pushed past Kate, scowling murderously. Kate's mother stood at the door, screaming after her. "And don't come back, you little whore!"

"Mum!" said Kate. She grabbed her mother's arm and wheeled her around, pushing her back into the house. She was rocketed back to her teenage years, feeling the neighbours' scorn and disapproval beaming out from the surrounding houses as her mum embarrassed her yet again. "What on earth? What's going on? Who was that?"

Her mum looked at her with a disbelieving expression.

"What d'you mean, who was that? That was *Courtney*, wasn't it? Little whore. Who'd she think she is, coming round here and trying to hit me up for cash?"

Kate felt a quick jab of shame. Courtney was one of her six half-siblings. Her own sister, and she hadn't even recognised her. When had she last seen her? Over a year ago, at least.

"Oh," she said feebly. Then, collecting herself, "Well, Mum, here I am."

"Yeah."

"I was going to ask what's been going on but I see that plenty has."

Her mother tottered off into the messy living room.

"Where's my fags?" she muttered, hunting amongst the detritus of the coffee table.

"How about a cup of tea?" said Kate. She wanted to deflect the inevitable offering of "a glass of something."

Mary Redman had found her cigarettes and lit one. A thin

ribbon of smoke rose towards the ceiling, stained ochre by twenty year's worth of exhaled fumes. Kate turned towards the tiny galley kitchen that lay at the end of the hallway.

She hunted for teabags and mugs amongst the chaos. Mary leant against the doorframe, watching her.

"*That* cupboard," she said, eventually. Kate opened it and was nearly brained by a landslide of tins and cardboard boxes.

"Oh, leave it," said Mary, as Kate scrabbled about on the floor, picking things up. "What's up with you, then? What you been up to?"

Kate stood up. She mentioned the Fullman case, just the bare bones of it, all she was able to say.

"Awful," said Mary, taking a long drag. She shook her head. "Don't know what I would have done if one of you had been taken. And that poor girl with her head smashed in!" Kate winced. "Poor little baby. His mum must be frantic."

Kate poured boiling water onto the teabags and nodded. She thought of Casey in her expensive prison, hemmed in by paparazzi, lost and alone in her glossy kitchen. A greater contrast to the one that she was in could scarcely be imagined.

"Here you go," she said, handing her mother a steaming mug.

Mary placed it precariously on the counter.

"Surprised you're doing this case," she said, watching Kate closely. "Thought it might bring back a few bad memories."

Kate felt her shoulders stiffen. "I don't know what you mean," she said.

"Don't you?" said Mary.

"No," said Kate. She could hear it in her voice: the shut-down, the freezing of emotion.

There was a moment's silence.

"Oh, well," said Mary. She picked up her tea and turned away. "Don't know how you did it, myself. That was proper cold, Kelly, it weren't natural. Couldn't have done it myself. Don't know how you–"

"That's enough."

Kate's voice made them both jump. She stood for a moment, breathing deeply, trembling, trying to keep herself together. Her mother was looking at her in an odd way, sympathy and spite mixed together.

"Want a glass of something?" said Mary, after a moment.

"No thanks," said Kate, automatically. She looked out of the small kitchen window into the uninspiring garden: concrete paving slabs, a dying shrub in a pot, a handkerchief-sized, balding lawn. There was a white plastic table out there, with an empty whisky bottle on top of it, an inch of dirty water in the bottom of the bottle.

"What did Courtney want?" she asked, after a moment.

Mary sniffed. "Money. As usual. As if she don't already get enough from her dad."

"But is she okay?"

"'Course she is. Just being a teenager, that's all. All she cares about is boys and Bacardi Breezers and getting her nails done."

Kate lifted her shoulders. "I cared about more than that, when I was her age."

Mary looked at her with her mouth quirked up at the corner.

"Yes, love," she said. "But you weren't normal."

When Kate closed the door of her flat behind her a few hours later, she stood for a moment, drinking in the peace and serenity of her home. More so than usual, she could feel the calmness that its order inspired in her – the well-being that the neatness, the cleanliness, the carefully-chosen fixtures and ornaments and furniture evoked.

Kate paid for a cleaner to come every week, and she cleaned the place herself, just a quick once-over, every day. It didn't take long. She walked slowly through the small flat, relishing the peace and solitude, the joy of being surrounded by things that she'd chosen with care and attention. She moved about the living room, touching the back of the sofa, the well-filled bookcases, the silver framed photograph of herself on her graduation day from Hendon. She picked it up and regarded it closely, noting her beaming, proud smile, her younger, eager face. *Top of the class, Kate. You couldn't have done that if – if things had been different. You made the right decision – for both of you.*

She went into her small but sparkling bathroom and undressed, dropping her clothes into the wicker laundry basket in the corner. Her jeans and jumper had been clean, but they felt tainted by the hours spent in her mother's house, smelling of smoke and whisky fumes and something else, something indefinable but awful. Kate checked that a clean, white towel hung from the hook by the shower door, ready for her when she stepped out of the cubicle and saw that the clean bathmat was laid on the shining tiles of the floor. She cleaned her teeth and cleaned her face. Before the bathroom mirror clouded over with steam, she regarded her naked body. You couldn't tell. There was nothing on the surface that showed.

For the thousandth time, she pushed away the memories. Shut them away, push them back into the dark. She stepped under the hot gush of water, closing her eyes against the spray. The hot water against her back and neck was so comforting. She watched the foam-laden water stream away from her and down the plughole, and imagined all the mistakes and regrets of the past being carried away with it.

Chapter Eight

Gemma Phillips lived in a very small townhouse. It was one of a recently-built estate so new that the lawn of the tiny front gardens was like a small, green patchwork quilt, the lines of earth showing between each strip of sod. The houses were what Kate would term "cheaply smart." They looked fresh and desirable because the new paint gleamed, the tiles shone and the windows sparkled. *Give it five years*, thought Kate as she parked the car, *and they'd look considerably less attractive, as the shoddy materials and second-rate design began to show.*

She'd phoned ahead to check that Gemma was at home, for once not at the Fullmans' place. She did at least have a few days off now and then, it seemed. Kate rapped smartly with the new doorknocker, already loose on its nail.

Gemma was slow in answering the door. She peered somewhat suspiciously through the gap between the frame and the door, frowning a little when she saw Kate standing there.

"Good morning," said Kate briskly, stepping forward. This was almost always the easiest way to get in a house quickly – most people didn't have the nerve to hold their ground. Gemma was no exception. She stepped back and Kate pressed on.

"Lovely morning," she said, now fully in the hallway. "I was hoping to have a chat with you about a few things, as I said on the phone. Could we sit down somewhere?"

Obviously accustomed to taking orders, Gemma turned

obediently and led her into the small living room. Kate's heels clacked on the laminate flooring. The cheaply smart theme was echoed here in the interior decoration. There was a feature wall of gaudy wallpaper, large silver flowers and red tendrils entwined. There was a glass coffee table, a small black leather sofa and matching armchair. No books, but a pile of glossy magazines in a heap by the armchair. A large flat screen television dominated the small room.

Kate perched herself on the armchair. Gemma sat down hesitantly opposite her. She was wearing black leggings and a fluffy white tunic, belted tightly around her tiny waist. She looked odd in casual wear, not quite comfortable, as if her natural inclination was to be strapped into tight-fitting and uncomfortable suits.

"Do you want tea?" said Gemma, after a moment.

"Yes, lovely, thanks," said Kate. She almost always agreed to a drink in these circumstances – it gave you a good opportunity to have a look around. As Gemma jumped up and left the room, Kate allowed her gaze to drift about. It snagged on a large cardboard container resting at the side of the sofa, one of the bags which upmarket shops give to their customers to carry their goods away. Kate leaned closer. *Very* upmarket. She noted the Mulberry logo, the satin ribbons that tied the top.

"You've got a new bag?" she asked, as Gemma came back with two steaming mugs of tea.

Gemma nodded, after a moment's hesitation.

"May I see it?" said Kate. "I love Mulberry." A lie, she didn't know a Mulberry from a raspberry, but it might put the girl at her ease.

Gemma hesitated again. Then she pulled out the bag and extracted the handbag from within, all padded sides and gleaming clasps.

"Lovely," said Kate, examining it. "Quite pricey, though, aren't they? Thought you'd treat yourself?"

Gemma nodded. After a moment, she said, "I got my bonus. From Nick."

"Great," said Kate. Then feeling it was time to cut to the chase, she handed the bag back to Gemma and leaned forward.

"I was hoping you could help me, Gemma. In cases like these, it's important that we cover all the angles, so to speak – the background detail, the minutia – you know, in case there's a small point that's really important. Something that otherwise we might miss, but could be vital in solving the case. Do you see what I'm saying?"

Gemma was holding the Mulberry bag on her lap like a shield. She nodded, biting her lip.

Kate went on.

"It's useful to us to get a sort of picture of the people involved, their histories, their habits and so forth. As you've worked for the Fullmans for some years, I thought you'd be able to do this, give me an idea of, well, the sort of people they are. Are you able to do that?"

Gemma was still for a moment. Then, exhaling, she put the bag back into its container and sat back in her chair, crossing her long legs. "Yeah, I can do that," she said. "What did you want to know?"

"Can you tell me about Nick – Mr Fullman? What's his history? Where did he grow up?"

Gemma laughed. "He's an Essex boy. Funny, isn't it? You'd never guess it from the way he speaks. His dad was a builder, but he made money, enough money to send Nick to private school. That's why he talks the way he does, not all – well, Essex, you know. Not all rough."

"So he's from a wealthy family?" Kate asked. "Well, a prosperous family at least."

Gemma nodded. "I guess, although I remember Nick saying his dad lost loads a few years ago, when the credit crunch hit. I think Nick had to lend him some money, bail him out, you know."

"Nick wasn't affected by the property crash?"

"Not so much. He kind of diversified into commercial property then and that didn't seem to take such a hit. He always seemed to have loads of work coming in, anyway."

"You're obviously paid well," said Kate. Gemma looked a little offended, as people tended to do when money was mentioned. "Clearly you also work long hours. You work hard for your money."

Gemma looked mollified. "That's right. It feels like twenty-four seven, this job, sometimes."

"Nick obviously works very hard. Do you think that it ever put a strain on his marriage?"

Gemma sniffed. "Is that what Casey said? She doesn't know, she's born. It's not like she has to work hard. She just gets to sit around and spend his money."

"Do you think Mr Fullman resents that? I mean, does it seem as though he dislikes working so hard?"

Gemma laughed a laugh with no humour in it.

"Nick doesn't resent anything to do with work. He's, like, a workaholic. That's all he thinks about. I'm pretty sure that's why he and his last girlfriend split up, the fact that he spends all his time working. And they'd been together *ages*."

"If that's the case, do you think Mrs Fullman – Casey – finds that difficult?"

"I don't know." Gemma was rolling a strand of hair back and forth between long-nailed fingers. "She doesn't really talk to me much. She doesn't like me."

"Why is that?"

Gemma shrugged. "Probably resents all the time I spend with Nick. We work together a lot, you know. Casey's bound to be a bit jealous. Wives always are."

Kate hesitated, wondering whether to push this further. Ask too probing a question and Gemma would clam up – but then, she needed to know...

"Does Casey have any grounds for jealously?" she asked. "Is

there anything more between you and Mr Fullman than perhaps there should be between work colleagues?"

She braced herself for anger and indignation but to her surprise, Gemma seemed quite pleased at the prospect. A small, smug smile showed briefly on her face. After a moment, she shook her head.

"No," she said slowly. "There's nothing like that." She sat up in her chair suddenly. "But just try telling Casey that! She only thinks that because she–" Her voice stopped suddenly, and she dropped her eyes to her lap, picking at the arm of the chair.

Kate raised her eyebrows. "Because she what?" she prompted, after a moment.

"Nothing." Gemma took up her lock of hair again, looking away. "It's nothing."

The gates had clearly clanged shut and that was all she was going to say. Kate paused for a moment, re-running the conversation through her mind. There had been something – what was it? Oh yes...

"You mentioned Nick's ex-girlfriend, Gemma," she said. "You said they'd been together ages. Can you tell me a bit more about her? Presumably you met her."

Gemma's restless fingers stilled for a moment. "Rebecca?" she said. "Yeah, I met her. Several times. She's all right."

"She and Nick were together how long?"

"God, ages. Ten years, maybe?"

"They were married?"

Gemma shook her head. "No, they never got married. Don't know why. I think they were engaged, but they never actually got married." She leant forward a little, conspiratorially. "You know, I'm pretty sure Nick left her for Casey, you know. I don't know for certain, but after they split up, it was only a month or so before Casey appeared on the scene. And it was only a month or so after *that* that she got pregnant."

Kate tapped her fingers on her legs, thinking.

"So it wasn't because of Nick's work that the relationship broke down?"

"I don't know. I'm just guessing. All I know is that Nick was with Rebecca for *years* and then all of a sudden he was with Casey and getting married and having the baby and all that."

Kate nodded.

"How did Rebecca take that?"

Gemma's eyes flickered. "Okay, I guess," she said. She put the end of the lock of hair into her mouth, making her next few words indistinct. "I don't really know. You'll have to ask her."

Kate nodded again. There was a long moment of silence.

"Well, if that's all..." said Gemma, eventually.

Kate leapt to her feet.

"Yes, thank you, Gemma. That's all for now. Thanks for your help."

Was it her imagination or did Gemma relax, just a little? It was probably nothing, but Kate noted it just the same. She pulled on her jacket and gathered up her bag. Gemma stood up as well.

Kate took a last look around the room. A framed photograph on a shelf caught her eye.

"Is that your fiancée?" she asked, gesturing.

Gemma turned around to look. She blushed. "Um, no. That's my brother," she said.

"Oh, right," said Kate. "Nice-looking guy."

Gemma smiled unhappily. "I've got a picture of my fiancée around somewhere if you want to see it," she said after a moment. "His name's Paul."

Kate had already reached the front door.

"Another time, thanks Gemma. Thanks for the tea."

The door shut smartly behind her as she was three steps up the tiny front path. She looked back. Gemma was standing in the living room window, half hidden by the curtains. Kate raised a hand, and the girl turned sharply away, twitching the curtain shut.

Chapter Nine

OLBECK LOOKED UP AT THE sound of Kate's exclamation. "What's up?"

Kate looked at him, her eyebrows raised. "I've been looking up the prices of Mulberry bags."

Now it was Olbeck's turn to look surprised. "Going to splash out on one, are you?"

"Splash out is right." Kate tapped a few keys to print out the current picture on her computer screen. "If I had a spare few thousand pounds, I'd be spending it on something other than a big leather *bag*, for God's sake. I had no idea they were so expensive."

Olbeck perched himself on the edge of Kate's desk. "Is there a point to this?"

Kate looked up at him, tapping a pencil on the edge of her jaw. "Gemma Phillips has just bought a new one. A brand new one, of the most expensive type, if I remember correctly."

"And?"

Kate paused. "Well, even with a bonus, would someone on a secretary's wages be able to afford a Mulberry handbag?"

Olbeck shrugged. "She probably stuck it on a credit card." He grinned. "Or maybe she stole it."

"Ha, ha. She had it in the official bag, so I suppose not." Kate pushed her chair back from her desk, sighing. "You're probably right, it's nothing."

Olbeck patted her on the shoulder. "She has an alibi, you

know. We checked it out, first thing. She was out on a hot date – we've got witnesses placing her in a restaurant and then clubbing and finally the two of them entering Gemma's house at about four o'clock in the morning from the taxi driver who dropped them off. The whole night accounted for."

Kate half-smiled. "That would be with the fiancée. Paul somebody."

Olbeck snorted. "Fiancée? Hardly. If it's Paul Dinnock you're talking about, and it probably is, it was her first date with the guy. We contacted him and he gave us the full story."

Kate swung round on her chair to stare at him.

"Seriously, it was her first date? With this Paul?"

"Yes. I don't see why he would lie. He was quite open about it, the fact that they'd slept together. I didn't get the impression that it was anything other than a one-night-stand."

"Right," said Kate, slowly.

"Does it matter?" said Olbeck.

"Apart from the fact that she's a liar?"

"Is she?"

"Yes. She told me she was engaged to the guy. She called him her fiancée."

Olbeck raised his eyebrows.

"That's – odd. Slightly odd, at least." A thought seemed to strike him. "Or is it? Don't women lie about that sort of thing all the time?"

Kate grinned. "Well, that's just it. She lied to me about having a fiancée. Is that just embarrassment at being single – I got the impression that that was a bit of a sore subject – or is it that she's just a liar, full stop? And if she is, what else has she lied about?"

She related the particulars of her recent conversation with Gemma to Olbeck. He nodded at various points.

"We need to interview the ex-girlfriend," he said, when Kate had finished speaking. "Don't we?"

"I think so. If only to get a bit more background on the

Fullmans. I looked her up, her name's Rebecca D'Arcy-Warner. Minor aristocracy, daughter of a brigadier."

"Let's do it–" Olbeck broke off as the whirlwind that was Anderton was seen and heard approaching down the corridor. "After the meeting."

REBECCA D'ARCY-WARNER HAD AN ATTRACTIVE voice, low and clear and unmistakably upper-class. For all that, she sounded at first aghast and then suspicious when Kate had explained the reason for her call.

"I hardly think–" Rebecca said and then broke off. "I *heard* about it all, of course. I read about it in the papers. But what on earth has it got to do with *me*?"

Kate attempted to explain. She could almost feel the woman's disbelief radiating down the phone line.

"We're merely trying to gather some more background information," she finished, fearing that her words were falling on stony ground. "As you were with Mr Fullman for so long, you're probably just the person to fill us in on the background details."

"Well," said Rebecca, doubtfully. There was a pause. "I still don't see...but if you think I could help, I don't know–"

"We'd only take up a few minutes of your time, Ms D'Arcy-Warner," said Kate. "Should we come to you?"

"No. I mean, that's not very convenient at the moment. I could come to you – wait, I know. I'll be over at my father's house this afternoon. He lives at Cudston Magna. That's quite near you, isn't it? I could meet you there, if it's really only going to be five minutes. It's just that my father's not well, you see, and I don't want him confused or upset."

Kate hastened to reassure her. She and Olbeck set off for the hour's drive in his car, only slightly delayed by the now-traditional shovelling of accumulation from the front passenger seat to the back footwells.

Cudston Magna was a tiny village, virtually a hamlet, set amidst rolling green hills and pastures grazed by sheep and cattle. Cudston Manor was a beautiful piece of Georgian architecture with golden stone balustrades and two wings extending out to either side of the original house. Kate got out of the car, feeling insignificant.

Rebecca D'Arcy-Warner looked thoroughly at home here. She came down to meet them, shaking hands with the forthrightness of someone taught social grace from an early age. What surprised Kate was that she was considerably older than Nick Fullman, perhaps by as much as ten years, which meant she must be in her mid to late forties. She was an attractive woman, something of an Amazon in height and build, but with a mane of deep red hair and a broad, high-cheekboned face. She was certainly nothing like Casey Fullman in the looks department.

"I'm sorry for being so abrupt on the phone" she said, ushering them through the front door. "It just didn't seem like anything I could assist you with and I was worried about my father being worried, if you see what I mean. He's quite elderly, and I don't like him to be upset in any way. It's not good for him."

Kate nodded. Rebecca led them into a small, charming sitting room.

"I'm not sure how I can help you," she said, sitting down and clasping her hands together. There were no rings on her fingers. Kate remembered that she'd never actually been married to Nick Fullman.

Kate began.

"We were hoping you could tell us something about Nick Fullman. We'd like to know more of his background, from people who knew him well. I believe you were with him for some considerable time?"

Rebecca nodded. "Eleven years." Her face flickered for a moment and then cleared. "We met just before the millennium.

We both belonged to a property investor's network –that's where we met."

"You and Mr Fullman were engaged?" said Olbeck.

"Yes. We were engaged for two years."

"But – forgive me – you never married?"

Rebecca shook her head. She was sitting very upright and very still, her hands gripping one another. "No, we never actually got married."

"Why was that?"

She blinked. "Is that relevant?"

"I'm sorry but it may be."

Rebecca looked away. "I hardly see how." There was a pause and then she said, "Well, it's old news now, anyway. I'm not sure why it didn't work out. We just drifted apart really. It wasn't anything very dramatic."

"You didn't have any children together?"

Kate was watching closely. As she asked the question she saw the minute jerk of Rebecca's shoulders, almost too small to notice. Then the movement was gone, and Rebecca answered the question in a calm, steady tone.

"No, no children." She laughed, rather harshly. "I'm not very maternal, I'm afraid. Children have never really been in my life plan."

Olbeck nodded. "So there were no hard feelings between you and Mr Fullman when your relationship ended?"

"Well, nothing out of the ordinary. I mean, it was *painful*. We'd been together for years. It took me a while to recover. I mean, when your life's being going one way and then all of a sudden, there's an enormous detour...that takes a while to get over, doesn't it?" She gazed at them both, earnestly. Her words rang with sincerity. "But after the dust had settled, I could see – we could both see – that it was really for the best."

Kate waited for a moment and then asked, "Did you resent Mr Fullman marrying so soon after your relationship broke up?"

Rebecca blinked again. "Of course not." She gave a rather stagy laugh. "I mean – well, I wouldn't want to be uncharitable, but it did seem rather *too* sudden. And then of course, the baby was born so perhaps they had to get married, although in this day and age it doesn't seem very likely, does it? That she trapped him into it, I mean." Her gaze fell to her clasped hands. "No doubt he knew what he was doing."

"Are you still in regular contact with Mr Fullman?"

Rebecca laughed again. She seemed to use laughter as punctuation rather than as a method of expressing joy or excitement.

"I'm afraid I haven't seen Nick since we split up. Not since he moved out and that was, oh, nearly two years ago now."

Kate cleared her throat. "I understand that Mr Fullman is something of a, shall we say, a workaholic? He works incredibly hard?"

Rebecca nodded. "He works very hard. Such long hours...that was always a bit of a sore point between us. I mean, I have my business – I'm a property investor – and that takes up a fair bit of time but I have a *life* as well, you know. Nick doesn't ever stop. That's why he's so successful, of course. He's driven." Her voice faltered for a moment. "He works out what he wants and then he goes and gets it. That's admirable, in a way. It's something I learnt from him, that if you really want something, you have to put your all into it. You have to go out and get it. No matter what it takes."

The door to the sitting room opened with a creak, making them all look over towards it. An elderly man paused with his hand on the door handle, peering at them.

"Rebecca?" he said, in a gentle voice, quavering a little. Rebecca jumped up.

"It's fine, Dad. These are the people I was telling you about."

The man, clearly Brigadier D'Arcy-Warner, stood for a moment, his head swinging a little from side to side. Although in his eighties, or perhaps even older, he still had a head of copious black hair, scarcely greyed at the temples. Rebecca turned to the police officers.

"Well, if that was all, perhaps we could call it a day?"

Her voice was anxious. Kate and Olbeck exchanged glances and got up.

"Who are these people?" said Brigadier D'Arcy-Warner. He didn't say it in a rude fashion, but Rebecca blushed, the pink of her cheeks clashing with the red of her hair.

"It doesn't matter, Daddy, they're leaving now. Go back to the sitting room and I'll bring you through a cup of tea. Go on now." He hesitated, one faintly shaking hand resting on the door handle. "I'll bring you through a cup of tea."

The Brigadier nodded vaguely and turned away, out of sight. They all heard his hesitant footsteps fade from hearing.

Rebecca remained standing.

"He has dementia," she said, to their unspoken question. "Not too severe as yet, but he gets very confused...very confused. I try and keep him in a routine, calm and ordered, you know. It helps."

"Does he live here alone?" asked Olbeck.

"No, he has a home help and carers that come in every day. And of course, I'm here most of the time. I can set my own hours, so I'm here pretty much every day."

"You don't live here?"

"No, I have my own place just outside of Tornford." She half-smiled. "Nick and I bought it together, actually. But he moved out, obviously, when we split up and he bought that modern monstrosity."

Kate pricked up her ears.

"You've been to Mr Fullman's house, then?"

Rebecca shrugged. "Just the once. I had to drop off some of his things." She grimaced. "Once was enough."

Olbeck nodded. "It's routine," he said. "But I have to ask you where you were on the night of the crime. Saturday, the fourteenth of January."

Kate expected another outburst of incredulity but Rebecca just sighed. "Yes, I thought you might ask me that," she said. "I can see that you have to – what's the phrase? Eliminate people from your enquiries." Olbeck nodded encouragingly. Rebecca sighed again. "I'm afraid that, as usual, I was here, with my father. I stayed the night. I usually do if I get here late."

"Is there anyone who can verify your presence here?"

"I'm afraid not." She sounded regretful.

"What about your father?"

Rebecca looked shocked.

"Well, yes. He could confirm it – for what it's worth. But as I've said, he has dementia. And, if it's not essential, I'd really prefer that you didn't ask him. It would confuse him and if he knew anything about the – well, the murder – it would upset him terribly."

What isn't essential in a murder case? Kate thought. She and Olbeck left it at that, shaking hands and handing over their cards as a matter of routine. Rebecca watched them drive away from the front door, holding her arms across her body, one elbow in each hand.

"What did you think?" asked Kate, as they drove onto the main road.

Olbeck shrugged. "Hard-nosed career type, if you ask me." He looked over at her and grinned. "Like you."

Kate half laughed to cover her sudden intake of breath. Was that the image she gave out? *Why not, Kate,* she asked herself. *Isn't that what it's all about? Isn't that what you wanted?*

"She's got no alibi," was all she said.

"We could ask the Major."

"Brigadier. But I agree with her that it's probably not worth our while."

Olbeck flicked on the indicator. "I got the impression that it was a pretty lukewarm sort of relationship. Her and Fullman, I mean. What motive would she have for kidnapping his kid and killing his nanny?"

It was Kate's turn to shrug. "You're right. Still, that's one more off the list."

"Onwards and upwards."

They drove in silence for a moment.

"I get the impression you don't really care for ambitious women," said Kate, after a long moment of thought. Was it too soon to be having this kind of conversation? The last thing she wanted to be was antagonistic.

Olbeck looked astonished. "Where did you get that impression?" he said.

Kate spread her hands. "I don't know. Just what you said back there – and you having what sounds like a nice little domestic goddess at home." She glanced at him sideways. "Am I wrong?"

Olbeck spluttered. "You could not be *more* wrong. God, you make me sound like a complete sexist."

"Sorry."

They drove in silence for another minute.

"God," said Olbeck, shaking his head. "I am so not like that. Kate, you really couldn't be more wrong. I'm all for the emancipated woman, believe me."

Kate laughed, relieved at his tone. "Sorry. I misread you."

"S'alright."

The car turned, slowing. Kate drummed her fingers on her knees.

"So, what does Jo do?" she asked just for something to say.

Olbeck looked over at her. "Acting," he said, briefly.

"Really? God, that's interesting. Would she have been in anything I've seen?" Kate reflected for a moment. "Actually, probably not. I don't watch much TV, and I can't remember when I last went to the cinema. Or theatre."

They'd arrived at the station and Olbeck swung the car into a parking space.

"Come on," he said, clearly ready to move on from the subject. "Paperwork time."

"Oh, joy."

Chapter Ten

Kate was halfway through her reports when her phone rang. She placed the voice on the end of the line immediately.

"What can I do for you, Ms Darcy-Warner?"

"Call me Rebecca, please. I'm sorry to bother you but I–" She hesitated for a moment. Kate sat up a little, reaching for her pen.

Rebecca continued. "I'm afraid I wasn't entirely truthful earlier. No, that's not correct, I didn't lie. I'm afraid I didn't tell you a few things. That's probably lying by omission, isn't it?"

"Never mind about that now, Rebecca. Can you tell me now?"

"It's probably not even relevant…"

"Let me be the judge of that. Please tell me and then you'll have done your duty." Kate said that last with a smile in her voice, trying to break down the other woman's reserve.

"Yes," said Rebecca, hesitating again. Then she plunged on. "It's just that – Nick – well, there was another reason we split up. There always is, isn't there?"

"Yes, indeed. And that other reason was?"

"Well– basically, he was keeping some very odd company. Some very reprehensible company. I didn't approve."

"Can you be more specific?"

"He said they were business associates but – I just didn't like them. I work in the property business too and you hear things… these men were notorious." Rebecca lowered her voice so that Kate had to strain to hear her. "They were gangsters."

"Gangsters?"

"Oh it sounds so melodramatic, doesn't it? But they were definitely not the people to get on the wrong side of."

"And Mr Fullman was working with them?"

"Well, I don't know about working with them – but he was definitely meeting them. He met them several times. They even came to our house once before I put my foot down."

"Can you give me their names?"

"I'm afraid not, not definitely. You see, I refused to listen when Nick tried to talk about them. I really didn't approve. I think they were called Costa, or Costas. Something like that."

Kate tried to push for a few more details but Rebecca insisted she didn't know any more. Eventually Kate gave up and thanked her for calling.

"You're welcome," said Rebecca. There was a slight pause and Kate was just about to say goodbye before Rebecca said suddenly, "It's funny, about Nick. He looks so, so adult and successful and together. You wouldn't have thought anyone could put anything over on him. But underneath it all, he's just a scared little boy."

Kate's eyebrows went up. "Is that–" she began, but Rebecca was speaking again.

"Just a scared, uncertain little boy. Perhaps that's why he needed so much *mothering*." For a moment, bitterness pervaded her voice. "Anyway, I hope I've been of help."

Kate assured her that she had, and they said goodbye. Kate stared at the replaced handset for a moment, tapping her pen on the edge of the desk and thinking. Then she lifted the telephone again and asked to speak to Anderton.

"Costa?"

"That's right, sir. She said 'Costa' or 'Costas.'"

Anderton and Olbeck exchanged glances. Kate interpreted it. "You know the name then?"

"Yes," said Anderton. "You're new here, DS Redman, so I'll forgive you for not picking this up." He smiled briefly. "The Costa brothers are known to us."

"What have they done?"

Anderton looked at Olbeck, who took up the conversation.

"Fraud, arson, extortion – or at least, that's what we've tried to charge them with at various times. Sometimes successfully and sometimes not. They're extremely wealthy and have a crack team of lawyers on their side."

"They've both spent time in prison," said Anderton. "Both are currently free, though. And they were free on the night of January 14th."

"Hmm," said Kate.

"Hmm, is right," said Anderton. "A lead worth following up, I think. Talk to Nick Fullman about his association with the Costa. Ask him why he didn't think this little nugget of information was worth mentioning when we questioned him before."

"Would you suspect them of something like this, sir?"

Anderton shrugged. "I don't believe they've ever stooped to murder or kidnapping *before*. That's not to say it's out of the question. It's a lead."

Kate and Olbeck nodded and went to get up.

"Wait," said Anderton. "While you're with Mr Fullman, you can ask him about this little matter as well." He reached into a desk drawer and withdrew a small sheet of white paper, enclosed in an evidence bag. He handed it to Olbeck, who smoothed it out on the desk top and read it aloud.

"*'Ask Fullman about Councillor Jones'*. What's this? When did you receive this, sir?"

"This morning, in an anonymous envelope, in the post. Addressed to me."

"Councillor Jones?" said Kate. "That's the–" She groped for a moment. "That's the guy he was having a drink with on the night of Charlie's disappearance, right?"

Anderton nodded.

"Councillor Gary Jones is a District Councillor for Abbeyford. He's on the planning committee and the brownfield regeneration committee. Nick Fullman works in property. Now, there may be nothing more natural than the two of them being buddies, but I want it looked into. If someone wants to cause trouble, enough to go to the effort of writing, or typing, an anonymous note, there may be something in it."

He tweaked the note from under Olbeck's fingers and waved a hand at them both. "Off you go, then."

Outside Anderton's office, Kate turned to Olbeck.

"Phew," she said. "Where to start?"

Olbeck began to count on his fingers.

"We've got Casey to question about Ali Saheed, Fullman to question about the Costa brothers and Councillor Jones, Mrs Bright to question full-stop, Councillor Jones to question about Nick Fullman and the Costa brothers to question if only for a reason for their revolting existence."

Kate rubbed her forehead.

"Where do you want to start?"

Olbeck started to walk down the corridor. Kate hurried after him.

"I'll take the Costa brothers." He shuddered. "God, for my sins. Theo or Jerry can do Councillor Jones. Why don't you do Casey and Mrs Bright and we'll track down Nick Fullman together?"

"Fine," said Kate. "Let's check back later."

She said goodbye and hurried off to find her car keys.

Chapter Eleven

THE PAPARAZZI AT THE GATES of the Fullmans' house had thinned in numbers slightly, and their replacement was, at first sight, more picturesque. A heap of blooms, a mountain of flowers: bouquets, baskets, single-stemmed white roses. Blue ribbons everywhere, tied to the trees and the fence and the gateposts.

As Kate drove through, she caught sight of a tiny blue teddy bear with white, fluffy paws. A middle-aged couple stood by the makeshift shrine, reading the inscriptions on the bouquets. Who were they mourning, these people who'd brought the flowers? Dita or Charlie? *He's not dead*, said Kate to herself, fiercely, because at the thought of Charlie dead, something seemed to collapse inside of her. She knew, logically, that he probably was. But logic didn't seem to have anything to do with it. *I can't think of him dead*, she thought, fingers clenched on the steering wheel. *I can't.*

She thought of all the blue ribbons fluttering in the cold January wind and felt something else, a surge of anger. What good were ribbons? What possible difference would tying a ribbon around a tree make? Would it get them one step closer to Charlie? *Stupid, stupid*, she hissed through gritted teeth, parking the car a little too abruptly by the front door.

The sight of Casey shocked her out of her anger. *Zombie* was the word that first came to mind when the door opened. Hollowed eyes, blonde hair darkened and flattened by grease, Casey swayed a little on her feet. She turned, saying nothing, and walked back through the house like a somnambulist, the dirty ends of her tracksuit trousers trailing on the floor.

Mrs Bright was there in the kitchen, perched on a stool by the breakfast bar, the local paper spread out before her and a half empty glass of orange juice in front of her. Kate greeted her and asked where Mr Fullman was.

Mrs Bright rolled her eyes. "At work? Where else is he ever?"

Kate nodded. She hesitated again, wondering whether to question Mrs Bright or to follow Casey. She decided on the latter. Casey worried her, seriously worried her.

She knocked on the door of the bedroom, although it was half open and she could see the dirty soles of Casey's feet dangling off the edge of the enormous bed. There was no answer so she pushed open the door.

Casey was lying face down, her head buried in the pillows. Kate said her name, gently at first and then with more urgency. At last, Casey turned her head to look at her.

"What?"

"Casey, please sit up. I need to speak to you."

In the end, she had to help her up, almost prop her against the headboard. Casey's pupils were huge and she stared blearily ahead, saying nothing. Kate was uncomfortably reminded of a doll from her childhood, a rare toy she'd been given by a neighbour, which had had the same blank stare, the same empty eyes.

"Casey," she said once more. "I told you we'd find Charlie for you and we will. But you have to help us. I need to talk to you about Ali Saheed."

That broke Casey's stupor. She flicked a frightened sideways glance at Kate.

"Why?"

"It's important."

"I told you, he couldn't have done this. He wouldn't."

"Why would you say that?"

Casey paused for a second.

"He always said family was important, even though he didn't have any kids of his own. He likes children. He was really happy for me when I got pregnant. He said so."

Kate sighed inwardly.

"People don't always mean what they say, Casey. Believe me, as a police officer I know that."

Casey started to cry.

"This is a nightmare, it's a nightmare. I can't believe it's happening. I think I'm going mad."

Kate fought against the urge to hug her, pat her on the back, rock her into comfort again.

"I just need to know if–"

Casey interrupted her, her words barely audible over loud sobs.

"I'm being punished. This is my punishment."

Kate frowned. "What do you mean by that, Casey?"

Casey shook her head, crying louder.

"Is it something that you feel you've done?" Kate hesitated, unsure of whether to go any further. Should she call Olbeck or Anderton? Was this going to be a confession? She could feel her heart rate begin to speed up, the sickness rising in her stomach. What to do?

She pressed on.

"Is it something you've done to – to Charlie?"

Casey shook her head again, almost screaming

"No, no! I would never hurt my baby, never. What are you, *sick*?"

She rolled away from Kate, burying her head in the pillows again. She said something else but it was too muffled for Kate to make out.

Kate sat back, thinking hard. Guilt, but not at something to do with the baby...if she was telling the truth. She ran through the possibilities, internally. What the hell, she was probably right...

She pulled at Casey's arm, speaking sharply. "Casey. Casey! Sit up, please. I need to ask you something."

After a few moments, Casey sat up again. She looked at Kate, sullenly.

Kate took the bull by the horns. "Did you have an affair with Ali Saheed?"

The expression on Casey's face, aghast and guilty, told her everything she needed to know. After a moment, Casey dropped her eyes. She gave a tiny nod of the head, so tiny it was almost imperceptible.

Kate sighed. "When was this?"

Casey looked up at her for a split second and then looked away.

"Not since the baby," she said quickly.

"Not since the birth or not since the pregnancy?"

Casey's voice wobbled. "Not since the birth. Of course not. Not for months."

"Was it just a one-off?"

"No. We – we were together on and off for years. But secretly, you know. I don't know why..." Her voice faded for a second. "I don't know why we didn't get together properly. Ali said it wouldn't be very professional."

But shagging his clients was? Kate mentally filed away her sarcastic comment without voicing it.

"So you've been in an on-going relationship with Mr Saheed for years?" A nod from Casey. "Does Mr Fullman know?"

Casey blanched. "God, no. He would kill me." She grabbed at Kate's arm, her eyes huge. "You won't tell him, will you? Please God, don't tell him. He'd kill me." She started to hyperventilate. "Oh Christ, oh God, why did I tell you? Don't tell him, please don't tell him..."

Kate hastened to soothe her as best she could.

"Casey, please don't worry. We'll do all we can to keep this between us."

Casey put her head in her hands. The part of her hair showed a inch-thick strip of dark brown hair, visible against the blonde streaks.

"I can't believe this," she whispered. "I know my affair was wrong but I *know* Ali, I know he wouldn't do this."

Kate took a deep breath. "I need to know all about this, Casey. Can you tell me?"

Silence from the woman on the bed.

"Casey. You have to talk to me. When did you two first, er, get together?"

Casey kept her head in her hands, but she began to speak, slowly and with a gasp in her voice.

"It was about five years ago now. I needed an agent and someone told me about him and so I rang him up. And then we met and there was, oh, I dunno, an instant attraction, I guess. And he was a good agent. He got me lots of work. Magazines and that TV show. We were never really a couple though, you know. We were just, just…"

Kate groped for the appropriate term. "Friends with benefits?"

Casey nodded. "Sort of. I mean, I guess I knew he had other girlfriends and I used to date a few guys myself. But somehow we always ended up sleeping together again. And then I met Nick and got pregnant, and then it just seemed wrong. I just couldn't do it any more."

"So you sacked him as your agent?"

Casey nodded. "I thought that would be the easiest way for both of us."

Mentally, Kate rolled her eyes. "You didn't really expect Mr Saheed to think that? He loses his client and his girlfriend in one go?"

Casey put her hands up to her eyes again. "I don't know," she cried. "I just had to, I couldn't – couldn't have Nick finding out, you don't know what he would have done."

Kate's antenna went up, quivering.

"You think Mr Fullman would have reacted angrily?" *Stupid*

question, Kate. She rephrased it. "I mean, obviously he would be angry, very angry, but you were scared of his reaction?" Casey didn't react. "Physically scared?"

Casey did nothing for a moment. Then she gave another small nod.

Kate drummed her fingers on her knees.

"Does Mr Fullman ever threaten you? Is he ever violent towards you? Or abusive in any way?"

Casey took her hands down from her face, wiping the tears from under her eyes.

"No," she sniffed. "He's not that bad."

Kate opened her mouth to ask another question but a knock on the door made them both jump. Mrs Bright stood in the doorway.

"Just came to see if you wanted a cup of tea?" she said, her eyes going straight to Casey's tear-stained face.

"We're fine, thank you, Mrs Bright," said Kate, inwardly cursing her for the interruption. The moment had gone, she could feel it.

"I want one," said Casey loudly, confirming Kate's realisation that the moment of confession was over. She got up from the bed, allowing Casey to swing her legs to the floor and followed her through to the kitchen.

Mrs Bright made Casey a cup of tea, and her daughter took it wordlessly. The brief spasm of defiance that she'd displayed seemed to have dissipated. She eyed Kate for a moment, blankly, and then turned and trailed away, back to the bedroom.

Kate let her go. She had Mrs Bright to talk to and this would be the perfect opportunity.

"I will have a cup, if there's one going, Mrs Bright," she said.

Sheila Bright nodded. Kate watched her make the tea. There was a huge, domed cluster of diamonds on her ring finger, sparkling over the other gold and platinum rings that cluttered her fingers.

"Are you married, Mrs Bright?" asked Kate.

Sheila handed her a mug of tea, the bag still in it, liquid slopping over the side.

"I was," she said, briefly. "Got divorced years ago."

"Is Casey your only child?"

A nod.

"So Charlie is your only grandchild?"

The artificially smooth face contracted for a moment. "Yes."

"It must be very distressing for you," said Kate. She took a sip of the awful tea. "We're doing all we can to find him."

Mrs Bright nodded. Kate pressed on.

"How did Casey find motherhood?" She revised her question quickly. "How is Casey finding motherhood? It's quite hard, the first time, isn't it?"

"She's okay," said Mrs Bright, non-committally. "As all right as she can be. She has a lot of help. Had a lot, poor Dita."

"Does Mr Fullman help her out with the baby?"

Mrs Bright laughed soundlessly. It was the first sign of animation she'd shown.

"Nick, help out? When would he have time? He's always at work isn't he? Besides..." She stopped talking, raising one glittering finger to her mouth for a moment.

"Besides, Mrs Bright?" prompted Kate.

Sheila Bright flicked her a sideways glance. "It's difficult for men, isn't it?" she said, evasively. "They don't always deal with babies too well. You know."

"I'm afraid I don't know, Mrs Bright. Can you elaborate?"

"Well, they get jealous, don't they? Only natural if they've been the centre of attention for so long. All of a sudden, there's someone else getting all the attention, isn't there? It's no wonder some men feel a bit pushed out."

"You're saying Mr Fullman felt pushed out when Charlie was born?"

Sheila Bright's face clearly wasn't capable of showing extreme emotion, but she looked a little uneasy. "Well, sort of," she said.

"Nothing bad or anything. I had the same thing with my ex-husband when Casey was born. It's normal."

"Is it?"

"Yes, it is," said Sheila Bright, shortly.

Kate put her mug down. "Do you think Mr Fullman resented his baby?"

"Don't be stupid," said Sheila Bright. Then she coloured a little. "Sorry. I didn't mean anything. All I meant was that men find it hard, don't they, that's all. Nothing worse than that. They get over it, anyway, once the baby's been here for a while. It all settles down."

They get over it, anyway... Kate thought about that as she drove away from the house. Did they? Had Nick Fullman gotten over it? Had he even had a chance? Was the bit about his behaviour true and, if it was, did it mean anything? She turned the car lights on, illuminating the road ahead, and pulled out of the driveway, keeping her face turned from the gates and the fluttering mass of ribbons, staring straight ahead into the gathering dusk.

Chapter Twelve

"Interesting," said Anderton. Kate and Olbeck were sat in his office, ostensibly facing his desk but actually turning this way and that in their chairs to keep him in view as he paced up and down.

"I don't know why I didn't think of it earlier," said Olbeck. "Saheed was obviously pretty cut up about the fact that he never saw Casey Fullman anymore."

A search of Ali Saheed's flat had yielded nothing of interest, except a half-full wrap of cocaine and some fairly vanilla pornography. Kate swivelled in her seat, trying to catch Anderton's eye.

"Casey is clearly scared of her husband," she said. "She said several times 'He'll kill me.' It wouldn't surprise me if he's abusive, emotionally abusive if not physically."

"And where is your evidence for that, DS Redman? A lot of wives would be very scared of their husbands finding out they'd had a five-year affair. It doesn't mean that they're all married to perpetrators of domestic violence."

Kate took a deep breath. "No, I appreciate that, but–"

"But what? You have no evidence of abuse. None. Dig around if you must, talk to a few more people. You can't assume from a throwaway comment – a throwaway comment from an extremely emotionally distraught woman – that it means anything of significance."

"Actually, sir," said Olbeck, seeing that Kate was momentarily wrong-footed. "It would be useful to get a bit more background on this development. Casey says no one knew, but in my experience, someone always knows."

Kate was thinking hard. There was something Gemma Phillips had said – what was it? She scrolled back through her mental files, searching for the pertinent phrase. What was it? She thought of her last interview with Gemma: the Mulberry bag, the false fiancée, the smile at the suggestion of an affair with Nick – *ah*. That was it. What had Gemma said when confronted with that very suggestion? She'd retorted something about it being Casey who'd told Kate that. What else? *But just try telling Casey that! She only thinks that because she–*

"Gemma Phillips," she said, slowly. "She knows. Or she knows something. I have a feeling she knows more about this than she's letting on. I'll talk to her again."

Anderton finally came to a halt and looked at her.

"Do that," he said, briefly. "Where are we with the other things?"

Olbeck consulted his notes.

"Jerry interviewed Gary Jones about his association with Nick Fullman. Insisted there was nothing more than a business acquaintanceship and that he wanted Nick's advice on investing in property. They were apparently discussing buy to let investments during their meeting on January 14th. Nothing else. "

"Have you spoken to Fullman about this, yet?"

"Not yet, sir."

"Well, do it. Quickly. What about the Costa brothers?"

"My report's here, sir." He handed over a file. Kate flashed him a glance, and he shook his head, minutely.

"Fine," said Anderton. "Redman, what about Gemma Phillips?"

"I haven't had a chance yet, sir. I was with Casey and Mrs Bright yesterday. I'm going there right now."

"Right," said Anderton, glancing through Olbeck's file. He didn't look up at her. "Get on with it, then."

Kate rang the Fullmans' house and got Mrs Bright on the end of the line.

"Gemma?" said Mrs Bright in answer to Kate's question. "No, she's not here today. I don't know if she's been in today or not, to be honest."

Kate asked, fairly hopelessly, to speak to Nick, and to her surprise was speaking with him in a matter of seconds.

"Nick Fullman here."

What are you doing at home? She managed not to voice the question with some difficulty. Instead, she asked whether Gemma was expected in the office at all today.

"She's not been in today," said Nick, conventionally enough. Then his tone began to change to one of outrage. "She's been really slack as a matter of fact, asked me for a couple of days holiday, which I could really have done without at this time, but I said yeah, no problem. Then she's supposed to be back today and she doesn't turn up, she's not answering her phone..."

"She hasn't been in contact?" said Kate. She was conscious of a faint, creeping unease.

Nick Fullman's hard, angry tones came down the line.

"Not a phone call, not a text or an email. I'd go round to her place myself but I can't leave Casey. I don't know what's the matter with her, She's not like this usually."

"I'll call on Ms Phillips myself," said Kate. Two memories popped up: Casey's white face as she said *Don't tell him, he'll kill me* and Gemma's face at the window of her house, looking furtively out at Kate from behind the curtains. That creeping feeling of unease was getting stronger.

"What's up?" said Olbeck, as she put the phone down. Kate explained in a few sentences and he nodded his head.

"Think we ought to take a look?"

Kate was already gathering up her coat. "I do. Let's go."

They didn't talk much on the drive there. The house looked as normal when they parked outside, a light on in the front room, the closed curtains glowing gently. Kate and Olbeck looked at each other.

"Come on," said Kate, and they got out of the car and knocked at the door.

There was no answer.

Kate banged the cheap, loose brass knocker once more. Then once more. Then she knelt and shouted through the letterbox.

"Gemma! It's DS Redman, Kate Redman. Are you there?"

Silence. Olbeck moved to the living room window and knelt, peering through the minute gap between the edge of the curtain and the windowsill. Then he straightened up.

"Let's get that door open," he said, and something in his voice made Kate shudder involuntarily.

The two of them got the door open in three shoulder charges. Inside the house was warm and stuffy, a faint breath of something in the air almost too intangible to notice. There was still enough for the two of them to approach the half-open living room door with dread.

Gemma Phillips lay slackly on the sofa, one outflung arm brushing the floor. Pulled tightly around her throat was a silk scarf, its marbled blue and green pattern horribly matched to the cyanotic hue of her dead face. Her mouth hung open and her eyes were closed.

Kate and Olbeck stood and looked for a long moment. Kate could hear her own fast breathing echoed in Olbeck's but neither of them said anything – they just stood and looked at poor Gemma, lying there dead on the sofa until the silence stretched out interminably and Olbeck finally reached for his phone.

Chapter Thirteen

"She was killed with this," said Doctor Telling, indicating the silk scarf coiled incongruously in a metal kidney bowl on the autopsy table. "Obviously. But it wouldn't surprise me if she was drugged first. I'll have to wait until the stomach contents have been analysed before I can say for certain. But from the posture, the looseness of the limbs…yes, I'd say it was highly possible she was drugged first."

Anderton nodded. They were all there in the autopsy theatre – Kate, Olbeck and Anderton – watching Doctor Telling perform her work on Gemma Phillips.

"So she wouldn't have known anything about it?" said Kate. She looked at Gemma's face, plainer than ever now stripped of life and make-up, and felt a terrible sadness.

Doctor Telling shrugged her thin shoulders.

"I'm not sure. I wouldn't have thought so."

"I hope you're right," muttered Kate, almost under her breath. Olbeck patted her on the shoulder.

"Poor girl," he said. Kate thought he was referring to Gemma, but who knew?

Back in the station control room, Anderton regarded the scene of crime photographs from Gemma's house.

"No sign of a struggle," he said. "No sign of forced entry. She almost certainly knew her killer."

"Almost certainly?" said Kate. "I wouldn't have thought there was any doubt about it."

Anderton glanced at her.

"No doubt you are right, DS Redman. I never like to make emphatic statements such as yours until I'm absolutely certain of the facts."

"That's right," said Olbeck, and Kate gave him an annoyed glance. "We're assuming that Gemma's murder is a direct result of Dita's murder and Charlie's kidnapping. But what if it's not? What it it's completely unrelated, just a bad coincidence? What if one of her internet dating buddies killed her?"

"Oh, come *on*," said Kate. "That's ridiculous. It's got to be connected."

"We have to look at every possibility."

"Mark's right," said Anderton, interrupting Kate as she was taking a deep breath, about to launch into a tirade. "But you're right as well. I want you to have a look at her bank statements. Go through them with a fine-tooth comb if necessary. Go through her *house* with a fine-tooth comb. Get the evidence."

Kate shook herself, trying to calm down. "Yes, sir."

"Get on with it then. I'll swear the warrant for you."

Kate remained standing. "What about the Fullmans?"

Anderton glanced at her.

"I'll deal with them. Get on with looking in Gemma's affairs. Olbeck, you too."

"Has Nick Fullman got an alibi for the night of Gemma's murder?" asked Kate, stubbornly.

"Are you trying to tell me how to do my job, DC Redman?"

"No, sir." *Stop it Kate, you're antagonising him. Just leave it.* "I'm just anxious to cover all bases, like you said." *Just shut up.*

"Come on," said Olbeck, propelling her towards the door. "Bank first. You can drive."

Out in the corridor, he shook his head. "God, girl, don't you know when to shut up?"

Kate twitched her shoulders crossly. "Oh, leave it out, will you? It's just – you know we need to look at the Fullmans. At Nick Fullman particularly."

Olbeck raised his eyebrows.

"But not Casey?"

Kate shook her head.

"Well," said Olbeck. "You're probably right. But you can't go steaming in and accusing people without evidence, as well you know."

"Are you telling me I don't know that?" said Kate. "For fuck's sake, Mark. That's why we need to be checking alibis and so forth."

Olbeck chuckled. "That's the first time I've heard you swear."

"I can assure you that it won't be the last."

"Look, Anderton's no fool. He'll dig up anything that necessary."

They had reached the car. Kate flung herself into the driver's seat.

"You suspect him, then?" said Olbeck quietly as he got in next to her.

Kate glanced over. "Don't you?"

"It's possible," said Olbeck cautiously.

Kate made a noise indicative of impatience but said nothing else, putting her foot down on the accelerator.

The manager at Gemma's bank was forthcoming and led them to a private room at the back of the bank with the paperwork all ready for them. Kate spread the statements out on the table and waited for the manager to leave.

"Plain as day," she said as the door shut. She pointed. "Look, here and here. Large cash sums deposited."

"Blackmail payments," said Olbeck.

Kate nodded. "It's possible. As you might say."

He gave her a half-grin.

"The dates tally. Look, the first thousand goes in here, two days after Dita's death. Then another a week later. Big one, that one. She must have used some of the cash to buy that Mulberry bag."

"Someone didn't want to pay out any more and killed her instead?"

"It looks like it. She must have known who took Charlie, or killed Dita, or both." Kate stared across the room at the bank wall, unseeingly. "I *knew* she knew something. Secretaries always know something. I should have pushed her harder to talk."

"You didn't know she was going to be killed. Everyone's always hiding something in a murder case, you know that. It's finding out what's important and what's not that's difficult."

"I know. It's just..." she let the sentence tail off in a sigh.

Olbeck gathered up the papers.

"I know. It's shit. But let's get this stuff back to the station and get to her house."

"It has to be someone in that house," said Kate as they left the building.

Olbeck looked across at her.

"You're probably right," he said. "But we need to–"

"Get the evidence, I know," said Kate. They got into the car. "What happened with the Costa brothers?"

Olbeck exhaled loudly. "The usual. Superficial charm, then outrage and bombast at the accusation that they had anything to do with this case at all. 'I've got two sons of my own, Detective Sergeant Olbeck', as if that precluded any parent from doing anything criminal at all at any time. Both with rock-solid alibis for the night of the 14th."

"What about the night Gemma was killed?"

"How would I know? It hadn't happened when I interviewed them."

Kate slapped her forehead. "Duh. Sorry."

"You buffoon."

Kate grinned, despite herself. "You've got a good vocabulary for a copper."

"Oh, cheers," he said sarcastically. "'For a copper'. Do you mind? I get enough of that at home."

Gemma's little house had a forlorn appearance, made worse by the police tape cordon and the little straggle of curious onlookers. Kate wondered whether people would come and tie ribbons to the railings outside to join the few pathetic bunches of flowers that had been laid on the pavement. Pink ones, naturally. She gritted her teeth.

Ravinder Cheetam, Rav to his colleagues, and Jerry Hindley were already there, working methodically through cupboards and drawers. They nodded at Kate and Olbeck.

"There's more designer stuff here than you shake a stick at," said Rav. He held up a Prada bag. "Clothes in the bedroom. New iPad. Looks like she was spending for England."

Kate stirred the tissue paper that had drifted onto the floor with her foot. "Shame she never got to enjoy any of it."

"Right."

"Jane and Theo are interviewing the neighbours," said Jerry, to Olbeck. Kate couldn't put her finger on it, but she had the impression that Jerry didn't much like her. It annoyed her, but this wasn't the time or place to worry about it.

"I'll look upstairs," she said.

Gemma's bedroom was mostly white and pink, the bed unmade, a hot-pink quilted throw half-slipped to the floor. A grubby pair of slippers with the backs trodden down peeked out from under the bed. The sight of them made Kate feel sad again. She began to work through the bedside cupboard, finding the usual stash: condoms, tissues, old pens, broken necklaces, a vibrator shoved right to the back. In the base of the cupboard were several self-help books dealing with relationships. More glossy magazines. An older model mobile phone.

She moved to the wardrobe, which was stuffed with clothes, mostly the formal work suits that Gemma had so often been seen in, but some dresses, shirts, short skirts to show off those long legs. What seemed like hundreds of pairs of shoes. Kate thought of her own pathetic collection of footwear at home, a black pair of heels, work shoes, trainers, Birkenstocks. Sometimes she felt as if she was slightly weird, unfeminine, not in the least like women that the media and society kept trying to tell her were doing it right. Mind you, Gemma had seemed to be very much that type of woman, and where had it got her?

She got down on her knees to search under the bed, pulling out more shoe boxes, dust-covered hair clips, old tissues. The tips of her fingers touched something hard and square. She pulled it out – a photograph album. Leafing through it, she could see that the photographs were reasonably recent. Strange, to have a photo album at all – most people used digital albums. The photos were all of Gemma and Nick. *All* of them, Kate realised. Nothing revealing, just everyday shots of the two of them in the office, at various building sites and properties, a couple of party scenes where they shared the same frame. How strange. Poor Gemma must have had a massive crush on her boss. Had it been reciprocated? Was Casey as ignorant of her husband's affairs as he was (as far as Casey knew) of hers? Kate made a mental note to talk to Nick herself and to hell with Anderton if he didn't like it.

There was a photograph near the end of the album that snagged her eye. In it, Gemma and Nick stood side by side, smiling, and on Nick's other side was a woman that after a moment Kate was able to place as Rebecca D'Arcy-Warner. Nick and Gemma were smiling into the camera, full, beaming smiles but Rebecca was looking out of shot and the expression on her face pulled at Kate, nudged her somewhere. It was a look of – what? Misery? Hunger? Something of the two, perhaps. It was an expression she'd seen somewhere before without being able to place it. It made her uneasy - it had a connection with something unpleasant in her memory. With what? She couldn't remember. No doubt it would come back to her. She couldn't tell where the photograph had been taken. The background was blurred – it looked something like a stone wall. She regarded for a moment longer and then shut the album.

Back at the station, Jane and Theo related the findings of their interviews with the neighbours.

"Nothing of great interest," said Jane. She was short and plump, with glorious red curls of the kind you don't see much anymore. *Pre-Raphaelite*, said Kate to herself, watching her talk. What a satisfaction it was to be able to find the right word. What a satisfaction it was to know you were at least adequately educated, even if you'd had to educate yourself.

"Although several people did report seeing a tall man in a Barbour jacket walking towards the house that night," said Theo. "Not actually in Gemma's street, but in the street leading to it. It's probably nothing, but we'll chase it up. Unfortunately it was a bad night, lots of rain and cold so everyone was indoors with the curtains closed."

"We need more background on Gemma Phillips," said Anderton. He turned to Kate. "Would you talk to the people who knew her best? The Fullmans to start with. I'll come with you."

"Yes sir," said Kate, inwardly cheering. Perhaps Anderton had forgiven her for her outburst the previous day.

Nick Fullman opened the front door to them himself. For the first time since Kate had met him, he was dressed casually, in jeans, socked feet and a grey sweatshirt, his dark hair unbrushed, his jaw dark with stubble. He looked stunned, bludgeoned by the knowledge of his assistant's death. Kate wavered a little in her suspicions of him. He looked truly *shocked,* and that was something that was very difficult to fake.

In the kitchen, Nick sat down at the kitchen table. Casey was nowhere to be seen. After a moment, he collected himself and asked whether they wanted coffee.

"I'm not sure where it all is," he said, gesturing to the cupboards. "But if you want one–"

"No, thank you, Mr Fullman." Was the man so babied, so pampered, that he'd never made his own coffee? "We wanted to talk to you about Gemma Phillips, if you feel up to answering some questions? I can see that you've had a shock."

"I have. I can't take it in. Not after everything else. Gemma – I mean, why? Why would someone kill her?" He looked up at them. "She was killed, wasn't she? I mean, I was told she was but –"

"But what, Mr Fullman?"

"I don't know." He shrugged his shoulders. "I thought, it's stupid but perhaps she'd taken Charlie and she – she was so remorseful she'd – you know, killed herself." He looked at their faces. "No, okay, it's a stupid theory."

"I'm afraid there's no doubt that she was murdered, Mr Fullman. Did you really suspect her of having something to do with Charlie's abduction and Dita's death?"

"Well, no – it's just that your mind comes up with all these strange ideas..." He trailed off, running a hand through his messy hair. "I trusted her. I really did trust her, I had to. She had access to everything, all my accounts, business dealings. Like a PA does. That's what I couldn't understand, that I trusted her and yet I still thought – thought she might have done it."

Olbeck and Kate exchanged a glance.

"When did these...suspicions first arise, Mr Fullman?"

"No, you've got it wrong. They weren't really suspicions. I was just thinking – you know – forget I said it. It's really not important now, is it? Not now that this awful thing has happened."

"You weren't angry at her? When you had these ideas?"

"No, and I just said, it wasn't important. It was a throwaway comment, that's all. Just a theory and a pretty stupid one, I know that."

"That's fine, sir," said Olbeck smoothly, as Kate opened her mouth to ask another question. "We're just trying to establish what happened on the night Gemma died. You said she'd asked you for a few days holiday, is that right?"

Nick nodded.

"Yeah. She rings me up and asks for a few days off, doesn't give me any kind of excuse except to say that she just needs a bit of time off after all that's happened."

"Was she in the habit of asking you for time off at short notice?"

"No, she wasn't. She took the odd sick day here and there but she'd never really asked for time off out of the blue for no good reason."

"She'd worked for you for quite a long time, hadn't she?"

Nick shrugged.

"I guess so. A few years."

"So would you say you were close friends? Close colleagues?"

Nick stared as if they'd asked him the name of Gemma's first pet or favourite shade of blue. "I suppose so," he said, after a moment.

"Can you tell us about her? One of the things we try and do is construct a picture of the victim, their likes and dislikes, their history, family and friends and so forth. Can you help us with that sort of thing?"

"Well..."

"It would be a great help to us if you could."

"Well, I'll try," said Nick Fullman. His mouth twisted. "I need Gemma for this. She'd know what to do." His voice thickened and he stopped talking for a second, pinching the bridge of his nose hard. "Sorry, I just–"

"Take a moment if you need one, sir," said Anderton. Kate drummed her fingers on her knees impatiently.

Nick took a deep breath and sat back. "Gemma's thirty-five, I think. *Was* thirty-five. She didn't like celebrating her birthday much, I can't even remember when it was, around June, I think."

"Was she a good secretary?"

"Pretty good. I mean, she could be a little bit lazy sometimes, and she clearly didn't have anything like I do invested in the business – by that I mean it wasn't important to her, not really. I could see that it was just a job to her, but she was okay."

"You two spent long hours working together, didn't you?" asked Kate.

Nick looked at her narrowly.

"Yes."

Kate hesitated, not sure whether to get this personal just yet. Would Anderton head her off? She made up her mind to go ahead. "Long hours and close working conditions can mean that people get, well, more involved with one another than they might do normally."

Nick was still staring at her.

"And?" he said.

"Was there ever anything more between you and Miss Phillips than an employer/employee relationship?"

"Why the hell would you ask that?"

"Could you please answer me, sir?"

Nick dropped his eyes to the table.

"Of course not," he said. "I'm a married man, for a start."

So what? Since when had marriage vows ever stopped anybody? She thought for a second of a name she'd left in the past long ago, the silly sixteen-year-old it had belonged to. Had marriage vows stopped that teenager from doing what she did? She cleared her throat.

"There was never anything between you at all?"

"I said no, didn't I?" said Nick, irritably. He looked at her and she realised he disliked her as much as she disliked him. Anderton raised a placatory hand.

"Thank you, sir. My colleague is just trying to ascertain the facts. One thing we do need to know is what you were doing on the night of Gemma's death."

If the question about an alleged affair hadn't shaken Nick Fullman, this one did. He sat back in his chair, blinking.

"You can't seriously suspect me of – of this. What are you saying?" He was gripping the table with both hands. "You're not serious?"

Anderton attempted to soothe him. "It's routine, Mr Fullman, you must know that. We have to ask everyone connected with the case to establish their whereabouts at the time of the crime."

Slowly, Nick relaxed his grip on the table. He sat back, flexing his fingers a little. His hands shook.

"Fine, fine, I see that," he muttered. "It just gave me a shock."

"So can you confirm your whereabouts between the hours of seven pm and one am on the night of January twenty-fourth?"

"I was..." he began, and then apparently had to stop and think. "I was at the office. I had to work late. It was flat out, particularly as Gemma hadn't been there that day. I couldn't believe she'd just left me to get on with it. I couldn't *believe* it. Oh God–" He clearly recollected what had happened to his absent assistant. "I didn't mean...anyway, I was at work. In the office."

"Can anyone corroborate that? Did you speak to anyone? Did anyone call in to see you?"

Fullman thought for a moment. "I'm not sure. I – wait, I did make a few phone calls. I–" He stopped talking suddenly.

"Who did you speak to?" There was silence. "Mr Fullman?"

"No one in particular," said Nick, reluctantly.

"Come now, Mr Fullman. Who did you speak to?"

"Um, a friend of mine on the Council. We're friends..."

"Would this be Councillor Gary Jones?"

Fullman looked shocked. "Yes, how did you know?"

"Never mind that now. You spoke to Gary Jones at what time?"

"I don't know, I can't remember. It was late, after nine."

"A strange time to be making a business call," said Kate, earning herself a glare from Nick Fullman.

"It might be to you, Sergeant, but not to me. Besides, it was a personal call, not a business call."

"That's fine," said Anderton, seeing that Kate was about to

speak. "The telephone company can provide us with details of your calls." Fullman shifted in his seat again. "We can also confirm your conversation with Councillor Jones himself."

There was a moment of silence in the kitchen, an oddly loaded period of quiet. Then Anderton spoke again. "If you have anything else to tell us, Mr Fullman, I suggest you do so now."

Nick Fullman looked frightened. Kate was reminded of what Rebecca D'Arcy-Warner had said. *Underneath it all, he's just a scared, uncertain little boy...*

"Is there anything you have to tell us, Mr Fullman?" repeated Anderton.

"No," said Nick Fullman, almost inaudibly. Then he said it again, in a firmer voice. "No, there's not."

Chapter Fourteen

Olbeck was surveying the slipping piles of paperwork on his desk with dismay when the desk phone rang, almost hidden under a pile of reports. He pushed the paper to one side, cursing as several folders crashed to the floor, and lifted the receiver.

"DS Olbeck."

The voice on the other end of the phone was quiet.

"I don't want to give my name."

"Fine. How can I help you?"

It was a man's voice, oddly furtive.

"Did you get my note? About Councillor Jones?"

Olbeck mentally sat up straighter.

"We did. Do you have some further information for us, sir?"

There was a moment's hesitation. Then the anonymous voice spoke again.

"Ask Councillor Jones about contaminated land and building on it. Ask Nick Fullman about his new development."

"Can you be more spe–" began Olbeck and then there was the click and burr of a broken connection. He regarded the buzzing handset for a second before replacing it.

"What is it?" said Kate, who had been listening alertly from the other side of the desk.

"The plot thickens. I'll tell you in the car. Come on, we're going to do some digging."

Kate raised her eyebrows.

"Not literally, I hope."

"You never know."

Olbeck drove to Wallingham, pulling up on the edge of a building site. Kate stared through the windscreen at the activity going on: the hauling of bricks, the earth movers, the scaffolding.

"I didn't think you were serious about the digging."

Olbeck grinned. "Don't worry, I just wanted to have a look."

"What is this?" asked Kate, pretty sure she knew the answer.

"Nick Fullman's new development," said Olbeck. Kate nodded. "This is the main project he's working on at the moment."

"Right," said Kate. "And your anonymous caller believes that this land is actually contaminated?"

"That's what they said."

"Contaminated with what?"

"I have no idea."

"Where's their evidence?"

"For all I know, they have none. It could be complete fantasy. Or a personal vendetta against Gary Jones. Or Nick Fullman."

Kate sighed. "So where do we go from here?"

Olbeck took his notebook out of his pocket and started writing.

"We get samples taken for evidence of contamination. If there's something dodgy, then we've got something to go on. We can start questioning people."

"We need to question them anyway. Gary Jones, Nick Fullman and those brothers. How do they tie up with this?"

Olbeck tapped his pen against the steering wheel. "They freely admit to *knowing* Nick Fullman. But I agree with you. They're in this somewhere. The question is, is it actually relevant to the kidnapping and the murders? Or is it just coincidence?"

Kate put her hands in her pockets, hunching her shoulders against the chill wind. She watched the excavators pushing mounds of earth up from a gigantic hole dug in the ground. Pallets of bricks and concrete blocks were stacked up against the chain link fence, and she saw the yellow mass of a digger move slowly along behind the makeshift barrier.

"Let's organise the samples," she said, eventually. "And see where that takes us."

"I'll get Theo to do it. Come on, it's freezing, let's go back."

THE NEXT DAY KATE FOUND herself driving towards Essex, visor tipped down against the winter sun. She found Mr Fullman Senior's place without much drama, pulling into the driveway of a much-extended Thirties house and slotting the car behind a large, black Range Rover.

The woman who answered the door was the person she'd spoken to on the phone. Evie Fullman was John Fullman's second wife, a fact she appraised Kate of almost as soon as she was in the door.

"Oh, no, I'm his step-mother, love," she said, ushering Kate though to the kitchen and perching on one the stools by the breakfast bar. "John's first wife died young, not long after Nick was born, poor soul. He felt it, you know. Well, you would, wouldn't you?" She hopped off her stool and stood poised by the kettle. "Tea?"

"Yes, please. Thank you for seeing me, Mrs Fullman."

"Ooh, call me Evie, please. It's no problem. Anything I can do to help. I can't sleep for thinking of poor Charlie, you know. That poor little mite." She turned her head away sharply, looking at the boiling kettle as if it fascinated her. "Anyway, what was it you wanted to know?"

Kate had heaved herself rather awkwardly up onto a stool.

"I wanted to know about Nick, Mrs Fullman – Evie. Nick and Casey. Presumably you've known Nick for some years? When did you and Mr Fullman marry?"

Evie pursed up her lips, pouring the tea with skill.

"Now that would be telling. All of – ooh, twenty years or so, now. Gawd, doesn't that make me sound ancient?" She handed Kate a mug of tea and hopped up onto her perch again. There was something very birdlike about her: she was a small woman, bosomed like a pigeon, her hair teased into a brittle beehive. Kate felt there was something familiar about her and after a moment, it came to her. Evie reminded her of her mum, except with an added dash of vigour and intelligence and, let's face it, she probably wasn't a piss-head.

"Tea all right, love?" said Evie, with her head on one side.

"Lovely, thanks," said Kate. "So you've known Nick since he was a little boy? You said he was badly affected by his mother's death?"

Evie nodded. "Yes he was. Well, you would be, wouldn't you? There's nothing like your own mother, is there?" Kate winced. "He felt it badly, and I don't believe John really knew how to handle it, to be honest. Well, he's a man, what are you going to do? You didn't talk feelings in them days, not really."

"How do you and Nick get on?"

Evie eyed her. "Fine, love, as far as I know. We don't see him very often."

"Sorry, I meant more – how did you get on in his childhood? Did he resent his father marrying again?"

That was probably slightly too personal a question, but Kate thought she'd chance it.

"Oh, right you are. Well, it's funny you should say that because you'd have thought that he'd be one to be very jealous. But he wasn't. I think he was quite pleased to have a step-mum. He said as much to me, one day. Made me well up, that did."

"You thought he'd be jealous? Is he a jealous type of person?"

Evie nodded. "He's very intense, love. Always has been. He feels things – and when he was a little boy, he didn't mind showing it. He and his Dad..." She paused for a second to take a sip of cooling tea. "His dad's very old school. He's proud of Nick, of course he is, but they ain't got much in common anymore. Makes them both feel a bit lonely, I think, when they're together."

Kate said nothing, turning her tea cup around in her hands. Then she asked about Casey.

"Nick's wife," she nearly said second wife, "Nick's wife, Casey. How do you get on with her?"

"Me?" Evie raised her eyebrows. "She's a nice girl. Not got a lot to her, to be honest. Not what I'd call a strong personality. That probably suits Nick, though. Always the same with these, what-do-yer-call-em, charismatic men, isn't it? Got little, pretty, quiet wives in the background."

"Would you say it was a happy marriage?"

Evie laughed and then looked sober. "Gawd, I shouldn't be laughing, not with how things are. But, just thinking about it, yes, it seems happy enough for two people who've only been married a year." She winked. "Get to twenty years and then ask me, love, that's when you can say it was happy or not."

Kate smiled. She was thinking that if she were Nick Fullman, she'd have been quite pleased to have this woman for a stepmother too.

"He was with his previous girlfriend for a long time, wasn't he?" she commented.

"Rebecca?"

"Yes," said Kate.

There was a slight change in the atmosphere, almost too subtle for Kate to notice but it was there, just the slightest chill in the air. She mentally sat up a little, alert.

"Rebecca," repeated Evie. She hopped back off her stool and went to the counter, hand poised over the kettle. "More tea, love?"

"No, thanks," said Kate. "Can you tell me anything about Rebecca D'Arcy-Warner?"

Evie had her back turned, busying herself with the kettle.

"Oh, she was a nice girl too," she said. The unspoken "but" hung in the air.

"But?" said Kate.

Evie turned back around to face her. Behind her, the kettle threw clouds of steam into the air.

"Well, for starters, she was a bit out of Nick's league, wasn't she?" Not waiting for an answer, she went on. "She was a cut or five above him, I'd say, and it showed. He felt that, too. Not so much when they were together but when they came here…or saw his old friends…" She trailed off, regarding the teapot blankly. "I always thought there was something a bit…oh, well, it doesn't matter now."

"What do you mean, Evie?"

"Oh, nothing really."

Kate hesitated, wondering whether to push it. Then Evie went on.

"She wasn't a happy girl. Well, woman. No, that she wasn't. That family – well, there were a few stories about her people, posh as they were."

"What do you mean?"

Evie pulled herself back onto her stool, slowly.

"Perhaps it's like that with all those old families," she said, settling herself. "They go back so far, there's always a few who are not quite right."

Kate mentally shook her head.

"Would you say Rebecca, then, was 'not quite right?' Is that what you're trying to say?" Evie said nothing for a moment. Kate persisted. "I know I sound really nosy, but it could be important. Evie?"

Evie pulled out a packet of cigarettes from her cardigan pocket. Without answering, she lit one with a pink plastic lighter and regarded the blue coil of smoke rising slowly from the tip.

"I'm not sure," she said, reluctantly. "It's just something that Nick said once. She'd had some sort of breakdown. Mentally, I mean."

"When?"

"Ooh, I don't know."

"When he was with her? Or afterwards?"

"I'm not sure."

"Was it serious?" Kate wondered whether this was relevant or not. Was she wise to keep pushing for information?

"I don't know, love and that's the truth." Evie gazed at her, blandly, her bouffant head cocked to one side.

"Well..." said Kate, hesitatingly.

"He wasn't kind to her," said Evie, suddenly. She tapped non-existent ash from her cigarette into the ashtray.

"Who wasn't? Nick?"

"I mean, I'm fond of him but even I could see he wasn't kind. Told him too, I did. Never did hold back with giving my opinions."

"You're saying Nick wasn't kind to Rebecca?" Kate checked. "In what way? Was he abusive toward her?"

Evie's eyebrows went up. "Nick? Gawd, no. Not like *that*. I meant, it wasn't kind of him to keep her hanging on like that."

"How do you mean?"

"Well, girls can say they're not interested in getting married, but you show me one who really isn't. They can say it all they like but they don't fool me."

Kate shifted a little.

"Some women really don't want to get married," she said stiffly.

Evie gave her a wry look.

"Righto. I don't buy it myself. Even the gay ones want to get married nowadays, don't they?"

Kate refused to be sidetracked by this interesting side issue. "Rebecca and Nick were together for a long time. They did get engaged."

Evie snorted. "Engaged, yes, but what does that mean? She was pushing for something more, and Nick threw that her way to keep her happy. Didn't mean it was ever going to actually *happen*."

"And it didn't," said Kate, almost to herself. She was thinking hard. "Rebecca said that her relationship with Nick fizzled out, that they both realised it was for the best when they split up. Do you think that was the case?"

Evie shrugged. "Love, when you get to my age you realise you don't know much about other people's relationships. All I know is what I said to Nick. That girl wanted to get married and you kept her hanging on for it. That's not kind."

"And how did he react when you said that?"

Evie looked uncomfortable. "He laughed." There was a moment's silence. "He didn't mean it to be cruel. He just didn't see what he'd done wrong."

Kate nodded.

"How is he with Charlie?" she asked, switching tack.

Evie looked wary. "What do you mean?"

Kate smiled, trying to put her at her ease. "Is he a hands-on dad, would you say? Was he excited to be a father?"

Evie stubbed out her cigarette. She hopped down from her stool once more and began to to wash up her tea cup, slowly rinsing it under the tap.

"I suppose so," she said, over the noise of rushing water. "It's hard when they're tiny babies though, isn't it? Men don't really get it. They're all for their mums, then, aren't they? Dads aren't really needed."

"Would you say he'd bonded with the baby?"

"Bonded?"

"Yes. Was he affectionate with Charlie? Did he–" Kate stopped herself. "Does he love him?"

Something of Evie's vivacity dimmed a little. She had a tea towel in her hands and she folded it very exactly, lining up the edges and hanging it over the back of one of the kitchen chairs. Kate had the feeling she was stalling for time.

"He was fine with him," she said, shortly. "As fine as he needed to be. There wasn't much he could do with him, was there, Charlie being so young. They just want their mums at that age." Kate flinched, unable to help herself.

There was a moment's silence. Kate knew she should keep questioning Evie, knew she should delve deeper into this line of enquiry, but she was suddenly taut with pain and she didn't think she could trust her voice.

Driving away from the house, uncomfortably full of tea, Kate heard the buzz of an incoming text message on her mobile. She pulled over and checked it. It was from Jay, her younger half-brother, one of her mother's second family and her favourite sibling. Smiling, she opened up the message to find the smile dropping from her face. *Sis, pls call me. Mum in hosp. J xx* read the text.

Kate leant her head against the steering wheel for a moment, swearing softly. This wasn't the first time she'd received news like this. The first time had had her tearing to the hospital in question, even running a red light on the way, such was her hurry. She'd virtually sprinted to the ward to find her mother fast asleep in a hospital bed and apparently undamaged except for the reek of whisky fumes that permeated her clothes. *Shame they don't have drunk tanks in hospitals*, Kate had hissed furiously to her when she finally woke up.

Now, she just *knew* it would be something similar. She battled with her conscience for a moment and then texted Jay. *Anything serious? Am flat out at wrk. Let me know, K xx*. She drove on, listening out for the chime of an incoming text, hoping against hope that she wouldn't hear it.

Chapter Fifteen

"Got something you might find interesting," said Olbeck the next morning, waving a handful of paper under Kate's nose. She looked up from the screen of her mobile – Jay had finally texted her back. *Broken ankle. Sis CALL ME pls x*. She sighed.

"What's up?"

She shook her head. "Nothing that can't wait. What am I going to find interesting?"

Olbeck drew up a chair and fanned the papers out in front of her. "Soil samples from the Wallingham site."

Kate raised her eyebrows. "That was quick. And?"

"It was only quick because apparently the lab had already had several samples posted to them – anonymously. So when our environmental scientist sent ours through, they matched them up pretty quickly."

"Someone had already sent some through?"

Olbeck nodded. "Probably our mystery caller, don't you think?"

Kate bent over the papers.

"I can't make heads nor tails of this," she said after a moment. "Is it contaminated, or isn't it?"

Olbeck grinned. "Once you get past the geek speak, I think the consensus is that although it's nothing too drastically poisonous, the general opinion is that planning permission should not have been granted without, shall we say, some heavy decontamination of the land involved."

"And I assume that hasn't happened?"

"Nope."

"Hmm."

Theo walked over, having clearly overheard what they were discussing.

"Another thing," he said, perching on the side of the desk and knocking over Kate's empty mug. "Whoops, sorry. Anyway, I was doing a bit more digging back into the building regs and paperwork for the site, and guess whose subsidiary company comes up as a part-backer of the development?"

Kate struck a dramatic pose, hand to her forehead. "Could it possibly be...the Costa brothers' company by any chance?"

Theo grinned. "Got it in one."

Olbeck and Kate exchanged glances. Olbeck looked excited but Kate was surprised at her own lack of interest. She had played along with her colleagues, who were clearly pleased at their discovery. but beneath the surface, she was thinking, *So what? That's not it, that's not why this happened.*

Olbeck picked up on her lack of enthusiasm. "What's the problem?"

"Nothing," she said. She didn't want to say anything, given that her misgivings were based purely on instinct. "It's a good lead. Where to from here?"

"You finally get to have the pleasure of the Costa brothers."

"Fabulous. I can hardly wait."

The first and older Costa brother, Stelios Costa, lived in exactly the kind of house that Kate was anticipating: huge, new, brash, vulgar. After a ten minute standoff at the security gates, these were finally swung back by invisible, electronic means, and Olbeck drove slowly onto the forecourt of the house, parking beside an enormous silver Range Rover. *Anyone thinking that crime doesn't pay is wrong in the most literal way, unfortunately,* thought Kate, and she got out of the car feeling cross.

Stelios Costa was standing by the front door of the house, arms folded, watching the two officers approach him. He was a big, powerfully built man, running a little too fat, dressed casually in jeans and a navy hooded sweatshirt. He was smiling, although not by much. He looked Kate up and down in an appraising manner as they came close and she quickly put on a bored expression, to disguise the annoyance she felt.

"Officers," said Stelios as they came to halt in front of him.

"May we come in, sir?" said Olbeck, flashing his warrant card.

"Put that away, Officer Olbeck , I know who you are. And no, you may not come in without a warrant, and I doubt you've got one of those, have you love?"

He addressed this last remark to Kate, who mentally drew an imaginary truncheon and battered him over the head with it. In reality, she smiled slightly and insincerely.

"We have a few questions to ask you–"

Stelios sighed theatrically and cast up his eyes. "I know nothing about the Nick Fullman case, I have no comment, I have nothing to say."

"Interesting that you knew we were going to ask you about Nick Fullman," said Olbeck.

Stelios sneered. "Of course you were. And I may as well tell you now, as I told you before, that we do know him. We are part-backers of his new project in Wallingham. That's in the public domain."

"So you've got nothing to hide."

"That's right."

Kate smiled, or at least widened her mouth. "Is the knowledge that planning permission for those flats was granted despite the land being contaminated in the public domain as well?" she asked. *Take that, you arrogant bastard.*

Stelios looked at her steadily. "Now where did you hear a thing like that?" he asked. A slight shift in his stance made Olbeck take a protective step closer to Kate.

"It's what we know, *sir*," she said, with what she hoped was just the right amount of calculated insolence. "We have samples proving contamination."

Stelios looked at her a moment longer. Then he shrugged. "I have nothing to say, officers," he said. "Talk to the council. It's nothing to do with me."

"You have nothing to say on the matter?"

"I've got nothing to say. That sounds like a council matter to me. If you want to question me further, you can talk to my lawyer."

Olbeck and Kate exchanged a silent glance. They both knew it was pointless going on. The only way they could put the pressure on would be by arresting the man, and they had no grounds to do that.

"We may need to talk to you again, sir," said Olbeck, in a vaguely threatening tone. Stelios looked amused.

"I'll look forward to it," he said. He watched them walk away. Kate just knew he was grinning broadly behind their backs.

Back in the car, they looked at one another.

"Now what?" said Kate.

Olbeck shrugged and started the engine. "We'll dig into it. Talk to the council. Get that slimy bugger Gary Jones to sweat a little."

"You think he's been taking back-handers?"

"I do. But it's not really our concern. That's a matter for the Fraud boys and for the council."

"Mmm."

Kate watched the road slip away beneath the windscreen, the white lines in the centre of the road merging into one long, light strip in her vision.

"I'm going to talk to Fullman," she said, eventually.

Olbeck glanced over. "I wouldn't."

"I think he needs to start talking a bit more than he has."

They drew into the station car park. Olbeck drew the car to a standstill.

"I wouldn't," he repeated. "Let Anderton take the lead."

Kate sat still for a moment, chewing her lip. Then she grabbed her bag and slid from the seat. "I'll risk it," she said. "I won't be long."

Olbeck sighed and handed over the car keys.

"New girl," he said. "Too bloody keen by half."

Kate winked. "It'll wear off soon enough."

She slammed the driver side door, adjusted the seat and drove off, tipping him a salute as she drove past. She could see him in her rear view mirror as she waited to join the main road, shaking his head slowly.

REFUSING TO LISTEN TO THE small voice inside her that was telling her not to be so hasty, she drove to Nick Fullman's office in Wallingham, negotiating the unfamiliar one-way system. Wallingham was a large market town, much developed over the past century and was currently bustling with shoppers, office workers and mothers pushing buggies. Kate averted her eyes from these last whenever she could. She parked the car in the spare parking space outside the offices, smoothed her hair, checked her warrant card and phone and got out.

She hadn't called ahead, but he was in, of course he was. Mrs Bright must be sitting with Casey – or had he left her on her own? She flashed him a big, bright smile.

"Good morning, Mr Fullman. Are you able to answer a few questions for me?"

She pressed forward as she spoke, and he fell back, allowing her into the building.

"I'm surprised to find you at work, sir," Kate said, unable to help one little dig.

Fullman scowled. "As you know, Detective Sergeant, I'm a busy man. Now with Gemma gone, I'm twice as busy. Will this take long?"

"I hope not, sir." Kate found herself a black leather chair opposite Fullman's mahogany desk and seated herself without waiting to be asked. There was a moment's silence. Nick Fullman sat down opposite her, his brows drawn down. He wore one of his expensive suits and a snowy-white shirt, but his eyes were ringed with shadow and he was unshaven. Kate wondered how much sleep he'd been getting over the past few weeks. Not a lot, by the look of him. Kate mentally shuffled the topics that she had to question him about and picked the first and hopefully least contentious.

"Can you tell me about your relationship with Rebecca D'Arcy-Warner, Mr Fullman?"

Nick Fullman had clearly not been expecting this. His eyebrows went up.

"Rebecca?" he said. "What about her?"

"I understand that you had a very long term relationship with her."

"Yes. And?"

"Why did you split up?"

"Why do you want to know? What possible relevance can it have?"

"Please just answer my question, sir. Why did you split up?"

Nick stared at her. "We just grew apart," he said, stonily.

"There was no other reason?"

"What do you mean?" He didn't wait for her to answer. "What has she said?"

Kate took the plunge. "She mentioned that you'd been keeping what she called 'reprehensible company.' The Costa brothers? Rebecca said she didn't approve."

Nick's eyes bulged. "What? She said that?"

"Is it true?"

"I – I–" he blustered for a moment and then sat forward, putting his large hands on the desk. Kate was reminded rather uneasily of his physical presence. "I have met them, yes. That's all. They own a lot of property. That's all. That's how I met them."

"You don't have any business dealings with them?"

"Well–"

"You haven't, for example, been involved in one of their latest building projects?"

Nick stared at her. "What do you mean?"

"I mean the latest development of new-build flats in Wallingham, Mr Fullman. The development built on brownfield land. The development that was apparently granted permission despite being on contaminated land?"

Nick's hands were shaking. They both looked at them before he removed them from the desk and tucked them out of sight.

"I don't know what you're talking about," he said, feebly.

"You don't, sir? Despite your close friendship with Councillor Jones? Councillor Jones who heads the planning department and has final say over permission granted for new buildings?"

Nick seemed to recollect himself.

"So what?" he said, sitting up a little straighter. "If there's a problem with the planning permission, you should be talking to the council, not to me. It's nothing to do with me."

"Isn't it?"

"No."

"Your development of flats, sir. The Costa brothers are part-backers of the project, isn't that right?"

There was a moment's silence. Nick turned his face away from her. "I have nothing to say on that matter, officer."

Kate itched to arrest him. She opened her mouth to start the words of the caution, thought again, shut it. She didn't know why, but she suddenly knew that the contaminated land issue wasn't the reason for Charlie's disappearance. Anderton would scoff, but she *knew*. She remembered Charlie's little face in the magazine, so tiny and vulnerable. She thought of Mrs Bright and Evie, both mothers and grandmothers, and the words they'd both used to describe Nick. *Jealous, difficult, resentful...* His child was gone and had he even wanted him in the first place? Hot, bitter anger suddenly rose up in her, almost choking her. She couldn't keep the words back any longer.

"Do you *want* us to find your son, sir?"

Nick's head whipped around to face her again. He looked stunned.

"What do you mean? Of course I do."

"Do you, sir?"

"Yes!"

Kate looked him directly in the eye. "Do you want us to find your son, sir?"

Nick put his hands on the desk again and leaned forward. "Are you mad? What do you mean by that?"

Kate spoke quietly. "You've not bonded with your son, sir, have you? You hired a nanny to take care of him from birth. You kept him in a nursery way away from your bedroom. You've never changed his nappy or fed him or taken care of him yourself, have you, sir? Why is that? Do you resent him?" Nick was staring, aghast.

Kate felt the words coming out of her mouth, unable to stop the torrent of accusation. "You didn't want him, did you, sir? You were jealous of him, weren't you? Jealous of a baby screaming all the time, waking in the night, getting all the attention, all the attention that should have been yours? What happened that night, Nick? Did it all get too much for you? Did you–"

"That's enough!" Nick Fullman was on his feet, facing her across the table, shaking. Kate found herself on her feet too. Her legs felt as though they were going to collapse beneath her.

"How dare you, how dare you–" Nick tripped over the words. "Get out of here. Get out!"

Kate recollected herself. What the hell had just happened there? She attempted to say something, something placatory.

Nick Fullman was coming around the desk. She flinched,

unable to help herself. He stopped a few feet away, staring at her with loathing. "Get out," he said, quietly and with menace.

"Sir–"

"Now!"

She backed away until she was at the door, and then turned, trying not to scurry. She could barely hear anything over the thump of blood in her ears. She reached the car, fumbled for the keys, dropped them, bent to pick them up, dropped them again. When she was finally in the driver's seat, she sat for a moment, swallowing convulsively.

What the hell, Kate? You idiot, she told herself in fury. *What have you done?* Through the window of the office, she could see Nick Fullman pick up the phone, and the dread and sickness inside her leapt up another notch.

Chapter Sixteen

BACK AT THE OFFICE, SHE went to the women's toilets and stood for a moment, regarding her face in the mirror. That last scene with Nick Fullman replayed itself in her head. What had she *done*? She'd virtually accused him of murdering his own son. She thought of Anderton saying 'get the evidence' and winced. What evidence did she have, apart from her own dislike of the man? For a moment she thought she was going to be sick.

There was that awful hollow feeling inside, the *I've fucked up badly* feeling. A feeling she hadn't had for years, not since she'd looked at the blue line on a pregnancy test at age sixteen and realised, with a wave of horror and misery washing over her, that she had just ruined her life. And here she was, years later, ruining her life again.

Kate ran the cold taps over her wrists. Perhaps it would be okay. Perhaps Fullman wouldn't do anything. *Fuck, please don't let him do anything.* She pulled a paper towel from the dispenser and dried her hands. Then she pinned a neutral expression to her face and went back to the office. Through the inner window, she could see Olbeck put the phone on his desk back down with a bang, soundless through the glass. Then he threw the pencil he was holding across the desk. She squared her shoulders, took a deep breath and went into the room.

Olbeck didn't look up at her arrival.

"You all right?" said Kate, pleased that her voice sounded so normal.

"Fine." He looked a little ashamed of the abruptness of his answer. "Domestic dramas. As usual. How was it? Get anything useful?"

I accused Nick Fullman of the murder of his son. Virtually. On no evidence. Kate mentally shook herself. She wasn't going to mention anything about the conversation – the argument – that she'd just had with Fullman. What could she say? She recollected her talk with Evie, a million years ago, it now seemed.

"Nick Fullman's a jealous commitment-phobe who kept his last girlfriend hanging on waiting for marriage and drove her mad in the process. Apparently."

Olbeck winced.

"What's wrong?"

"Nothing."

"Anderton wants an update."

Kate felt her stomach drop. "Now?"

"Yes. You have to see him the second you get in, apparently."

Kate slung herself into her chair. "Great." She swallowed down the nausea that was rising fast. "I'll go right away."

Olbeck stared at her. "Are *you* all right?"

Well, I'm about to be utterly bollocked. If not fired.

"I'm fine," said Kate shortly, and left the room.

Anderton was seated at his desk when Kate walked into his office. This was the first time she'd seen him in a stationary position since she'd known him, and from this she realised that she was in very deep trouble indeed. She closed the door behind her, noting with detached interest that her legs were actually shaking. She wasn't sure whether to sit down, but she didn't want to fall over in a heap.

"Sit down," said Anderton briefly, and Kate subsided gratefully into a chair.

"I expect you know why you're here," he went on. Kate opened her mouth to say something, and he raised a hand, silencing her.

There was a moment of quiet.

"Do you remember me saying at the start of this investigation that I didn't want anyone steaming in, upsetting people with their own clumsy prejudices?"

Kate swallowed.

"Yes, sir."

"So why, in fact, have you done just that when I expressly asked you not to?"

Kate's heartbeat thumped in her ears. She gripped the sides of her chair. "Sir, I–"

"You are a police officer, DS Redman. You work on evidence. Where is your evidence for accusing Nick Fullman of the murder of his child and his nanny?"

Kate closed her eyes briefly. She could actually feel sweat beading on her upper lip.

"Sir, I'm sorry–"

"Do you realise the damage it does to a case when accusations are flung around with no evidence to back them up? Do you want to further jeopardise the safety of a vulnerable baby because of your own emotional issues?"

Kate's heart was thumping.

"No, I'm sorry, sir. I can't tell you how sorry I am." Anderton didn't say anything for a moment, and she pressed on. "You must admit that we have to at least look at the possibility that Nick Fullman is inv–"

Anderton's shout and bang of his hand on his desk made her jump.

"Do you not think that that's been in the back of my mind since this case began, Detective Sergeant? Do you not think that perhaps the reason we haven't moved forward on that assumption is that there is simply *no evidence*? If Nick Fullman is guilty, do you want to see the case thrown out by the CPS at the first hurdle because we haven't got a single scrap of evidence with which to charge him? Do you?"

Kate could feel tears pressing at the back of her eyes. *Don't cry, Kate, whatever you do, don't cry.* She dug her fingernails into her legs.

"No, sir." She wanted to say something more but at that second, she couldn't trust her voice.

Anderton sat back in his chair, exhaling. There was a moment's silence, during which Kate tried to breathe normally.

Then Anderton sat forward.

"You're a promising officer, DS Redman. I had excellent reports of you from Bournemouth. You'll go far, I have no doubt."

Kate blinked. "Thank you, sir."

"I should tell you, though, that I had serious doubts about allowing you onto this case."

Kate held her breath, knowing he was about to say more.

"I had serious doubts because of the nature of the case and because of, shall we say, your personal history."

Kate looked across the table. Anderton was sitting very still, his hands on the desk in front of him. She felt pinned to her chair by his eyes. Her heart began thumping so heavily she was surprised it wasn't audible to the grim-faced man sat opposite her.

"What do you mean, sir?" she said, cursing the feebleness of her voice. Why was she asking, anyway? She didn't know what the answer was, but she was damn sure she wouldn't like it.

Anderton spoke quietly.

"I knew you would find this case an emotive one, DS Redman, because you yourself had a baby taken from you at roughly Charlie Fullman's age."

Kate said nothing for a moment. For a second, she thought she was going to be sick.

Anderton was still speaking.

"I'm sorry to remind you of what was no doubt a painful time for you, DS Redman, but I'm sure you can appreciate my concerns and more particularly now in the light of recent developments."

"He wasn't taken away," said Kate, hoarsely.

"I'm sorry?"

"My – the baby. He wasn't taken away."

"No, that's true. You gave him up for adoption, didn't you?"

Kate nodded, mutely, unable to speak. She wanted to ask, *How did you know*? but of course it would be in her notes, on her profile.

Don't cry, Kate. Don't cry.

Anderton was regarding her silently. She felt flayed, her skin raw and prickling with shock. This was the nightmare come to life, the thing she'd been dreading since that last meeting with the adoption agency twelve years ago. She wanted to get up and walk out of the office, but she couldn't trust her legs.

"It must have been very painful for you," said Anderton eventually, quietly. Kate couldn't even nod for fear of dislodging the tears that were trembling on the edge of her eyelids.

"I don't know if you've ever had counselling..." he said, watching her. She managed to shake her head, carefully. She couldn't have stood any type of counselling – having to sit there and pull all those painful memories back out again, having to face up to what she'd done. Instead she'd kept those memories locked up in a box, somewhere deep inside of her. Covered over with dust and locked away.

"Perhaps you should think about it," Anderton said. He sat back in his chair, sighing a little. Kate turned her face up to the ceiling, blinking. Anderton went on. "I want you to go home now, DS Redman. Take the afternoon off. Calm down. Come back tomorrow, and we'll start again."

"Yes, sir," said Kate. She cleared her throat. "Thank you, sir."

She took a deep breath and got up. Anderton raised one finger to stop her.

"One more outburst like that," he said. "And you are off the case. Not just off the case, in fact, off the force. One more. Do I make myself clear?"

Her tears had gone, and this time she managed to nod.

"Yes, sir."

He swung round in his chair, dismissing her.

"Off you go, then."

Chapter Seventeen

KATE CLOSED AND THEN LOCKED the door behind her. She stood for a moment in the hallway of her flat, palms extended slightly, turned outward, trying to drink in the calm that normally descended when she returned home. She breathed in deeply, trying to block out Anderton's words and the memories that those words conjured up.

After five minutes, she realised it wasn't going to be possible. Those words kept reverberating. *You gave him up for adoption, didn't you? You gave him up for adoption, didn't you?* Kate put her hands up to her face. She *would not* cry. She wasn't a crier. She felt the tears brimming. She would not.

She stumbled into the living room, lounge – what the fuck did it matter what she called it? Why was she trying to escape what she was, pretend her past didn't matter, try and be something she wasn't? *That was proper cold, Kelly, it weren't natural.* Her own mother had said that about her. Was it true? She'd given her baby away. He was gone, taken away, as lost to her as Charlie was to Casey.

No, not that. She'd signed him over. She'd allowed them to take him from her. She saw his face again, the face she saw whenever her defences were down. His little old-man face. He hadn't looked anything like her, apart from his long fingers and his dark curls of hair. She could still remember, twelve years later, the sheer, grinding agony of the labour pains. How it felt as if she was splitting in two. The hoarseness of her voice a day later, from all the screaming. The ache, the misery of every muscle in her body having strained to push her boy out.

Her boy. But he wasn't, was he? At least Casey had had that, had had her Charlie for three months. What had Kelly had, for she was still Kelly then? Her birth name had gone with her baby. And what had she got to show for it? For a second, she saw the future and it was dark and empty.

She'd reached the sofa, and her face was buried in its cushions. Her nails sank into the fabric of the seat. She could see his little face in her mind's eye, right there, pink and crumpled and with that fluffy, dark birth hair. With a gasp of pain, she realised she had no idea what colour his hair would be now. Was he even alive? She groaned into the cushion, mouth agape.

After five minutes, she sat up. Grief battled against self consciousness. She knelt for a moment, wiping her eyes and hiding her face, as if there was someone else in the room, judging her.

She drifted into the kitchen and switched on the kettle, automatically. Then, disregarding the cup and sachet of camomile tea that she'd prepared, she went into the hallway and looked up at the hatch in the ceiling.

Twenty four minutes later, Kate levered open the dusty lid of the box she'd brought down from the attic. Her fingers shook as she put the box lid aside and lifted out the contents. For a moment, she was ashamed of the thick layer of dust that coated the lid of the box and then thought of how ridiculous that sounded. Even she didn't dust her *attic*, for God's sake.

Here were the scan photos, encased in a twee little envelope with a cartoon picture on the front and a caption in scribbly font that said *My Baby*. He wasn't, though, was he? He hadn't really ever been hers. Kate drew in a breath that was dangerously close to a sob. She took out the first photo, taken at twelve weeks. Twelve weeks from conception and here was a photograph. Even now she found that incredible. Here he was, curled like a bud but still recognisably human. Arms extended, little legs, the unmistakeable bump of his nose and curve of his forehead. Here was the scan at twenty weeks, much more baby-like now. Little skeletal face turned towards the camera. Fingers, toes. He had one hand up to his cheek, as if sleeping. Had he been asleep? Kate remembered the sonographer prodding her swollen belly, trying to get him to move. He had moved, hadn't he? She allowed herself to remember. Twenty weeks and he was a lively one, rolling and kicking and punching her from within.

A teardrop fell onto the scan picture and Kate wiped it away gently. How had she got through nine months of pregnancy knowing that she would lose him? Don't say that, don't say *lose him*, as if it's something that happened accidentally. As if it was nothing to do with you. *You gave him away.* Kate felt a kick in her belly again, as if a phantom baby was protesting within her. How had she gone through nine months of pregnancy without going mad?

You're more malleable when you're young. You're better able to take things. What you lack in wisdom, you make up for in shock absorption. You're like a young tree; you can bend in the storm but you won't break. Kate thought of Courtney, sixteen years old. If Courtney had a baby in the next year, Kate would be horrified. She was a *child*. *As I was*, she thought. *As I was*. What had he been thinking, that man in the pub? What had he been doing, seducing a child? *Come off it, Kate. You loved being taken for someone older than yourself. All teenagers do. You knew what you were doing.*

She wiped her eyes and turned her attention back to the box. Here was the letter from the hospital, telling her of the miniscule risk of Down's Syndrome for the baby. She'd paid for that test, it hadn't been offered as a routine option. Of course it hadn't, she was only seventeen years old. Why had she paid for it, why had she cared, knowing she wouldn't be keeping the baby anyway? Because she'd wanted to know. He hadn't had Down's Syndrome, anyway. He'd been perfect.

She lifted out the last bundle of papers. These were all from the private adoption agency, all with that distinctive blue and orange logo on the headed paper. It was good quality paper, thick and creamy. Arranging adoptions was obviously a lucrative business. Why had she used a private agency? Because she'd thought that if you had money, you'd make a better parent? She *had* thought that. Kate cringed in shame. *Stupid girl, stupid idiot.*

She looked again at the letters and wondered whether they'd meant the logo to look quite so much like a colourful embryo. Perhaps it was deliberate, reminding all the hopeful, would-be parents of what they couldn't have. The fuckers. She could feel her teeth set in a something that wasn't a grin. Kate felt as if that logo was burned into her retinas, something she'd be seeing every time she closed her eyes at night. She'd probably see it on her death bed. She skimmed through the papers, hesitating over the very last one, a sealed envelope. It was a copy of the letter she'd written to the baby, for him to open on his eighteenth birthday. If his adoptive parents gave it to him, that is. Perhaps they'd burned or torn it up and thrown it away. She picked it up and put it down again. She couldn't read it, not yet. It was too painful.

Why had she kept all of this? Was it because she was afraid to throw away official papers? Did she worry about forgetting? She almost laughed at that, a thin, gaspy wheeze. As if she would ever forget. *I know why I've kept them*, she thought. *It's because I knew one day I'd have to do this. Look through them. Face up to what I've done.*

She put the papers back into the box, neatly, and shut the lid, returning that blue and orange logo to darkness. Then she opened it and took them out again, unable to leave them alone. She went and made herself that camomile tea, but she didn't drink it. She held it to her chest and sat on the sofa and wept, for her lost baby, for her seventeen-year-old self. For all the mistakes she'd made, the regrets of the past and her fears for the future. Wept open-mouthed, tears dropping onto her legs, onto the papers on her lap, marking those official words.

Chapter Eighteen

"You all right?" said Olbeck, the next morning, noting Kate's red eyes.

"I've got a cold," said Kate. She sniffed. "I'll be fine."

"What did Anderton want?"

"Nothing."

He gave her a wry look. "Really?"

Kate swung her chair away. "I don't really want to talk about it, Mark. Sorry."

"All right. Hey, don't worry, we've all been there. He does this, you know, if you stuff up. Don't take it personally."

Kate turned back to him. "Fine, I won't. Can we leave it now?"

Olbeck raised his hands above his head in a "don't shoot" gesture.

"Leaving it right now." He paused. "Anyway, Anderton wants us to double check alibis for the night of Gemma's death. I'm doing Saheed, but I can do Rebecca Thingy as well if you like."

Kate hesitated. If she took on Rebecca's, it would mean another drive down to Cudston Magna. Could she bear to be in the car by herself for an hour, trapped with her own thoughts? Olbeck was looking at her. She battled with herself and then her conscience won.

"It's all right, I'll do hers," she said, getting up and reaching for her car keys.

It was a beautiful day, the first sunshine for a long time. As Kate waited at a traffic light, she looked at the hedgerow by the car window and saw the first, tiny green buds unfurling. Spring is coming. She felt a little bit better than she had done. *One day, this will all be in the distant past*, she thought, *and perhaps it won't hurt quite as much as it does now*. Twelve years was nothing, it was the blink of an eye. Then it caught her again: her tiny baby boy was now a twelve year old. She caught her breath and blinked hard against the tears, stretching her eyes wide to stop them falling.

The car behind hooted and she realised the lights had changed.

The Georgian manor looked just as imposing as it had the first time. Kate realised as she pulled up outside and parked the car that she hadn't rung ahead to announce her arrival. What was the matter with her? *You're losing it*, she chastised herself. She took a moment to compose herself, sitting behind the steering wheel, smoothing her hair back with one hand.

She rang the doorbell once, waited five minutes, and then rang again. Nobody was home. What a waste of a journey... She was just turning to go back down the steps to her car when the door opened, slowly and hesitantly. Brigadier D'Arcy-Warner stood on the threshold, blinking and peering at her rather like a mole peering out of a burrow.

Kate got out her warrant card.

"Is your daughter in, Mr D'Arcy-Warner?" As she said it, she was suddenly conscious that she'd used the wrong title. "My apologies, um, Brigadier. Is Rebecca in?"

"Rebecca?" said the Brigadier in a puzzled tone.

"Yes, your daughter. Is she here?"

"No," said the Brigadier, after a long moment. He pulled the door open a bit wider. "Do come in, my dear. I'll make you a cup of tea. Do you like tea?"

"Oh no, that's..." Kate realised he'd turned away, leaving the door open. She hesitated for a second and then followed him into the hallway.

The Brigadier plodded slowly across the black and white tiles towards a door at the far end of the hall. As Kate hesitated, he turned back.

"Come here, my dear."

Kate walked across the acres of tiling until she was level with him. He stood, peering at her in the dimness.

"Are you a friend of Rebecca's?"

"I'm a police officer, sir. Is Rebecca here?"

The Brigadier's bushy eyebrows went up. "A policeman, eh? Have you come about the burglary?"

"I'm sorry?"

The Brigadier indicated another door on the right of the corridor. "There's been a burglary," he said. "In the study. Have you come about that?"

Kate hesitated for a second.

"Could you show me, sir?"

The Brigadier led her to a small, wood-panelled study. A desk stood by a window, with drawers akimbo and papers scattered over the surface and drifted onto the floor.

"It's here," said the Brigadier. He regarded the mess for a moment. "I think it was a burglary. It may have been me. I get in a mess sometimes."

Kate sighed inwardly.

"Sir, can you be more specific? Has there actually been a burglary?"

"No," said the Brigadier, sadly. Another mass of paper slipped from the desk to the floor. "It must have been when I was looking for something. It's hard to remember things, sometimes. You'll know that, when you get to my age."

"Yes," said Kate, remembering what Rebecca had said. *He has dementia.* Did he really, though, or was he just old and forgetful? Would he remember whether his daughter had been with him on the night of Gemma's death? Was it even worth asking? *Perhaps I'll be like that when I'm his age and then I'll be happy not to remember everything.*

She opened her mouth to ask the question, but the Brigadier had already started walking towards the door.

"You stay here, my dear," he said. "I'll bring you your tea. I can do that."

Kate began a sentence and then thought better of it. Was he even able to find the kitchen? Where were the live-in carers, the home-helps that Rebecca had mentioned on their first visit? She saw no point in hanging around waiting for the Brigadier to remember how to boil a kettle, but she decided to wait for a moment. He closed the door of the study behind him, leaving Kate in the room.

She stood for a moment and then went to the chair by the desk, moving a mass of papers from the seat to the floor. What a mess. She looked out of the window at a little flowerbed and a slice of lawn. What must it have been like to grow up here? She sat back against the chair, allowing her eyes to drift from the window to the surface of the desk, from the open drawers to the piles of paper on the floor. Then she froze.

There was the logo, the blue and orange logo. The curled, embryonic shape. The logo she'd seen last night, on the paper from the adoption agency. There it was, on a letter on the floor, peeking out from underneath a pile of other letters. Kate leant down, her heart thumping. She knew she hadn't been mistaken, but peering closer confirmed it. It was the same logo. It was a letter from the same adoption agency. She twitched at it and saw the salutation, *Dear Ms. D'Arcy-Warner...*

"Here you go, my dear," said the Brigadier, crashing open the door. Kate jumped and sat upright. He came into the room, balancing a cup on a saucer.

"Tea for you," he said proudly. Kate took it, barely able to mutter her thanks. It was stone cold.

"OLBECK, IT'S ME. I NEED you to get onto the Wenlove Agency. It's an adoption agency, Wenlove Agency, W-E-N-L-O-V-E. Talk to the MD, ask about Rebecca D'Arcy-Warner. It's urgent."

"What the hell? What's happened?"

"Just talk to them. Actually don't, just get me the number. I'll be back in twenty minutes, and I need to talk to them."

Twenty minutes was pushing it, but Kate put her foot down. Damn the speed limits. She wished Olbeck was here, driving, so she could have time to think. What did it mean? Did it mean anything? She remembered Rebecca sitting opposite her, very upright, clasping her ringless fingers together. *I'm not very maternal, I'm afraid.* Had *she* had a child adopted? Kate slid to a stop at a red light, cursing the delay. Should she pull over and call the agency, right now? No, she needed to be in the office. *Come on, come on.* The light changed and she shot forward.

Back at the office, she appraised Olbeck of the situation.

"But how did you know it was the Wenlove's logo?" he asked.

Kate had been dreading this bit.

"I just know," she said, praying he wouldn't ask for more details. "I can't go into it now but I know it, I know it was the logo of a private adoption agency. Just take it from me."

Olbeck nodded.

"Theo pulled up the info. Managing Director is a Graham Winterdown. He pulled the old 'that's highly confidential card' when I spoke to him, until I told him it was a double murder enquiry."

"So he knows we're coming?"

"He does. Come on, I'm driving."

Chapter Nineteen

Graham Winterdown was a small, neat man, with a fussy beard and smooth, long-fingered hands. Kate disliked him on sight. Walking through the reception area, she was transported back twelve years, when she'd come here once before to sign the papers. To sign over her boy. She clenched her fists and then consciously forced herself to relax them. She'd made two visits here, one for the paper signing and one more, to meet the prospective parents. The people who would be raising her child. Kate caught her breath in a gasp of pain and then stopped, struck by something that had just occurred to her. The adoptive parents... the woman's face... her train of thought was derailed as they were ushered into the managing director's office.

"This is very irregular," said Winterdown disapprovingly as they sat down in chairs opposite his desk. "I appreciate that you need the information but I'm very worried about the security of our clients' details."

"Any information will be safe with us," said Kate. She took in the luxurious fittings of his office: the mahogany desk, the crystal carafe of water perched on top. On the far wall was a large, black and white photograph of a smiling baby dressed in a pair of striped dungarees.

"What was it you wanted to know?" asked Winterdown after offering refreshments and having them refused.

Olbeck had explained the purpose of their visit during his telephone call. He repeated as much to Winterdown.

"Ah, yes." Winterdown extracted a file from the drawer of his desk. "I just wanted to be sure that I had the facts right, as it were."

Kate longed to arrest him for being a smug, sanctimonious git.

"You've been in correspondence with Rebecca D'Arcy-Warner," she said, sharply. "We need to know why."

Winterdown raised his eyebrows at her tone but didn't comment. He offered the file in his hand to her.

"We did indeed have some correspondence with a Ms D'Arcy-Warner," he said, as Kate took the file. "All of the paperwork relating to the lady is in that file. She applied to us to become an adoptive parent two years ago now."

"And did she become one? An adoptive parent?"

"She did not."

Olbeck and Kate exchanged glances.

"Why not?" said Olbeck.

Winterdown moved a pen into alignment with the edge of his desk.

"There are many reasons someone wouldn't make a suitable adoptive parent," he said, after a moment. "We have very stringent criteria before people are approved to adopt. It's all in the best interests of the children."

"Of course," said Kate. "But can you be more specific? Why was Rebecca turned down? Or did she change her mind?"

"No, she didn't change her mind."

"So you turned her down?"

"We did." He clearly realised he was expected to elaborate. "There were certain...pointers, shall we say, that led us to believe that she was not entirely a – stable person. Not suitable for adopting a child."

"She had a history of mental illness?"

Winterdown looked shocked.

"My goodness me, no, nothing like that. Under interview though, she made several comments that in the light of day seemed inappropriate in an adoptive parent. Anyone who wants to adopt must realise that the whole thing *must* proceed with regard to what's best for the child. Not what's best for themselves."

"She was eager to adopt, though?"

"Very much so."

Kate was riffling through the papers in the file.

"We must take these, Mr Winterdown." Had he overseen her son's adoption? "How long have you worked here?"

"I'm sorry?"

"How long have you been Managing Director here?"

His eyebrows went up again.

"For the last – let me see – six years? Yes, I think it must be six years."

Olbeck was giving her an odd look. She closed the file.

"We'll take this, Mr Winterdown. I'll give you a receipt for it, and you can be assured that we'll be very careful with it."

"You all right?" said Olbeck when they were back in the car.

Kate nodded, brushing at her eyes. She sniffed.

"Still got that cold, I see," he said, in a neutral tone.

They drove for a moment in silence.

"We need to get a warrant to search her house," said Kate. "The mansion and Rebecca's own house."

"Do we have the grounds?"

"I think so. For a start, she's lied to us. You heard her tell us she wasn't maternal yourself. She said children weren't in her game plan, or something like that. And yet, two years ago, she's trying to adopt a child."

"Perhaps that's why she told us that. You know, she gets turned down for adoption and decides that she isn't ever going to be a parent and pretends that's been her plan all along. Protesting too much, you know."

"It's still a lie."

"I know," said Olbeck, indicating to turn off the main road. "I just don't know if it's enough."

"I never did check her alibi for the night of Gemma's death. We need to question her."

"I know. Let's go there now."

He pulled the car over and called the station, asking Theo for her home address and punching it into the sat nav.

While this was happening, Kate was thinking hard. There was something nagging at her, something that was important. Something to do with Gemma. What was it? She scrolled back through her memories, thinking back to the last time she was at Gemma's house. Oh yes, there it was. She opened her mouth to tell Olbeck and shut it again. *Tell him and you'll have to tell him why you know what you do...* Kate battled with herself. *Tell Olbeck and you'll have to tell him everything.* Could she bear for anyone else to know? Anderton knowing was bad enough. But it was important. Kate knew it was important. She made up her mind.

"There's something else," she said, reluctantly, as the car began moving again.

Olbeck glanced over at her.

"Yes?"

"Yes." She took a deep breath, steadying herself. "There's a photograph of Rebecca D'Arcy-Warner at Gemma Phillips' house. In that weird photo album full of photos of Nick Fullman."

"Yes?" said Olbeck, clearly expecting more.

"It's of the three of them together. I'm not sure where it was taken. Rebecca has this look on her face, a very intense expression. It bothered me because I knew I'd seen that exact type of look before, but I couldn't remember where."

"Right," said Olbeck. "And?"

Kate knew she was dragging this out because she didn't want to tell him. *Come on, get a grip.* She took another deep breath. She was trembling.

"When I was seventeen," she began. For a moment, her voice failed. "When I was seventeen, I had a baby adopted."

There it was, the bald statement. Olbeck said nothing but he gave a little whistle of surprise.

"Okay," he said, eventually. They were both looking straight ahead, Olbeck out of necessity, Kate because she didn't want to look at him. She swallowed.

"I'm sorry to hear that," said Olbeck. "That must have been really hard."

Kate tried to say "it was." For a moment, the tears threatened to overcome her. She swallowed again and again.

"It was," she said, when she could trust her voice. "But I'm telling you this for a reason, I don't want to go into too much detail. But the look on Rebecca's face in the picture, it's the same look as the one on the face of the adoptive parents that I met. The woman – the mother – when – when I had my son adopted. She looked just like that. "

There was a moment's silence.

"You're sure?" said Olbeck. He glanced over at her. "I'm really sorry about that, Kate."

"S'okay," said Kate, in a watery voice. She concentrated on breathing in and out. "I am sure, though. I couldn't forget it. The look on her face – the woman's – when she saw the picture of my son."

She pinched the bridge of her nose. "Believe me, it's the same look."

"I believe you. I can't see it helping us much though. I mean, a look is not evidence."

"I know that," snapped Kate, taking emotional refuge in anger. "It's another reason why we have to interview her now, today."

Olbeck checked the sat nav.

"We're almost there. Hold tight."

No one came to answer the door, even after repeated pealing of the doorbell. The house was a semi-detached Edwardian building, handsome and well-kept. Kate peered through the front bay window at a pleasant, tidy sitting room.

"Are you looking for someone?" asked a woman who was walking up the path of the house next door. She was a middle-aged lady with greyish-blonde hair, clothes and accent impeccable.

"Rebecca D'Arcy-Warner," said Kate. "Have you seen her recently?"

"Not for weeks," said the neighbour. "It's funny you ask because I was thinking to myself it's ages since I've seen Rebecca, and I was almost wondering whether she'd moved. Not that she'd have gone without saying goodbye, I'm sure."

"Thank you, Mrs – ?"

"Mrs Smithson, Barbara Smithson." She looked startled at the production of their warrant cards. "Oh dear, there isn't any trouble is there?"

Kate hastened to reassure her. "We're just anxious to have a chat with Ms D'Arcy-Warner," she said. "Are you close friends with her?"

"Well, not especially close, I suppose. We're *friendly*. Well, you have to be, being neighbours, don't you?"

Olbeck stepped forward.

"May we have a word with you, Mrs Smithson? Me and my colleague would like to talk to someone who knows Rebecca, even if it is on a casual basis."

"Rebecca's a very nice person. She would always sign for any parcels if they came while I was out, and when my husband and I went away on holiday last year, she kept an eye on the house for us, watered the plants, that sort of thing."

"So she was a good neighbour?" asked Olbeck, nursing a mug of weak coffee.

"Yes. I mean, I don't know her *well* or anything like that, but she is certainly a very pleasant person."

Kate sat still with difficulty. She felt fizzy with energy, itching to *do* something. What she didn't want to do was sit around drinking yet another hot drink and listening to the meaningless pleasantries of this neighbour. She forced herself to sit still.

"Rebecca's not married, is she?" said Olbeck.

Mrs Smithson shook her head. "No, she's not."

"Does she have a boyfriend? A partner?"

"I wouldn't know. I don't think so. I've not seen her with anyone here."

"Has she had many visitors in the last few weeks that you're aware of?"

Mrs Smithson sat, twisting her hands. "I'm not sure," she said, nervously. "I haven't noticed anyone in particular."

This was useless. Kate tried to beam her thoughts into Olbeck's head. If he wasn't going to make a move soon, she would do it for him. "Well, that's–" she began, standing up, when Mrs Smithson exclaimed.

"Oh, I almost forgot. I took in a parcel for Rebecca myself, not that long ago. That one up there." She indicated a box on the kitchen dresser. "I expected she'd call round for it, but I haven't seen her for so long, I quite forgot about it."

"May I have a look?" said Kate, not waiting for an answer. She lifted the box, shook it and then opened it. Mrs Smithson made a small noise of protest, but by that time, both Olbeck and Kate could see what the parcel contained. It was a baby monitor.

Kate called Anderton as they drove to Cudston Magna. She appraised him of the situation in a few short sentences.

"Good, do just that," he said after she stopped speaking. "Don't go in hard, though. This could be very tricky."

"But I can arrest?"

"Yes, of course. I'm sending Theo and Jerry over as well for back up."

"Thank you, sir."

Chapter Twenty

She and Olbeck didn't speak for the rest of the journey. He was concentrating on driving, and she held onto her knees, gripping tightly to stop her fingers shaking. At last, they were turning down the driveway of the manor house, the gravel making a rushing noise under the wheels. The house looked peaceful, its many windows glittering in the weak spring sunlight.

No one came to the door. Kate tried it and rattled the door handle.

"Locked," she said to Olbeck.

"Let's walk around, there must be another way."

"We could break it down."

Olbeck hesitated. "Let's–" The door began to open, slowly and creakily.

The Brigadier stood on the threshold, blinking at them. "Yes?" he said, screwing up his eyes against the brightness of the day after the dimness of the hallway.

Kate held up her warrant card.

"Police, sir. We urgently need to speak to your daughter."

"Yes?"

He hadn't moved. Kate made a noise of impatience and pushed past him into the house. She looked up at the staircase and there, frozen on the top step, was Rebecca D'Arcy-Warner. Their eyes locked.

"Rebecca–" Kate began and then the woman on the stairs whirled around and ran.

Kate didn't stop to think. She let her legs carry her up the staircase, her arms pumping, heart racing. She heard Olbeck shout something, but by that time she was up on the landing. A door slammed at the far end of the corridor.

Kate ran quickly down the hall and wrenched open the door. Inside was a bedroom, with the unlived stillness of a guest room. Rebecca appeared to have disappeared into thin air. Kate bent down and checked under the bed. Against the far wall was another door. Bracing herself, Kate yanked it open.

Another staircase, a plain wooden one this time. How big was this house? Kate's heart was thumping. She knew she should wait for Olbeck, the two of them should go together, but she couldn't. She ran up the stairs, past a large window. Outside, she could see Theo's car drawing to a halt, scattering gravel. She ran on, through another door and into another corridor. She seemed to be in the upper stories of the house now. She stopped for a second, holding her breath and trying to listen above the rushing of blood in her ears. Above her head, a floorboard creaked.

She opened a door to an empty room, save for a drift of cardboard boxes in the corner. She tried another door which led to a small and shabby bathroom. This was hopeless. Rebecca could be anywhere. Her radio crackled, making her jump.

"Where the hell are you?" Olbeck hissed at her over the airwaves.

"Don't know. Have you spotted her?"

"The Major says there's an attic, a big one. We're coming up. Wait for–"

"I don't have time to wait!"

"Kate–"

She'd turned and started running again.

She found another corridor after the third door she tried opened. This was a smaller hallway, uncarpeted and ending in a small, steep flight of steps. Kate pattered along. The stairs ended in yet another door. Kate went through it and stopped dead.

She was standing in a small, white-painted room with a cream carpet. There was a cot. There was a Moses basket. There was a white-painted chest of drawers, with baby clothes stacked along the top. There was Rebecca D'Arcy-Warner standing at the far end of the room, a sleeping baby in her arms.

Kate stood stock still. She breathed out slowly.

"Charlie," she said.

Rebecca's eyes were fixed on her face. She was standing by another door, a small one, barely half the size of a normal door. Keeping her eyes on Kate, Rebecca extended a free hand and turned the handle of the door.

"Rebecca," said Kate. "I can help you. Please give Charlie to me."

Rebecca said nothing. Her face was a curious, blank mask, devoid of expression. She stooped, never taking her eyes off Kate and bent to get through the small doorway.

"Wait–" said Kate, moving forward, but Rebecca and the baby were gone.

Kate rushed forward and crouched, pushing herself through the doorway. She straightened up and realised she was on the roof of the house. This part was flat, covered with some sort of tarred covering. The wind hit her, whipping her ponytail up. She looked around wildly. Rebecca and Charlie were standing by the edge of the roof, where a tiny iron balustrade provided no stability at all against the long drop. Rebecca's red hair swirled around her face, and Charlie's blanket fluttered in the wind.

Kate inched forward. Rebecca took a step nearer the edge of the roof.

"Wait," said Kate. Her voice was shaking. "Just wait. I can help you."

Rebecca said nothing.

"Look," said Kate. "I'm stopping right here. I won't come any closer. Why don't you come over here a bit and we can talk? We can talk about anything you want to talk about."

Rebecca remained silent.

"We can talk about Charlie, if you like. Or Nick. Or anything. Why not just come over here a bit and I can help you with whatever it is you need help with."

"Nick," said Rebecca suddenly. Her arms tightened about Charlie. "*Nick.*"

"You must be very angry with him."

Rebecca made a gasping noise, air rushing inwards.

"Angry? Angry doesn't even come close to it. Do you know what it feels like to lose the chance of having a child? To wait and wait for your partner to grow up and want to be a father?"

"That must have been so hard," said Kate. She took a tiny step forward and then another.

"*Ten years* I waited for him to propose. Ten years, I waited for him to give me a child. Ten years of watching my fertility just drain away. He kept fobbing me off. He kept telling me 'one day.'"

"That's so cruel," said Kate, stepping a little bit nearer.

"I just waited and waited. Don't rush him, I told myself. Don't rush him. All the while, it was just getting harder and harder. We used to go to weddings... other people would get married, but not us. I used to have to watch other women get married, have babies, everyone was having babies – but not me. I kept thinking there was still time. Do you know what it's like to watch your chances just evaporate into thin air? Whilst everyone else around you gets what they want?"

"I know," said Kate, holding out her hands, palm up. "I know."

"He was such a *child*. That's what he wanted – a mother. That's why he was with me. He knew I'd mother him. He just kept fobbing me off!"

"I'm sorry, Rebecca."

"He robbed me!"

"It must have been so awful for you," soothed Kate. She looked at Charlie, sleeping so peacefully in his kidnapper's arms. One little hand opened and closed like a starfish.

Rebecca suddenly seemed to become aware that Kate had nearly reached her. She gasped and stepped nearer the edge.

"Wait!" said Kate. Her stomach churned. "I can help you. I know you don't want to hurt Charlie, do you?"

Rebecca looked down at the baby. Her face contracted for a moment.

"I never meant any harm," she whispered.

"You're fine, you're fine," said Kate, shivering in the cold wind. "I can help you. Won't you give me Charlie to hold for a moment?"

Rebecca tightened her grip.

"Ten years," she said. "Ten years of being told he wasn't interested in marriage and children. And within a year he'd married someone else and was a father."

"It's so hard," said Kate. She held out her arms. "Why not let me hold Charlie for a bit? Or shall we take him back inside? It's getting cold out here. Don't you think we should take him back inside?"

Rebecca was trembling

"I knew the security code," she said. "I knew the number he used. You'd think most people would use something like their birthday or their *loved one's* birthday. That would be the normal thing to do." She laughed a mirthless laugh. "Nick used the date he made his first million." She laughed again and the laughter trailed off into something that was closer to a sob.

"You poor thing," said Kate. "Let's go inside, shall we? Shall I hold Charlie for a bit?"

Rebecca didn't seem to have heard her. She was staring down at Charlie's peaceful face.

"I only wanted what was mine," she said. "He's mine. He should have been mine."

"Of course he is," said Kate. "He's beautiful. Could I hold him for a second?"

She held her breath. Rebecca stared at the baby. Then she slowly extended her arms. Kate inched forward, barely breathing. She felt the light weight of the baby and slowly, oh so slowly, drew him towards her.

"He's a beautiful baby, Rebecca," she said, her voice shaking. She didn't dare step backwards yet for fear that Rebecca would grab him back. "He's so lovely."

Rebecca looked at the baby wrapped in his blankets. She put one finger out – Kate managed not to flinch – and touched the baby's firm little cheek. He turned his face towards the touch, making little sucking motions with his tiny mouth.

"Charlie," whispered Rebecca.

Then she turned and stepped off the edge of the roof, lifting her feet to clear the iron balustrade. Kate heard her intake of breath as she stepped out into nothingness, into the void, but there was no sound, no scream as she fell, no sound at all until her body hit the ground far below.

Chapter Twenty One

ANDERTON LOOMED ABOVE THE TABLE, carrying a tray filled with clinking glasses.

"Your cranberry juice, DS Redman " he said, placing the drink in front of Kate. "Don't drink it all at once."

"I won't."

"Sure you don't want a proper drink, DS Redman?"

"For Christ's sake," snapped Kate. "Just call me Kate, all right?" Anderton said nothing. "Sir," she added.

He grinned and gave her a strange look, wry and approving at the same time, as if she'd passed some sort of secret test.

"Cheers," said Olbeck, clinking his pint glass against Anderton's and then against Kate's dainty pink drink.

They all drank for a moment and, in unison, put their slightly emptier glasses back on the table.

There was a moment's silence, broken only by the beeping of the slot machine in the corner of the pub.

"How did she think she was going to get away with it?" said Kate, knowing someone would have to start, and it may as well be her.

"Public school arrogance," said Olbeck. "They think they're invincible. They are never wrong."

Kate raised her eyebrows at him.

"I know," he said. "I went to public school."

Kate was intrigued, but this wasn't the time to pursue it. She turned to Anderton.

He turned his pint glass around slowly, inking wet rings of condensation into the scarred table top.

"The backdrop, shall we say, to this case goes back a long way," he said. "Back ten years ago, at least, when Rebecca D'Arcy-Warner was rich, some would say beautiful, successful and in love with Nick Fullman. She had everything she wanted except the one thing she really wanted, the thing she thought would come naturally. The one thing that she naturally assumed would be the next thing on the list."

"A baby," said Anderton. "But no baby was forthcoming. She pressed Fullman about it, about marriage too, although I'm willing to bet that she would have had the baby with him without the marriage certificate, if it had come to that. But the fact was, Nick Fullman didn't want a wife and he certainly didn't want a baby. We can speculate why he and Rebecca got together in the first place, but after ten years it was clear that Nick Fullman had no intention of changing the status quo. Perhaps he wanted a mother figure, having lost his own mother so young. Who knows? What he didn't want to be was a father."

Kate raised a finger. "She said that – Rebecca – something about him needing a lot of mothering. She told me that."

Anderton looked at her and nodded slightly, before continuing.

"Rebecca and Nick eventually got engaged. Was this after a lot of pressure from Rebecca? A lot of emotional blackmail? Who can say? I'm sure to Rebecca this meant that she could finally see the end prize in sight – marriage and a baby. But as we all know, from Nick's stepmother Evie, he had no intention of actually going through with the marriage. It was a sop to Rebecca's feelings – some might say a calculated move to keep his life on the calm, even keel he wanted it to be–"

"Didn't want to lose his rich girlfriend, more like," said Olbeck.

"Maybe. Maybe. Whatever the reason, Nick Fullman had no

intention of marrying Rebecca and no intention of having a child with her, in or out of wedlock."

"Bit of a bastard, wasn't he?" said Olbeck.

Anderton looked at him.

"Was he? Perhaps. He's not the only man to not want to rock the boat, to be happy with his life as it is. Perhaps he was fooling himself as well as Rebecca. Perhaps he thought he'd change his mind."

"Perhaps he didn't want to hurt her," said Kate.

Anderton nodded.

"The road to hell, and all that," he said. "Hey, Mark? Sound familiar?"

Kate was astonished to see Olbeck blush and drop his eyes to the table. There was an awkward moment of silence before Anderton began speaking again.

"Like so many people stuck in a mediocre relationship, Nick Fullman didn't do anything drastic until he'd actually met someone else. He met Casey Bright at a media party and they fell in love, or lust, or whatever you want to call it. And of course, that gave him the impetus to finish, finally, his relationship with Rebecca."

"Typical man," said Kate. "Won't jump ship without a life raft waiting for him. They never just *leave*. It's always for someone else."

Anderton tipped back the last of his pint.

"You may be right there, DS - Kate. Whatever reason Nick had, it came as a total shock to Rebecca. She was devastated. I think it wouldn't be too far off to say that she almost lost her mind over it. In one fell swoop, she'd lost her partner, her upcoming marriage and of course, any chance of a baby as well."

Kate cleared her throat.

"She could have - couldn't she have tried something else?"

"She tried adoption."

Kate felt her face grow hot, not so much because she was

embarrassed – she was over that now – but because she knew the men would *think* she was embarrassed. She drank the remainder of her drink to hide her confusion.

"She tried to adopt," repeated Anderton. "But as we know, she was turned down. We've had a look at her medical records. She had a history of depression, a suicide attempt at university – what they call a passive attempt, a cry for help, but still – and digging deeper, there were other indications of mental instability. She had a history of self-harming. Nick Fullman confirmed that."

"And then, of course, Nick and Casey had a baby. That must have been the straw that broke the camel's back. This man, who'd avoided marrying her for so many years, had robbed her of her chance for a family, goes and marries someone he'd known for a matter of months – weeks, even. And they have a baby. To Rebecca, that must have been the tipping point."

Kate got up and bought the next round of drinks. Anderton waited until she'd sat down again before he continued speaking.

"She planned it carefully. She knew the security codes to the Fullmans' house and she probably knew where the CCTV cameras were as well. She had money, a lot of money, and we all know how much you can do – can get away with – if you have money. And perhaps she had something even more valuable – someone on the inside who would help her."

"Gemma," said Olbeck.

Anderton nodded. "Gemma was obsessed with her boss, Nick Fullman. They had slept together, of course, early on in their working relationship. Poor Gemma was in love, or lust, with Nick and hated Casey. Perhaps she thought that with Charlie out of the way, the Fullmans' marriage would break up, and she'd be left to pick up the pieces. Who knows? Perhaps she just wanted the money."

"It was Rebecca who paid her, then?"

"Yes. Whether Rebecca cooked up this plan together with Gemma or whether Gemma just twigged that it must have been

Rebecca, is something we'll possibly never know. I'm inclined to believe that Rebecca *didn't* include Gemma in the plan from the start, but once Charlie had gone, Gemma started to do a bit of digging. She had access to a lot of information through Nick Fullman's business interests. Perhaps she went to see Rebecca and told her that she knew. Who knows? She had Rebecca over a barrel, anyway. Charlie's kidnapping and Dita's death…"

"Yes, Dita," said Kate. "What happened there?"

Anderton gently rolled his pint glass between his hands.

"I think it was accidental. Dita surprised her in the act of lifting Charlie from the cot and Rebecca panicked and hit her with the metal torch she was carrying. She's a tall, strong woman, and she swung as hard as she could. I don't believe she actually set out to kill her. Rebecca was the tall man that Nicholas Draker saw in the woods, of course."

"And the one in the Barbour jacket outside Gemma's flat."

Anderton nodded.

"Rebecca clearly decided that Gemma was too much of a threat. It would have been easy for her to go to Gemma's house on the pretext of paying her next blackmail payment. Then drugging Gemma's drink while she was out of the room and then – well, you know what happened next."

Kate shook her head.

"She must have been mad."

"She thought she had no choice. She can't keep paying off Gemma forever. What was the alternative – losing Charlie, going to prison? She was determined not to lose him. She'd already done so many bad things to get him."

Kate recollected something.

"She said that was what she learned from Nick," she said slowly. "She said something like 'You have to decide what you want and go and get it, no matter what it takes.'"

"Yes. It sounds slightly less admirable if you think about what it really means – stopping at nothing to get what you want, no matter how unreasonable. No matter who you hurt along the way."

"She was obsessed," said Olbeck. "But did she think she was going to get away with it? How was she going to keep hiding him for ever? What about her dad finding him?"

"I think her plan was to pretend that he was hers by adoption. Keep Charlie hidden away in Cudston Magna until the hue and cry dies down and then pretend she's adopted him. She lived a fairly solitary life – there weren't many people to question the arrival of a child in her life anyway. Her father is senile and anything he says can be dismissed as the meanderings of old age. There were no home-helps or carers, of course, coming to the house. Rebecca was the only one there most of the time. Perhaps she planned to get a false passport for him. She knew the Costa brothers. That sort of thing would be exactly the kind of service they'd provide for a fee. She gave us their name in an attempt – another attempt – to make more trouble for Nick Fullman. I don't think I'm exaggerating when I say that the idea of having him found guilty of Charlie's disappearance, possibly under arrest for the murder of his child, was almost as big as incentive as having Charlie himself."

"But there was no body," said Kate.

Anderton shrugged. "I'm not saying he would have been arrested. But Rebecca probably would be happy for him to remain under a cloud of suspicion for the rest of his life."

Olbeck shook his head.

"What a bitch."

Anderton swilled the rest of his pint and stood up.

"Selfishness. That's what every crime comes down to in the end. Selfishness. Someone who thinks what they want is more important than anyone else."

"Yes, sir," said Kate.

Anderton picked his coat. "Good work, though, team. See you tomorrow. Goodnight."

Kate and Olbeck remained silent for a moment after his departure, staring into their drinks, lost in their own private thoughts. Finally Olbeck roused himself.

"Want another?"

Kate shook her head.

"Bedtime for me. I'm knackered."

"I'll walk you back to your car."

The night was cool, a chilly wind blowing. Kate hunched into her coat, tucking her cold hands under her armpits. They walked in silence back to where Kate's car was parked on a side-street.

"Who was our mystery caller?" said Kate, recalling the missing piece of the puzzle.

Olbeck laughed.

"Disgruntled council worker called Tom Farrow. He'd been made redundant from the planning department and decided to get his own back on the boss. He was the one who sent off the soil samples as well."

Kate nodded. There was a moment's silence.

"Well, goodnight then," said Olbeck.

Kate hefted her keys in her hand.

"What did Anderton mean?" she asked. "When he said something about good intentions to you?"

Olbeck's smile died.

"Oh, you know–"

"No, I don't."

Olbeck shrugged. He had his chin sunk into the neck of his jumper, hunching his shoulders against the cold.

"He's talking about Joe," he said. "He thinks – well – he thinks I'm not being quite fair to him."

Kate's eyes widened. "Him?" she said. Then she laughed. "Oh, sorry. It's not funny. It's just I didn't – sorry."

"Yeah, I'm gay," said Olbeck. "Anyway. Anderton's right. I'm not being fair. He thinks I'm stringing Joe along a bit. I – well, you know how it is."

"Tell me about it in the morning," said Kate. "Not that my

track record with men is anything but disastrous, so don't listen to my advice anyway."

Olbeck grinned. "Night, then."

"Good night."

When Olbeck arrived home, he could hear sounds from the television in the living room. He hesitated outside the door for a moment. He could picture what lay behind the door: a log crumbling to ash in the fireplace, a single table lamp casting a warm golden glow over the room. Joe with his legs thrown over the arm of the chair, a glass of red wine on the coffee table in front of him. A cosy, domestic, harmonious scene. *I don't want that.* The thought was there: immediate, unbidden, inescapable. He sighed and took a deep breath and opened the door.

"You're home early–" began Joe, but Olbeck was already speaking across him.

"Look Joe," he said. "We need to talk."

KATE HAD CIRCLED THE HOSPITAL entrance twice before she spotted her mother, hobbling out towards the entrance, crutch tucked under one armpit. An unlit cigarette held in her free hand. She sighed and drew into one of the parking bays at the front.

"Over here, Mum."

"Thanks, love."

Mary Redman settled herself into the passenger seat and lit up. Kate set her jaw and opened her window.

"How's the ankle?"

"Not too bad. They've given me loads of painkillers. I'll be fine."

Kate thrust away the thought of what those painkillers would be liked mixed with whiskey. *Perhaps I should stay with Mum tonight?* She shuddered inwardly at the thought, and the quick stab of guilt made her say, in softened tones, "I'll see you're fine and settled before I go."

"Thanks, love."

They drove in silence and clouds of smoke for a few miles. Kate was concentrating on finding her way on these unfamiliar streets when her mother spoke up.

"Solved that case, then?"

Kate glanced at her.

"That's right. He's back where he belongs now."

"Thank God," said Mary, comfortably. She rolled down her window and pitched her cigarette butt out. Kate winced.

Back at her mum's place, Kate helped her up the bumpy path and to the sofa, carefully lifting the plastered ankle onto a cushion. She made a cup of tea, put the ashtray within reaching distance of Mary and made sure she had a glass of water on the table. Then she stood back, hesitantly.

"Are you sure you'll be all right?"

"I'll be fine, love. Go on home now. You must be tired."

Kate still hesitated. "Can you, you know, get to the loo okay on your own?"

Mary rolled her eyes. "'Course. Look, stop worrying. Always were such a worrier, weren't you? Even as a child."

Kate bit back the retort that she'd had to be the one who worried about things as her own mother clearly hadn't worried about anything, except where her next drink and smoke was coming from. She bit her lip, turning a little. She could see out of the window into the tiny garden next door, where washing flapped on a line. Her eyes fastened on one of the garments fluttering in the wind – a blue and brown striped babygro.

She kept facing away from her mother, holding each elbow in her opposite hand.

"Did you – did you really think I made a mistake?" she said, her voice so faint she could barely hear it herself. "With – with the baby? Did you really think I should have kept him?"

There was a silence behind her. Kate kept her eyes on that tiny piece of clothing, snapping and flexing in the breeze.

Then Mary said, "You did what you had to, I suppose."

Kate blinked hard. Anderton's words were reverberating around her skull. *Selfishness. That's what every crime comes down to in the end.* Well, she hadn't committed a crime, but she felt as guilty as if she had, She was as selfish as the next person, wasn't she? *Aren't you, Kate?*

"I told myself I was doing it for him," she said slowly, almost to herself. "I told myself it was the best thing for him."

"It might have been."

The babygrow blurred in Kate's vision.

"I did it for me, though," she whispered. "It was what I wanted. I told myself I was doing it for him, but I wasn't."

There was a long moment of silence. Kate took a deep, shuddering breath.

There was the click of the cigarette lighter and the familiar smell of cigarette smoke wending its way up to the tarred ceiling.

"Don't go upsetting yourself," said Mary. "You thought you were doing the best thing at the time. Just like every mum does, love."

When Kate arrived home, she took her usual shower, scrubbing her skin and her hair, washing her sins away. She put on her softest, most comfortable pair of pyjamas. Then, as the kettle boiled, she reached for the box under her bed, the box from her attic. She levered off the box lid, clear from dust now, and reached in. The envelope felt heavy in her hand. Would her boy open it on his eighteenth birthday? She hoped so. She curled herself up on the sofa and put the envelope up to her closed eyes for a moment, steadying herself. Then she opened it, drawing out the many sheets of paper with trembling hands and smoothing them out.

She took a deep breath, and she began to read.

THE END

Requiem

A Kate Redman Mystery: Book 2

Chapter One

The girl's body lay on the riverbank, her arms outflung. Her blonde hair lay in matted clumps, shockingly pale against the muddy bank. Her face was like a porcelain sculpture that had been broken and glued back together: grey cracks were visible under the white sheen of her dead skin. Her lips were so blue they could have been traced in ink. Purple half-moons pooled beneath the dark fan of her eyelashes.

"So, what do you think?" asked Jay Redman.

His half-sister cocked her head to one side. "It's very… powerful," she said cautiously. She reached a finger out toward the scene, realising something.

"It's *not* a photograph, is it? Wow, it looks just like one."

Jay Redman's painting technique was called 'hyperrealism'; it mimicked the precision of a photograph, but the image was delineated in paint. She looked at her little brother with a mixture of affection and exasperation. She appreciated the gesture, and God, Jay had real talent, but what on Earth made him think she'd want a picture of a dead girl hung above the fireplace? It was like looking at a crime scene photograph.

"It's great, isn't it?" said Jay. He adjusted the frame slightly, straightening it like a proud father pulling the shoulders of his son's first school blazer into shape. "Best thing I've done so far."

"Yes, indeed!" said Kate, trying to sound enthusiastic.

"It's for our end of year show. My tutor thinks it's great—he thinks it might even win the Bolton Prize."

"That's the top award, isn't it? That's brilliant, Jay. Why are you giving it to me?"

"I thought you'd like to have it for a while," said Jay, still staring proudly at the painting. "It's a housewarming present. On loan."

"Well, thank you."

"I'm calling it 'Ophelia Redux.'"

Kate felt another burst of affection towards her sibling. How wonderful it was to have someone in the family who knew Shakespeare, who had even *read* Shakespeare. It was clear why she and Jay got along so well, and it was something more than the fact that Kate had practically brought him up. There was no one else in the Redman family and its many offshoots who could talk about things other than reality television and the latest tabloid headlines. Kate had pulled herself up by her bootstraps, and here was Jay, doing the same, even if the path he was taking was a different one to hers.

"It's great, Jay," she said, and her pride in her younger brother gave her tone a warmth which made her sound sincere. Jay beamed.

"I'm well proud of it," he said, reminding his sister that he did, in fact, have some way to go before he shook off his roots entirely. She gave herself a swift mental kick for being so judgemental.

"It's well good," she said, grinning. "Now, have you seen the rest of the house?"

"Can you show me after a drink?"

"Of course, sorry." Kate headed for the kitchen, still a little unfamiliar with the layout of her new house. She'd been here all of a week, and the rooms were still packed with boxes. "Tea?"

"Haven't you got anything stronger? We *are* supposed to be celebrating your move, you know, sis."

"Um..." Kate opened a few kitchen cupboards hopelessly. There was probably an ancient bottle of wine packed in one of the many cardboard boxes but where, exactly?

Jay rolled his eyes.

"Luckily for me, I know what you're like." He put his hand into his ragged green backpack and pulled out a bottle of champagne with a flourish. "See how good I am?"

"Jay, that's brilliant. How do you afford champagne on a student's budget?"

"Ah," said Jay. "Now there you have me."

"You didn't steal it?" gasped Kate, horrified.

"*'Course* not, sis, what do you take me for?" He leaned forward conspiratorially. "It's not real champagne. Just cheap fizz."

Kate smiled, relieved. "It'll do fine. As long as you don't mind drinking it out of mugs."

"Classy."

"I think you mean 'bohemian.'"

Kate sat on the sofa she'd brought from her old flat, and Jay took the new armchair she'd splashed out on when she moved. They clinked mugs and sipped. Kate found her gaze being drawn to the painting of the girl once more.

"Who's the model?" she asked. She looked at the mock-dead face, noting the fine bones under the unnatural pallor of her skin.

"My mate, Elodie."

There was a casualness in Jay's voice that didn't deceive Kate, especially with all her experience with reading what was unsaid.

"Girlfriend?"

Jay slugged back the rest of his champagne. "Nope, just a mate."

"Right," said Kate. She tipped a little bit more fizz in Jay's mug. "Is she on your course?"

Jay was in his second year at the Abbeyford School of Art and Drama, a further education college that specialised in the visual and dramatic arts. Kate had been thrilled when he'd decided to study there; her home town of Bournemouth was well over an hour's drive away from her new location, and while Jay had still lived at home, she'd not seen much of him.

"Nope. She's a musician, goes to Rawlwood."

Kate raised her eyebrows. "She must be good, then. They hardly accept anyone there, unless they're the new—um." She groped for a famous classical musician. "A new Stradivarius, or something."

"Eh?"

"I mean, it's really hard to get a place there."

Jay rolled his eyes. "Well, it probably helps that she's the Headmaster's daughter."

"Seriously?"

"Yep. But, actually, she *is* a talented musician, really good. She plays violin in this great band. Lorelei."

"Lorelei?"

"That's the band name. They play sort of folk rock. It's good—" Jay said, seeing Kate's unconvinced look. "Actually, there's a gig on tonight. I meant to tell you. Did you want to go?"

"Tonight?" asked Kate, doubtfully.

"Oh, come on," said Jay. "I know you normally need your plans signed off three weeks in advance before you commit to anything, but come on, sis, it'll do you good. You need to get out sometimes, you know. Start meeting people. Start joining in."

It was Kate's turn to roll her eyes. "I'm not a hermit, you know. I do have a social life."

"I'm not talking about hanging out with all your copper mates. That's not a social life—that's *work*. You need to get out and meet some normal people."

Kate laughed. "You're telling me police officers aren't normal people?"

Jay gave her a wry look and reached for the last of the champagne.

"No, sis, they are not. They are definitely not."

Kate twiddled her mug around in her hands. She'd planned a nice dinner for Jay's first visit to her new house, and then she'd assumed they'd sit in front of the fire and chat. That was what she felt like doing.

But his remark about her needing to know plans weeks in advance had stung a little. Was she really that inflexible?

And when was the last time she'd actually *been* out, anyway? Somewhere that wasn't with her friend, and fellow officer, Mark Olbeck? She groped for a memory and realised that it must have been sometime in the summer: her friend Hannah's party. And now it was November. *All right, so I've had to organise a move in the meantime but honestly, I'm twenty eight, not eighty eight...*

She put the mug down and made up her mind.

"Sure, let's go. It'll be fun."

"Oh, cool, sis. You'll enjoy it. Elodie's great. You'll like her."

The faraway look in his eyes as he mentioned his friend's name troubled Kate a little. She wondered whether Elodie knew how Jay felt about her. Well, she'd be able to see for herself later.

"Where's this gig?"

Jay tapped his phone's screen and began to scroll through his text messages.

"Arbuthon Green," he announced a moment later. "There's a pub there, the—"

"Black Horse," said Kate, sighing.

"You know it?"

"Yes." There had been several arrests there recently for drug dealing, but she wasn't going to mention that to Jay. So a night out at a dodgy pub listening to a student band? She was glad she hadn't drunk more than a mouthful of champagne; she'd be able to drive now and make a quick getaway if necessary.

"What about dinner?" she asked.

"Plenty of time for that later," said Jay. "I'll shout you some chips if you like."

"Perfect," said Kate ironically, standing up. "Come on." She nearly added 'let's get it over with,' but she didn't want to dampen Jay's obvious excitement. It would be nice to spend some time with her brother, anyway. She hadn't seen him for several months, after all.

"How's Mum?" she asked, once they were in the car and making their way to Arbuthon Green.

Jay looked at her in surprise.

"She's fine. Why? Haven't you seen her lately?"

Kate lifted one shoulder in a non-committal shrug.

"Not very lately. I've been so busy. With the move and everything."

Jay had his knees resting on the dashboard, and he was tapping them with his hands in response to some inner music.

"Mum's all right. She's got some new bloke on the go."

Oh God. Kate recalled some of the other 'blokes.' The fellow alcoholic, the married man, the other married man, the petty thief. She suppressed a sigh.

"What's he like?" she asked as they pulled into the car park of the Black Horse.

"All right, actually," said Jay, sounding surprised. "Seems fairly normal. Not like the others."

"Well, that's odd in itself," muttered Kate, almost under her breath. Then she dismissed her mother from her mind and concentrated on finding a parking space in the busy car park.

The pub was packed, standing room only. Jay and Kate battled their way through to the bar. Kate was already regretting her decision to come. She didn't want to stand up for two hours, shifting her weight from foot to aching foot, drinking warm orange juice and listening to some crappy amateur band. She felt a bit cross with Jay. Months since she'd seen him and now they weren't really going to have a chance to catch up at all...

She bought them both a drink after a long and frustrating wait at the bar. They battled back through the crowds to a spare square foot of space over by the back wall that was rather too near the toilets for Kate's liking.

The noise in the pub made it difficult to talk. There was a moment of silence between brother and sister as they sipped their drinks. Kate looked out at the heaving crowd. Lots of students, couples, noisy groups of young people. Denim, leather, piercings, spiky heels, band T-shirts. She looked down at her neat blue jeans and cashmere jumper in a tasteful shade of beige. Suddenly, she felt acutely out of place. Hot on the heels of that feeling, a much sharper surge of loneliness peaked. She felt totally apart from this raucous, happy crowd; it was as if she were observing them from afar, always on the outside looking in.

That's what being a police officer does for you, she thought, but she knew it wasn't just that.

She caught the eye of a man in the crowd who'd turned to look her way, as if attuned to her sudden emotional state. He looked familiar. She opened her mouth to greet him, looked closer, and shut it again. She didn't know him. Kate sipped her drink, cautiously looking back at the man, who'd turned to face the stage again. He still looked familiar. Kate mentally shrugged. She'd had this feeling before, and it usually meant she'd recognised someone she'd met in the course of her duties. Well, that was one way of putting it. Quite embarrassing, actually, running into someone you'd arrested.

She looked again at the man. He did actually have the faintly disreputable look of someone who might have rubbed up against the police at some point. His bone structure was good, you could even say he was raggedly handsome, but the overall impression was of good looks subjected to the major stressors of time, worry and hard living. He was staring at the stage, sipping a pint. Alone, like her.

No, not like her. She had Jay beside her, after all. She was aware that her brother had suddenly straightened up, quivering a little like a hunting dog spotting its quarry. There was an outbreak of noise from the expectant crowd: shouts, cheers, catcalls. Kate realised the band had made its entrance.

She spotted Elodie at once: blonde hair in an elfin crop which framed her fine-boned face. The girl had a violin in one hand, held casually but expertly against her hip, a bit like an experienced mother holds a baby. There was a male singer, hair a mass of knotty dreadlocks, nose ring glinting under the pub lights. A drummer and a guitarist, again both male, studenty, scruffy.

Elodie tucked the violin under her chin. The singer counted his band members in, and they launched straight into their first number.

Three songs later, Kate was surprised to find that she was actually enjoying herself. The band, despite their scruffy appearance, were polished performers; they were well-rehearsed and talented and still had the charming enthusiasm of an amateur group. The songs were good, alternating between rollicking, stomping pop and quieter, more melodic ballads. Elodie came into her own during the slower pieces, her nimble fingers drawing plaintive, beautiful sounds from the strings of her violin. She played with great intensity, closing her eyes, seemingly lost in her own world of music.

Kate watched her face as she played, noting the high cheekbones and the sharp angle of her jaw. A beautiful girl, and beautiful in an uncommon way. There were plenty of pretty girls in the room, but Elodie had something else, some other quality that drew the eye. No wonder Jay was smitten.

The band finished their set with a rousing, raucous little number that had the crowd cheering and clapping. Elodie flourished her bow, laughing while she took a bow, and then the musicians all left the tiny stage.

Jay turned to Kate, raising his eyebrows. "Pretty good, huh?"

"They were excellent," agreed Kate.

"Let's go backstage, and you can meet her."

They battled their way through to the back of the pub. 'Backstage' was a bit of a misnomer—the band was crammed into a fetid little room just off the corridor, along from the toilets.

Kate was curious to see how Elodie greeted Jay. She was starting to wonder whether Jay actually knew her as well as he had implied, but she had to know him fairly well to agree to something like modelling for his painting, surely?

Her doubts were dispelled as Elodie caught sight of them. She shrieked and hurled herself at Jay, hugging him and landing a misdirected kiss on his ear.

"You came! What did you think? Were we good? Did you see me fuck up that last song? God!"

The questions came rapidly. Kate, ignored for now, could see the manic glitter in Elodie's eyes—the dilated pupils—now that she was close to the girl. Drugs? She really hoped no one would pull anything out in front of her. She'd *have* to arrest them, and then Jay would never forgive her.

Jay was laughing. He turned to her and gestured.

"Sis, this is Elodie. Elodie, this is my big sister, Kate."

"Hello," said Kate, reaching out to shake hands.

"Hi!" said Elodie. She pulled Kate forward into a hug—Kate squeaked in surprise—and kissed her cheek. The girl's body was thrumming with energy, her cheek warm and damp against Kate's.

"I thought you were really good—" began Kate.

"Oh thanks, you know, first nights are always tricky. Totally nerve-wracking."

"You haven't played here before?"

Elodie shook her head, her eyes sparkling. Kate suddenly saw what she must have looked like as a little girl: mischievous and cherubic at the same time, with blonde curls and chubby cheeks.

"Kate's seen the picture of you," said Jay. "You know, *the* picture. She loved it."

Elodie shrieked. "Damn you, Jay, that river bank was cold. And the *mud*...he made me lie in the mud for *hours*."

Even over the hubbub of the crowded room, Kate could hear her beautiful accent, each vowel and syllable falling neatly into place. It was easy to see how Elodie was the daughter of the head of Rawlwood College. Privately educated, loved and cherished, she must have had the best of everything. A girlhood so different to Kate's that it was difficult not to feel a surge of envy.

"So you're Jay's big sister?" asked Elodie. "He often talks about you."

Kate smiled. "All good, I hope." A clichéd response.

"What do you do?"

Kate glanced at Jay, wondering whether to come clean. Being a police officer—and a detective especially—was like being a call girl or a gynaecologist. People were fascinated, and they wanted all the gory details, but at the same time, they were always a little uneasy in your presence.

"Um—"

She could see Jay shaking his head, a minute gesture easily passed between siblings.

It didn't matter anyway. She could see Elodie had lost interest in her answer; the girl's gaze was drawn up and over her shoulder. Kate watched the light die in Elodie's eyes, noticed the sudden dimming and shrinking of her personality. Elodie's smile faded. She muttered something like 'excuse me a minute' and pushed past Kate and Jay.

Kate turned round. The man she'd noticed earlier was standing in the doorway to the room, and Elodie was walking up to him, talking to him in a voice too low for Kate to make out their conversation. After a moment, they left the room together.

Kate frowned. Sensitive to atmosphere, she could feel the chill settling on the room. There was a sense that the party was over, that the best of the night was gone. She was suddenly aware of how tired she was.

She turned back to Jay.

"Do you want to make a move—" she began, stopping when she saw the bleak look on his face.

"What's wrong?"

Jay seemed to shake himself mentally.

"Nothing," he said, after a moment. She could see him forcing a smile. "I'm alright. Want a drink?"

Kate shook her head. "I'm bushed, Jay, and I've got to work tomorrow. Shall we head home?"

"I'm going to stay on for a bit."

"Really?"

Jay patted her arm. "S'alright, sis. Don't worry about me. You go on home and get some sleep."

"But how will you get back?"

"I'll get a cab. Don't worry."

Kate hunted in her bag before realising she didn't even have a spare key.

"I'll lock up, but just ring me on my mobile when you get back," she said. "I'll keep it by my bed."

"Yeah, cool." From Jay's distracted manner, she wasn't even sure he was listening. He was still staring at the empty doorway where Elodie and her male companion had been standing. Kate wavered for a moment, conscious of a faint nagging feeling of unease. Then she told herself not to worry. Jay was an adult, after all.

"See you later, then. I've made the spare bed up for you."

"Cheers, sis."

He hugged her goodbye, but she could tell his attention was still far away. *Oh well. Bedtime, Kate.*

She looked for Elodie as she walked to her car, thinking she might see her outside the pub door, smoking cigarettes with the little crowd that had gathered there. There was no sign of her. Kate stood for a moment, her hand on the handle of the car door, wondering whether to look for her, to say goodbye and thank you. Then she dismissed the thought.

At that moment, all she wanted to do was get home and climb into her new bed.

Chapter Two

When Kate got to the office the next day, Olbeck was already there, hunched over his desk staring blearily and uncomprehendingly at the screen. He gave Kate the big, forced smile of a man pretending he didn't have a hangover.

"Good night?" asked Kate.

"Mmmph."

Kate said nothing, but she reached into her desk drawer and drew out a packet of paracetomol, which she threw across the desk.

"I'm *fine*," snapped Olbeck as the packet landed on his keyboard. "Just tired, that's all."

Kate said nothing. Olbeck relented.

"Sorry. Thanks."

Kate got them both a coffee and sat down again. She looked again at the text message from Jay, who hadn't come home last night. *Got a bed sis, wont be hm, c u later xx.* Sent at 4.13am. Whose bed? Elodie's or some random pick-up? Or simply a friend? She tried not to worry. *He's an adult*, she told herself, not for the first time.

She looked across at Olbeck, who was wincing and rubbing his temples. She wasn't going to worry about *him*, either. He was an adult too, although he currently wasn't acting much like one.

Olbeck had split up with his partner, Joe, several months ago. Having been the one to instigate the break-up, Olbeck had been making the most of his newly-found freedom. Night after night, he'd been out clubbing, partying, drinking and dancing. When he wasn't out living it up, he was working all hours, clocking up the overtime, constantly in the office. To Kate, it seemed very much like the actions of a man who was trying not to face up to something painful. However, having had her head bitten off more than once when she'd tried to broach the subject, she'd decided discretion was the better part of valour and was currently keeping her mouth shut.

She dismissed both Jay's and Olbeck's private lives from her mind, mentally squared her shoulders, and turned her attention to the massive amount of paperwork littering her desk while trying to ignore the long-suffering groans Olbeck kept making under his breath.

"What have we got today?"

Olbeck shoved a file across the desk.

"That domestic assault case is coming up."

"I thought Rav was doing that one?"

"He is, but—"

The phone rang. Olbeck picked it up.

"Olbeck here."

He said nothing else, but there was something in the change of his posture that made Kate sit up. She sat with pen poised, feeling her stomach tighten a little. It was a sixth sense, that's what it was; you knew when something big had happened. Olbeck wasn't saying much, just asking a series of blunt questions and scribbling down the answers. He said goodbye and put the phone down.

Kate put her pen down.

"What is it?"

Olbeck stood up, reaching for his car keys.

"Dead girl in the river. Patrol just called it in."

"Oh, no."

"Afraid so."

"Where?"

"Arbuthon Green."

Kate was reaching for her coat and looked up in surprise. "Seriously? I was there last night. Just last night."

"Should I arrest you?"

"Ha, bloody ha. Come on, you can tell me what you know in the car."

It was a twenty-minute drive to Arbuthon Green, and their route took them past the Black Horse, shut up now at 10.30am in the morning. The pavement outside was littered with cigarette stubs and empty bottles. Olbeck drove on through streets of terraced houses, their walls grey with pockmarked pebbledash and festooned with satellite dishes. Abbeyford was a reasonably affluent town, but every town has its poorer areas. Arbuthon Green was one of them.

The river was a winding oasis of beauty in the squalor. A footpath ran parallel with the water, and the banks were fringed with graceful willow trees, frondy branches dipping into the water. The banks were shallow, covered in patchy grass or thick mud. As Kate and Olbeck walked towards the little knot of people further up the footpath, they could see the pale shape of the body on the bank. No tent had yet been erected to screen the body from public view.

"Where's Scene of Crime?" Olbeck muttered, almost to himself, as they walked along.

Kate said nothing. As they got closer, she was aware of a sensation very much like shock that was beginning to set in. it was worse than shock: a sense of unreality, a feeling of dislocation. She could see the girl properly now; she was lying on her back, arms outflung. There was mud in her blonde hair, and her face was blue-lipped, ghastly pale.

"Oh my God."

Olbeck turned as Kate stopped walking.

"What's wrong?"

Kate was staring at the body. For a moment, she wondered whether she was still at home in bed dreaming.

"The body…it's the scene—"

"Kate, talk to me. You're not making sense."

Kate turned a pale face to Olbeck. "I know her. The girl. I met her last night."

Olbeck's face mirrored the shock on her own.

"You're kidding."

They'd reached the scene now. There were several uniformed officers, a shivering man in a wet tracksuit and Theo Marsh, one of Kate and Olbeck's colleagues.

Behind Theo, Olbeck saw the white vans of the Scene of Crime Officers draw up.

Theo raised a hand in greeting, and then frowned when he saw Kate's expression.

"What's up?"

Kate was breathing deeply, trying to get a hold of herself. She kept seeing the painting hanging even now on her living room wall: Elodie's mock-dead face, her blue lips. All brought to reality right in front of her. How was it possible? She brought a hand up to her face, pinching the bridge of her nose hard.

"First time, is it?" one of the uniforms asked in a bored and patronising manner.

"No, it bloody isn't," snapped Kate. She wheeled on one heel, not waiting to hear his response, and walked rapidly away along the riverbank. She took just ten steps before stopping, but it was enough to take her away from the body. The feeling of unreality receded slightly. She stood, back turned to the scene, watching the ripples on the surface of the river. Sticks and rubbish had drifted up against the muddy banks. Half a pumpkin floated by, one carved eye socket and several grinning teeth still evident, reminding Kate that Halloween had come and gone.

She heard Olbeck and Theo walk up behind her.

"Kate? You all right?"

She turned round. SOCO had already begun to cordon off the riverbank. The man in the wet tracksuit was being shepherded towards a waiting police car.

"I'm all right. It was just a shock."

"Mark says you know her," said Theo. He looked worried and young. This was a situation they'd discussed before, over drinks. *What if the victim was someone you knew? What would you do?*

Kate opened her mouth to tell them about the painting—and then shut it again.

"I met her last night for the first time. She's called Elodie. She's a musician, goes to Rawlwood College." She remembered what Jay had told her. "I think her father's the headmaster there."

Olbeck's eyebrows went up.

"God. If you're right, this is going to be..." He didn't need to elaborate to his colleagues.

"Are you sure it's her?" asked Theo. "I mean, if you've only met her once and with the water damage, and all..."

Kate was conscious of a sudden spurt of hope. How wonderful it would be if it *wasn't* Elodie. *Wonderful? Listen to yourself, Kate. You're talking about someone's daughter, someone's child.*

She dismissed her inner critic and walked up to the tape line, staring at the body. Once again, she was reminded of the painting. The posture, her face. Was it possible that the painting had actually caused her to misidentify the body because of the resemblance? Kate looked closer and her heart sank. It was definitely Elodie.

She walked back to the others, shaking her head.

"As far as I can see, it's her."

"Shit," said Theo. "We'd better tell Anderton as soon as he gets here."

"He's on his way now?" asked Olbeck.

Theo nodded. Kate watched the river slipping slowly past. She hadn't thought this far ahead yet. Anderton was the DCI for Abbeyford and surrounding areas; he was Kate's immediate boss. He would have to know about the picture. He would have to know everything. Kate remembered Jay sitting across from her on her new chair, tipping his mug full of champagne towards her, smiling.

Who's the model? My mate Elodie.

"Kate?"

Kate realised she was standing with her eyes tightly shut. She gave herself a mental shake. *Get it together. You have no idea what's happened as yet, so stop panicking.*

"Here's Anderton," she said as she saw his car draw up, pleased her voice sounded so normal.

The three of them walked towards their DCI. Anderton had just returned from holiday—three weeks at his holiday home in the South of France, Olbeck had explained to Kate—and he was certainly tanned, his grey hair lightened by the sun. But he didn't look much like a man who'd enjoyed three weeks of relaxation. His brows were drawn down in a frown and there were dark circles under his eyes. *Probably doesn't want to be back at work, and who could blame him*? thought Kate as she returned his subdued greeting.

"Suicide, murder or accident?" said Anderton as they walked back towards the crime scene.

"We don't yet know, sir," said Kate. She pictured the painting hanging on her living room wall and heard her voice falter a little. When was she going to have to mention it?

"Well, any ideas at all? What have you people been doing all morning? Have I just been dragged down here to stand around like a spare part?"

Kate flinched under his tone. He could be brusque, she knew that, but he was not normally so rude.

"A jogger discovered the body at about seven this morning," said Olbeck, hastily. "He thought someone was drowning, waded in and pulled them out, although obviously the girl was long dead by then."

"So the body was found in the river?"

"That's right, sir."

Kate grabbed Olbeck's arm. "Is that right? The body was pulled out of the river?"

"Yes," said Olbeck, looking down at her hand on his arm with a quizzical expression. "Didn't I say?"

"No, you bloody didn't!"

All three men were now looking at her strangely. Kate tried to pin a neutral expression on her face and tried not to show the waves of warm relief washing over her. The resemblance of the body on the riverbank to the picture on her wall was coincidental, that's all. Oh, wonderful relief. For a moment, she felt dizzy with it.

"Something wrong, Kate?" Anderton spoke in a voice that implied she had to tell him.

Kate struggled and managed to subdue her euphoria. "Sorry sir, nothing wrong. I just hadn't been informed of all the facts, that's all." Olbeck shot her a hurt look, which she ignored. "I wasn't aware that this wasn't the original crime scene."

Anderton exhaled in disgust.

"You lot are not impressing me this morning. Theo, tell me something useful, for Christ's sake."

"Yes, sir." Theo almost stood to attention. "As Mark said, the body was discovered by a jogger, Mike Deedham, this morning at about seven am. He often runs along this path, according to him. He said he saw something in the water—in fact, he said he saw 'someone' in the water—and thought they were drowning, plunged in, dragged them out onto the river bank and then realised they were, well, dead already."

"Humph." Anderton looked over at the police car where the man in the wet tracksuit had been taken. "That's *his* story. We'll have to take a much more detailed statement. Anything else? Do we know who the victim is yet?"

Olbeck nudged Kate's arm and she shot him an annoyed look.

Anderton intercepted it. "Kate Redman, what is the matter with you this morning? Do you know who the victim is, or not?"

Kate spoke. "Yes sir. She's a young student called Elodie, I'm not sure of her last name." Olbeck nudged her again. "For fuck's sake, Mark! Let me finish. She's a musician, a student at Rawlwood College."

Anderton studied her face.

"And how do you know all of this?"

Jay's face swam in front of her eyes. Kate swallowed. "Because I met her last night, sir."

Anderton's grey eyes regarded her steadily.

"Is that so?" he said. "Well, you'd better tell me all about it."

Chapter Three

Elodie Duncan lived—had lived—with her parents in a house on the grounds of Rawlwood College. The house was named Rawlwood Cottage, which was something of a misnomer, as Kate and Olbeck discovered. They drove up the long and winding gravel driveway to the impressive Victorian building that stood in a clearing of evergreen and deciduous trees. Hidden from view from the main road behind a bank of trees, the house was very large, the gables and window frames painted black, original stained glass in the front door. There were two cars parked neatly side-by-side in front of the house: a dark purple Volvo and a newer model Beetle in silver.

"Did Elodie have a car?" asked Mark as they made their way to the front door.

"I don't know—" Kate was unable to say more, as the door opened before she'd even raised a hand to the doorbell. The man who had opened it was in his late fifties: tall, rather handsome and dressed in a well-cut tweed jacket. There was something slightly wrong with his appearance, something so subtle that Kate could hardly put her finger on what it was. Then she realised it was his tie. It was a colour that clashed slightly with the tweed of his suit and the knot was tied badly, obviously in haste.

"May I help you?"

"Mr Duncan? Thomas Duncan?"

"Yes? What's the matter?"

Olbeck and Kate showed their warrant cards. "We're police officers, sir. May we come in for a moment?"

Mr Duncan remained where he was for a moment, one hand on the half-open door. He closed his eyes.

"What's happened?" he said, in a voice almost too faint to be heard.

"May we come in, Mr Duncan?" Kate wasn't going to do this on the doorstep, whether or not the house was isolated.

The headmaster opened his eyes.

"Yes, of course," he said. He seemed to pull himself together a little. "I'm sorry. Come through..."

They followed him through the hallway and into a sitting room to the left. A woman was perched there on the very edge of the sofa, clasping her hands together. She was blonde, petite: an older, faded copy of Elodie.

"This is my wife, Genevieve Duncan," said Thomas Duncan. Kate had the impression that the two of them had been sitting there all night, waiting. Were they waiting for their daughter, who was never coming home? She took a deep breath. This was the worst part of her job, the very worst. It never got any easier.

"Mrs Duncan, Mr Duncan, I'm very sorry to have to tell you that I have some very bad news." Say it quick, don't ever drag it out. People at this point know the worst has happened, there was never any need to prolong the agony. "This morning, we found the body of a girl which we believe to be your daughter Elodie. I'm so sorry—"

Mrs Duncan burst out in screams, in full-blown hysteria: piercing yells, tears streaming down her pale cheeks. Mr Duncan knelt by her, his face grey. She threw her hands over her face, writhing and kicking like a toddler having a tantrum.

Kate looked at Olbeck. He met her eyes, but there was no need to say anything. There was nothing they could do but wait.

After a seemingly endless stretch of time, Mrs Duncan's sobs tapered off into gasping breaths. She lay back against the cushions of the sofa, still hiding her face. Kate had seen that impulse in people before: the wish to shut out the knowledge, an attempt to physically block off the horror.

Mr Duncan sat by her, his hands dangling between his knees.

"I'm so very sorry," Kate said, quietly. "This must have been a terrible shock to you. I'm afraid I will need one of you to come with us to identify her."

She looked directly at the headmaster. "Mr Duncan, are you able to do that?"

Mr Duncan got up from the sofa, moving like a man twenty years older than himself.

"Me? I don't know if I could bear it." He looked at his wife, helplessly. "No, I must, I can see that I must."

"Is there someone who could stay with your wife to give her some support? DS Olbeck will stay here as well, but perhaps a friend..."

"I don't know, I—"

"I don't want anyone," said Mrs Duncan, in a voice ragged with tears.

Kate nodded slightly at Olbeck. She stood back slightly to let Mr Duncan make his slow and shaky way past her to the hallway.

At the mortuary, he stood in silence, with Kate beside him, regarding Elodie's body. His gaze lingered on her pale face. The dead never look as though they are sleeping, not when looked at properly. Something—call it the soul, the spark of life—something indefinable has gone. The dead look truly dead.

Kate thought of her first glimpse of Elodie; the girl's impish grin and vivid personality shining out from the stage. And now this, a whole person reduced to a hollow shell, lying on a cold metal table. She felt tears come to her eyes.

As if he could sense her pain, Mr Duncan began to speak, falteringly, almost as if he were talking to himself.

"She was always special. She had a glow about her, something special—everyone around her could feel it. She was eight years old when I met her, and I could see it then. Oh yes," he interjected as Kate made some kind of noise in response, "I'm her stepfather. But that never mattered. She always felt like mine, just as if she were my real daughter. Yes, mine..."

His voice faded away. Kate sensed a huge tidal wave of emotion, held back by the flimsiest of barriers.

"Always special," said Mr Duncan, his voice shaking. The dam broke. He put his hands up to his face, tears running down between his fingers. Kate put a hand on his trembling arm.

"It shouldn't be like this!" he cried, and then his words were lost in a torrent of sobs. Kate, feeling her uselessness, kept a steadying hand on him, muttering the usual soothing words.

Later, after driving Mr Duncan home, Kate and Olbeck conferred briefly with the family liaison officer now stationed at the house. Mrs Duncan was sat at the kitchen table, staring out at the garden, a cup of tea untouched before her. Kate wondered whether to interview the parents now or whether to wait until the first shock had worn off a little. She decided on the latter.

"God," said Olbeck as they got into the car. He leant his head against the back of the car seat and closed his eyes. "That was a bad one."

"Especially on a hangover," said Kate unsympathetically.

"You have no idea." He sat up again, rubbing his temples. "Actually, I need a drink."

"No, you don't."

"I do. A bloody big one."

"I'll buy you one."

Olbeck looked at her in surprise. "You will?"

"A giant coffee," said Kate, smiling a little. "Perhaps even a muffin to go with it."

"Huh." Olbeck slumped again. "We'd better get back, anyway."

Later that afternoon, Kate, Olbeck and Anderton returned to Rawlwood Cottage. Normally, the three of them would use the time in the car to discuss the case, bring forward points they thought worthy of discussion, make suggestions about where to go next. Today, though, they sat in silence, all three of them busy with their own thoughts. Kate stared out of the window as they turned into the driveway, past the crumbling stone gateposts and through the banks of trees still clothed in their autumn leaves. She was thinking about the painting. When was she going to mention it? *Was* she going to mention it? Wasn't it just a coincidence that the crime scene so closely resembled the picture? *The body was found in the river*, she told herself, trying to ignore that small voice inside that told her that it could still be important.

"Kate! Wake up. We're here."

Anderton's voice made her jump. She gave herself a mental shake and got out of the car, smoothing back her hair and trying to get herself back into the right state of mind for this interview.

The Duncans were sitting in the living room. Mrs Duncan hunched into an arm chair; her husband perched on the edge of the sofa. The family liaison officer, a PC called Mandy, stood up as the other officers came into the room. Anderton introduced himself and his team.

"I'll make us all some tea," said Mandy. Kate smiled at her as she walked past to the kitchen. Briefly she wondered how many millions of cups of tea the liaison officers made in the course of their careers.

Anderton began with a few words of sympathy. Mrs Duncan kept her eyes on the arm of her chair, her fingers rubbing and picking at the fabric.

"I don't know what we can tell you," said Mr Duncan. "We don't know any more than you do. Elodie went out last night—she was in a band and they were playing at a pub, The Black Horse. I don't know what happened."

"Did you expect Elodie to come home last night?"

"She was meant to."

Anderton leant forward a little.

"Does that mean that you did expect her home, or not?"

The Duncans exchanged a glance. Then Mr Duncan said, reluctantly, "We did expect her home but…we weren't sure whether she would be or not."

Mrs Duncan gripped the edge of the seat arm, the bones of her fingers showing bluish-white through the skin of her hands.

"She's been so odd recently…" she began falteringly, and then obviously realised the mistake in her use of the present tense. Tears began to stream down her cheeks, but she kept speaking. "She was so secretive, moody—we used to get so upset with one another, I don't know…I didn't know what to do."

Anderton looked at Kate, and she responded to his unseen cue, taking up the baton.

"Were you worried when Elodie didn't come home, Mrs Duncan? Had she done this before—stay out all night without letting you know when she'd be home?"

Mrs Duncan nodded.

"The past few months have been particularly bad. She was so argumentative. Nothing her father or I could do was right. Ever since her eighteenth birthday, she's just run wild." She stopped abruptly and put her face in her hands.

Kate turned to Mr Duncan, who was staring blankly at the carpet.

"Did Elodie have a boyfriend?"

"No."

He said it harshly, almost angrily. Then he seemed to recollect himself. "I'm sorry. She did have a boyfriend for a few months, but that didn't last long. There wasn't anyone else."

Kate glanced at Olbeck, who looked back at her expressively. How much did these parents actually know of their daughter? She wouldn't have been the first teenager to hide an unsuitable boyfriend from their knowledge.

"We'll need the name of Elodie's ex-boyfriend, please, and

also the names of her friends, the people she used to spend a lot of time with."

Neither of the Duncans spoke for a moment. Then Mrs Duncan, fingers unconsciously pulling at the fabric of the chair on which she sat, said, "His name was Reuben, Reuben Farraday."

"Is he a pupil at Rawlwood College?"

"He is not," said Mr Duncan. "He and Elodie met at a concert. I'm afraid I have no knowledge of where he is now." He and his wife exchanged another look. "I'm afraid I didn't much approve of him."

"Was that why they split up?"

"I don't know." His tone indicated that he would prefer not to continue talking about this particular subject, which normally would mean that Kate and the team would start to push harder. But these parents had just lost their daughter and, after a tiny shake of the head from Anderton, Kate switched subjects.

"You mentioned Elodie's behaviour had changed over the past couple of months, Mrs Duncan. Did you know why that was?"

Mrs Duncan shook her head. "Every time I tried to talk to Elodie about how badly she was behaving, she just got worse. Eventually, I just didn't dare to bring it up anymore."

"How was she behaving badly?"

Mrs Duncan wiped her face. "I thought I'd already said. She was rude, moody. Such hard work to be around. She didn't want to do anything with me, with Tom, with anyone."

"So she didn't go out much?"

An incredulous look. "She went out *all the time*. She was never at home. But she would never say who she was going out with."

"Did she ever bring any friends home?"

"Amy came over sometimes." Mrs Duncan sniffed. "She's known her for years. She's a nice girl."

"Amy is Elodie's best friend? What's her surname?"

"Peters." Mrs Duncan hesitated, pulling again at the arm of

the chair. "She hasn't been round for a while. I think Elodie and she had an argument."

"An argument? What about, Mrs Peters?"

Mrs Duncan shook her head.

"I don't know. I don't know anything."

There was a moment's silence. Kate thought back through the conversation, making a mental list of the words used by Elodie's mother. *Moody, difficult, secretive...* She recalled the manic glitter she'd seen in Elodie's eyes, and her heart sank a little. As if reading her thoughts, Mr Duncan asked in an almost inaudible voice, "How did she die?"

Mrs Duncan winced as if he had shouted. Anderton shook his head slowly.

"We don't yet know, I'm afraid. The post-mortem will tell us more."

Mr Duncan opened his mouth as if to ask another question and then shut it again. There was a lengthy moment of silence in the room. Kate caught sight of a photograph of a younger Elodie on the mantelpiece, framed in silver. She had an impish grin on her face and was staring out of the frame, pointed chin lifted. She looked as though she were laughing at them all.

Chapter Four

Kate had attended many post-mortems in the course of her career, but they had yet to become commonplace. She steadied herself with a deep breath. She always felt something like awe at the magnitude of death—how a whole, remarkable person could be reduced down to a waxen reproduction of themselves. The pathologist performing the autopsy was someone Kate hadn't met before, a young man called Stanton. She had hoped it would be Doctor Telling, who she rather liked for being quiet and gentle and skilled at her job, but she was apparently on holiday for three weeks. Kate's mind conjured up a rather bizarre mental picture of the gaunt, pale doctor sunning herself on a beach somewhere, still dressed in her pathologist's scrubs. She dismissed the thought, as it was provoking an inappropriate grin, and brought herself back to the task in hand.

Anderton had cried off, citing a meeting, but Olbeck had met her at the coroner's offices, turning up looking rather better than he had done yesterday. Presumably he'd not been out partying to the early hours the night before. Kate could understand his decision to stay in; she could think of few things worse than having to observe an autopsy with a raging hangover. She said as much to Olbeck.

"What would you know about it?" he said, rather grumpily. "You never *get* hangovers. You hardly bloody drink."

"I can still imagine it."

"Well, anyway. Let's get on with it."

Dr Stanton had a rather brusque manner, tersely commenting as he performed the various tasks that would untangle the mystery of Elodie's death.

"Are there any indications of suicide?" asked Olbeck, who'd disappeared halfway through the operation to answer a text message, rather to Kate's annoyance.

"Most definitely not," said Stanton. He turned away from the table, leaning back against the instrument bench against the wall. "There's no water in the lungs, which is always a good indication."

"Ah."

"And more pertinently than that, the hyoid bone is fractured."

Kate knew the significance of that. "So she was strangled?"

Doctor Stanton looked at her appraisingly and then smiled rather flirtatiously.

"The indications are there. Bruises on the neck as well."

"Right."

"I don't believe we've met before, have we? This will all be in my report, by the way. I'm happy to talk you through it—perhaps over coffee afterwards?"

Olbeck was grinning. Kate sighed inwardly. Flirting was one thing, but doing it over the body of a dead girl was distasteful in the extreme.

"That's fine, thank you. I can read it later."

Stanton shrugged. "There's one thing you should know."

"Which is?"

"She was pregnant."

Kate felt the familiar little tremor inside her, as if a tiny foot had swung against her lower belly. When would she stop feeling that?

She cleared her throat. "How pregnant?"

"Not very. First trimester. About ten weeks, I'd estimate."

Olbeck had stopped smiling. "That's something her parents didn't know."

"Or they didn't tell us." Kate tried to run a hand through her hair, knowing it was pure displacement activity, before realising it was tied back tightly. "We'll need to talk to them again anyway." She remembered something else. "What about drugs? Any indications?"

Stanton had begun to peel off his gloves.

"You'll have to wait for the tox tests. I should have the results within a week. There was plenty of alcohol and not much food in her stomach."

So Elodie had been drinking despite her pregnancy. Had she even known she *was* pregnant? Who was the father? If Elodie had known she was pregnant, had she told anyone else? Looking down at the body, shrouded now in dull green cotton, Kate felt tired. So many questions... It was hard to know where to begin.

"Do you know the time of death?" asked Olbeck.

Stanton was rinsing his hands under the tap. He pulled a handful of blue paper towels from the dispenser on the wall, dried his hands and threw the crumpled up ball of paper into a wastebin next to him.

"It's hard to say exactly, as well you know. But—like I say in my report—you can narrow it down to between about 3am and 5.30am the night before last."

"He fancied you," said Olbeck, when they were back in the car.

"No, he didn't."

"Yes, he did. It was obvious. You were definitely in there."

Kate snorted. "Even if I was, I'm not going out with a *pathologist*, for God's sake. Can you imagine going to bed with one, for a start? You'd always be wondering where their hands had been. Ugh."

Olbeck chuckled. "Perfect partner for a necrophiliac."

"Well, quite." Kate flicked the indicator on to turn left. "As for me, it's thanks but no thanks."

"All right, all right. I get the message." Olbeck checked his phone and made a satisfied noise.

Kate glanced over. "What's up?"

"Nothing," he said, smugly.

Kate sighed. "Don't tell me. Your hot date for tonight."

"Got it in one."

"You have more hot dates than I have hot dinners," grumbled Kate. "And what was with the texting during the PM? That's not professional, Mark."

"Oh, leave it out, Kate. It could have been work-related for all you know."

"Well, was it?"

Olbeck was silent for a moment. "It might have been."

"*Was* it?"

"No." He grinned a little sheepishly. "But come on, it was only a minute. Besides, don't tell me you've never done anything unprofessional at work." He laughed a little. "Wait, what am I saying? This is DS Redman we're talking about."

Kate said nothing. She knew he was just teasing her, but his words had brought the painting sharply back to the forefront of her mind. Was she going to mention it? Should she? *Of course you should, and you know it*, a little voice whispered. Hard on the heels of that thought came the question, *Does Jay know yet? Am I going to have to tell him?* Kate shivered inwardly, already dreading the moment.

Chapter Five

THE CRIME SCENE PHOTOGRAPHS WERE already pinned up to the whiteboards when Kate entered the office the next day. The night before, she'd taken the picture down and put it away in an upstairs cupboard. Then she'd locked the cupboard door. She'd tried to call Jay, but the call had gone straight to his voicemail, so she'd hung up without leaving a message. Cowardly but... Kate's train of thought was derailed as Anderton crashed through the door.

"Morning team, morning team." He strode up to the whiteboards and pinned up another photograph beside the one of Elodie's body. This new picture made a cruel contrast: it was a recently taken shot, professionally posed, obviously a school picture. Elodie in the dark blue and silver uniform of Rawlwood College, shoulders held back, pointed chin lifted, blonde crop neatly brushed. She looked younger, somehow, than she had when Kate had met her. Perhaps it was the uniform. Perhaps it was the expression on her face, eyes big and dark, a hint of anxiety in her gaze.

Anderton seemed to have recovered his mood and was back to his normal ebullient self. The rest of the team took up their usual positions, angled to keep their chief in sight as he paced up and down the room.

"Elodie Duncan," said Anderton. "Our victim. Eighteen years

old, a pupil at Rawlwood College, daughter of the College's headmaster."

"Stepdaughter," said Olbeck.

"Yes, that's right. Stepdaughter." He stopped pacing for a moment, clutching his hair with one hand. "Her body was found at 7.06am two days ago by a jogger on the footpath that runs along the river by Arbuthon Green. Cause of death now confirmed as manual strangulation. Kate!" Kate jumped. "Wake up. Anything pertinent from the PM?"

Kate took a deep breath.

"She was pregnant. Early stages, about ten weeks."

"Aha," said Anderton. He turned and put a finger out, touching the school picture of Elodie almost tenderly. "That's interesting. Do her parents know, I wonder?"

"That's what we thought," said Olbeck. Kate hadn't had a chance to talk to him yet. She looked over at him, noting with irritation mixed with concern that he looked even rougher than he had done the other day. What was the matter with him? He was acting like a teenager. Immediately her thoughts snapped back to Jay, and by association, the painting. *You've got to do something or stop thinking about it,* she told herself. *This is how madness starts.*

Anderton was still talking.

"We've spoken to Elodie's parents. They're not telling us much at the moment, but it seems our girl's been moody, difficult, argumentative. Out of control, in her parents' eyes. Now this may be nothing more than the usual teenage rebellion, but it may not be. I want all her friends interviewed. Let's see what they can tell us. I've already cleared it with her father that we can use a room at the College for as long as we need for interviews. We need to find this ex-boyfriend of hers too."

Jerry raised his hand.

"What about the bloke who found the body?"

"Yes, indeed. I want to hear his story myself. Told us he

thought he saw someone drowning, jumped in to try and save them, pulled out the body. Now he may be telling the truth, or it may be his way of covering up something more sinister. *Kate*."

Kate came back to reality with a start. "What, sir?"

"Did you have a late night, or something? Wake up. What's the jogger's name?"

Kate groped for a moment and then thankfully her memory returned.

"His name's Michael Deedham."

"Deedham, right. We need to interview him again. Mark, Kate, come with me after this meeting, and we'll knock that off to start with." Anderton reached the wall, turned sharply on his heel and began pacing back the other way. "Right, what else?"

Kate thought it was time she made a real contribution. "Mark and I will start interviewing her friends. They may know a lot more about Elodie's life than her parents do."

"Good point." Anderton shot her a piercing glance. "Didn't your brother know her?"

Kate felt her heart rate begin to speed up a little. She could see the painting in her mind's eye: the river bank, the mud, Elodie's dead face. She swallowed.

"That's right." She paused for a second. "I'm not sure how well he *actually* knows her though."

"Well, it'll do for a start. What about girlfriends? Her mother mentioned her best friend, whose name escapes me at the moment. Anyone?"

Olbeck shifted his position, leaning against one of the tables.

"Amy Peters," he said, looking down at his notes. We'll track her down."

"The ex-boyfriend, too," said Kate. "Reuben Farraday."

"Her teachers," said Theo.

"Good, good. All this needs to be followed up. Jane, get onto the CCTV from that stretch of the river. In fact, from anywhere near the last place she was seen alive, which was the Black Horse."

Jane's red curls bounced as she nodded.

Anderton finally came to a halt.

"Right, that'll do to go with. Anyone else got anything to say?"

"You haven't mentioned the pregnancy, sir," said Kate. "Do we mention it in our interviews?"

"Christ, yes. How did I forget that?" Nobody answered him, although there were a few disconcerted glances exchanged. It was unusual for Anderton to admit to a mistake and even more unusual for him to make one. "So, Elodie Duncan was...what was it? Ten weeks pregnant when she died. Now, the question is, does this have any bearing on her death or is it coincidence? Why didn't her parents mention it? Do they even know?" He ran both hands through his hair and dropped them to his side. "Yes, mention it. Well, see how the conversation is going and use your discretion. I want to know whether it's important or not. Right, team, you've got your orders. Start digging. Get—"

"The evidence," they all chorused, finishing his sentence. Anderton grinned.

"That's right. Okay, Kate, Mark—let's go."

The jogger who'd reported the discovery of the body, Michael Deedham, lived in a red-brick Edwardian villa in Charlock, the neighbouring suburb to Arbuthon Green. Both Charlock and Deedham's house were a great deal more prosperous and respectable-looking than the poky terraces and down-at-heel flats that made up most of Arbuthon Green. Deedham was an athletic-looking man of around forty, balding and muscular. He had looked more at home in the damp tracksuit he'd been wearing when Kate and Olbeck had seen him at the crime scene than he did in the well-cut suit he was wearing when he opened the door to them. Although they'd rung ahead to announce their visit, he still looked a little disconcerted at their appearance.

They were ushered into a sitting room at the front of the house that was furnished with a battered leather Chesterfield and a rather jarringly modern armchair. Children's plastic toys and a jumble of wooden train set pieces were scattered over the worn Persian rug.

"Sorry about the mess," said Deedham, kicking a battered plastic doll and a few toy cars over to the skirting board. "Two kids under three, what can you do?" He didn't seem to require an answer. "What can I do for you?"

He had a brisk manner which Kate associated with teaching for a living. She asked him what he did for a job.

"I'm a management consultant," he said. "With Seddons Hargrove." Kate nodded to give the impression that she actually knew what a management consultant was. What was it exactly that they did?

Olbeck and Anderton had seated themselves on the Chesterfield, leaving Kate to choose the modern chair. She perched somewhat gingerly on its edge.

"We'd just like to talk to you again about the events of the day before yesterday," began Anderton. "Take us through the timeline, so to speak."

Deedham had taken the only other chair in the room, a rickety wooden one. He frowned.

"I've already given a statement."

"I know, sir," said Anderton smoothly. "This is very much standard procedure. There's nothing to worry about."

"I'm not worried. I just don't understand why I have to go through it all again. It was a pretty distressing experience."

"It must have been. So, you were on your usual morning run?"

Deedham sighed and gave in.

"That's right. I run every morning, sometimes in the evenings as well. I'm training for the London marathon, and I have to put in the hours, because I'm deskbound for the rest of the day. Anyway, I was doing the usual route, along the path by the river, and I spotted something white in the water."

"Could you see it was a person?"

"Not at first—I just saw this large, white thing in the river, then this hand came up." He raised his own arm to demonstrate. "And I think, my God, it's someone drowning. So of course I kicked off my trainers and leapt right on in."

"You didn't realise that the girl was already dead?"

Deedham looked annoyed.

"No, I didn't. Not until I got her out onto the bank anyway. Look, what was I supposed to have done, leave her to drown?" He pulled himself up. "I mean, I thought she was drowning. Jesus Christ, next time I won't bother."

"All right, Mr Deedham. We know you were trying to do the right thing. We just have to have everything absolutely straightened out, to make sure we've got everything down correctly."

Deedham ran a finger around his collar, as if it had suddenly become too tight.

"I tried mouth to mouth," he said in a clipped tone. "Now you're probably going to tell me I was wrong to do that as well."

Kate and Olbeck exchanged glances.

"Of course not, Mr Deedham," said Kate, taking up the conversation. "That was very public-spirited of you. I suppose even though you knew she was dead, you thought there might be a chance to bring her back to life?"

Deedham nodded. All of a sudden his eyes filled with tears.

After a moment, he said with a catch in his voice, "I didn't try for long. I could see it wasn't going to work. She was cold as anything, lifeless—like a doll, really..."

He trailed off into silence. Anderton let it spool out for a couple of seconds and then asked, "Did you know Elodie Duncan, Mr Deedham?"

Deedham stared.

"*Know* her? What, aside from pulling her out of the river?"

"Yes. Did you know her in—life, shall we say?"

Deedham was still staring. "No. I'd never seen her before in my life."

"Are you sure?"

"Yes, of course. Why?" Nobody answered him. "I promise you I'd never clapped eyes on her before, poor girl."

"You know that she was the daughter of the Headmaster, Thomas Duncan, at Rawlwood College?"

"Was she?" Deedham rubbed his balding head. "No, I didn't know that."

"Have you any connection to the College?"

Deedham got up out of his chair and stood behind it, gripping the back of it.

"No, I haven't got any *connection* to the College. I don't understand all these questions. What are you implying?"

"It's standard procedure, sir," said Kate, knowing that Anderton liked her to step in at these moments. *It's something about the softer voice, Kate,* he'd said when they'd talked about it. She'd called him an utter sexist, but it did seem to work when a suspect was becoming aggressive. "I'm sorry if you find this intrusive, but you have to understand that in a murder case, we're operating from a standpoint of complete ignorance. We have to ask a lot of questions to try and see where we're going."

Deedham looked at her. She smiled, and he looked a little mollified.

"You're being very helpful, sir," Kate added. "We are very grateful. As I'm sure Elodie's parents are for what you tried to do for their daughter."

"Okay," said Deedham, shortly. He sat down again, pulling at his jacket sleeves. "I'm being totally honest with you. I'd never seen her before or heard of her, and I had no idea she was anything to do with whatever it was College. That's all."

There was the sound of the front door banging open and then the squeal of young children's voices out in the hallway. A few seconds later, the doorway opened and a yelling toddler barrelled into the room. The little boy came to a screeching halt as he realised there were three strange adults in the room.

"It's all right, Harry, it's all right," said Deedham, picking his son up. The boy hid his face in his father's broad chest. A woman put her head around the door.

"Oh, sorry," she said, looking puzzled.

"It's the police," said Deedham. His wife's face clouded. "They want to know whether I knew Elodie Duncan."

"Who?"

Deedham looked at the police as if to say 'you see?'

"That poor girl I pulled out of the river."

"Knew her?" His wife came fully into the room. She was a small woman, neat and pretty, with a chin-length bob haircut. She had a baby settled on her hip, a girl of about eight months who looked at the police officers with round eyes and began sucking her small thumb.

"Of course he didn't know her," said Mrs Deedham. "He'd never seen her before in his life."

The little boy in Deedham's arms began to struggle. His father put him down on the floor, and he immediately ran over to a box of toys in the corner of the room and began throwing them aside, clearly searching for a particularly loved one. The officers exchanged glances. The time for questioning was obviously at an end. They got to their feet.

"So what do you think?" asked Olbeck as they drove back to the station.

Anderton was driving. Technically, his work status warranted a driver, but Kate had noticed that he always preferred to drive himself. He liked to be in control.

He shrugged and made an indeterminate noise.

"I don't know. There's nothing about his statement that doesn't add up but...I don't know."

"I know what you mean," said Kate. "He's very defensive."

"It's not so much that." He slowed the car for a T-junction, glancing at her in the rear view mirror. "There's something about him I don't like. I can't put my finger on it. It may be important—then again, it may not."

"Should we talk to his wife?" asked Kate. "See if she says anything that, well, doesn't quite tally?"

Anderton pondered. "Yes. But it's lower priority at the moment than the other interviews. We start at Rawlwood College tomorrow, nine sharp." They were approaching the station. He caught her eye again. "You talked to your brother yet?"

"Not yet, sir, sorry," said Kate, adequately disguising the drop of her stomach. "I haven't been able to get hold of him. I'll try again once I'm back at my desk."

Chapter Six

Kate called it a night at nine thirty that evening. She said goodbye to Olbeck, still hunched over his keyboard, and let herself out of the office, raising a hand to the duty sergeant on the front desk as she left the building.

Settled in the driver's seat, she checked her phone before she drove off. Nothing from Jay. Where the hell was he? She'd now left him three messages. Trying not to worry, she put the key in the ignition, locked her driver side door and drove off.

Kate's new house was situated at the end of a terrace of Victorian buildings at the end of a cul-de-sac. The last streetlight lay twenty feet from her garden gate, meaning her walk up the path to the front door was always slightly nerve-wracking after dark. *I must get an outside light*, she told herself yet again, knowing she'd forget about it once she was through the front door.

As she opened the squeaky little iron gate to the path up to the door, a dark shadow moved. A hand reached for her. There was a moment of cold terror and her hand holding the front door keys came up like a flash; they were a tiny weapon, but it could be the difference between life and death...

She let out her breath in a half-scream as she realised it was her brother.

"Jay, you idiot, you scared the absolute shit out of me!"

Jay said nothing. He stood there, dumbly, shaking his head. Kate could smell the booze on him from three feet away.

"Are you all right?"

He finally spoke. "No, I'm not," he said, in a slurred and teary mumble. "Sis, I'm so not okay. I didn't want to scare you, I didn't know where to go—"

Kate had the front door open now and the hallway light on. She gently pushed Jay into her house before her and turned him to face her. He looked awful: unshaven, red-eyed, hair unbrushed and greasy.

"You've heard about Elodie," she said. It was a statement, not a question.

"Yes," said Jay and burst into tears.

She let him cry, leading him to the sofa and wrapping him up in one of the blankets she kept there. Then she made him a cup of hot chocolate, listening to his sobs gradually tapering off, like a toy winding down. By the time he'd drunk his hot drink, he was dry-eyed again, his chest only occasionally heaving.

"I'm really sorry, Jay," said Kate eventually. "It's awful. You must be feeling desperate."

Jay's mouth crimped. For a moment, she thought he was going to start crying again, but he managed to control himself.

"I can't believe it," he said. He leaned forward and put the mug down on the floor with a shaking hand. "I can't believe it. She was so amazing. Why would anyone do this?"

Kate could only shake her head.

"It shouldn't have happened!" he cried and then buried his face in his hands, sobbing. Kate was reminded of Mr Duncan at the morgue, saying almost those very words.

"Jay," she said gently, after a moment. "We'll need to take a statement from you. I can't do it myself but Mark—you remember Mark?—he can do it for you. You can come to the station with me tomorrow."

Jay shook his head. "I can't. I don't want to have everyone laughing at me for crying, and I can't talk about Elodie without crying." He wiped his face. "I can't, sis."

Kate picked the empty mug from the floor.

"We'll talk about in the morning," she said, before remembering that she had to be at Rawlwood College for the first round of interviews. "Actually, I've got to go out early. You sleep in, have a shower, have some breakfast. We'll talk later when I get back."

When she was finally in bed, she lay wide-eyed in the darkness, staring up at the dim ceiling. She wondered whether Jay was lying awake in the next bedroom too. She hoped not. She rolled on her side, pulling the duvet up to her ear. She hoped she wouldn't dream, but she could sense that the riverbank and the mud and Elodie's white face were lying in wait for her, out there in the dark.

"You look as bad as I do," said Olbeck the next morning when he knocked on Kate's door. "Don't tell me you went on a wild bender when you left the office last night."

"I could make a smart remark about that, coming from you," said Kate as she flopped into the passenger seat. "And I won't even start on the 'bender.'"

Olbeck laughed. "So how come you look so rough?"

"I'm not that bad, am I?" Kate flipped down the visor to look in the little mirror and groaned. "Crap. Where's my hairbrush?"

As she brushed her hair, she told Olbeck what had happened last night.

"Poor kid," said Olbeck. "I'll do his statement."

"I told him you would," said Kate. She tied back her now-neat hair. "I obviously can't do it myself, and he needs someone to be—well—gentle with him."

Olbeck glanced over at her. "Did he say anything about the night she died? Did he see anything?"

Kate dropped her hairbrush back into her bag and snapped it shut.

"He didn't say," she said, shortly. "He wasn't anywhere near her when I left that night, I know that."

"All right, all right," said Olbeck, peering through the windscreen. "You need to talk it through with Anderton later. Where's the bloody turn off for the College?"

The road they were travelling along ran along a high brick wall, ten feet tall. Olbeck spotted the turning, and the car swung into the winding drive of Rawlwood. They drove along through a thin bank of trees before the open lawns of the College began, and the building loomed into view, huge and black in full Gothic splendour.

"My God," said Kate, looking at the turrets and bell tower and the mullioned windows. "It's Hogwarts."

"My school was a bit like this," said Olbeck, slowing down to look.

"Wow. Mine definitely wasn't."

"Yes, well, don't envy me," said Olbeck. Kate was surprised at the bitterness in his voice. "Just because it looks fantastic on the surface doesn't mean it was wonderful underneath."

"True." For a moment, Kate was going to ask Olbeck about his school days. He'd been to private school, she knew that, although she didn't know the specific school he'd attended. He never talked about it.

Kate stared out the window as they approached the visitors' car park. There were little huddles of students here and there, walking back and forth between the buildings, all dressed in the navy and silver uniform: the same uniform worn by Elodie Duncan in the photograph pinned to the crime room whiteboard. Several carried musical instruments in cases. One tiny, redheaded girl was struggling along with a case that was almost bigger than she was. As Kate watched, a grey-haired man, clearly one of the teachers, intercepted her and lifted the case from her small hands. The two of them walked off together, chatting, the case—was it a cello?—between them.

The two of them got out of the car. Kate stood, getting her bearings. It was difficult to know whether there was an unusual amount of activity because of what had happened to Elodie or whether this was just a normal day at Rawlwood. It would be easier to ascertain once they'd spent some time here.

They found the school reception and were guided to the south wing of the school by a rather superior school secretary, who glided along in front of them, occasionally nodding from side to side and snapping out descriptions such as 'large common room,' 'bursar's room,' and 'dining hall,' as they swept past glimpses of wood-panelled rooms and lofty-ceilinged halls. She delivered them to a much less grand room furnished with a few odd tables and chairs. One of the chairs was occupied by Anderton, who was speed-reading through a pile of papers on the desk in front of him.

"Morning you two," he said without raising his head. Kate and Olbeck stood aside to allow the secretary to sweep back out of the room with an audible sniff.

"Did you get the impression we're not welcome here?" murmured Olbeck.

Kate shrugged.

"We're never welcome anywhere," she said. "Morning, sir."

Anderton pushed the chair back and stood up.

"Right," he said, sweeping the papers away from him. "Now, here's where we'll start—"

There was a commotion outside in the hallway, raised voices, a scrimmage of feet. Two seconds later, a teenage girl came barrelling through the doorway, all long legs and a fall of long brown hair.

"Police—are you the police?" she demanded breathlessly. Without waiting for an answer, she flung her school bag down onto the floor and raised both hands to her head, staring at the officers, wild-eyed. "I've got to talk to you, like, immediately. Are you the police?"

"Yes, we are," said Kate, raising her hands in a 'calm down' gesture. "What's the matter? Do you want to talk to us about—"

"Elodie? Yes, of course I want to talk to you about Elodie! Or rather about *him*. I need to talk to you about *him*!"

The officers looked at one another.

"Who are you talking about?"

The girl looked at them as though they were crazy. Worse, as if they were stupid. "I'm talking about Reuben Farraday," she said. Then she burst into tears. "He always said he'd kill her, and now he has!"

Chapter Seven

THE THREE OFFICERS STOOD NONPLUSSED for a moment. Then Kate stepped forward, raising her hands in a calming gesture once again. The girl was still sobbing wildly.

"Okay, okay," soothed Kate. "Calm down. What's your name?"

The girl turned out to be Amy Peters, the best friend that Elodie's mother had mentioned. Kate led her to a chair and sat her down, rummaging in her bag for a clean tissue.

The girl only cried for a few more minutes. Then she sat up, threw her hair away from her tear-stained face, and raised both hands to her temples as she took a few deep breaths. There was something stagy about her mannerisms, something not quite natural, as if she was exaggerating genuinely felt emotions. Perhaps she was. Hadn't Mrs Duncan said something about Elodie and Amy having a falling-out?

"Miss Peters?" said Anderton. "Anything you can tell us will be helpful. You think Reuben Farraday had something to do with Elodie's death?"

Amy stretched her eyes wide.

"Well, of *course*. He was a nightmare to Elodie, simply a nightmare. He used to threaten her *regularly*."

"In what way?"

Amy took a handful of hair and held it back from her head. Kate could tell that she was the kind of girl who used her hair as a form of punctuation: pulling it, twisting it, throwing it back to give emphasis to her words.

"Elodie and Reuben split up about six months ago," she said. "You know that, right? Ever since then—"

"Excuse me, Amy, but why did they split up? What was the reason?"

Amy gave her a look of scorn mixed with incredulity. She had all the superiority of the elite mixed with the ringing self-confidence of the average teenager. Kate was half amused, half annoyed.

"He was possessive," Amy said dramatically. "*Extremely* possessive. Always wanting to know what she was doing and who she was with, never letting her have a moment's peace. For God's sake, she got enough of that at home. Reuben just couldn't accept that she didn't want to spend all her time with him, that she had other friends as well. He was a *nightmare*."

"Other friends? Did Elodie have other boyfriends as well? Is that what you mean?"

Amy stared, her lip curled. "*No*. She wasn't *unfaithful*. Of course not! She just didn't want to spend all her free time with him, God, what little she had. She said she just felt completely suffocated by him, and so she dumped him."

"When was this?"

"I told you. About six months ago. And ever since then, he's been calling and texting and generally being a complete nightmare to her. He wouldn't leave her alone."

"Did her parents know about this?" asked Anderton.

Amy sniffed. "Not really. Elodie always said she could handle it. She didn't believe he was actually serious." For a second, her actressy manner departed, and she was just a young girl with tears in her eyes. Her voice shook a little. "She always said it was just words, that he didn't mean anything by it. I feel awful because I believed her. I thought she knew what she was doing. And now it's too late."

She hung her head, the curtain of hair sweeping forward and hiding her face.

Olbeck cleared his throat. "What sort of threats did he make, Amy?"

There was no response from Amy for a moment. Kate saw a tear fall from underneath the curtain of hair onto the dusty floor.

"Amy?"

Amy sat up, throwing her hair back and wiping her face.

"I'm sorry," she said. "I'm just very upset. Elodie was my *best friend*."

"What sort of threats did Reuben make, Amy?" asked Olbeck, patiently.

"Terrible ones. When they first split up, he told her he'd kill her."

"You heard him say that?"

"I *saw* it. On Facebook. He deleted it a few hours later, though."

"Did you ever see him physically threaten or assault Elodie?"

Amy pouted. "No, not as such. He used to hang around sometimes and try and talk to her when we got out of class. God, he was such a *stalker*. I don't know why Elodie wasn't more scared of him." Her big blue eyes filled up with tears again. "She should have been. Look what happened."

"Right, Amy, thank you," said Anderton. He put a hand under the girl's arm and helped her up. "DS Olbeck will take a full statement from you now, and you can rest assured we will be questioning Mr Farraday very closely and very soon."

Amy sniffed again and tucked her hair behind her ears. She bent to pick up her school bag.

"I can't believe it," she said, tucking the strap over her shoulder. "First Violet and now this. I sometimes feel this school is *cursed*."

Olbeck led her away to a desk in the corner. Anderton and Kate exchanged glances and Kate cast up her eyes very slightly.

"Teenage girls," she said quietly.

Anderton looked suddenly grim.

"Don't remind me," he said. "I've got two of my own."

"What about Farraday?"

"I think it's about time we pulled him in, don't you?"

"Should I—"

Anderton was already reaching for his jacket. He shook his head. "I need you supervising things here, Kate. I'll handle it. Start working through this list."

"Okay," muttered Kate, dissatisfied. She would rather be out there, taking action, pulling in what sounded like their prime suspect, rather than taking statements from a lot of overly dramatic, snobby students in here. She chastised herself, *Come on, this is important too*. She watched Anderton leave and turned back to see Amy swishing her hair back yet again in the corner. Her teeth clenched with irritation. Then Kate suddenly realised she'd missed something. She walked over to where Olbeck was taking Amy's statement and waited for an appropriate pause.

"Amy," she said, when she could. "What did you mean by what you said just a moment ago?"

Amy looked at her, wide-eyed. "What do you mean?"

"You said something about the school being cursed. What was that again?"

Amy looked a little ashamed of her dramatic phrase. "Oh, nothing. It was just after what happened to Violet last year—"

"That was it," said Kate. She picked up a chair and joined them at the desk. "What did you mean by that? Who's Violet?"

Amy curled a lock of hair around her fingers, rubbing it against her lips.

"Violet Sammidge," she said, in a small voice. "Don't you remember? She committed suicide last year."

Olbeck and Kate looked at one another.

"I think I remember that," said Olbeck. "In fact, I do remember that. Very sad. She was a pupil here, wasn't she?"

Amy nodded. "We were both in the drama group. She was

younger than me, and that's how we met, in drama. She hanged herself in the cloakrooms. It was awful."

"It must have been," said Olbeck. He was looking at Kate in a familiar way. They never asked each other 'is that important?' in front of suspects or witnesses, but she had got to know the look he gave her when he was thinking it. So she got up smartly, thanked Amy and went back to her desk.

It was a long day. Kate interviewed a seemingly endless line of teenage boys and girls and several of Elodie's teachers. Her music teacher, Graham Lightbody, she recognised as the grey-haired man who'd helped the tiny girl carry the huge cello case. He was a soft-spoken, urbane man, given to thoughtful pauses; he took his time to reflect on her questions before answering in measured tones. He too spoke about how special Elodie had been.

"We have a lot of students here with talent, Detective Sergeant. People expect to come to Rawlwood because we nurture the best students. Elodie Duncan was very good. Not the best we've had, I couldn't say that, but I fully expected her to make a great career for herself in the arts."

Kate nodded.

"People with great talent aren't always very happy," she said. "Did Elodie strike you as a happy person? Do you think she was generally content?"

Lightbody smiled. "She was a teenage girl, Detective Sergeant. You're not very old yourself. Surely you can remember being a teenage girl?"

Kate forced a smile. She would be quite happy for most of her teenage years to be wiped from her memory. *No you wouldn't*, whispered a voice. *You wouldn't want to forget him*. As if there was any chance of *that*. She sighed inwardly before turning her attention back to the interview.

"What do you know of Elodie's ex-boyfriend, Reuben Farraday?"

Lightbody raised his eyebrows. "I'm afraid I know nothing of him. He wasn't a pupil here."

"You weren't aware of any threats he'd made against Elodie? Any threatening or violent behaviour?"

"Dear me, no. Not at all. Is he a suspect in her death?"

Kate didn't answer him.

"Did Elodie ever seem scared of anybody?"

"No. Not that I knew. But I'm afraid, Detective Sergeant, that I didn't know her very well. She was a beautiful, talented girl, but as to what she was like as a person, I couldn't say."

Kate nodded. After a few more questions, she brought the interview to a close, thanked Dr Lightbody for his time and handed over her card. Once he'd left the room, she looked over at Olbeck, who was busy writing up the first of many reports.

"That's me done for the day."

Olbeck clicked his pen closed with a flourish.

"Me too. Let's head back and see how Anderton's getting along with young Mr Farraday."

"You read my mind."

Chapter Eight

BACK AT THE STATION, OLBECK paused outside the interview room. "Coming in?"

Kate shook her head. "I'll just watch."

She went to the viewing room, nodded at Steve, who was monitoring the video feed, and settled down in front of the screen. Reuben Farraday was a good-looking young man with a flopping fringe of dark hair and good cheekbones. Elodie and he must have made a striking couple. Kate looked closely at his face. He was attempting a surly nonchalance, but she could see the fear in his eyes. A solicitor sat next to him—not the duty one but a glossy young woman wearing an expensive trouser suit. His parents were not in attendance; well, now that she considered it, they wouldn't be. He was legally an adult.

"So, Reuben," said Anderton, leaning forward. "I've been told that you and Elodie split up some time ago."

"Yeah," said Reuben.

"Was it an amicable break up?"

Reuben scowled. "It was all right."

Anderton let the silence stretch out for a beat. Then he said, "We've been informed that you made specific and multiple threats to Elodie Duncan once your relationship was over. Can you confirm if that is true?"

Reuben's eyes widened. The solicitor opened her mouth, but he spoke before she could.

"That's not true!"

Anderton looked down at his notes.

"You didn't, for example, threaten to kill her in a post made on Facebook?"

"You don't have to answer that," interposed the solicitor, smoothly.

Reuben was shaking his head. "That's *so* not true. I don't know who told you that. Who told you that?"

Anderton declined to answer him. He sat back and his tone of voice changed. Before he had been brusque; now his voice became gentler, almost fatherly. Kate smiled. She knew the old 'good cop, bad cop' cliché but Anderton was the only officer she knew who managed to flip between the two all by himself.

"Now, Reuben, we've been told that you and Elodie had quite an intense relationship. You were apparently quite serious about one another. It must have come as a shock when your relationship broke down."

Reuben looked at him with a wealth of expression. He might be scared, but underneath it all he was still a teenage boy.

"I don't know who you've been talking to. Elodie and me, we were okay. It wasn't the romance of the century or anything. Half the time—" He paused for a moment. Then he said slowly, "Half the time I just felt sorry for her."

Anderton raised his eyebrows. "What do you mean by that, Reuben?"

Reuben picked at a loose thread on the sleeve of his long black coat. He looked up from under his fringe at Anderton.

"She—Elodie—she had a lot of problems. She was—she could be hard work. But she was cool as well, you know?"

"What kind of problems, Reuben?"

Reuben broke the eye contact. "Oh, I dunno," he said. "She used to cry a lot. I didn't know what was the matter with her half the time."

Anderton nodded as if he understood. "Did she ever confide in you about these problems?"

Reuben shrugged. "Sometimes. Not really. Sometimes she'd start to speak, start to tell me something, and then she'd kind of clam up again. I used to ask her what was wrong when she got upset, and I thought she would be going to tell me but—but something made her stop."

"What do you think was the matter, Reuben?"

"I don't know. I told you, she didn't ever tell me."

Anderton cleared his throat.

"Were you and Elodie sexually involved?"

Reuben flushed, to his obvious mortification. "'Course," he said, uncomfortably. There was a beat of silence.

"But?" said Anderton.

Reuben looked away. Kate could see the heat in his cheeks even over the grainy image of the video feed.

"She didn't—well, she didn't really—" He took a deep breath. "She was kind of mixed up about sex."

"Meaning?"

Reuben dropped his head.

"She was all over the place," he mumbled. "Sometimes she'd be really into it, and sometimes she'd just get angry if I wanted to. I didn't know what was going on half the time."

"Mm-hmm," said Anderton, his face expressionless. Kate wondered if he was thinking about his own teenage girls. "So you're saying she could be a bit—well, a bit of tease?"

"No—not exactly..."

"Did that make you angry, Reuben?"

Reuben shook his head, not vehemently. It was more convincing than if he had been more emphatic. "I just felt sorry for her," he repeated.

"What do you think?" asked Olbeck when they met in the canteen during a break in the interview.

Kate stirred her coffee.

"I don't know," she said slowly. "On the face of it, there's everything to suggest it was him. Rejected ex-boyfriend, tempestuous relationship. The usual kind of thing. But—"

"I know what you mean," said Olbeck. "I was watching him the whole time. He looked scared but not—not guilty, if you see what I mean."

"A look is not evidence," said Kate, tipping him a wink. "Isn't that what you've said to me before?"

"Ha ha." Olbeck tipped up his mug and drained it. "He's got no alibi, as yet."

"Are you going to charge him?"

"Not sure. Don't think so. I don't think we got enough for it to stick, quite frankly."

"Have you quizzed him about the pregnancy?"

"Not yet. Anderton's keeping that up his sleeve for now. We've swabbed him for DNA obviously."

"Right." Kate picked up her bag and keys and stood up. "I'm off back to the Duncans' house. I need to have a look at Elodie's bedroom."

Kate braced herself before ringing the bell of Rawlwood Cottage. She fully expected Elodie's mother to present the kind of bleached, transparent countenance that only grief could produce. When Genevieve Duncan answered the door, she was certainly pale, her eyes ringed with shadow, but there was something else about her, some other kind of emotion running through her that Kate couldn't quite pinpoint. It shimmered around her like an aura.

"Yes, of course," she replied when Kate asked her if she could see Elodie's room. Mrs Duncan's voice was blank, and her eyes were staring at something in the far distance visible only to her.

"I'll leave everything as I find it," said Kate.

Mrs Duncan nodded. She didn't watch Kate walk up the stairs but instead drifted back into the living room, out of sight.

Elodie's room was large and about as far away from her parents' bedroom as it was possible to be, tucked up into the eaves of the roof. A former attic, the walls sloped sharply downwards from the ceiling, and the only window was small and many-paned. Kate stood in the doorway for a moment, getting the feel of it, snapping on her gloves. It was a pretty room, tastefully decorated. Kate could see that Elodie had stamped her personality over the space in a variety of ways. A huge poster of Jim Morrison covered almost all of one wall. Kate regarded it, feeling as if his dark eyes were watching her. Did teenagers really still listen to the Doors? There was a cork noticeboard next to the poster with a mass of ticket stubs and flyers pinned to it. Kate looked more closely. Glastonbury, Bestival, Isle of Wight festival tickets, some torn-off wrist bands and lots of smaller gig tickets were evident. Well, Elodie had been musical after all, nothing very surprising that she'd enjoyed going to see her favourite bands.

There were photographs on the walls, some framed, some just blu-tacked to the paint. Kate looked at one of Elodie and a girl she recognised as Amy Peters. Both girls looked younger, perhaps thirteen years old: still almost children. They had their arms slung about one another and were laughing, Amy facing the camera, Elodie looking off to the side.

There was a violin lying on the bed, still in its black case. Kate touched it tentatively, then unsnapped the locks and raised the lid. The violin was a beautiful thing, made of polished golden wood. Kate ran a finger softly over its strings. She had never learned to play a musical instrument, and at that moment, she felt the loss keenly. She'd always felt it was something she really ought to do, a skill everyone ought to have to be a fully-rounded person. Then she smiled. Even to herself, she sounded like Miss Bingley in *Pride and Prejudice*. "A woman must have a thorough knowledge *of music, singing, drawing, dancing and the modern languages..."* She thought, *Kate, you've got plenty of other accomplishments, Don't do yourself down.*

There were a few books by the bed, a rather incongruous selection of children's classics. *Winnie the Pooh, Watership Down, The Velveteen Rabbit.* Strange bedtime reading for an eighteen-year-old girl. But perhaps they were just there because they'd always been there since Elodie was a child. Kate picked each book up and shook it upside down to see if anything fluttered out. Nothing. She got on her knees and looked under the bed. You could find surprisingly revealing things under a bed sometimes. Kate remembered the strange photo album that had been under poor Gemma Phillips' bed back in the Charlie Fullman kidnapping case: her first case in Abbeyford. She remembered Charlie's mother, Casey, the little blonde trophy wife. Briefly, Kate wondered what had happened to her. The Fullmans' marriage hadn't lasted much longer than their courtship, if she remembered correctly.

Kate blinked, bringing herself back to the present. There was nothing under Elodie's bed except for an empty shoe box and plenty of dust. Kate got up, dusting off her trousers. She checked Elodie's wardrobe, stood against the only flat, windowless wall at the end of the room. There was something so sad about the clothes of a person who'd recently died; they drooped from their hangers more emptily than normal. Kate moved the hangers apart, checking between each dress and coat and shirt. Shoeboxes were stacked on the floor of the wardrobe. She brought them out into the light, one by one, opening the lid and checking the contents. Nothing untoward. Nothing until she reached the last one, when she pulled off the lid to reveal a plastic bag wrapped tightly round on itself. She could smell the contents nonetheless. She unwrapped it gingerly.

A bag of marijuana, home-grown by the look of it. Kate hefted it in one hand. Several smaller plastic bags of pills. By far the biggest bag in the box was filled with white powder. Kate recalled the manic glitter in Elodie's eyes the night they'd met. The night Elodie had died. Cocaine, then, or some such stimulant. She put all the drugs back in the cardboard box and folded it carefully into a large evidence bag. After a moment's thought, she put the evidence bag into her handbag and zipped it up, hiding it away from Elodie's mother's eyes.

Chapter Nine

"Well," said Olbeck when she showed him her find back at the station. "You can't tell me that's for personal use."

"Not unless she was spending every hour of the day off her face. And I think that would have been obvious to anyone, don't you?"

Olbeck took the bag from her. "We'd better get the usual tests done, just in case."

"I know."

"Find anything else? Anything at all? A diary, or something?"

Kate began to gather the various forms she needed to fill in. "Teenage girls don't keep diaries any more, do they?" she said. "They just post it all on Facebook."

"True." Olbeck leant back in his chair and pushed his hands through his hair. "The plot thickens. We've got a potential suspect in the ex-boyfriend, and now it seems that our murder victim was a drug dealer."

"We really need to ask her parents about the pregnancy—and this." Kate flourished the bag.

Olbeck nodded. "Let's talk to Anderton. Right now."

As they approached his office, the door stood ajar. Anderton was reclined in his chair behind the large desk, sitting still and staring into space. This was so unusual that Kate stopped dead herself, her hand raised to knock. She stopped short of touching the door as she took in the scene. Anderton was *never* still. Ceaseless, relentless energy was his defining characteristic. For a moment, Kate was infused with a sense of dread. Perhaps Anderton was ill. Really ill. He'd looked so tired lately: tired and somehow diminished.

"What's wrong?" whispered Olbeck behind her.

Kate shook herself mentally.

"Nothing," she said, and knocked.

Anderton took a moment to respond. Then he turned his head disinterestedly.

"Yes?" he asked, after a moment.

"We've had some new developments on the Elodie Duncan case," said Olbeck, sounding a little uncertain. Kate knew he was wondering what was wrong with Anderton just as she was.

There was a moment's silence that hung between the three of them. Then Anderton seemed to take hold of himself.

"Right," he said. He sprang up from his chair and Kate almost gave a sigh of relief. "Bring me up to speed then. What've you got?"

Kate told him of her find in Elodie's wardrobe.

"Right, right," he said, pacing to the window. He leant both hands on the sill for a moment before turning to face them. "Well done. This could be important."

"We were going to question her parents again. See if they know anything."

"Yes, do that. We're due the tox tests any day now, so we'll be able to see if our girl was partaking as well as supplying."

Kate thought of something.

"Elodie's baby," she said, a little awkwardly. She didn't like discussing things like this with either Olbeck or Anderton—they knew too much of her past. But it could be important…"Is it possible to get a DNA test done on the—the remains of the baby?"

Both men looked at her.

She added. "If we could, we could run the results through the database. See if there's a match on record."

"Mmm," said Anderton. He tousled his hair. "Might be worth a try. Look into it."

"I'll speak to the pathologist," said Kate.

Once they were outside Anderton's room, Kate turned to Olbeck.

"Stop grinning."

"I'm not. I'm smirking."

"I know what you're thinking, and you're wrong."

"Am I?" said Olbeck, innocently. "Sure it's not just an excuse to talk to our young pathologist friend?"

Kate snorted and turned to march off.

"Not everyone's as sex-obsessed as you," was her parting remark, flung over her shoulder.

Olbeck said nothing else on the journey to Rawlwood Cottage but kept the same infuriating grin on his face, humming a little tune. Kate tried to ignore him. Then she asked him whether he knew if there was anything wrong with Anderton.

The grin dropped from his face immediately.

"Why do you ask?"

"You know," said Kate. "He's not himself. There's something bugging him—or he's not well."

"I don't know," said Olbeck, worriedly. "He hasn't said anything to me."

"Hmm." Kate drew up outside the Duncan's house. "Okay, we're here. Do you want to take the lead, or shall I?"

"Drugs?"

Mr Duncan looked as if someone had just punched him in the face. He had been standing, but at the word, he sat down suddenly on the sofa behind him, as if his legs had suddenly given way.

"I'm sorry, Mr Duncan," said Olbeck. "I assume you weren't aware that your daughter had a large quantity of drugs in her bedroom? That she could well have been supplying them to others?"

Mr Duncan was shaking his head from side to side slowly, seemingly dazed.

"I had—I had no idea," he said. "I can't—can't believe it. Surely there must have been some mistake? Elodie...Elodie wasn't like that."

Kate was looking keenly at Genevieve Duncan.

"Mrs Duncan?" she prompted. The woman sat with eyes cast down, picking at the worn threads of the armchair once again. How many hours had she sat there, pulling threads from the arm in ceaseless anxiety?

"Mrs Duncan," said Kate again, more firmly. "Is this news to you?"

For a moment, she thought the woman would refuse to answer. Mrs Duncan put her hand up to her face, covering her eyes in a characteristic gesture.

"Mrs Duncan?"

"I found something," Mrs Duncan burst out. She lowered her shaking hand. "Just once. A plastic packet with something in it. I don't know what it was. Some sort of white powder. I'm not stupid...I—" She pinched her trembling lips together for a moment with her fingers, and then released them. "I asked Elodie about it."

"You asked her?"

"Yes. I had to, didn't I? My own daughter..." Mrs Duncan slumped against the back of the chair, her hands falling limply to her lap.

After a moment, Kate asked, "What happened?"

Mrs Duncan stared into space.

"Mrs Duncan?"

"She got angry," said Mrs Duncan, dully. "The way she always did. She had so much...*rage* inside her. I don't know where it came from... She got angry, and then she laughed and said that I didn't know anything. That I didn't understand and never had."

"Did you ever find anything else?"

"No. I never did. But I didn't look. Who knows what else she had in her room, what she could have been hiding?"

Kate knew the time was right for the second question, but she quailed a little at asking it. You needed the hide of rhinoceros to do this job, sometimes. Was that what was wrong with Anderton? Could he just not face the emotional payback any more?

Olbeck pre-empted her. He did that sometimes, knowing almost telepathically when to take over and face the outcome, letting Kate gather her defences together once more.

"I'm sorry to cause you both any more distress, but I have another question for you. Where you aware that Elodie was ten weeks pregnant when she died?"

Mrs Duncan made a noise, a kind of half-grunt, half-shout. She flinched back as if Olbeck had shouted at her.

"Oh my God," was all she said and then the tears began again. Mr Duncan gathered her into his arms, rocking and crooning to her like a child.

Olbeck gave them a couple of minutes. Then he asked the question again.

"No, of course I didn't know," Mrs Duncan almost shouted. Mr Duncan sat beside her, shaking his head.

"Mr Duncan? Did Elodie confide in you?"

He flinched. "No. No, she didn't. I had no idea, no idea about any of this." There was some kind of undercurrent to his voice, and it took Kate a few moments to realise what it was—anger. "I had no idea what she was up to. She didn't tell me anything." He glanced at his wife. "She didn't tell *us* anything."

"Who was it?" Mrs Duncan sat up, holding her arms across her body like a woman expecting a physical blow. Her voice was shaking so much it was hard for Kate to understand what she was saying.

"What do you mean, Mrs Duncan?" asked Kate.

"Who was the father?"

"We don't yet know, I'm afraid."

"Yet?" said Mr Duncan, his face grey. "You mean you *will* know?"

"No, we can't promise that, sir, I'm sorry. There's a possibility that we'll be able to run various tests that might give us a DNA profile, but it's not certain. I wouldn't want to give you false hope. Even if we do get a DNA sample, there's no way to know anything more unless we have an equivalent record on file."

"I see," said Mr Duncan. He put one shaking hand up to his forehead. "I don't know how much more of this we can take."

"We're very sorry," said Olbeck. "We'll keep you informed every step of the way."

Chapter Ten

"Can you drop me back at my place?" Kate asked as they were on their way home. "In fact, why don't you come in? We'll pick up Jay and take him back to the station to do his statement."

Olbeck concurred. As they drew up outside Kate's house, she realised someone else had parked in her driveway.

"That's not your car, is it?" asked Olbeck.

"No, it's not." Kate got out of the car, puzzled. The car was a large estate car, old but well-kept. She didn't recognise it. Halfway to the front door, it opened and out came someone she wasn't expecting or prepared to see: her mother.

"Kelly!"

Her mum flung her arms around Kate. Taken by surprise, Kate could only manage a feeble "Hi, Mum. What are you doing here?" in response.

Her mother didn't seem to notice her lukewarm greeting. She released Kate and stood back, beaming. Kate almost goggled. Her mother looked...well, *groomed* was the only word for it: her hair done, make-up on her face, her clothes different to the usual stained and worn tracksuit that Kate was used to seeing her wear. She looked *smart*, a word hitherto never associated with Mary Redman.

Kate pulled herself together.

"What are you doing here, Mum?" she asked. "Did Jay let you in?"

"Thought we'd see your new place, didn't we? I said to Peter, 'We may as well go and see Kelly while we're here,' and so we all came over. Very nice too, Kelly, shame you didn't invite us over before."

A man appeared in the doorway behind Mary. He was portly, middle-aged, with a neatly-trimmed beard. He was wearing brown cord trousers and a fisherman's jumper.

"Here he is," exclaimed Mary. "Here she is, Peter. This is Kelly."

Kate forced a smile. She shook hands with Peter, debating whether to insist that he call her Kate. She realised Olbeck was standing behind her, and she introduced him to her mother and Peter. Thank God she'd already told Olbeck she'd changed her name in her teens. As it was, he was not above calling her Kelly when he wanted to annoy her.

"Pleased to meet you," said Peter. He had a kind of tweedy, avuncular air about him, which was quite appealing. What *was* he doing with her mother? Kate found herself shepherding them all back into the house where she had a second surprise: her two younger half-sisters Courtney and Jade were in the garden with Jay, smoking cigarettes.

"It's the full family contingent," she said to Olbeck, trying to make a joke of it. He hadn't met any of her siblings before except Jay.

"Alright, sis," said Courtney, coming over and giving her a smoky hug. "When are you gonna get some real furniture?"

"What do you mean?" asked Kate, realising with a jolt that her seventeen-year-old sister was now taller than her. And Jade—she hadn't seen Jade for nearly a year. Her youngest sister was now a large, plump young woman, and she was wearing a pair of straining leggings and a top that did nothing to hide a mountainous pair of breasts. Try as she might, Kate could not suppress the thought that her fourteen-year-old sibling looked cheap and tarty. She gave Jade an extra warm hug to try and atone for her thoughts.

"Well, it's a bit old, innit?" Courtney looked disdainfully at the worn leather sofa that Kate found so comfortable.

"Oh well," said Kate rather helplessly. "I will when I get around to it."

She made tea for those who wanted it: Peter, Olbeck, and herself. Jay had stood silently through the greetings and tumult of the female Redmans, and he was now sat at the kitchen table with his eyes cast down. Kate wished she could get rid of everyone so she could talk to him.

Olbeck saved her. While Kate was showing her mother and Peter, at their insistence, round the house and into the garden, she saw Olbeck talking quietly to Jay. After about ten minutes, he came over to tell her he was taking her brother to the station to make his statement.

"Statement?" screeched Mary. "What's he done?"

"Nothing, Mum, I'll explain later," said Kate hurriedly, seeing Jay flinch. She squeezed his arm as he went past, hoping to catch his eye, but he flashed her a quick half smile and then he and Olbeck were gone.

Jade, Courtney and Mary surrounded her, bombarding her with questions.

"It's nothing," said Kate desperately. "He's just a witness, that's all. It's nothing—"

"Now, now," said Peter, unexpectedly. "Don't badger the poor girl. Why don't we all sit down and listen to what Kate has to tell us, if she's willing and able to?"

Mary shut up instantly. Courtney and Jade subsided after Peter raised his hand in a 'shushing' gesture and motioned for Kate to speak.

While Kate was explaining what had happened—all that she could say about the case—a small part of her was mulling over Peter's presence. Her mother was clearly smitten with him, and the girls seemed to like him. He seemed a nice enough man. But what was the attraction for *him*? Did he really like her mother? If so, *why*? Kate hated herself for thinking like that, but she'd faced the facts about her mother a long time ago. Mary Redman had a drinking problem, and she was feckless, short-tempered and unreliable. Where was the attraction in that?

They all left soon after. Kate shook hands with Peter at the door of her house as they were making their goodbyes.

"I didn't ask you how you came to be in the vicinity," she said. "Do you live around here?"

"Yes, duck—not far from here. Burton Abbot. You must come and visit me sometime."

"That would be lovely," said Kate politely. "I'm pretty busy with work at the moment, though. What do you do?"

"Me? I'm a driving instructor." Peter laughed. "Bit nerve-wracking at times, but I do enjoy it."

Courtney and Jade were getting into the back of Peter's car. Kate gestured to it.

"Do you use that for lessons? It looks quite unscathed."

Peter put an arm around Mary and began to shepherd her towards the passenger seat.

"No, I've got something a bit more modern for the learners," he said. "You might even have seen it around. Bright yellow Mini. Easy for other drivers to spot—and avoid! Pete Buckley's yellow peril, they call it."

Kate smiled and waved as they drove away. Once they were gone, she went quickly back inside to her desk and scribbled 'Peter Buckley, Burton Abbot' on a piece of paper and put it in her bag.

She stood for a moment in the hallway, hesitating. Then she climbed the stairs and went straight to the cupboard where she'd put Jay's picture. She drew it out carefully. It no longer induced in her a sense of nausea and panic, despite the resemblance to the crime scene photographs she'd seen every day at the office. She looked harder at the picture, noting that the leaves of the trees in the background were a bright, fresh green. There were wildflowers growing on the banks of the river. Kate noticed something she'd never noticed before: the crown of tiny daisies wound about Elodie's tangled blonde hair. Of course, she was supposed to be Ophelia, wasn't she?

"There is a willow grows aslant a brook
That shows his hoar leaves in the glassy stream
There with fantastic garlands did she come
Of crow-flowers, nettles, daisies, and long purples..."

Kate propped the picture against the wall and sat back on her haunches. It was coincidence, that was all. There was nothing to be afraid of. She would tell Anderton tomorrow, she told herself, and she ignored the tiny quake of fear that followed.

Chapter Eleven

"Cocaine," said Anderton. "And marijuana, but we don't care so much about that. The tox tests are back. Our girl tested positive for cocaine, which given DS Redman's discovery the other day, probably doesn't come as a great surprise to most of you."

He stopped, swivelled on one foot and began to retrace his steps. His team watched him, ranged around the room in their various seats. He tapped Elodie's school picture as he walked by it.

"Now, you're not telling me that an eighteen-year-old private school girl, daughter of the headmaster no less, is the sole mastermind behind the supply of Class A drugs to her school mates. Because I just don't believe it."

"Me neither," said Olbeck. "Who gave it to her?"

"Exactly, Mark. There's someone behind all this."

Kate was shuffling the various copies of the witness statements already taken from Elodie's schoolmates.

"Several people mention an older boyfriend. Well, they mention a man they'd seen with Elodie a couple of times." She hesitated. "I think I saw him myself, if it's the same guy. He was older than her, definitely older."

Anderton looked at her.

"Yes, you've mentioned him. What else can you tell us?"

Kate shrugged. "Unfortunately, sir, not much. I only saw him for a moment or so."

"Did you recognise him?"

Kate lifted her shoulders up again. "It's funny but when I first saw him, I *did* think I recognised him. Then I realised he just seemed familiar. I thought I might have arrested him at one time and that's where I knew him from. That's all. No name, nothing like that."

Anderton swung on his heel again.

"Well, we must find him. I have the feeling this mystery man is the key to what happened to Elodie. Find him, and we're a giant step forward." He pointed a finger at Theo. "Theo, go through the statements that mention him. Talk to those witnesses again, get them to see if they can remember any more. Kate, go with him. See if what they tell you tallies with what you remember of this man."

Kate nodded. She looked across at Theo, and he winked at her, which made her grin.

"Jane, where are we with the CCTV?" asked Anderton.

Jane hopped off the desk and handed over a mass of papers. "Several interesting sightings," she said, pointing to something on the camera printouts. "Two men here, and again here. Unfortunately we can't see their faces."

"Bloody hoodies," grumbled Anderton. "Do we have any sightings of Elodie?"

"Yes, she was on the camera outside the pub, leaving with a man—probably the one you saw her with, Kate—and walking into the car park. Unfortunately the camera on that area of the car park was on the blink and we've got nothing definite. She could have got into a car, she could have driven off somewhere, or she could have walked away. There are no cameras on that section of the river footpath."

"Shame. Okay, this'll do for now. What else?" He scanned the board and his scribbled notes. "Kate! DNA tests?"

"Sorry, sir, I haven't had a chance. I'll ring the pathologist today." She could see Olbeck grinning at her from across the room and mouthed 'sod off' at him.

"You won't have a chance *today*, you'll be out with Theo. Jerry, you do it. Right, what else? What else?" He came to a standstill in front of the boards, both hands churning his hair. "Mark, Rav, you're with me. We need to get young Reuben back in for more questioning. He's not off my hit-list yet, not by a long shot. And at some point. we need to go back and question our jogger—what's his name? Deedham."

Rav stuck his hand up smartly.

"We've done that, sir. Jerry and I went to see him yesterday. Still insists he didn't know Elodie Duncan. He's regularly seen jogging on that stretch of the riverbank, and his wife also insists he didn't know our victim. We did a bit of digging, but there's nothing. Nothing at all."

"Great," said Anderton. "I suppose his wife alibied him too?"

Rav nodded. Anderton threw up his hands in exasperation.

"Fine, we'll wash him out for now. What about Reuben Farraday? He got an alibi yet?"

"His parents," said Jane. She shrugged. "For what that's worth."

"Fine, fine," said Anderton through gritted teeth. "So we're absolutely no further forward than we were. Bring him in, anyway and let's get on with it. Oh—" Anderton sagged suddenly, as if struck by an unpleasant thought. His hands dropped to his side. His team stared at him.

After a moment, he went on.

"I can't actually, I've got a meeting. Damn. You two carry on and report back. I can't get out of this one. Unfortunately."

There was a moment's silence. Kate wondered if anyone else had caught the bleak look that flashed across Anderton's face, just for a split second. Then it was gone, and he was calling out his goodbyes, *carry on team, good work* and striding out the door.

Olbeck was looking after Anderton with a worried look on his face.

"Hey, Mark," said Kate, as much to distract him as because she wanted to know. "I hope you didn't find my family too overwhelming."

Olbeck turned to her, smiling. "Course not. Your brother's a nice kid."

"How was his statement?" asked Kate, speaking casually despite the sudden jump of anxiety that she felt.

"Quite straightforward." Olbeck sat down and rummaged through the paperwork on his desk. "Here you go. You can read it at your leisure."

"Thanks." Kate took it and skimmed it quickly, inwardly quaking. But there was nothing there that jumped out. Nothing that could be construed as...dangerous. She blew out her cheeks and put the paper in her desk drawer to read properly when she had some more time. There was something else that she had to do—what was it now? Oh yes...before she pulled the scrap of paper from her bag, she asked Olbeck another question.

"What did you think of Peter?"

Olbeck was texting again. "Who?"

"My mum's new man. The bloke with the beard."

Olbeck looked up from his phone. "I didn't really notice him much, to be honest. He seemed okay."

"Hmm."

Olbeck's eyes narrowed. "Why?"

"Oh, nothing." Kate swung her chair back and forth a little. "It's just—why would someone like that..."

"Yes?"

Kate cringed inwardly as she said it. "Why would a man like that be interested in my mum? What's he after?"

Olbeck stared at her for a long moment. Then he put down his phone.

"I don't understand you," he said. "I know this is a weird thing to say to a detective, but you are *so* suspicious. What do you mean, what's he after? Why can't he just be after your mum?"

"You don't understand," muttered Kate. She swung her chair away from him, avoiding his accusing gaze. "You don't know my mum. Why would someone like him be interested in someone like her?"

Olbeck scoffed. "Listen to you. I've only met your mum once, and she's not that bad, from what I could see. She's quite attractive. I can see why he'd be attracted to her."

"*Quite attractive*?"

"Yes." He grinned suddenly. "You look quite like her, actually."

"I do not!"

Kate fought a childish urge to put her fingers in her ears. She was suddenly furious with Olbeck. How dare he say that, how dare he compare her to her mother? *I am nothing like her*. She turned her back on him, picked the piece of paper out of her bag and fired up the various databases that she needed.

"What are you doing?"

She ignored Olbeck's question. She looked down at the piece of paper in her hand. Peter Buckley, Burton Abbot. Then, ignoring the voice inside that told her she was being unreasonable, suspicious, *paranoid*, she typed Peter's name into the appropriate fields.

"Are you checking up on him?"

"Shut up, Mark."

"You are, aren't you? Jesus Christ."

"Shut up, Mark."

Over the other side of the room, she could see Theo beckoning. She gave him a 'five minutes' gesture and turned her attention back to the screen. Nothing. No match. No records. A great swamping wave of shame washed over her. What on Earth did she think she was doing?

"You see?" said Olbeck from behind her shoulder.

"Oh, shut up."

She got up and grabbed her bag and coat. Theo was waiting for her by the office door.

"Nutter," said Olbeck, in a not unkind tone, as she walked off.

Theo drove. Kate hadn't worked alone with him for some time, and it felt rather odd to be sat next to someone who wasn't Olbeck. There had been a time, not long after she joined the team in Abbeyford, when Theo had taken her for a drink after work and made a pretty direct pass at her. She'd turned him down (not without some regret—he really *was* very good looking) and there had been a dreadfully strained couple of months before Theo had got himself a new girlfriend and had apparently forgiven her. All that was water under the bridge now. Kate liked him very much; he had the cockiness of attractive youth but was also whip-smart, ambitious and good at his job.

They presented themselves at the headmaster's office on arrival. Kate wasn't sure he would be there; perhaps he was still too grief-stricken to come to work. But after a moment's wait in the superior secretary's office, Mr Duncan came outside to shake their hands and greet them in a subdued fashion. He looked as if he'd aged twenty years in the few days since Kate had last seen him.

"Of course you may use the room," he said, in answer to their question. "You must have free rein..."

He trailed off, staring past Kate's shoulder and out of the window. Then he seemed to recollect himself.

"I'm sorry. Please go ahead with whatever you have to do."

"Poor bastard," whispered Theo as they left the room. Kate nodded.

She thought she knew the way to the room they'd used before, but she was mistaken. After several wrong turns down wood-panelled corridors, she stopped, irritated.

"This place is a bloody *maze*."

Theo gestured.

"I recognised that bit back there."

They retraced their steps to a small foyer, where glass fronted cases displayed various trophies and awards. There were several large class photographs, children lined up in rows with the teachers standing behind them. The names of the children were printed underneath. As Kate hesitated, wondering where to go, a name caught her eye.

"Violet Sammidge. Look, Theo. That's the girl who committed suicide here last year."

They both looked. Violet Sammidge had been a gawky, large-eyed girl with a mass of frizzy brown hair. She stared out of the photograph, grinning anxiously. Kate felt a flicker of something too intangible to name. A fluttering of clarity in the far corners of her comprehension, something so brief that it was gone almost before she could acknowledge it.

"Ah, Detective Sergeant," said an urbane voice by her shoulder. She turned to find Graham Lightbody, the grey-haired teacher, standing by her with an armful of files.

He saw what they had been looking at.

"What a tragedy that was," he said. His face contracted briefly. "I don't believe we've got over it yet."

"You taught Violet?"

"Taught her? My dear, she was my protégé. A quite exceptional talent. I was just devastated—" He broke off abruptly, staring at the photograph of the dead girl. After a moment, he went on. "She was an unhappy child, I could see that. Her parents had not long gone through a very messy and painful divorce when she began her lessons with me. I don't know how much I helped..." He trailed off again. "Not enough, it seems. Not nearly enough."

There was a moment's silence. Then Mr Lightbody pulled the files closer to his chest.

"You'll have to excuse me, Detective Sergeant. I have a class now."

He nodded to Theo and set off down the corridor, his footsteps echoing back from the panelled walls.

Chapter Twelve

THEY EVENTUALLY FOUND THE ROOM they were looking for and settled down to go through the statements.

"Who's first?" asked Theo

Kate read the name on the first statement and groaned.

"Amy Peters." She gave Theo a wry look. "You'll enjoy this one."

"Why?"

"She's young, lively and beautiful."

Theo brightened up. "Let's get started then."

Amy Peters entered the room in a slightly less dramatic fashion than she had the time before. There was still a hint of staginess about her, and the hair-tossing had not noticeably decreased.

"Of *course* I saw Elodie with a man. Several times. I told you this before."

"Perhaps you could just take us through it again, Amy," said Kate pleasantly. She kept her eyes on the girl's face. What had her relationship with Elodie *really* been like? Best of friends or something else? It was hard to see through the theatrical gloss of Amy's behaviour.

Amy cast Theo a flirtatious glance from underneath lowered lashes, smiled, and then turned back to Kate.

"I saw him a couple of times with Elodie. He was tall and pretty fit if you like the older man thing." She giggled and threw back her hair. "I even asked Elodie about him once, but she wouldn't tell me anything."

"Do you know when she met him? How long she had known him?"

Amy shook her head. "I told you, I only saw her with him a handful of times. Once, outside the school gates, she got into his car. And once in town. They were going into a pub."

"Which one?"

"I don't know. I can't remember. Just some dive, nowhere nice."

"Where was this pub?"

"On Castle Street, I think. I'd never actually been there myself." She cast up her eyes to the ceiling. "Elodie always did like slumming it."

The words, spoken in her beautiful RP accent, sounded even more disdainful than Amy had probably meant them to. Kate could see Theo's brows drawing down and knew that Amy had lost her admirer. *Arrogant little bitch.* Even as Kate was thinking it, she was chastising herself inwardly for using the words.

Kate let the silence draw out just a moment too long for comfort. It was a technique she'd seen Anderton use to effect more than once. Then she asked another question.

"Can you tell us something about Elodie herself, Amy? She's still a mystery to us. Her parents don't seem to have the first clue about what she was up to."

Amy looked at her, wide-eyed and innocently.

"What do you mean?"

"Did you ever see Elodie take drugs?"

The beautiful, wide eyes blinked.

"Drugs? Elodie?" Amy's gaze dropped away. "No. No, I didn't."

"Did Elodie ever sell *you* any drugs?" asked Kate, bluntly.

"No," said Amy. She gave her hair an indignant toss.

"Really?" said Kate. "You won't get into trouble for telling me the truth."

Amy looked at her directly.

"Elodie never sold me any drugs. I swear on my mother's life."

Kate held her gaze.

"Never, Amy?"

"I told you, no. Drugs are for losers." Amy tossed her head again. "We don't have that sort of thing around here."

"Balls, they don't," said Theo after the interviews, when they were walking back to the car and discussing what they'd heard.

"I agree with you," said Kate. "I'm pretty sure Amy's lying. She's got the faux-naivety thing down quite nicely though. I'll give her credit for being quite a good actress."

"We're still no nearer finding out who this older guy is."

Kate shrugged. "We know that Amy did actually *see* him. We can ask around at the pub she talked about. If we manage to get a name, we might be able to pull up a photograph."

Back at the station, Kate was caught up in the reams of paperwork that she'd been neglecting. She barely had time to grab a canteen sandwich and a hurried cup of tea, let alone have time to do any more thinking. After three hours of solid desk work, she stretched, yawned and sat back in her chair, grimacing at the ache in her shoulders. Opening her desk drawer to grab a fresh pen, she caught sight of the paper that Olbeck had given her that morning: Jay's statement. She took it up and read through it carefully, noting particularly what Jay had said he had been doing between the crucial hours during which the murder had taken place. Nothing very illuminating. He'd apparently been with one of the band members—the singer, Tom Hough—and they seemed to have spent a couple of hours wandering around Arbuthon Green, smoking cigarettes and 'losing track of time.' There was no mention of Elodie after she'd left the pub with her older companion. Kate frowned, thinking hard, tapping the paper on her desk. Then she made up her mind.

Anderton's office door was shut. This was so unusual that Kate stopped, momentarily wrong-footed. Of course, he shut the door when he had a meeting with one or more of the upper echelons of the police hierarchy. Kate bent awkwardly down to see if she could see more than one pair of feet beyond the opaque section of glass that ran along his office wall. Nothing. Was he even in? It was late—perhaps he'd left already. She knocked, hesitantly at first, and then louder when there was no response.

"Come in," was the quiet response to her second knock. Kate popped her head around the door. Anderton was sitting at his desk and for the strangest moment, Kate had the impression that he'd just raised his head from his hands.

"Yes, Kate?"

"I've got some more information for you regarding the case, sir," she said a little nervously. She hadn't really planned out what she was going to say. For a moment, she wished she'd gone away without knocking and left her revelation for another day. Anderton was looking at her with an expression she couldn't read.

"You've found Elodie's boyfriend?"

"Not yet, sir, no. We're further forward there, a bit. I wanted to tell you about something..." Kate hesitated, feeling something like a tremor of unease, a premonition of how this conversation would go. Then she plunged on.

Anderton said nothing as she told him of the picture her brother had painted, how the crime scene had reminded her of the picture but that it had to be coincidence, particularly as the body had actually been found in the river. How Jay and Elodie were friends but nothing more than that. How she had wondered whether it was even worth mentioning but thought she should for completeness. Anderton still said nothing. By now, Kate was gabbling, filling up the silence and feeling the metaphorical temperature in the room drop from neutral to icy to twenty below freezing.

Eventually she managed to stop herself speaking. There was a long moment of silence before Anderton opened his mouth.

When he did finally speak, his voice was ominously quiet.

"Why have you taken days to tell me this, DS Redman?"

At the use of her full formal title, Kate realised that Anderton was furious. She tried to speak calmly, hiding the fact that her heart was beating fast.

"I didn't think it was particularly important sir. I'm sorry—"

Anderton still spoke in that ominously quiet voice.

"Your brother painted a picture that closely resembles the crime scene of our murder victim—your brother, who was one of the last people known to have seen Elodie Duncan alive. Your brother, who by all accounts is infatuated with the victim. You knew all this days ago—and you didn't think it was particularly important?"

Kate swallowed. She knew she was, conversationally at least, one step away from plunging over a precipice.

"I...when I found that the body had been pulled from the river—it had to have been a coincidence—"

The ground crumbled beneath her. Anderton catapulted himself up from his chair, leaning over his desk to shout into her face.

"Coincidence, my arse! You kept this from me deliberately, Redman. You were protecting your brother—"

"I wasn't," gasped Kate, fighting the urge to run from the room.

"Don't lie to me—"

"I told him to make a statement! I, I encouraged him to come forward—"

"Why didn't you tell me about this earlier?"

"I—I didn't—"

"*Why?*"

Kate shut her eyes for a moment, unable to help it. She shook her head, unable to answer.

Anderton sat back down, breathing heavily. After a moment, he spoke quietly, but with an added, hissing emphasis.

"I don't care if it was your brother who did this. I wouldn't care if it was your *son*."

Kate flinched as if he'd slapped her. What was worse, after the initial shock of the words he'd used, was the realisation that he'd said them deliberately to hurt her; he had used the words he knew would cause her maximum pain.

Silence fell. After a moment, Anderton reached for the telephone on his desk. Kate kept her eyes on the floor, unable to look him in the face.

"Jerry," said Anderton in the receiver. "I'm swearing a warrant for the arrest of Jason Redman. I want him picked up and brought back here to answer some questions about Elodie Duncan's murder."

"No!" said Kate, unable to help herself. "It wasn't him! He wouldn't do it—"

Anderton ignored her.

"Quick as you can, Jerry, thank you. That's all for now." He put the receiver down.

Kate dug her fingers into her leg, willing herself not to cry. When she could trust her voice, she asked, "Can I sit in on the interview, sir?"

"Are you actually insane? Do you not see how inappropriate that would be?"

Kate did see it, of course she did. She nodded, eyes down. "What about Mark?"

"Don't make me laugh. You probably roped him into not saying anything too."

Kate gasped, stung into indignation by the unfairness of that remark. "He knew nothing about it, nothing."

"So *you* say. God help us, it's come to this that I can't trust my own officers."

Kate stood up, trembling. She'd made a mistake, but she was human. Jay was her *brother*. She'd never known Anderton like this. He could be brusque and demanding—but he'd never before been cruel. He'd never before been unfair.

"I am truly sorry, sir," she said. "I made a mistake and for that I apologise. But I was not trying to shield my brother, and I am not someone that you can't trust. And neither is Mark. And you know that. You *know* that, sir."

Anderton looked at her, expressionless.

"What's wrong with you?" Kate asked, and there was real puzzlement and concern in her voice, something that caused Anderton's granite face to flicker.

He leant forward and put his face in his hands.

"Get out," he said, his voice muffled by his fingers.

Chapter Thirteen

Kate walked back to her desk. Oddly, she no longer felt like crying. It was as if she'd been blasted numb, as if she had walked away from a serious accident apparently unscathed. But deep within her, something had been badly damaged. She sat down at her desk carefully.

She couldn't think about Jay yet. Whenever he came into her mind, it was his younger face that she remembered, the face of the little boy she'd loved and cared for over so many years. The thought of him being arrested twisted something deep inside her. Would he run or try to run? Would they handcuff him or would he come quietly? *Was he guilty?* She mimicked Anderton, putting her face in her hands to try and block out the thought.

Someone put a warm hand on her shoulder and she jumped.

"What's up?" said Olbeck, quietly.

Kate shook her head. Over Olbeck's shoulder, she could see the clock on the wall, its hands pointing to eight o'clock.

"Are you knocking off soon?" she asked.

Olbeck was regarding her with a worried look on his face. "I was," he said absently. "Why, are you heading home?"

Kate nodded. She thought of her silent house, Jay's things in the spare bedroom, perhaps a sign of a struggle.

"Why don't you come home with me?" she said. "Come and have dinner at my place."

"Well," said Olbeck, "I did sort of have something planned—"

"Please." *Don't leave me on my own.*

Olbeck looked at her appraisingly. Then he nodded. "Okay. Why not?"

As soon as he'd agreed, Kate felt guilty, guilty and ashamed of her own weakness.

"Oh, it's okay...if you've got something planned—"

Olbeck patted her shoulder again. "S'alright," he said. "I don't like him much anyway, to be honest. Might do me good to have a quiet night in."

"Thanks," said Kate, gratefully.

"Tell me all about it on the way home."

"Thanks," said Kate again, and she meant it from the bottom of her heart.

They bought takeaway Chinese on the way home and stopped off at the corner shop for a bottle of wine (for Olbeck) and a bottle of elderflower cordial (for Kate). There was a small section of DVDs for hire in one aisle of the shop and Olbeck stopped in front of the display.

"Let's get a film."

Kate cast a disinterested eye over the plastic cases. Then she realised that watching something mindless might actually take her mind of the terrible images that kept circulating.

"What do you want to watch?" she asked, praying he wouldn't choose something crime-related or anything gory.

Mark ran a finger along the cases and picked one out.

"How about this? British rom-com. Something fluffy."

"Fine," said Kate. She saw once again Anderton's face as he buried it in his hands. She blinked and that image was replaced by one of Jay in a police cell, young and small and scared. *Stop thinking about it*. She realised she was staring into space. Olbeck was already at the counter, paying for the DVD.

Once they were back at her house, she turned on the oven and put the takeaway containers inside it to keep warm. Then she told

Olbeck to follow her and led him up to the hallway cupboard on the landing upstairs, where she'd stored the painting.

"Here," she said. "What do you think? I mean, really think?"

Olbeck took it from her silently and regarded it intently. She watched his face, not knowing quite what it was she wanted to see there.

"It's not—not that bad, is it?" she said after the silence stretched too long.

"I don't know," said Olbeck in a low voice. "I don't know. In one way, it takes your breath away, how close it is but yet—when I look at it more closely, I can see that, well, there's nothing really much there."

"Yes, I think so too," said Kate. "The more you look at it the more you realise it's *not* much alike at all. Don't you?"

"Mmm." Olbeck sounded less convinced that she would have liked. After a moment, he propped the picture back against the wall and stood up.

"Come on, I'm starving. Let's eat and watch the film."

Back in the living room, Olbeck began to fiddle about with the DVD player.

"Can I make a fire?" he asked eagerly, like a small boy. Kate was amused, in spite of herself.

"Of course. Knock yourself out. I'll get the food."

Olbeck got the DVD working and knelt to build the fire. Once it was crackling to his satisfaction, he sat back on Kate's sofa and put his feet up. He looked around the neat, cosy, nicely-decorated room. It was funny—when he'd been with Joe, he couldn't stand to be in this kind of warm domestic setting; it made him want to run screaming down to the nearest dodgy bar and never go home again. At Kate's, it somehow felt different. Perhaps it was because he was just a visitor. *She'll make someone a wonderful wife someday*, he thought and decided with a grin to tell her that when she came back into the room, mainly to see the outraged look on her face.

Kate came back with a plate full of food and a glass of wine for him, but by that time, the moment had passed. She brought in her own tray and they began to watch the film.

"This is shite," said Olbeck, after about twenty minutes had passed.

"It's certainly low-budget," said Kate. She pushed listlessly at the remaining food on her plate—she'd hardly touched anything.

"It's pretty dated, isn't it? Look at the mobiles they're carrying."

Kate scoffed. "Trust you to notice that."

"I'm just going to the little boy's room. Don't bother stopping it."

Kate pushed a forkful of cold rice into her mouth and chewed slowly, staring at the screen, not so much because she was interested in what was happening, more that she couldn't be bothered to look away. The film changed scenes. Her eyes widened. Suddenly she sat bolt upright and choked.

Olbeck was halfway up the stairs when he heard Kate yell. He arrived back in the living room five seconds later, wide-eyed.

"What the hell? What's the matter?"

Kate was spluttering, covered in half-chewed rice. She clawed frantically for the remote, stabbing her finger at the screen.

"It's him, it's him! The guy, the man—it's him!"

"What the hell?"

"There, *there*. It's him, it's our guy. The one with Elodie. Look there—"

She paused the DVD. The actor on screen froze, staring out from the screen.

Kate wiped the last remaining grains of rice away from her mouth.

"Are you sure?" asked Olbeck.

"I'm sure. It's him. My God."

They looked at one another in shock. "I can't believe it. He's an actor. No wonder he looked familiar."

"He *was* an actor," said Olbeck, checking the back of the DVD cover. "I was right. This film's twelve years old. He might not still be an actor."

Kate was staring at the screen.

"It's definitely him," she said, after a moment. "Younger, but I can tell it's him. What's his name?"

"What character is he playing?"

"No bloody idea, I wasn't paying attention."

"Okay, we'll watch it. Sit quiet and listen out for his name."

They watched intently for several minutes.

"Arley. Arley? What kind of a name is that?" Olbeck muttered.

"Skip to the credits," said Kate, almost bouncing in her seat. Olbeck fumbled with the remote.

They watched the credits scroll up the screen. Kate pounced.

"There! Nathan Vertz. We've got it!"

She grabbed her laptop and brought it to life, typing busily into the browser bar.

"Checking IMDB?" asked Olbeck.

Kate nodded. She typed in the name of the film, clicked twice and gave a cry of triumph. She began to read aloud from the screen.

"Nathan Vertz. Former child star of the highly successful *The Butterkins Trilogy*, including *Meet The Butterkins*, *The Butterkins Abroad*, *The Butterkins Christmas*, Nathan Vertz also starred in the independent British production *Wine and Roses*." She looked at Olbeck, awed. "The Butterkins. God, what a blast from the past. Remember those films?"

"I used to love the books." Olbeck looked from the computer screen to the frozen image on the television. "I can't believe that's the same guy who played Toby Butterkin. God."

Kate was busy pulling up more information.

"Look, he's got his own Wikipedia page."

They both regarded the laptop screen. The main picture was of an adorable little boy, his cheeky smile framed by a mop of blonde ringlets.

"You'd never think it was the same person," said Olbeck sadly.

"Nathan Vertz is his real name," said Kate. She traced a finger along the screen. "Born in London...got the part of Toby Butterkin when he was eight. God, that's young. Hmm...hmm...one of the stars of the highly successful franchise... blah, blah...career declined in adulthood...drink and drug dependency..." She looked at Olbeck. "We need to run a check on his name."

"Right. We will. Tomorrow."

Kate paused, halfway to the door.

"What about now?"

"Kate," said Olbeck. "It's almost midnight. It can wait until tomorrow morning."

Kate looked as though she were about to argue. Then she sagged a little.

"Okay. You're right. It's just..."

She let the sentence trail away. Olbeck got up, stretching.

"Jay will be all right, you know," he said, gently. "They'll treat him just as they would anyone else."

"That's what worries me."

Olbeck found his coat and pulled it on, wrapping his scarf around his neck.

"He'll be fine," he repeated. "You can go and see him in the morning. He might even be released before then."

"I know," said Kate. She cleared her throat. "Thanks, Mark. Thanks for being here tonight. And we found our guy. Imagine that."

"*You* did," said Olbeck. "God, imagine if we'd both been out of the room. He was only a bit character—we could have missed him."

"Well, you picked the DVD," said Kate, with a tired smile. "It must have been fate."

She saw him to the front door. He gave her an awkward hug and said goodbye.

"Try and get some sleep."

Kate nodded. Just as he was turning away, she spoke.

"There's something wrong with this case, Mark."

He turned back, surprised.

"What do you mean?"

"I don't know," said Kate, rather helplessly. "We're missing something, I'm sure of it. Something big. I've never known a case where—oh, I don't know. Where I know something is hidden but all I can see is the surface. Like the river."

"In the picture?" said Olbeck, puzzled.

"Yes. No. I don't know exactly what I'm trying to say."

"That makes two of us."

"It's just…I have a feeling we're missing something, something important." Kate hesitated. She tried to recall where it was she'd felt this most strongly before, but the memory eluded her. "I can't explain it."

"Tell Anderton. Go and see him tomorrow and tell him."

"Tell him what? I don't know what it is myself. Besides—" Kate swallowed, remembering the scene of the afternoon. "He hates me at the moment."

"No, he doesn't." Olbeck yawned. "Listen, I've got to go. Like I said, try and get some sleep. It'll all seem better in the morning."

Chapter Fourteen

KATE HAD HOPED THAT SHE'D be woken the next morning by the sound of the doorbell. She wanted to open it to find a dishevelled Jay standing on the doorstep, having been released without charge.

She was disappointed.

It was a beautiful sunny morning, warm for late autumn, but she showered and dressed feeling like a grey cloud was hanging over her. The excitement of last night's discovery had ebbed away and now she was dreading seeing Anderton, dreading hearing what had happened with Jay. She wanted to go back to bed, pull the covers over her head and sleep until this nightmare was over. Instead, she squared her shoulders, smoothed back her hair and headed out the door.

Olbeck was already at his desk, looking bright-eyed and bushy-tailed. He waved as he saw Kate come through the door.

"Wait 'til you see this."

Kate slung her coat on the back of her chair.

"I have to go and check on Jay first."

"I've done that. Told him you'd be down to see him."

"Oh, thank you," said Kate, absurdly near tears due to Olbeck's kindness. "I'll go right now."

As it turned out, Jay was asleep in his cell when arrived. She looked through the viewing hatch at her little brother, curled on the uncomfortable bed under the one inadequate grey blanket. He had one hand under his cheek. Kate remembered how he used to sleep like that as a child.

"You want me to wake him up?" asked the PC who was on guard duty.

"No, don't," said Kate, quickly. She looked at her brother with tenderness. "Let him sleep. He needs it. Just tell him I was here when he wakes up."

"All okay?" asked Olbeck when she got back to the office.

Kate shrugged. "Let's not talk about it. Thanks for going down before."

"It's nothing. You're welcome."

"What have you got on Nathan Vertz? Has he got a record?"

Olbeck rolled his chair back from his desk for emphasis.

"Ooh, yes he has."

Kate felt a welcome pulse of excitement, something to distract her from the thought of Jay locked in a cell downstairs. "Really?"

"Yup. See here."

He handed over some print outs. Kate read through the first one and her eyebrows rose.

"Domestic violence. I *see*."

Olbeck was grinning. "Read on. See exactly what he was accused of."

Kate did so. Then she whistled, slowly.

"Attempted strangulation. My God."

"His first wife. Well, his only wife, but she divorced him, unsurprisingly."

Kate read on. "He did six months for that. *That* wasn't on the Wikipedia page."

"Well, that was clearly written by a fan. Anyway, it's not the only time he's been violent. He was arrested for assaulting a member of the paparazzi before the domestic violence charge."

"Back when he was still famous," mused Kate. "How the mighty have fallen. It's sad, really."

"I'll reserve my sympathy for someone who really needs it," said Olbeck. "Anyway, I've brought Anderton up to speed."

Kate couldn't help the drop of her stomach but she managed to hide it at the sound of his name.

"Good," she said. "Let's go and talk to Mr Vertz."

Nathan Vertz lived in Arbuthon Green in a terraced house, one of many on a down-at-heel street. Black bin bags were piled in the street outside every house—it was clearly the day when the dustbin collectors were expected—and several bags had burst or been torn open, scattering rubbish along the street. Kate and Olbeck paused outside the gate of Number 22. The curtains were drawn at all of the visible windows.

"God, when you think about the money he must have had..." said Olbeck, making a face of disgust. He kicked at a soggy newspaper that had wrapped itself around his shoe.

"I know," said Kate. "I think he actually went bankrupt. Come on, let's get him out of bed."

She rang the doorbell repeatedly. When it wasn't answered, she knocked. After a full five minutes, the door opened slowly and Nathan Vertz stood there in the doorway, blinking in the sunlight. A waft of old cigarette smoke and body odour made Kate want to wrinkle up her nose.

"I'm Detective Sergeant Kate Redman, and this is Detective Sergeant Olbeck," she said, snapping her card in his face. He recoiled slightly, shaking his head. "We'd like to talk to you about the murder of Elodie Duncan."

His eyes widened. For a second, Kate was convinced he was going to run—forward between them or backwards into the house—she could see that change of stance, the minute quiver as the impulse flooded his muscles. She tensed, almost as instinctively, ready to chase. She could feel Olbeck do the same.

The moment was over and gone in a moment; Nathan Vertz clearly mastered his sudden impulse and some kind of energy went out of him, an almost imperceptible change in his posture. He sighed.

"You'd better come in," he said quietly.

The interior of the house was a surprise. Given the area's general sense of squalor and Nathan Vertz's own grubby appearance, Kate was expecting dirt, frowst, filthy carpets, stale smelling rooms and piles of clutter. Instead, they found rooms that wouldn't have looked out of place in an interiors magazine. The walls were white, the floorboards sanded back and polished. The furniture was old but very well made, some of it clearly valuable. Dotted here and there on the dust-free surfaces were small sculptures, well-framed artwork, a crystal bowl of beautiful autumnal flowers that lit up the corner of the room.

With the backdrop of all this beauty and order, Nathan Vertz presented a strange contrast. His uncut hair fell in greasy spikes on his forehead, although, if she looked closely, Kate could still see the natural curl that had given him the mop of blonde ringlets in the photograph of him as a child.

He sat down on the nearest sofa, an old but sturdy leather Chesterfield, rather like Kate's own. She felt a secret pride that her own furniture was similar to this man's lovingly collected antiques.

Vertz looked down at the floor. He was sitting slumped, his hands dangling over his knees.

"We're enquiring about the death of Elodie Duncan, Mr Vertz," said Olbeck. "I believe you knew her?"

Vertz said nothing.

"Mr Vertz?"

"I knew her," said Vertz, heavily. "How well, I'm not sure. We went on a few dates."

"Can you elaborate?"

"What do you want me to say?"

"We want you to tell us the truth, Mr Vertz. When you say you went on a few dates, does that mean you were Elodie Duncan's partner? Her boyfriend?"

Vertz was silent.

"Mr Vertz?"

He shook his head.

Olbeck glanced at Kate.

"Mr Vertz," she said sharply. "Obstructing police in the course of their enquiries is a crime. Do you wish to continue this conversation down at the police station?"

Vertz said nothing for a moment. Kate breathed in sharply, ready to start giving the words of the caution. Then he spoke.

"I don't care." He wasn't looking at the officers but staring at the wall, slumped against the side of the sofa. "I don't care about anything anymore."

Kate and Olbeck exchanged glances. Then they got to their feet.

"We're continuing this conversation back at the station, sir. I suggest you come with us right away."

Vertz was silent on the drive back to the station. Olbeck sat next to him in the back seat. Kate drove, trying not to wrinkle her nose as the man's stale smell permeated the air of the car's interior. Kate looked at him in the rear view mirror. He was staring down at the floor.

She couldn't work him out. He was clearly depressed, but there was something else, something underneath the surface that was making her uneasy. There it was again, that sixth sense, that feeling that she was missing something. Undercurrent: that was the word she was looking for.

She let Olbeck take him to one of the interview rooms, one of the less-pleasant ones on the ground floor. Then she ran down to the holding cells.

Jay had been released. Kate had expected to feel jubilant at the news—that must mean that they hadn't found any more evidence with which to hold him, or God forbid, to charge him. But instead, she felt worry begin to gnaw at her, cramping her stomach. Her brother was young. He was struggling over the death of his friend; he'd just been through the trauma of an arrest and a night's imprisonment, not to mention the intimidating questioning session he would have gone through with Anderton and Jerry. Would he be all right? She tried to call him, his mobile going straight to voicemail. Then she called her mother—same thing. Eventually, Kate managed to get through to Courtney, who said she'd keep trying until she got through to him. Kate thanked her, told her she loved her, and hung up, running frantically up the stairs to the interview room before smoothing her hair down, trying to get her breath back and opening the door.

Chapter Fifteen

"DS Redman has entered the room," said Olbeck, also giving the time.

Kate sat down opposite Nathan Vertz. He gave her a dull look, almost bovine in its weariness, before resuming his apparent examination of the table-top.

"Mr Vertz, you have been seen with Elodie Duncan on more than one occasion." Olbeck was clearly still referring to the suspect as a 'Mister.' How soon this changed would depend on the responses he was given. Kate was less patient and often dispensed with the title in the first few moments.

Olbeck continued.

"Several witnesses have confirmed that you were with Elodie on the night that she died. I will ask you again: did you have anything to do with her death?"

"No."

"Can you confirm the time and place you last saw Elodie on the night of the eighth of November?"

"No comment."

"What do you think happened?"

There was a flicker on Vertz's set face. "I don't know."

Olbeck sat back in his seat, clearly suppressing his irritation. He looked over at Kate, giving her tacit permission to take over.

Kate sat up, pulled her shirt sleeves down straight over her wrists and put her shoulders back.

"Are you musical, Mr Vertz?"

This was clearly not the question he'd been expecting. He gave her a glance of surprise, the first sign of animation she'd seen.

"I was, once." He pushed the hair out of his eyes with the back of his hand. "I was a good singer, once."

Kate recalled something about the Butterkins films—hadn't they been adapted for the stage as well?

"That's something that you and Elodie had in common," she said. "She was very talented musically."

He was looking at her properly now, as if she'd suddenly come into focus.

"She was. She was amazing."

"Did she ever play for you?"

Vertz actually smiled. Dirty as he was, unsavoury as he was, Kate could suddenly see his appeal for Elodie: the smile made him look eager, boyish, and vulnerable in an attractive way.

"She did, many times."

Kate contrasted that remark with Vertz's previous assertion that he and Elodie had been 'on a few dates.'

"So you did actually spend quite a lot of time together?"

Vertz looked uncomfortable. "I suppose so."

"Did you ever meet her family?"

"No."

"Did she ever talk to you about her family at all? Did she mention her relationship with her parents?"

A flash in Vertz's eyes but he shook his head.

"No."

"Did you meet Elodie's friends?"

"No."

"None of them? Amy Peters?"

"No."

Kate cleared her throat.

"What about Jason Redman?"

"No." Vertz was sounding bored.

Kate sat back. It was Olbeck's turn.

He didn't disappoint her.

"Elodie Duncan was in possession of a large amount of cocaine, Mr Vertz. Do you know anything about this?"

Vertz didn't react. "No comment."

"Did you give it to her?"

"No comment."

"You have numerous convictions for drug related offences, Nathan." Ah, there. He'd lost the Mister. Kate was surprised it had taken this long. "Your girlfriend—your dead girlfriend—had drugs in her possession. Are you expecting me to believe there was no connection between these two facts?"

Vertz stared out of the tiny window, set high up in the wall. "No comment."

They kept it up for another hour, digging away, trying to find a weak spot. Vertz ignored the questions, or answered negatively, or replied 'no comment.' The only time Vertz showed any sign of animation was when Elodie's talent for music was highlighted.

Eventually, they had to let him go.

"Bugger," said Olbeck as they watched Nathan walk away from the station with his head down.

"We should have charged him" said Kate. "Kept him in." After all, Anderton had done just that to Jay, hadn't he? How was that fair? "He knows more than he's saying."

Olbeck gave her an old-fashioned look. "Well, of course he does. He's guilty as sin in my opinion."

"So why didn't we bloody charge him?" Kate snapped. She turned on her heel and walked back to her desk, pulling out her chair with an irritable tug.

"Temper," said Olbeck, sitting back down. "And actually, I agree with you. I'm going to update Anderton and see what he wants to do."

"Fine. Do that."

Kate reached for the phone as soon as he'd walked away and dialled the coroner's office.

"Doctor Telling? It's Kate Redman—fine, thanks. How was your holiday?"

She leant back, tapping a pencil on her jaw. Doctor Telling had a very quiet, measured voice, the sort where you instinctively relaxed listening to it. Kate had always thought that if the pathology thing didn't work out, the good doctor had an excellent career ahead of her as a voiceover artist for relaxation and meditation tracks.

"Sorry, I didn't quite catch that—the *Arctic*? Oh, a cruise. Well that's sounds…yes. Did Doctor Stanton tell you what we wanted? Oh you have—brilliant. Yes, I'm sorry, we only got one of the samples very recently, today in fact. Sorry—yes, please. No, I'll wait."

She held the receiver to her ear as Doctor Telling made rummaging and mouse-clicking noises on the other end of the line. Then that quiet, comforting voice came back on the line.

Kate's eyebrows rose.

"Seriously? That's great. Yes, if you could send over the info, we'd be really grateful. Thanks so much."

Kate put the receiver down, obscurely comforted that Doctor Telling had been somewhere suitably weird for her holiday. She threw her pen over at Olbeck, who had just come back to his desk.

"The DNA results are back. Telling's sending them over now."

"So," said Olbeck. "Don't keep me in suspense. Who's the daddy?"

WHEN KATE ARRIVED HOME THAT night, she found two waifs and strays on her doorstep—Courtney and Jay. They were sat side by side, huddled in their coats and smoking cigarettes. The area around their feet was littered with cigarette butts.

"You must be freezing," exclaimed Kate. She opened up the door and ushered them both in. How long had they been sitting out there? "How long have you been sitting out there?"

"Fucking ages," muttered Courtney. She was hunched over by the kitchen counter, her hands in her armpits. Her beautiful, sulky face was pinched, her nose and cheeks reddened by the cold.

Jay stood silently. Kate gave him a quick hug, feeling the sharp bones of his ribcage under her hands. She stood back and took him by the arms, looking into his face.

"It'll be all right, Jay," she said gently. "They haven't charged you with anything. It'll be all right."

He looked at her quickly and then away. For a moment she thought he was going to say something, and then he shook his head, gently detached her hands and walked away.

"There's just one thing," Kate said awkwardly. "You can't stay here. I'm really sorry, but I don't think it would be appropriate." She paused, hating the sound of her voice and her mealy-mouthed words. "I think you'd be better off somewhere where people don't know where to find you."

Jay laughed harshly.

"That's my digs out then. I'm not going back there anyway. I don't want everyone looking at me and thinking I did it."

Kate put both hands to her head and rubbed her temples. She was so tired: her eyes ached, her back ached, her feet ached.

"How about I drop you at Mum's? You can stay there for a while."

Courtney looked as though she was about to protest. Kate looked over at her sister. "Is that a bad idea? What about your dad?"

Courtney shook her head. "He's up in Scotland. Has been for ages."

"Oh. It'll have to be Mum's place, then. She won't mind." Kate hoped fervently that this were true. "Stay here tonight—both of you stay—and I'll run you both back tomorrow before work."

She ran a bath for Jay, found something to watch on television for Courtney, and put a couple of frozen pizzas in the oven. They ate the pizzas in a fairly companionable silence, and then the two youngsters disappeared out the back to smoke a last cigarette before bed. Kate bundled herself up in her coat and swept up all the butts from outside her front door. She put aside the uncharitable thought that if they had money for cigarettes, why on Earth did they always plead such poverty?

When she came back inside, Jay had already gone to bed. Courtney was glued to her phone screen with the television playing unheeded in the background.

"Well, I'm off to bed," said Kate. "Do you want to bunk in with me or would you rather have the sofa?"

"Sofa, sis, ta."

Kate fetched the remaining spare duvet and a pillow. Courtney stood up while Kate made up the sofa with the bedding. While she was smoothing out the pillow case, she could feel Courtney fidgeting behind her. She turned and raised her eyebrows.

"You okay?"

"Yeah," said Courtney. She seemed about to say more, but then her mobile pinged and she turned her attention back to the screen.

Kate hesitated for a moment. She had a feeling that Courtney had wanted to ask her something or tell her something.

"Courtney? Are you—is there something wrong?"

Courtney actually looked up from her phone. She looked frightened for a moment. Then she shook her head.

Kate stood, irresolute. Then she yawned and gave up. She was just too tired to get to the bottom of whatever it was—and it probably wasn't even important.

She yawned again and said goodnight.

Chapter Sixteen

It was a silent drive on the way to Mary Redman's house the next morning. As Kate drove past her mother's place, looking for a parking space, she saw a bright yellow Mini parked on the scrubby front lawn.

"Is Peter living here now?"

"Yeah," said Courtney.

Kate pulled the car into the kerb.

"Must be a bit crowded. With you two girls here as well." Courtney had been living with her father but clearly had decided a room at her mother's place was preferable to moving to Scotland.

Courtney shrugged. She looked at Kate, opened her mouth and then shut it again.

"What—" Kate was interrupted by Jay getting out of the car and slamming the door shut.

As they walked up the front path, past the Mini, the dirty net curtains at the front window flickered. Peter's face peered out, and momentarily, a frown crossed his face. The curtains were pulled across again, hiding his face from view. By that time, though, Kate had already processed that look.

When Kate had been a 'bobby on the beat,' very early on in her career, she'd been out with her Sergeant, a bluff Northerner called Wittock. He'd told her about what he'd termed 'coppers' senses': something almost indefinable that every good police officer developed. It was almost a sixth sense: the ability to deduct that something was awry from the smallest of gestures or inconsequential details.

"It takes time," Wittock had said. "But you'll get it. If you're any good at your job. You'll start to notice things, without even realising you're noticing them, if you see what I mean."

Kate had found he was right. And now, just on that one look from Peter, a momentary expression on his face seen in the fraction of a second, her copper's senses were screaming.

When he opened the door, he was all smiles and solicitous attention for Jay, ushering them all inside with warm greetings.

"Mary's out shopping," he said, gesturing for them to go through into the living room. It was much cleaner and tidier than it had been last time Kate had been here, although the stink of old cigarettes had not noticeably lessened. "Jade's at school, obviously. How are you, Kate?"

"Fine, thanks," said Kate, keeping a smile on her face. Jay sloped past them and she heard him walking heavily up the stairs. Courtney followed him a moment later.

"How about a cup of tea?"

"Lovely," said Kate, automatically. She'd noticed a laptop on the coffee table, the screen facing away from the room.

Peter followed her gaze.

"Just doing my accounts," he said. "Worst thing about being self-employed, the bloomin' paperwork!"

"I can imagine."

"I'll get you that tea. Sit down love, and I won't be long."

"Thanks," said Kate, her cheeks beginning to ache from smiling. Peter went off to the galley kitchen at the end of the hallway, leaving the door open behind him.

"Milk and sugar?" he shouted from the kitchen.

"Just milk, please," Kate shouted back. Quickly and quietly, she walked to the laptop so she could see the screen and gently tapped the spacebar to take off the screensaver. She was expecting a password request to come up, but there was nothing. There was nothing on the screen except the usual Outlook interface, emails and a little calendar. Nothing untoward.

Kate quickly ran her eye down the list of emails. Only one caught her attention and that was because the subject matter was a girl's name: Alice. She opened it, glancing towards the open door. What on earth was she going to say if Peter came back and caught her? The email opened. Kate scanned it quickly.

>   **From:** gil450231@gmail.com
>   **To:** pbuckley@hotmail.co.uk
>   **Subject:** Alice
>   **Message:** got those files you were looking for. Check new website https://www.nys1o16.com.

Nothing untoward there either. Kate tried to memorise the address and then whipped out her mobile and took a photograph of the screen. She could hear the kettle in the kitchen come to the boil. Quickly, she closed the email to bring back the original screen, tiptoed back to the sofa and sat down, checking the photograph had saved correctly. Then she put her phone away, just as Peter appeared in the doorway with two steaming mugs.

They made chit-chat while Kate tried to drink her hot tea as quickly as she decently could. Then she said goodbye to Peter, hugged Courtney and Jay who were listening to music and smoking cigarettes in Courtney's bedroom, and told them both to give her love to her Mum.

"Where've you bloody *been*?" said Olbeck as Kate dropped into her chair at the office. "We've pulled Nathan Vertz in again, under caution this time."

"Good," said Kate. "Are we questioning him?"

"Nope, Anderton's doing it. We've been sent over to Vertz's

place to pull it apart. We'll take Jane and Rav as well if they're free."

The four of them drove in two separate cars to Arbuthon Green. It was intensely cold: the first real frost of the season. The grubby terraces were almost transformed, glittering under a powdery dusting of ice.

Nathan Vertz's house was warm and clean and quiet.

"Wow, nice," said Jane, looking around with eyebrows raised. "You'd never think he had a place like this."

"I know," said Kate. She rubbed a finger along her jaw, wondering whether to say what she wanted to say. "I think—"

"Hey, look at this," said Rav, who was opening cupboards. "Awards. Not for the *Butterkins*, surely?"

"Don't be such a snob," said Olbeck. "They were really popular once. Made millions for the British film industry."

"Well, what happened to it all? Vertz's share, I mean." Rav took an award out of the cupboard, turning it over in his gloved hands. "*People's Choice*." He glanced at Olbeck. "See, it's hardly an Oscar, is it?"

Kate and Jane took the upstairs rooms, leaving the men to cover the ground floor. Nathan Vertz's bedroom was as beautifully decorated as the rest of the house; the walls were painted a pale, chalky green, the large bed made up with white linen. The duvet and pillows were rumpled and dragged half onto the floor. There was a small, delicate little wooden table by the bed, a lamp with a fawn silk shade still switched on. Kate turned it off. She pulled out the drawer of the bedside table. Inside was a collection of letters and postcards. Kate drew them out and sat on the edge of the messy bed to read through them. Beneath her feet was the scrape of something heavy being moved as the men began to shift the furniture.

"Look," she said to Jane after a moment. The other woman came over and Kate handed her the topmost letter.

"It's from Elodie."

Jane read silently for a moment. Then she looked at Kate.

"A love letter."

Kate fanned out the rest of the papers in her hands. "Lots of love letters. I didn't think anyone wrote love letters any more."

Jane took another one, a postcard of a Turner landscape. She read the inscription on the back out loud.

"'Remembering that afternoon in the cornfields. I love you.'" She turned it over and looked at the picture of the front, flipped it back again. "It's dated...August this year."

Kate pulled the drawer completely out and looked through it.

"There's nothing there from him to her," said Jane, sorting through the stack of correspondence.

"Well, would there be?"

"I guess not. Were there any letters from Vertz at Elodie's house when you searched it?"

Kate sat back on her haunches and stared at Jane. "No. No, there wasn't. Not a single thing."

"Well," said Jane, hesitatingly. "That's odd—isn't it?"

"Yes, it is," said Kate. She pulled herself to her feet with a groan. "I mean, he could be the sort of guy who doesn't ever write letters but...it's a bit odd."

She scanned the letters. "Look, here. She says, 'Thanks for your beautiful letter.' So he must have written at least one."

Jane opened her mouth to reply but before she could say anything, there was a shout from downstairs.

Kate and Jane arrived in the living room to see the sofa pushed back against the wall, the rug rolled up and a section of the floorboards upended.

Rav was grinning like a child who had just discovered a playmate during a game of hide and seek.

"The motherlode."

Kate looked down into the space beneath the floorboards

revealed by the upended wood. Several plastic-wrapped packages, a scuffed black rucksack, a half-empty sack of glucose powder, a set of scales.

"Well, well," said Olbeck. "At least one part of the mystery is cleared up." He carefully opened the rucksack with gloved hands without moving it from its original position. "Look here. Must be..." He riffled through the wads of neatly bound bank notes in the bag. "Must be thousands here."

Jane was already on the radio arranging for crime scene photographers. Kate, who was nearest the front window, noticed several cars drawing up outside the house. For a second, she thought it was some of their own officers before the cameras appearing put paid to that idea.

"Press are here," she said.

Jane rolled her eyes. "That didn't take long."

"We'd better get some uniforms here, cordon it off."

Kate drew the curtains across the windows. Rav was already phoning for reinforcements.

Olbeck drew Kate aside.

"Let's get back to Anderton, let him have the latest. This could be the trigger he's been waiting for."

Chapter Seventeen

ANDERTON WAS QUESTIONING VERTZ IN one of the interview rooms when Olbeck and Kate arrived back at the station. Nathan Vertz looked even more dishevelled than he had done the day before, eyes ringed by shadow, his face pale and pouchy. Kate and Olbeck waited outside while Anderton paused the interview and left the room, joining them in the corridor.

"What have you got for me?"

They told him. Kate was thankful she was able to be calm and professional. It meant the embarrassment of being in Anderton's company after their last disastrous meeting was somewhat mitigated.

All three went back into the interview room and Kate was sure that, this time, Anderton would take no prisoners. She kept the folder containing Elodie's letters on her lap, ready to hand it over at the right time.

Vertz flicked a single glance at her as she sat down before lapsing back into blankness. Again, she had the impression that there was something there under the surface, something hidden but dangerous. She'd felt it before, with someone else, someone quite different to this unshaven, slouched man before her. Who had it been?

She thought back and realised it was Mrs Duncan, Elodie's mother. Some other feeling had been there under the grief, barely glimpsed, like the tiniest tip of an iceberg poking out from chilly, black waters.

"So, Nathan," said Anderton quietly. "You maintain that the extent of your relationship with Elodie Duncan is that 'you went on a few dates.' Do you wish to amend that statement?"

Vertz said nothing but kept staring at the table top.

"I put it to you that you had a longstanding and deep romantic and sexual relationship with Elodie Duncan."

Silence from Vertz.

"Can you confirm if that is the case?"

Vertz continued to stare at the table top.

No one spoke for a few moments. Then Anderton took up the gauntlet again.

"A large quantity of cocaine was found in Elodie Duncan's possession after she died. My officers have just informed me that an even larger quantity of cocaine and other assorted illegal substances was found hidden away at your house today. Do you have anything to say about that?"

Nothing. Kate suppressed an irritated sigh. Stonewalling during an interview was an effective technique but surely there was something they could do to break him down... She pressed the side of her foot against Anderton's under the table and passed him the folder of love letters.

He didn't break stride in what he was saying but took the folder from her, continuing to ask Nathan Vertz his questions.

"Did you give that cocaine to Elodie Duncan for her to sell for you?"

"No comment," muttered Vertz. The solicitor beside him shifted uneasily.

"Did Elodie try to rip you off? Did you kill her?"

"No she didn't. And no I didn't."

"Who do you think killed her?"

There was a sudden stillness in Vertz. Kate was reminded of

an animal that had just scented its prey. Or was it an animal who had just heard the hunter stalking it?

"I don't know," he said in a quiet voice. There was something hidden in his statement that made Kate want to shiver.

Anderton let the silence after his remark continue for an uncomfortably long time. Then he slowly held up one of Elodie's letters and began to read from it aloud.

"'My darling Nathan, can't wait to see you again tonight. I know we only said goodbye a few days ago but it just seems too long before we can be together again. It's only when I'm with you that I really feel like myself—'"

Vertz went pale.

"Where did you get that?"

Anderton ignored him. He let the letter fall to his lap and picked up a postcard.

"'Hey, my sexy Nat, saw this and thought of you—'"

Vertz snatched for it, and Anderton pulled his hand back.

"That's mine!"

Vertz was on his feet. Kate and Olbeck leapt to theirs, and the uniformed officer in the corner did likewise. The solicitor, a grey-haired man in his sixties, looked as though he was ready to run out of the door.

Anderton hadn't moved. Without taking his eyes from Vertz's face, he slowly drew another postcard and held it, preparing to read from it.

"Stop."

Vertz's voice broke in a sob. Suddenly, he flopped back onto his chair, burying his face in his hands.

After a moment, Anderton spoke quietly.

"You loved Elodie Duncan, didn't you Nathan?"

Vertz was crying, harsh, open-mouthed sobs. The tears were running between his dirty fingers.

Anderton repeated his statement.

"You loved her, didn't you Nathan?"

Vertz nodded. After a moment, he spoke, his voice hoarse.

"I loved her. We—we found each other—we knew each other. We both knew what it was like..." His voice trailed away into a mumble. Then he cleared his throat and spoke again. "I didn't kill her. I would never hurt her."

"You have a police record for assaulting your wife," said Anderton. "A serious assault. Are you telling me you've changed that much?"

"That was different. Elodie was different."

"What happened that night?"

Vertz shook his head. "I don't know. I don't know."

"Did you kill Elodie Duncan?"

"No, I didn't. I would never hurt her." He began to cry again. "I wouldn't do that."

Anderton placed the letters back into the folder, gently. He closed it and gave it back to Kate. Vertz tracked the movement with his eyes.

"Those are mine."

"You will have them back, Nathan," said Anderton. Then he said, in the same gentle voice, "Are you aware that Elodie was pregnant when she died?"

If Vertz had been pale before, it was nothing to the colour he became. He looked almost transparent.

"What?" he whispered.

"Elodie Duncan was pregnant when she died," said Anderton, looking straight at the man. Some premonition made Kate brace herself, shift herself just a little closer to the edge of her seat.

Anderton continued.

"It was your baby."

Vertz exploded. Roaring, he flung himself forward, shouting something incomprehensible. Anderton and Kate dived, one to each side, and then Olbeck was on Vertz, the officer flinging himself forward, shouting for reinforcements. Anderton pushed Kate towards the door as the uniformed officers stampeded into the room, piling themselves on the struggling Vertz. His wordless shouts resolved themselves into a recognisable word.

"*No, no, no...*"

He continued to scream as they dragged him from the room. Kate could hear him as he was pulled towards the cells, getting fainter with every step.

His cries were abruptly cut off as the heavy metal door to the cells swung closed with a crash. The silence left behind seemed deafening.

Anderton still had his hand on Kate's arm. They both looked at it as if suddenly remembering it was there. Anderton removed it quickly.

"You all right?" he asked.

Kate nodded. She was still trembling slightly from the backwash of adrenaline.

"He wasn't expecting that," she said.

"No, he wasn't," Anderton agreed. He pushed his hands through this hair and dropped them to his sides, exhaling loudly. "There'll be no more out of him tonight. He won't be in any fit state."

Kate nodded. She knew that Vertz was probably being sedated right about now. She took a deep breath. Her trembling gradually stopped, but she felt empty, hollow, and suddenly depressed.

"Fancy a drink?" said Anderton suddenly.

Kate looked at him in surprise, so shocked she didn't at first know how to answer.

"Now?" she managed, after a moment.

"Yes, right now."

She was still so surprised she agreed without thinking.

Once they were in the pub and sat down with their drinks, the awkwardness between them threatened to return. Kate cast about for something to say, something to break the conversational deadlock, but she couldn't think of anything that didn't have some sort of negative connotation. She took a hurried sip of her orange juice.

"Do you ever drink?" asked Anderton abruptly. "Alcohol, I mean."

Kate shrugged. "Sometimes. At Christmas. It's just not my thing."

"Why is that?"

"Does there have to be a reason?"

"There normally is."

Kate sighed. "My mum's a drinker. Not exactly an alcoholic but—well, perhaps she is an alcoholic. I don't really know. She drinks too much, anyway." Talking of her mother reminded her of Peter and the email she'd discovered. She must look into that when she got home later. "It's just not something I enjoy, I'm afraid."

"Don't apologise." Anderton turned his pint glass around a few times. "You'll probably outlive us all." He looked up into her eyes. "Or perhaps you've got plenty of other secret vices."

Kate smiled in order to hide the sudden physical jolt his words had given her. "I do have a secret fondness for *Gardener's World*."

Anderton actually laughed. Then the smile from his face dropped abruptly and another awkward silence fell.

"Sir," said Kate after a moment, rather hesitatingly. She wasn't exactly sure what she wanted to say. "This case—"

"What about it?"

Kate sat up a little straighter. Then she shook her head. "I'm sorry, I don't know what I'm trying to say. I'm confused."

"Please tell me you're not hiding anything else from me that I need to know."

"No," said Kate, shocked and a little hurt. "All I mean is—oh, I don't know. There's something more to this case than what we're seeing, what we're investigating. Can't you feel it too, sir? There's something underneath it all that we haven't got yet."

Anderton was regarding her intently. "I think I know what you mean."

Kate dropped her head momentarily into her hands. When she raised it, she looked Anderton directly in the eye.

"There's so much *rage* in this case," she murmured. "Everyone connected with Elodie is just so angry. Vertz. Her mother. Her stepfather. There's this constant, simmering undercurrent of anger everywhere."

"Yes, there is."

Anderton suddenly sounded exhausted. There was another beat of silence. Kate was about to speak again when he pre-empted her.

"I owe you an apology, Kate."

Kate went blank for a moment.

"You do?" she said.

"Yes. I was totally wrong to speak to you like I did the other day. It was extremely unprofessional of me, and for that I sincerely apologise."

Kate muttered, "That's all right." What else could she say?

Anderton leaned forward a little.

"I'm not used to apologising," he said. "'Never apologise, never explain.' That was always my motto."

"Everyone thinks it was Churchill who said that," said Kate. "But it was actually some Victorian admiral, I can't remember his name."

Anderton grinned. "I'll let you off. Anyway, things... circumstances change. I'm sorry."

"It's fine," said Kate, a little awkwardly. "I should have come to see you first of all, anyway. It was my fault as—as much as yours."

Silence returned but this time it was easier. They had nearly reached the end of the drinks, and Kate opened her mouth to ask if he wanted another. Again, he pre-empted her.

"My marriage is breaking down," he said. Kate was again

so surprised she was struck dumb. Anderton went on. "Well, breaking down is too positive. It's broken. It's over."

"I'm sorry."

Anderton leant back in his chair, staring up at the ceiling.

"When you came into my office the other day, I'd just finished a call to my soon-to-be-ex wife. I was barely thinking straight, I was so upset. And then you came in and told me something that, ordinarily, would just merit a brief ticking off. It seemed like the last straw, just then. I blew up—"

"I know," said Kate. "I was there."

Anderton gave her a tired smile. "You chose the worst possible moment and bore the brunt of it. I'm sorry."

Their eyes met again, and Kate was again aware of something she'd been forcing down for so long that she'd almost forgotten it was there. Her attraction, her desire for Anderton crystallised in one long, charged moment. What made it worse was that she knew he was suddenly aware of it too. There was a breathless pause in which all the hubbub surrounding them faded away and there was just the two of them, eyes locked, leaning towards each other over the table.

Anderton put a hand over hers.

"Kate—"

Kate shot to her feet, knocking over her glass, dislodging his hand.

"Just going to the loo—back in a moment."

She hurried down the stairs to the toilets in the basement of the pub, almost falling in her haste to get away from him. She locked herself in a cubicle and sat on the closed seat for a moment, her hands over her eyes. *He's married, he's your boss; don't go there. He's married, he's your boss; don't go there.* She was shaken with the intensity of her desire, by the raw, urgent hunger she felt for him. *He's married, even if it's over. He's your boss. Just get up, go back, smile, say goodbye, and leave.*

As it turned out, she needn't have worried. When she got back to the table, Olbeck and Jerry were there, deep in conversation with Anderton. He looked up briefly as she came back and smiled, a quick flicker meant solely for her. Kate sat down, grateful for the company of the others.

For the rest of the evening, she barely said a word.

Chapter Eighteen

THERE WAS NO WAY THAT anyone would be questioning Nathan Vertz the next morning. Kate had been informed that when the doctor's sedative had worn off, Vertz had launched a bleary attack on his cell door: kicking it, shouting, rebounding off the frame to stumble to his knees. The doctor had been called again and had examined him, announcing that no interrogation would be possible for some time. Two representatives from the Mental Health Team were called and spent several hours with Vertz in his cell. Anderton had him under twenty-four-hour observation. Kate knew as well as Anderton that if a vulnerable suspect wanted to kill themselves, they would do their best to find a way.

"I've not lost one on my watch yet, and I'm not about to start now," Anderton said, striding ahead of Kate down the corridor back to the office. "We've got another day, and then we'll have to charge him or let him go again."

"I know," puffed Kate, hurrying to keep up. She wondered whether she'd mistaken that electric moment between the two of them the night before. Thank God she hadn't done anything about it. Best to put it to the back of her mind once more and focus all her energies on the job.

This good intention buoyed her up for all of five minutes once she sat down at her desk. She was very tired after a restless night with bad dreams and fractured sleep. She made herself a strong coffee, rubbed her eyes, and sat down to bury herself in paperwork. For once, she was glad of Olbeck sitting across from her and moaning softly that his head was killing him. He still found time to respond to whomever it was that kept sending him text messages, sending his phone buzzing and skittering across the desk like a large, shiny insect.

"Would you turn that off?" snapped Kate eventually, unable to take any more.

Olbeck gave her a hurt look. Kate pinched the bridge of her nose and tried to concentrate. Something was nagging at the back of her mind. Something about a phone message. She stared mindlessly into space for five minutes before she remembered.

She took out her own phone and hunted through the applications until she came to her photograph storage. There was the one she'd taken of the screen of Peter Buckley's laptop, the picture of the email that had piqued her curiosity.

From: gil450231@gmail.com
To: pbuckley@hotmail.co.uk
Subject: Alice
Message: got those files you were looking for. Check new website https://www.nys1o16.com.

Kate brought up an internet browser on her computer and typed in the website address. A blank blue screen came up with a password-protected log-in box in the middle. Kate frowned. She tried typing in Peter's name and 'password,' then his email address and 'password.' Error messages came up. She sat back, blowing out her cheeks. There was no way she was going to be able to guess his password, and she didn't know whether the site would automatically log her out after a certain number of erroneous attempts. She tapped her pen against her jaw for a moment and then picked up the phone.

"I'm heading down to IT," she said to Olbeck after a short telephone conversation. He grunted, finally intent on his work.

"Hi Sam," said Kate to Sam Hollington, the youngest, newest and keenest member of the Abbeyford team's Information and Technology Department.

"Hi Kate. What've you got for me?"

Sam had a round face, round wire-framed spectacles, and a mop of curly black hair. He reminded Kate of a Labrador puppy, in the nicest possible way.

"Can you check out a website for me? Who owns it, who the domain is registered to—anything, really."

"No probs. Gimme the URL and leave it with me."

Kate resisted the urge to pat him on the head. "You're a star. Thanks Sam."

"When do you need it?"

Kate paused, her hand on the door handle.

"No real hurry," she said. "It's probably not important. Whenever you can do it."

"Righto."

Checking her watch as she reached the ground floor—IT was located in the depths of the basement—Kate could see it was nearly one o'clock. Lunchtime. She hesitated, debating whether to drag Olbeck to the canteen or head outside to grab some fresh air and a sandwich. The lure of the outside won. She pushed the door open to the station foyer and immediately spotted Jay and Courtney, waiting side by side on the uncomfortable chairs against the wall. Both of them looked scared and small and young.

Kate reached them in three large strides. They both stood up together and the three of them stood in an odd little huddle for a moment.

Kate put both of her hands on their arms, one on each.

"What's wrong?"

Jay swallowed. His face was noticeably thinner, his eyes ringed with shadow.

"I've come to change my statement," he said.

The floor rocked for a moment. Kate closed her eyes and opened them again.

Courtney put her hand into Kate's, much as she had when she was a little girl.

"Sis—"

"Why—why now, Jay?" whispered Kate. She had a sudden, piercing flash of memory: baby Jay in her mother's arms, smiling gummily up at his big sister, clamping his tiny fingers around Kate's thumb. He used to grab onto her fingers while she was feeding him and pull her hand up and down as he sucked at the bottle, surprisingly strong for a baby. She fought the urge to turn him around bodily and push him back out the door into the street, before it was too late.

"I have to, sis," he said. He was deathly pale, but his chin was up, his shoulders squared. Kate knew she couldn't stop him. She stepped back, Courtney's hand slipping from hers.

Kate handed Jay over to Theo and watched as the two men walked away along the corridor to the interview rooms. Her ears buzzed. What was Jay going to say? What was he going to confess to? A bubble of nausea came up into her throat.

Courtney was still standing beside her, almost hanging onto her arm. Kate turned to her little sister.

"Do you—do you know this is about?"

Courtney, her eyes huge, her mouth pinched, nodded.

Kate swallowed. "I can't talk to you right now, Courtney. Don't wait. You should go home."

Courtney shook her head.

"I want to wait for Jay."

How could Kate tell her that she might wait all night, all the next day? How could she tell her that he might not be released at all?

She put her hands on Courtney's shoulders.

"Don't wait here, darling. It might take—it might take a long time. Why not go home?"

"I don't want to."

"All right," Kate said helplessly. "How about I give you some money and you find yourself a coffee shop or something? Have a look around the shops?"

For a second she thought Courtney was going to argue with her. Then the younger woman's eyes fell and she nodded.

"Okay."

Kate pulled her into a quick hug.

"Give me a sec," she said, her mouth against Courtney's messy hair. "Let me get my purse. I won't be long."

She ran along the corridor and up the stairs, not waiting for the lifts. What room had Jay been taken to? At her desk, Kate grabbed her handbag and riffled through it for her purse. The phone on her desk rang.

She hesitated. For a moment, she was determined not to answer it. Then duty got the better of her and she snatched it up.

"Kate Redman."

"Kate, it's Sam." For a second, she had to think about who that was. Because of her state of mind, it took her a moment to recognise his voice.

"Sam, I'm kind of busy right now—"

"It's about that website you asked me to look at." Now she could hear the shock in his voice. "I think you need to see it."

"Oh God—" Kate squeezed her eyes shut for a second. "Can't it wait?"

"I think you need to see it."

Kate breathed out as slowly as she could, tamping down a scream of frustration. It wasn't Sam's fault, after all.

"Okay," she said, after a moment. "I'm on my way."

She pounded back to the foyer, tucked a tenner in Courtney's hand and kissed her. "Now, don't *worry*," she emphasized, gently propelling her sister out of the station entrance. "Come back in a few hours. Text me and I'll come down and meet you."

Courtney gave her a wan smile and trotted obediently down the station steps at the entrance. Kate watched her cross the road and waved when she turned back for a last look before disappearing around the corner. Then Kate swivelled on her heel and ran back across the foyer, heading for the steps to the basement. She had to physically force herself past the turn off to the interview rooms. What in God's name was Jay confessing to in there?

Sam met her at the door to the IT department. His round, friendly face was pale, his freckles standing out.

"What is it?" asked Kate, trying not to sound as impatient as she felt.

He said nothing but beckoned her towards his desk. His monitor was showing a screensaver of a poster from the film *Watchmen*.

"I know you didn't ask me to hack into it," Sam said, bent over his desk and keying in what was obviously his password. "But I thought I'd give it a go. Anyway—"

"You can do that?" Kate said, moving closer.

Sam gave her a worried grin from over his shoulder. "Yeah, of course. But anyway, I wish I hadn't." He straightened up and looked around to see if anyone was near them. "Look."

He moved away from the screen. Kate heard herself grunt, an involuntary noise of shock. Hand to her mouth, she took in the images on the screen. Nice Young Sluts! screamed the header. Kate's gaze moved from one girl to the other. Incredibly, some were smiling, or at least their teeth were bared. Most were not.

"Oh my God."

Sam and Kate exchanged a glance of shared horror. Then Kate put her hand over her eyes.

"Put the screen saver on again. Please."

Sam tapped keys. Kate sat down heavily in his seat.

"Did you find out who it's registered to?" she said, after a moment of catching her breath.

"Of course. That's the first thing I did. The WHOIS was cloaked, but I soon got past that." He took a sheet of paper from his in-tray. "It's all on there. There you are. Registered to a G. Lightbody. The sick bugger."

Kate grabbed the paper from him and tried to hold it steady in her shaking hand. There it was, in black and white. She stared at the name and then past it, seeing nothing, her mind whirring. There was a moment of blackness, of staring into the void, and then a massive flare of light, comprehension exploding in a burst of sparks. She actually saw it, like fireworks in her mind.

"What should I do?" said Sam. "I'm kind of freaked out by that being on my computer."

Kate leapt up.

"Get everything you can on it," she said, already moving away. "Screenshots, print outs, anything. Whatever trail you can find from that site. IP addresses, any emails, *anything*. Get everyone onto it."

"Really?" said Sam. "Everyone?"

"Everyone. Thanks Sam. Got to go!"

She was already running by the time she got to the door. She leapt up the stairs, paused for a quick scan of the foyer—no sign of Courtney—before running up to the office. Olbeck was there, just putting on his coat.

"Come with me," gasped Kate, so breathless she could barely form the words.

"Where are we going?"

She grabbed his arm and pulled.

"Anderton's office. Right now."

Chapter Nineteen

AT NINE O'CLOCK THAT NIGHT, Kate was slumped on her sofa with Courtney, the two of them digesting a greasy Chinese takeaway. Watching television, she had the surreal experience of seeing herself on the news. It had happened a couple of times before, but she still hadn't got used to it. There she was, flanking Graham Lightbody as he was escorted from the grounds of Rawlwood College. Anderton loomed on the other side of him. Lightbody was a small man, but he looked even more shrunken on the screen. He'd been trembling as they walked away towards the police car.

Kate could see her own face on the screen, just briefly in the shot as she got into the car after their suspect; she was frowning and trying not to. She wondered whether the viewers of the local news would notice. Would they realise it was because she was concentrating hard on not punching Graham Lightbody in the face?

"Look, it's you," exclaimed Courtney. "Look, sis! You're on the news."

"I know." Kate struggled up to a sitting position.

"You're famous."

"Hardly. Anyway, everyone will be looking at him, not me."

"That sick bastard." Courtney looked towards the floor, her hair falling forward to hide her face. Kate knew she was thinking about Peter Buckley. Had *he* been arrested yet? She hoped so. Anderton had expressly forbidden her to be a part of that team.

Kate had capitulated without protest, knowing she wouldn't be able to trust herself with either Peter Buckley or her mother.

As if summoned by thought, Kate's mobile rang and the name Mary Redman flashed up on the screen. Caught unawares, Kate had time to think *why don't I have her number saved as 'Mum?'* She pressed the button to take the call before she could come up with the answer.

"You bitch, Kelly!"

From years of experience, Kate could usually gauge her mother's precise level of drunkenness simply by the slur in her voice. This time, Mary's inebriation was harder to place, though, given the fury that was emanating from the receiver.

"Mum—"

"Don't fucking 'mum' me! I bet you were just waiting for the chance to ruin things for me, weren't you? It's those coppers who have ruined you, you think the worst of everyone, you can't even treat your own mother with a bit of respect—"

Courtney was looking at her, wide-eyed. Kate tried to smile reassuringly through the battering of her right ear drum.

"Mum—"

"You're a liability, Kelly, you never had no respect for me, ever—"

"You're drunk," said Kate. She said it coldly, trying to keep a lid on her own anger.

"So what if I fucking am? You're driving me to it."

"I want to talk to you when you're sober."

"I know why you did this," said Mary, half sobbing. Kate heard the smash of a glass on the other end of the line and winced. "You're jealous. Jealous of me."

Kate laughed mirthlessly. She could feel her hold on her temper gradually slipping, like an oiled bottle through slick fingers.

"Yeah, right, Mum. I'm jealous."

"Too right you are. Perhaps if you got yourself a man, you

wouldn't go around trying to ruin everyone's else's. Eh? Eh, Kelly? Tell me I'm wrong. Tell me I'm wrong! Tell me—"

Kate pressed the 'end call' button as viciously as she could. Then she threw the phone down hard on the sofa and fought the urge to punch the cushion next to her while screaming out her rage. Instead, she dropped her head into her hands, breathing raggedly. After a moment, she felt the timid touch of Courtney's hand on her trembling shoulder.

"Sis?" Courtney whispered.

Kate sat up and smoothed her hair back, breathing deeply.

"It's all right," she began. "Listen, Courtney—"

The doorbell interrupted her.

"Who's that?" Courtney said, getting up and moving towards the door.

"Wait." Kate put a hand out to stop her. She had a horrible feeling it might be press, although that might just be paranoia from watching herself on the news. She peeked cautiously out from behind the living room curtains. It was a man on the doorstep but who it was, she couldn't quite make out...in that moment, the figure turned, and she realised it was Jay.

"Are you okay? Are you okay?" was all that she could say, moments later, as she stood with her arms around him on the doorstep, the two of them swaying slightly. The police had let him go. She tightened her arms around him for a moment, squeezing him so he cried out in mock protest.

Kate released him. By now, Courtney had come into the hallway. She shrieked and flung herself at her brother.

"Jesus," he gasped, staggering backwards. "I'm all right. Let me sit down, at least."

The two girls half dragged him into the living room and pushed him down onto the sofa.

"They let you go," said Courtney, still hugging him.

Jay smiled up at Kate. He had a strange kind of euphoria about him—a shaky sort of smile pinned to his face. He put one arm around Courtney and leant back, sighing out what sounded like a long-pent-up breath.

Kate sat down on the other chair. She was so relieved she was almost shaking. If they'd released him, then that meant...

"What happened, Jay?"

"Can I have a drink first?"

Kate got him a glass of wine, the last of the bottle that Olbeck had brought with him on the night they'd first seen Nathan Vertz on the small screen. Jay tossed it back in three mouthfuls.

"I needed that," he said with a gasp in his voice.

"What *happened*?"

"I changed my statement."

"They didn't charge you?"

"*Charge* me? Of course not. Charge me with what? I got a caution, that's all."

"A caution..." Kate got up and began pacing around the room. Then she came and sat down again.

"Tell me—tell us about it."

Jay put a hand to his forehead for a second, rubbing his temple.

"It was all over the papers...about Nathan Vertz, I mean. How he was under arrest for Elodie's murder." Kate nodded, listening intently. "Well, sis, that's when I knew I had to do something. I knew he couldn't have killed her."

"How did you know?" whispered Kate. Despite the fact he'd been released, despite the fact he was her brother, a tiny part of her was dreading hearing him say the words *because I killed her*.

But of course, he hadn't. Jay confirmed that with his next sentence.

"I knew he couldn't have killed her because he was with me most of the night. We were definitely together during the time of the murder."

"With you?"

"Yeah." For the first time, Jay dropped his gaze.

"Right," said Kate. "Clearly you mean—what do you mean? What were you doing?"

Jay had a small, sheepish smile on his lips.

"Massive amounts of charlie, sis. I'm sorry."

"Charlie? Cocaine? Oh Jay—" Kate checked herself, the first exclamation of anger choked down. Now was not the time for a lecture on the perils of drugs. "All right, I'm not thrilled to hear that. But we'll get to that later. You and Nathan were together on the night Elodie died?"

"Yeah. Most of the night, actually. You know how it is—" Now it was Jay's turn to check himself. "All right, so you don't know how it is. Anyway—I knew he wasn't anywhere near Elodie for most of the night. Tom vouched for him too."

"Tom?"

"Lorelei's singer. He wasn't with us all night—he just bought some weed off Nathan and went home—but he was there for some of it."

Kate sighed and sat back against the back of the sofa. She looked at her brother with a mixture of pride, anger and exasperation.

"Why now, Jay?" she asked. "Why come clean now? When I think of all that time I spent trying to persuade you to even give a bloody statement... Why on Earth didn't you mention this when they arrested you, for God's sake?"

Jay rolled his eyes. "Why d'you think? I didn't fancy getting banged up in the slammer for doing Class A's, did I? I knew they had no evidence that showed I had anything to do with Elodie being killed. I mean, I know that because I didn't do it. I was *going* to mention it if I thought they wouldn't let me go. Tom would have backed me up if he had to, just like he did for Nathan."

"So you put yourself back in danger of arrest to clear Nathan Vertz's name?" said Kate, slowly. "Why? He's not your friend. I didn't even know you knew him."

"I barely do know him. That wasn't why I did it." Jay looked

Kate directly in the eyes, as if to give extra weight to his next few words. "I did it for Elodie."

"Elodie—"

Jay nodded. "I did it for Elodie. She loved Nathan. I mean, she really loved him. I didn't like him, I didn't like him giving her drugs, but it was her decision, after all. He didn't push her into it. She loved him, and he loved her."

"But what about you?" Kate leant forward and put her hand on Jay's arm. "You loved her too, didn't you?"

Jay had a strange expression on his face, half smile, half grimace. He shook his head.

"I liked her," he said slowly. "I fancied her. I thought sometimes I *did* love her, or that I was in love with her, whatever you want to call it. But there was something that put me off. Elodie was hard work. She wasn't…there was something wrong with her. Something damaged. Christ knows I've had enough practice at spotting that. Know what I mean, sis? Eh, Courtney?"

His two sisters didn't agree or contradict him. They were all at that moment thinking of their mother and their chaotic childhood, the childhood that they seemed to have come through in one piece, if only just.

Kate glanced at her mobile phone, half hidden beneath a cushion. *You bitch, Kelly*. What kind of mother said that to her own child?

Jay went on. "I guess I just knew, somehow, that I had to leave her well alone. I knew she'd be bad for me."

Kate opened her mouth to speak, but he hadn't finished.

"Maybe I should have, though," he said quietly. "Maybe I should have. I don't know. Right now, I'm feeling like I—I let her down. That I should have tried harder to help her. That's why I had to do what I just did. Because I feel like I let Elodie down, and I should have done more to help her. This is the only thing I could do."

His voice broke and he put a hand up to his eyes. Courtney put an arm around him from where she was sitting next to him on the sofa and laid her cheek against his shuddering back.

Kate sat back, easing the ache in her shoulders.

"What about you, Courtney?" she asked, feeling as if she may as well uncover all the dark secrets at once. "What were you trying to tell me the other day? Was it about Jay? Or was it..." She stopped and swallowed. "Was it about Peter?"

Courtney didn't blush. Instead her features seemed to shrink a little, pulling together as if something were tightening inside her. Kate saw, and her heart sank.

"Oh Christ," she said. "Did he do something to you? What did he do?"

Courtney shook her head violently, and Kate remembered to breathe again.

"Not me," she said. "He never laid a finger on me. I saw him taking photos of Jade."

Kate's lungs locked up again. "Photos? What kind of photos?"

Courtney shook her head again, her big, dark eyes wide.

"Not *those* kind. Just pictures on his phone. But I just—I didn't like it. I thought it was weird. 'Cos Jade didn't know he was taking them. I didn't know who to tell, what to do or nothing."

Kate pressed her trembling hands together. She thought of her little sister, fourteen years old, and Peter Buckley lurking behind doors and windows with his phone, snapping away. If she saw that man again, she would kill him and sod her job. She took a deep breath.

"Did you tell Mum?"

Jay half laughed. Courtney, looking miserable, nodded. "What did she say?"

"She just went crazy mad. Shouted a lot and told me I was wrong."

Kate sat silently, almost felled again by another wave of anger, this time against her mother. How could Mary be so blind, so unreasonable; how *could* she? To think of poor Courtney, trying to do the best she could for her baby sister, verbally and possibly physically abused by the one person who was supposed to keep her daughters safe... For a moment, she found herself reaching for her mobile, determined to have it out with her mother, before sanity prevailed and she sat back against the cushions of the sofa, clenching her teeth with suppressed rage.

She pulled herself together. Courtney and Jay were looking at her anxiously. She sat up straight and tried to smile reassuringly at them. She wasn't a mother (*not a* real *one at least*, that hateful little voice whispered) but with these two, she felt like more than a big sister. They were her responsibility. They had to be, because who else was going to look after them?

"All right," she said eventually. "Try not to worry, Courts. I won't let anything happen to Jade. I promise you."

Later, when both Jay and Courtney were asleep, Kate sat up in her own bed with her laptop warming her legs under the covers. She brought up the internet browser and typed Nathan Vertz's name into the search box. Patiently, she followed each link, reading about the Butterkins films, interviews with Nathan as a boy, his Wikipedia page again. At one point, she got up and made herself a strong coffee, shivering in the cold kitchen as the kettle boiled. Back at the computer, she dug down into the third and fourth page of links, forcing her eyelids to remain open. Why was she doing this? What was she hoping to achieve? She asked herself this, several times, but still she kept reading.

A name caught her eye in the metadata of one of the links to Vertz's name—the name of a now-notorious television presenter of the seventies and eighties. Curious, Kate clicked on the link, which brought her through to a newspaper article reporting on the out-of-court settlement by the presenter to the family of Nathan Vertz. She rubbed her tired eyes and read on, several phrases leaping out at her. *Sexual abuse of a minor...civil case... payment of thousands...several other cases due to come to court...*

Kate thought for a moment, biting her lip. So Nathan Vertz had suffered sexual abuse as a little boy? Or had accused someone of abusing him, at least?

She read through the reportage again. What kind of parents accept an out-of-court settlement for something so serious? She leant back against the headboard and closed her eyes. No wonder Vertz was depressed.

She could feel herself falling backwards into sleep. Yawning, she closed the laptop, put it on the floor next to her bed and lay down, pulling the duvet cover up to her chin.

Chapter Twenty

The water of the river was green, translucent, dappled with sunlight. It was not cold, but as warm as a bath, as warm as the waters of the tropics. Kate swam easily through the waterweeds, which tangled and tugged at her arms and legs. Brightly-coloured fish wound in and out of the water plants, the kind of fish never seen in a British river but only in the land of dreams; their appearance caused Kate no surprise.

As she swam, she became aware of someone beside her and turned. It was Elodie, dead Elodie, the bones of her skull showing beneath the bleached skin of her face. Kate felt no fear; she was glad to see her. The two women swam side by side through the wavering, pellucid water. Then Elodie reached out for Kate, the hard bones of her skeletal hand winding around Kate's living fingers. She was pulling Kate through the water, up, urging her on, up, up...until Kate's face broke through the surface of the river into the dazzle of light beyond...

Kate woke then, her eyes clicking open just as if someone had thrown a switch in her brain. She stared up at the barely visible ceiling, looking blankly through the early morning darkness. She could still feel the touch of Elodie's hand in hers, a fading ghost-memory. Then she sighed out loud. The pieces were falling into place, click, click, click... there were no fireworks this time, no bright flare of comprehension: just a gradual clearing of the fog, the surface of the river becoming transparent so the hidden, drowned things beneath became visible.

It was six o'clock in the morning; too early to call. Kate got up, showered, dressed and breakfasted, moving quietly so as not to wake the others but jittery with impatience. At quarter to seven, she picked up the phone.

Anderton answered on the third ring. He sounded as wide awake as she was—perhaps he was an early riser. Or perhaps he'd been waiting for her to call.

He didn't say much but listened intently.

"Where's the evidence?" was all he said after Kate finished speaking.

"I need to talk to Sam. It'll be there, I'm sure of it."

"You're probably right. Meet me at the office and pick up Mark along the way."

Before she left, Kate checked on her siblings. Courtney was buried beneath a bunched duvet, one bare foot poking out the side of the bed. Kate gently covered it up again. Jay was crashed on the sofa, one hand beneath his cheek once again. Kate left them a brief note, scrawled two kisses on the end of it and put on her jacket, winding a scarf tightly about her neck. It was bitterly cold, the sky a leaden grey, a promise of snow in the icy air. She closed the front door almost noiselessly behind her.

She and Olbeck didn't speak much on the way to the office. She'd explained her theory, and he'd sat silently for a few minutes, his quick mind processing what she'd said.

"Don't say anything yet," Kate said, seeing he was preparing to speak. "Let's just see what we've got before we go any further."

"Okay."

They went straight to the IT room, which was bustling with activity. Sam was hunched over one of the impounded laptops, clicking the mouse with bleary determination. He looked up as Kate and Olbeck approached. His round face was pallid with exhaustion, dark circles under his eyes echoing the curve of his glasses.

Kate explained what they wanted as quickly and succinctly as she could. Sam nodded.

"I'll bring it up."

Anderton was already in his office, pacing back and forth. Kate and Olbeck had only just settled themselves when Sam bustled through the doorway with a bundle of papers in his arms.

"Is this everything?" asked Kate.

Sam shook his head. "Not quite. It's everything we could pull from the first two school iPads, Peter Buckley's laptop and Graham Lightbody's home computer. We're still working on the others."

"That's fine," said Anderton, crisply. "Well done, Sam. Excellent work." Sam smiled tiredly and straightened up a little. "Keep at it and let us have it when you do."

He waited until the door closed. Then Anderton spread the sheets out across his desk.

"Cross check against this list," he said. "We may as well see what we're dealing with here at the same time."

The room filled with the busy feel of intense concentration. Looking at the sheets of paper in her hand, Kate could clearly see the email trails between Peter Buckley and Graham Lightbody's many email accounts. Swapping passwords for closed forums, sending links to protected sites. How long had the two of them known each other? How had they met? The name Alice cropped up several times. A victim of their sick fantasies? An abused child? Kate could feel her mouth turning down. Then she realised. Alice, as in *Alice in Wonderland*. Kate remembered reading about the real-life Alice in a magazine article, recalled the rumours and innuendo that circled around the relationship between Lewis Carroll and his seven-year-old muse, Alice Liddell. Kate could recall them now; those weird, provocative photographs of the little girl who'd inspired the classic, taken by the writer of the book. She shuddered.

It was Olbeck who found what they were looking for. Kate and Anderton noticed it seconds after he did. There was a moment of breathless hush. Olbeck put one finger out, gently, touching it to the name they were looking for. He looked up at the other two.

"Of course," Anderton said, softly. "The spider at the centre of the whole rotten web."

They made their way to Anderton's car. As they passed the door that led to the cells, Kate remembered Vertz and asked about him.

"Released on bail," said Anderton, stepping quickly from stair to stair. "He'll be up for possession, intent to supply and a few other things I can think to throw at him, but we couldn't hold him on the murder charge."

"No, I know," said Kate. "So, he's free then?"

Anderton had reached the car. He held the back door open for her, courteously.

"For now," he said. "Why? What's the problem?"

Kate hesitated. Until that moment, she hadn't thought that there was a problem. Now, she was conscious of a faint, creeping sense of unease.

"Nothing," she said, after a second's thought. She ducked into the car and clipped on her belt. "There's no problem."

"He *was* assessed by the Psych Team," said Anderton, starting the car. "They clearly didn't think he was too much of a risk to himself."

"Yes, I know." Kate saw Olbeck turning round in his seat to catch her eye. He didn't have to say anything—one glance was enough. "It doesn't matter."

Olbeck turned back in his seat to face the front. Anderton glanced at him and caught Kate's eye in the mirror. He didn't say anything, but he pushed down on the accelerator with just a little more pressure.

They didn't say anything else for the duration of the drive. At one point, they passed the river, sparkling in the weak winter sunshine. How cold it must have been for Mike Deedham, jumping in to save Elodie, who was then far beyond saving. When could she have been saved? Why hadn't anyone helped her, when it hadn't been too late?

Kate found she had her eyes shut. She opened them to see the car pulling into the driveway of their destination. The trees were bare, skeletal now: rustling heaps of dead leaves piled against the banks. Anderton was slowing the car. Kate stared at the house before them, willing it to look normal, untouched, unchanged from when she'd last seen it. She spotted the half-open door straight away, but what with the noise of the car and the crunch of its wheels over the gravel, the three officers didn't hear the screaming until the engine was switched off.

They were out of the car in seconds and running towards the open door, Anderton in the lead. He kicked the partly open door open and as they stampeded into the hallway, the screaming became much louder, as if they'd been listening to it underwater and had just cleared the surface. Kate saw a bloodied hand print on the cream paint of the hallway wall, smeared but still recognisable. Drips of blood made a gory trail along the corridor. Then they were in the room with the screaming woman.

Genevieve Duncan was crouched in a foetal position in the armchair where Kate had seen her sitting before, where she'd pulled and picked at the arms. She had her hands up to her face in a characteristic gesture, her open mouth a black, vibrating hole beneath her clenched fingers. The body of Mr Duncan lay on the living room carpet. Because of the pattern of the carpet, the blood stains surrounding him were not immediately obvious, but when Kate saw the damage done to his head and face, she felt like screaming herself.

They found Nathan Vertz in the garden, sitting slackly on the steps that led down to the lawn. He was staring into space, his bloodstained hands hanging loosely at his sides. He didn't try to run or evade arrest. Kate had the impression, as Anderton cautioned him and Olbeck snapped the cuffs around his spattered wrists, that he was somewhere far away, a refugee in a distant land, hiding inside an inner landscape where, perhaps, he'd found some measure of blank and noiseless peace.

Chapter Twenty One

The woman in front of them sat tensely, sometimes clasping her hands together in front of her, sometimes holding each elbow, hugging her body protectively. Her face, the template for Elodie's golden looks, was rigid; the jawline was sharp, the cheekbones showing bluishly through the skin. Kate wondered whether Genevieve Duncan ever relaxed, if she ever sat in a loose, unstructured way. Well, even if she had once, she would probably never do so again.

As reserved as the woman's posture was, the same could not be said of her voice. She was talking in an endless, brittle monotone, floods of words—all the words, Kate sensed, that she had wanted to say for years but could, or would, not.

"It was always about *her*," said Mrs Duncan. Her hands pressed together once more. "I was always second-best, always. Even with my first husband, Elodie's father... The way he used to fawn over her was just sickening. After she was born, he barely gave me a second glance. Perhaps that would have changed, I don't know... He killed himself, you know, oh, not deliberately, but he drank too much and smashed himself up in his car. Elodie was only five. It was difficult, just the two of us. Two *females* in one house. That was something my mother always said to me: a house isn't big enough for two women, and she certainly made sure that was true in ours—"

Kate sat opposite from her, keeping as neutral a face as she could. Anderton and Olbeck were also in the room, sat slightly back from the table. The duty solicitor, a care-worn, grey-haired woman in her fifties sat next to Genevieve.

"Then I met Tom. I thought he was the answer to my prayers, a nice, handsome, well-off man willing to take on another man's daughter. I was so happy when he proposed." Mrs Duncan gave a laugh that was half sob. "And it was all to do with Elodie. She was all he wanted. Do you know what it's like to have your husband reject you for your own daughter? Do you have any comprehension of how humiliating that was? It was never about me. It was all about *her*."

Kate could see Olbeck struggle not to show the distaste this woman's self-pitying rant was engendering. She had no such qualms herself.

"Your husband was sexually abusing your daughter, Mrs Duncan," she said, making no attempt to hide the disgust in her voice. She wondered whether Anderton would pull her up. He remained silent.

Mrs Duncan looked at her with scorn.

"She encouraged him," she said, and this time, Olbeck did make a sound, a smothered exclamation of outrage. "She must have encouraged him."

"She was *eight years old* when they met," said Kate. "How can you say that?"

Mrs Duncan seemed not to hear her. She was staring at her hands knotted together on her lap, at the wedding ring on her finger that gleamed under the harsh strip lights.

"He used to read her bedtime stories," she said, *apropos* of nothing. Kate remembered the childish books by Elodie's bed and inwardly shuddered. Was that when the abuse had started? Was Elodie's bedroom so far away from her parents' room because she was trying to get away—or was it that her stepfather had given her that room to be sure of not being overheard?

"Did you daughter tell you she was being abused?" Kate asked.

"Did she *try* to tell you? Did she ask you for help?" She could feel her own hands clenching into fists under cover of the table. She remembered her own mother's reaction to Courtney's plea. "Did you even listen? Or did you tell her she was making it all up?"

"Kate..." said Anderton, and Kate subsided, choking down her anger.

There was silence for a moment. Genevieve Duncan continued to regard her hands as if they fascinated her. Perhaps, thought Kate, they did, considering what they had done.

Anderton spoke quietly.

"Here's what I think happened on that night, Mrs Duncan. Perhaps you'll tell me if I'm right or wrong."

Mrs Duncan gave no indication that she'd heard him. Anderton pressed on regardless. "Elodie got home late that night. She'd quarrelled with Vertz, nothing major, just the normal kind of lovers' tiff that happens now and again. Perhaps that's why she didn't go home with him. If only she had, she might still be alive."

Kate was watching Genevieve Duncan's face keenly. At Anderton's last remark, it contracted very slightly, a bare flicker of the muscles that was quickly controlled. How tightly had this woman kept her emotions over the years? Kate thought of a spring, wound tighter and tighter...until one day, it snaps.

Anderton went on speaking.

"Your husband went to her room, as he was wont to do. Was it every night, Genevieve? Did he ever leave her alone?"

Mrs Duncan said nothing, but a tide of red suffused her face. Was it embarrassment—or fury?

"I think you heard him leave your bed," said Anderton, watching her closely. "You followed him up to Elodie's room. I don't think it was what you saw that compelled you to act. After all, I don't believe for one second you didn't know your daughter was being abused, night after night. No, that wasn't what made you snap. That wasn't what made you do it."

He stopped speaking for a moment. Some sort of titanic

struggle was going on under the skin of Genevieve Duncan's face; years of suppression and denial were being beaten back by the tides of anger.

Anderton spoke again.

"The baby," he said softly, and Mrs Duncan made some sort of noise, a half-choked cry, as if she'd just been struck.

"The baby," repeated Anderton, relentlessly. "You heard Elodie tell her stepfather she was pregnant. You immediately jumped to the conclusion that it was your husband's baby. And that was the tipping point."

"She *said* it was his," gasped Genevieve Duncan. "She told him! She was evil, she was sick...it would have been an abomination..."

"Elodie was wrong," said Anderton. "It was Vertz's baby."

Mrs Duncan was shaking. She looked at Anderton through reddened eyes.

"You killed your daughter," said Anderton, in a deceptively gentle voice. "You and your husband, aghast at what you'd done, realised that you couldn't confess. The scandal would be catastrophic, especially for you, who'd spent so many years in denial of the reality of your family's situation. How could you be brave enough to own up to what you'd done? That admitting your actions would mean everything coming out in the open, everyone knowing the grim truth. What did you do with Vertz's letters to Elodie, Genevieve? Did you burn them?" He paused for breath. "Was it because you couldn't bear to see yet another man loving your daughter? The daughter who, in your eyes, had taken all the love that was meant for you?"

Kate was watching Genevieve's face closely. She could see the change of expression, the eyes filming over a little, the metaphorical shutters coming down. The habit of denial was just too strong.

"I don't know what you're talking about," she said in a choked voice. "I think you want to drive me mad."

"Why put her body in the river, Genevieve? Why do that?"

The woman opposite was silent. Then she laughed a laugh that was not quite sane.

"Ophelia," was all she said.

Kate went cold. She realised that Jay's painting *had* been involved, yet not in the way she'd thought. Had Elodie showed her parents the painting? Had they wanted to incriminate Jay, to find a credible suspect? She actually shuddered. Then she realised that it was more than that. Elodie wasn't Ophelia, was she? Ophelia was sat in this interview room, clasping her hands together: a woman driven mad by the cruelty of a man who couldn't, who wouldn't love her.

There was a long moment of silence.

Genevieve Duncan sat up a little straighter. She seemed to gain a little bit of control over herself.

"I wasn't in my right mind that night," she said. She looked Anderton full in the face. "No, that was it. She'd driven me mad by her behaviour. She wasn't—she was so—sick, so *damaged*. It was a kindness. I wasn't in my right mind. No, I wasn't in my right mind."

That was the last thing she said. She withdrew into herself then, staring at her hands, twisting her wedding ring about her thin finger. Nothing that Anderton or Kate or Olbeck could say shook her into talking again. After twenty fruitless minutes, they gave up and Anderton rang for an officer to escort her to the cells.

There was silence for a moment after Mrs Duncan was taken away. Then Anderton sprang up from his chair.

"Come on," he said. "Debrief time."

When they were all gathered in the incident room, Anderton took up his usual position, pacing back and forth before the whiteboards. He had something in his hand, some thin slip of paper. As he reached Elodie's school photograph, he took what was in his hand and pinned it up on the board next to Elodie's image. It was a photograph of Nathan Vertz as a little boy. Kate recognised it as a publicity shot from the first Butterkins film.

Anderton tapped each photograph.

"Two children," he said. "Two abused children. That was their connection, that's what underpinned their relationship. Do you remember what Vertz said? Anyone?"

Olbeck raised his hand. "He said, 'She knew what it was like.' Something like that, anyway."

Anderton nodded.

"Nathan Vertz entered show business at any extremely young age. He was a little boy, vulnerable and unprotected. I'm sure I don't need to remind you that predators can be found in any sphere—anywhere where children can be found."

Kate nodded, thinking of the crisis currently engulfing the BBC. Vertz had named his abuser, but had the accused been the only one to hurt him? She thought of a little blonde boy, a vulnerable child, the parents who should have protected him too interested in chasing fame and fortune to defend their son. She felt a little sick.

"Vertz and Elodie were drawn towards each other, as damaged people so often are. Vertz was a drug dealer, and Elodie was a drug user, so it could be that their relationship was pragmatic, one of convenience—but I'm not convinced. I think they had a genuine love affair. I think they loved each other as fully as two people who'd never been shown any real love could."

Kate remembered Jay saying much the same thing the other night. For a moment, she gave thanks. No matter what her mother's failings had been, at least Kate had always had someone to love. She'd had people to love her back—her brother and sisters.

Anderton was still speaking.

"Thomas Duncan met Genevieve and Elodie when Elodie was eight years old, as we know. Hideous as it is to contemplate, it's quite probable that he married the mother to enable him to abuse her daughter. He certainly wouldn't be the first paedophile to actively target a single mother to gain her trust and have unfettered access to her children."

Kate thought of her own mother, of Jade and Peter Buckley, and felt sick again. At least she had the satisfaction of knowing he would almost certainly be going to prison, although she hated the idea of her sisters having to give evidence at his trial.

"As you also know, the scale and extent of the abuse at Rawlwood College is still being uncovered. We have several teachers, as well as the headmaster himself, who regularly groomed and abused the children in their care. They targeted the vulnerable ones, the ones who wouldn't speak out."

He pinned a third photograph up on the board, one of a girl with frizzy brown hair. Placed side by side, you could see the resemblance in all three photographs, something in the eyes. A hunted, anxious expression. Kate had seen it, momentarily, at Rawlwood College, before being distracted. It was impossible to see their haunted young faces without tears coming to your eyes.

"Violet Sammidge," said Anderton. He placed a tender finger on her photographed face. "She was one of Graham Lightbody's victims. Possibly one of Duncan's too. She was a young girl, deeply affected by her parents' divorce. An easy target." For a moment, anger vibrated in his voice.

Jane raised her hand.

"You don't think she was murdered too, guv?"

Anderton shook his head. "No, not at all. It was a clear case of suicide. Although..." He paused for a moment, rubbing his chin. "Although you could say she was driven to it by the dreadful actions of Lightbody. So in a sense, he is responsible for her death. Unfortunately, we can't pin that on him."

"He'll get his punishment," said Olbeck, grimly.

"Let's hope so."

Anderton resumed his pacing.

"On the night of the murder, we know Elodie went home after the gig at the Black Horse. We know that her stepfather went up to her room." Kate could see the disgust on her own face mirrored in those of her colleagues. Anderton looked at her. "We have Kate to thank for highlighting the abuse."

Kate shrugged. "Once I'd realised, it just seemed so obvious. But I was wrong as well. I thought her stepfather had killed her."

Anderton tousled his hair and let his hand drop.

"No, Genevieve was the person who strangled Elodie. It's a horrible thought, a mother killing a daughter, but that's what happened. I don't think we'd have to dig too deeply into Genevieve's background to find another story of abuse in *her* childhood. Not that that's any excuse for what she did."

Kate waited until he paused and asked her question. "So Duncan knew Genevieve had killed Elodie?"

"Knew? He almost certainly witnessed it. Why didn't he stop her? Was it because he too thought he was the father of his stepdaughter's baby? Was he in shock? Who knows? He can't tell us."

"Did Nathan Vertz think Thomas Duncan had killed Elodie?" asked Olbeck.

Anderton nodded. "I think so. It tipped him over the edge. He knew about the abuse, of course, but it was the revelation of the baby that drove him to kill. Perhaps all the rage and shame and anger at the abuse he'd suffered in childhood came flooding out. Thomas Duncan became the symbol for what had happened to him as a little boy."

"Poor man," said Kate.

"Yes," said Anderton briefly. "So we have the Duncans colluding to dispose of Elodie's body. You know, Kate, I think they *did* put her body in the river in the hope it would incriminate your brother."

"It nearly did," said Kate, remembering Anderton's rage at her seeming deception. Their eyes met for a moment, and she felt another surge of the attraction that she thought she'd nearly succeeded in tamping down. Did he feel it too? She dropped her gaze, willing herself not to blush.

Anderton cleared his throat.

"A sad case," he said. He turned to the whiteboard and touched the picture of each child gently, just once. "A very sad case. Thank you all for bringing it to the only possible conclusion."

LATER THAT AFTERNOON, KATE SIGNED the last report, capped her pen and pushed her chair away from her desk. She looked over at Olbeck.

"I'm done for the day."

"Good for you. I've still got loads to do."

"Leave it for now, Mark. I'm going for a drive. Why don't you come with me?"

Olbeck considered. Then he stood up and took his coat from the back of his chair.

As they walked towards Kate's car, his phone chimed as a text message came through. "Another new date?" asked Kate, trying to keep the disapproval from her voice as they got into her car.

"Same one, actually," said Olbeck, clipping on his belt. "It'll be our third date."

"Oh, right," said Kate, eyebrows raised. She turned on the engine. "Is it serious?"

Olbeck scoffed. Then he reconsidered.

"Don't know, actually," he said, sounding surprised. "It might be. I like him."

"Good."

Olbeck smiled slyly.

"What about you?"

"What do you mean, 'what about me?'"

"When are we going to get you fixed up?"

"Oh, Mark." For a moment, Anderton's face came into Kate's

mind. She dismissed the jump in her lower belly. "I'm all right on my own."

"Sure?"

"Sure," said Kate, trying to sound firm.

They found a parking space not too far away and got out. It was one of those beautiful winter days with pale sunlight and high, wispy white clouds, the leafless trees like living sculptures. Kate and Olbeck walked along beside the river, their feet scuffing over frost-hardened ridges of mud. As they got closer, Kate could see all the flowers, laid out like a colourful carpet along the riverbank. She and Olbeck stopped a little way away and regarded the heaped blooms. She thought again of the painting with Elodie on the riverbank, pale and blue-lipped, entwined with flowers.

Something caught her eye, a tiny gleam of pale yellow, right at the water's edge. She looked harder and then nudged Olbeck.

"Look."

Olbeck followed her pointing finger past all the gaudy, plastic-wrapped hothouse flowers to the little blossom growing through the frozen mud.

"A primrose?" he said. "Growing in November?"

"Yes."

"That's weird. It's been so cold, you wouldn't have thought it would live."

They regarded the flower for a moment, its delicate yellow petals trembling in the cold wind.

"It's for Elodie," said Kate softly.

Olbeck looked at her quizzically. "It's not like you to be sentimental."

Kate thought of something else Jay had said, that Vertz had said, that even her stepfather had said.

"Elodie was different," she said.

Olbeck was silent. Kate took one last look at the primrose and turned away.

"Come on, time to go home."

They walked back along the riverbank, quietly, shielding their eyes against the sunlight that gleamed from the surface of the glittering river.

THE END

Imago

A Kate Redman Mystery: Book 3

J's Diary

THE FIRST GIRL'S DEATH WAS an accident.

I lifted my pen off of the paper and thought for a bit. My pen was poised to cross it out – the impulse trembled up my arm – but in the end, I left the sentence as it was.

I don't really know why I started writing this diary, account, whatever you'd call it. I suppose I wanted a record of what's happened in my life since the first one. Ever since I realised what I had to do to become complete – to unfold into a whole person rather than inhabit the empty shell of one – there's been another urge, almost as strong: the need to write down *why* I do the things I do. I'm not trying to justify anything to anyone, in the unlikely event that someone reads these diaries. The key thing, I suppose, is to be true to myself, to be truthful when I'm talking to myself as I am here, setting down these words. That's the only meaningful thing to do. If I'd only been true to myself from an early age, none of the bad things would have happened. Or maybe they would. Who knows?

So, in the interest of truth, the first death wasn't really an *accident*. I've just checked my dictionary and the definition of "accident" is something like *an unfortunate event that happens unintentionally*. Her death was certainly unfortunate – for her –

and it was, at the time, unintentional. I didn't plan it; I didn't spends hours and days fantasising about bringing it about as I have done with the other ones. So you could say it was accidental, I suppose, although I'd have a hard time convincing a jury.

It won't come to that, though. Now I'm getting good at this. It's a new skill, as well as a calling, and I've always been a fast learner. It makes me shiver in anticipation when I think that I could go on like this, year after year, getting better each time. Each time more perfect and more fulfilling than the last one. All those girls out there, for me. None of them have any idea that I am watching and waiting, waiting for the next time...the next death. None of them have any idea because I am in disguise. They don't fear me. Quite the opposite. It makes it twice as fun. Fun. That's certainly a surprising choice of words, especially for me, but that's what it is. It *is* fun – as well as the greatest pleasure I've ever known. Why don't they tell you this? Why do they lie? I feel like I'm the keeper of a secret only a few have discovered.

I know the next time will be soon; I've learnt to recognise the signs. I think I even know who it will be. She's oblivious, of course, just as she should be. All the time, I watch and wait, and she has no idea, none at all. And why would she? I'm disguised as myself, the very best disguise there is.

Chapter One

Kate ran.

Her breath rasped in and out of her lungs; her leg muscles burned. A drop of sweat rolled into the corner of her dry mouth. It felt as if she'd been running forever, weaving among the people on the pavements, the shock of her feet hitting the concrete reverberating through her muscles. Every fibre of her being cried out for her to stop, but she couldn't – she was afraid. The man was a sadist, a brutal sadist. She struggled on up a slight incline, her face burning, her lungs crying out for air. At the top of the hill, she had to stop, bent double, gasping for breath. The man following her at an effortless, loping run drew up alongside her.

"Come on, Kate. We've still got two miles to go."

"I can't," gasped Kate, when she had enough oxygen in her lungs to speak. "I'll be sick."

"You won't."

"Will."

The man appeared to relent. "All right. Take a two-minute breather."

Kate staggered over to a convenient bench and fell onto it. She put her roasting face down between her knees.

"Can't – do – this," she said, between gasps.

Detective Sergeant Mark Olbeck sat down beside her and stretched his legs out in front of him.

"It's only a bloody half marathon, for God's sake," he said. "Thirteen miles. It's nothing."

Kate sat back up again, marginally more comfortable, although still breathing hard.

"I'm too – unfit. Someone else will have to – do it."

"You'll *get* fit. That's the whole point of us going out running. Come on, you said you'd do it. It's for charity, remember."

"I can't get fit enough in three weeks."

"Well that's all the time you've got. You've got to be part of the team. If you pull out now, we won't have enough people."

Kate knew this was right. The Abbeyford Charity Half Marathon team from the police station had consisted of Olbeck, Detective Constable Theo Marsh and Detective Constable Ravinder Cheetam until Theo had broken his ankle playing football and had to drop out.

"There's Jerry. And Jane."

"You know as well as I do that Jane's got two small children and no partner. She can't go out in the evenings at the drop of a hat. And Jerry would probably have a coronary or something if we made him run, the poor old bugger."

Kate leant back against the back of the bench and closed her eyes. She knew all this already, which made her feel even worse about her lack of enthusiasm.

"Don't get comfortable," warned Olbeck. "Come on. On we go."

Kate heaved the deepest sigh her abused lungs could muster. Then she lurched to her feet, and they jogged on through the streets of Abbeyford.

They stopped at the bridge that spanned the river Avon, leaning against the stone parapet and watching the glittering waters slide beneath them. It was a beautiful summer's day, the sky blue but wisped with a filmy curtain of white cloud, the sun gaining in strength by the hour.

"You know, Mark, I'm really not sure I can do this," puffed

Kate. She leant her head on her folded arms for a moment and then raised it, looking out at the sparkling water.

"You'll be fine," said Olbeck. "And you'll feel very proud of yourself when you finish."

"I've done plenty of things I'm already proud of," said Kate. "I don't feel that putting one foot in front of the other very quickly qualifies as any kind of great achievement."

Mark grinned. "God, you're narky today."

"It's the unaccustomed blood rushing to my head."

There was a muffled buzzing from Mark's back pocket. He fished his phone out, frowned and answered the call.

"Hello sir. No, we're not doing anything."

Kate waited, knowing it was something serious. She had that familiar feeling she got every time a new case began: tension, anxiety and yes, shamefully, a little bit of excitement, which was tempered with relief – at least she wouldn't have to do any more running that day.

Olbeck said goodbye and put the phone back in his pocket. His partner raised her eyebrows.

"That was Anderton."

"So I gathered. What is it?"

"Dead woman, down by the canal. We've been called in."

"Let's go, then."

Abbeyford was a large market town in the southwest of England. In addition to the river Avon, one of several so named in the country, the town also had a canal running through it. In earlier times, goods had been brought to the town from neighbouring cities, and canal boats pulled by horses moved slowly along the paths by the water to be unloaded at the tiny docks. The canal freight trade had long since gone, and the canal docks in Abbeyford had gradually fallen into disrepair and, eventually, disrepute. The warehouse windows were all broken, the glass in the few remaining panes dulled with dirt and moss. A long-ago fire had gutted one of the buildings, leaving its blackened girders exposed like the charred bones of an animal. Rubbish, dead leaves and dirt were heaped in every corner.

Kate had never been to the area before; she was barely aware of its existence. Perhaps the other Abbeyford residents had a similar knowledge of this part of town, and this was why the killer had chosen to dump the body here. Or had killer and victim met here?

As it turned out, Kate wasn't off the jogging hook after all. She and Olbeck were close enough to the site to make their way there on foot, and Olbeck had insisted that they run, "to get in some more training." Kate arrived at the scene knowing that her face was tomato-red and that her tracksuit was stained with patches of sweat, but after one look at the huddled body of the woman on the ground, these minor concerns faded away.

Scene of Crime officers had already erected the tent that hid the body from prying eyes. Kate and Olbeck ducked under the flap that covered the entrance. The victim was a small, thin woman, with long, dark hair tied tightly back in a high ponytail. She lay on her side, curled in a foetal position, her back to the detectives. One dirty-soled foot was bare; the scuffed silver ballet pump that had fallen from it rested a few inches away. Kate couldn't see any obvious wounds, although the mottled, bare legs were spattered with small amounts of blood.

She studied the scene as intently as she could in the short time that she had, taking in everything that she could see. *Get a feel for the scene*, Anderton was always telling them. *It's amazing what you can pick up without even realising. It can come in very handy as the case progresses.* Kate knew she would never again have this first impression, so she observed with laser-intensity focus, trying to burn the image onto her retinas and into her mind.

Detective Chief Inspector Anderton was there along with Detective Constables Jerry Hindley and Ravinder Cheetam – Rav to his friends and colleagues. The three of them were in a huddle, talking quietly, whilst behind them, the scene was being preserved, photographed and otherwise documented by the Scene of Crime officers. Anderton looked up as Kate and Olbeck approached.

"You got here commendably quickly," was his opening remark. "Glad to see all this running's starting to pay off."

Olbeck gave Kate a 'you *see*?' look but said nothing. He nodded at Jerry and Rav.

"Let's go outside," said Anderton. "Too many people in here."

Outside, the air felt fresh and the sunlight was warm and welcoming on Kate's upturned face.

"What's been happening?" she asked.

"The body was discovered this morning," said Anderton. "A couple of hours ago, so that makes it, what – twelve thirty or so?"

"Who found it?" asked Kate.

"Two young lads. They were a bit reticent about why they were down here in the first place. Probably here to do some tagging or something. They're back at the station at the moment, giving their statements."

"Cause of death?" asked Olbeck.

"We don't yet know. Stanton should be able to tell us more when he's finished – talk of the devil—" Anderton looked up as the white-clad figure of the pathologist emerged from the tent. "Stanton. Stanton!" he called. "What's the quick and dirty?"

Doctor Andrew Stanton joined the group, brightening a little as he realised Kate was amongst them. He had an undisguised admiration for her, which always led to a day's worth of teasing from Olbeck after the three of them met.

"Hi guys. Hi Kate," he added, with special, caressing attention. The other men grinned, and Kate managed to grit her teeth and smile politely at the same time.

"What have we got?" asked Anderton.

Stanton immediately became professional.

"Stab wounds, several of them, mostly through the lower thoracic region. Stomach and lower chest."

Anderton shook his head.

"Definitely one for us, then. Oh well. Any sign of sexual assault?"

"Difficult to tell. I'll be able to give you a better answer once we've done the PM."

"Right," said Anderton. "Stab wounds. That puts another possible spin on things." He didn't elaborate on what this spin could be. "Any chance of fixing the time of death?"

Stanton shrugged.

"Probably sometime early in the morning, very early. Two or three o'clock. You know I can't be accurate at this stage. You'll have to wait for the PM."

"It gives us a starting point," said Anderton, briefly. "Okay, thanks, Andrew. We'll speak later."

Once Doctor Stanton had left, Anderton ducked into the tent, quickly followed by Rav and Olbeck. Kate found herself standing alone with Jerry Hindley, and her heart sank a little. Jerry was the colleague she knew and liked the least. From the very start of her career at Abbeyford, he'd made it plain that he didn't like her. She'd asked Olbeck and Theo why this might be, and they'd explained that it was probably jealously. "You got the promotion he'd been angling for, Kate," Olbeck had said, and although this sounded plausible, it seemed strange that he'd still be acting hurt and resentful two years later. Again she reminded herself that she didn't care about the opinion of someone so petty and sexist. Occasionally she'd attempt to be friendly, wondering whether he'd ever respond in the same way. She tried again now.

"What do you think happened, Jerry?"

He sighed in an irritated manner. "Didn't you hear the guv? We don't know anything other than what you just heard."

Kate said nothing more. Why did she bother? Was she trying to make him like her? Why? She didn't care about his opinion, did she?

She was relieved to see the other officers exit the tent and make their way back to where she stood.

"Do we have an ID on the victim yet, sir?" Kate asked Anderton, provoking an irritated sigh from Jerry. She ignored him.

Anderton shook his head.

"There's no ID at all on the body. No cards, no purse, no bag."

"Really? That's strange. You'd expect her to have a purse at least, even if she didn't use a handbag."

"Exactly," said Anderton. "It was almost certainly removed from the body by our perpetrator." He looked at the still surface of the canal. "We're going to have to have that searched. It could easily be in there, as well as the murder weapon."

Olbeck was glancing around at the buildings surrounding them.

"Any cameras here?" he asked. "CCTV footage would help."

"I can't see any," said Kate, scanning the scene. "It doesn't look the sort of place where people would care about vandalism or theft."

"Right, well," said Anderton. "We need to start digging. We don't know whether the murder actually took place here, although from the blood found at the scene, it seems likely. We don't know who the victim is. We don't know what the murder weapon was – yes, some kind of knife, but what kind? We're currently operating from a standpoint of complete ignorance, and that's not a position I like to be in." He paused for breath. "Let's get back to HQ, and we'll take it from there."

Chapter Two

"The weapon that created these wounds was unusual," said Doctor Telling. She was washing her hands as she spoke, speaking over her shoulder to Kate, who had arrived too late for the actual post mortem. "Very unusual in this kind of case."

"Really? It was a knife, I assume?"

"Oh, yes, that's without doubt. But a knife with a serrated edge. A steak knife or something like that."

"A *steak* knife?" Kate's eyebrows rose. "That is odd."

Doctor Telling finished drying her long, thin fingers. She smiled her unearthly smile. "Yes, I don't believe I've ever come across one used as a murder weapon before. Have you found it, by the way?"

Kate shook her head. "No. No sign of it."

"It should be easy to match it to the wounds if you do."

"Right. Anything else that's pertinent? I know I'll get your report but—"

"Quite a lot." Doctor Telling was taking off her stained white coat. She dropped it into what was obviously a laundry basket. Underneath she wore a rather incongruous floral blouse. "She was a drug user – injection marks all over her. She'd had at least one child. And while I didn't find any semen, there were traces of condom lubricant."

"Hmm," said Kate. "So our perpetrator is savvy enough to cover up. Was she raped?"

Doctor Telling shrugged her thin shoulders. "Possibly. It's unusual for a rapist to use a condom, but it's not unheard of. There's no obvious damage, no bruising or abrasions. It's hard to tell. Do you have an ID on the victim yet?"

"We're running the fingerprints through the database now."

"I think it's likely that the victim was a prostitute."

"Based on what you've told me, I think you're right."

The Abbeyford police station was undergoing something of a renovation. The reception area was now equipped with some fairly convincing wood-grain laminate (Kate deplored the use of laminate but could see that polished wooden floorboards were out of the question, simply as a matter of cost) and had been repainted a fresh and sprightly green. The interview rooms had also been repainted, and Anderton's office now had new carpet.

The room currently being renovated was the team's main office, which meant that everyone had been required to grumblingly pack up all their files and office paraphernalia and shift all their computers to a different room. At least it gave everyone the opportunity to complain about the unfamiliar office chairs and the distance to the coffee machine. It also meant that team meetings now tended to take place in Anderton's freshly carpeted office, which hadn't really been designed for large meetings. There was always a scrimmage for chairs. Today, Kate had successfully acquired one over by the window. She tried to flex her stiff legs, which were still aching from yesterday's exercise session.

Now that meetings were held in his office, Anderton was unable to start things off, as he used to do, by crashing through the door like a human whirlwind. He was also clearly unable to pace about as much as he wanted to. It made Kate chuckle inwardly to see him start out with a firm stride only to bring himself up short as he realised the limitations of the space available.

"Right, team, let's get on. Excuse the by-now-familiar cramped conditions. Anyone know when we move back to the incident room?" No one knew, although Jane tentatively volunteered that it might be next week. "God, let's hope so. Can't work under these conditions. Anyway, where were we?"

Anderton came to a stop in front of the much-reduced set of whiteboards that had migrated over to his office during the renovation. Several crime scene photographs were pinned up already, demonstrating the curled shape of the dead woman, one shoe lying beside her pale, dirty foot.

"You'll be pleased to know that we're now much further forward than we were this morning – we have ID'd the victim. Amanda Renkin, more commonly known as Mandy Renkin. Twenty-six years old, a known prostitute and drug user. The usual, sad story: chaotic childhood, in and out of care homes. Pregnant at seventeen, baby removed from her care shortly after birth." Kate flinched, still unable to hear those words without some sort of emotional reaction. Would she ever be able to?

Anderton continued.

"Convictions for soliciting and drug use. Nothing that comes as any great surprise, poor woman."

"Did she work alone?" asked Olbeck. "I mean, did she have a pimp or something?"

"That's something we'll have to find out. We don't even know if she worked the streets. She may have had a place that she used. Something we need to find out. Talk to some of the usual girls, see if they can tell us anything. Jane, Theo, get onto the CCTV, if there is any in the area. If not, look at what's nearest, see if you can find anything. Jerry, Rav, if there are any residential areas near the crime scene, talk to people. See if they saw or heard anything."

Kate raised her hand.

"Shall Mark and I do her address, sir?"

Anderton nodded. "Yep, first thing. See what you can find. Talk to her relatives, talk to her friends, if she had any. Now I'm sure I don't need to remind you all that the most likely perpetrator in this kind of crime is an ex-partner or even a current partner. Don't let the fact that she was a prostitute blind you to that. Dig into her background. Did she have a husband or boyfriend? Who was the father of her child?"

Anderton came to the edge of his desk and hoisted himself up, sitting on the edge with his legs swinging. Somehow, the boyish movement went straight to Kate's heart. Suddenly moved, she blinked and looked away.

That moment, though it had been brief, kept recurring to Kate when she was back at her desk. She had begun the slow, wearisome task of checking her share of the background facts that Anderton had brought up. She'd long been aware of her attraction to her boss and had managed to keep it a secret from him, from the rest of the team and, with surprising success, from herself as well.

She gave herself the usual stern talking to, reciting an inner monologue that pointed out the sad predictability of being attracted to your boss; the foolishness that resulted from such a breach of professional behaviour; and the fact that it could only lead to humiliation, scorn and misery. How pursuing her feelings would be professional and probably social suicide. Staring blankly at her computer screen while the same old words went round and round in her head, Kate could only think one thing: *I don't care. I still want him.*

With a massive effort, she shoved those treacherous feelings back down into the depths of her subconscious and turned her attention back to the case.

"Get anything?" asked Olbeck from across the desks.

Kate tapped the keys to print out some data.

"Got an address. Looks like some sort of hostel or something like that. Saint Andrews Mission, Church Road, Arbuthon Green."

"That's a homeless charity, I think." said Olbeck, getting up. He perched himself on the edge of Kate's desk and she realised he was dressed in a tracksuit. "Catholic. Shall we go and check it out?"

"Yes," said Kate, standing up. She swung her car keys in an ostentatious circle. "And we're *driving*."

"Fine," said Olbeck, grinning. "Just means we'll have to do an extra training session tomorrow. No drama."

Kate said nothing but suppressed a silent scream.

St Andrews Mission was located in what had obviously once been a village school, Victorian-built, with the usual attention to decorative detail and handsome arched windows. What had once been the playground at the front of the building was now paved over to make space for several cars to park. Kate was pleased to see the old school bell still remained up under the eaves and pointed it out to Olbeck as they got out of the car.

The reception area was painted in industrial green. A low, scuffed table sat by the front desk with a variety of leaflets, advertising counselling services, mother and baby groups, drug and alcohol support groups. A small number of battered chairs stood against the wall, and the reception desk was located behind a glass partition. Behind the reception desk, there was a door with a security key code pad on it.

The grey-haired woman, dressed in a white blouse, who staffed the reception desk looked up as the officers approached.

Kate introduced herself and Olbeck. The woman looked apprehensive.

"Oh yes, we did speak on the phone earlier, I remember," she said. "I'm Margaret Paling."

"Do you run this place?" asked Kate.

"Oh no, dear, I'm just one of the volunteers. You'll need to talk to Father Michael, but he's out at the moment."

"We'd like to have a quick chat with you, Mrs Paling, if we may. I understand you knew Mandy Renkin?"

Margaret Paling nodded. She was fingering a rather lovely rhinestone brooch pinned to the lapel of her blouse.

"It's Miss Paling," she said. "I'm not married. But I'd be happy to have a chat. Would you like to come through, and I'll make us some tea?"

Kate and Olbeck were ushered through the security door into a lounge-type area, which sported several worn sofas and armchairs. There was a bookcase with a small selection of second-hand books, a magazine rack stuffed with lots of dog-eared celebrity gossip magazines and a box full of children's toys.

"We'll go through to Father Michael's office," said Margaret. "The residents aren't normally up this early, but if you want to talk privately it's best we use the office." She saw Kate's expression. "Oh, I know. Ten thirty in the morning is isn't very early, but these girls – well, they're not very *disciplined*, shall we say. Mind you, having said that, a couple of them are actually in work at the moment, and they're out, obviously, and the children are in school."

"Children?" said Olbeck.

Margaret nodded as she opened the door to a small office.

"We have two family rooms here," she said. "Of course, they're always in use. In fact, we're full to the brim at the moment."

She bustled around, making the tea. Kate had expected to see the usual chipped and battered mugs, milk in a plastic bottle and sugar clumped together in a metal bowl. Instead, Margaret set out a rather nice old tea set, complete with milk jug and dainty sugar bowl. A wisp of steam rose from the spout of the teapot.

"What lovely china," said Kate. "Royal Doulton, isn't it?"

Margaret looked gratified.

"That's right," she said. "Been in my family for years. May as well get some use out of it." She looked as though she was about to say more for a moment, but she didn't. She handed Kate and Olbeck their cups. It had been a long time since Kate had drunk tea from a delicate china cup and saucer. It was good tea, hot and strong.

"You knew Mandy Renkin?" asked Olbeck.

Margaret nodded, fingering her brooch again.

"I knew her, but not very well. She hadn't been here long and it seemed as though—" She faltered, looking awkward. "Well, it's not for me to say, but it did seem as though she might not have been here very much longer. We're very strict on our no alcohol and no drug use policy here – we have to be – and, well…"

"Mandy was using drugs?" asked Kate.

Margaret nodded again. "I don't know for sure, but I know that Father Michael had, well, *words* with her to that very end. They had quite an argument, actually."

"When was this?"

"I'm not sure. I only heard it about it from someone else, one of the other volunteers. Perhaps two weeks ago? I couldn't say for sure."

"We'll speak to Father Michael when he comes back," said Kate. "He runs the hostel, then?"

"Yes, he's the supervisor here. It's a Church-funded charity."

Olbeck carefully placed his empty cup back on its saucer and transferred both to what was obviously Father Michael's desk.

"Could we have a look at Mandy's room, Miss Paling?"

Margaret looked worried but nodded.

"Yes, of course. I'll take you there right away."

"When do you expect Father Michael back?" asked Kate, as Margaret led them back through the sitting room, through another door, along several corridors, across a paved courtyard and finally into another building, a modern block of apartments.

"I couldn't say for sure. Perhaps after lunch?" Margaret stopped before a door numbered 14. She unlocked it and pushed it open gently.

"This is Mandy's room."

Chapter Three

THE TWO OFFICERS STEPPED INSIDE the dim room. The blind at the window was pulled down and the air inside smelt stale. Kate nodded at Margaret in a way she hoped was polite but dismissive.

"Thank you, Miss Paling. We'll take it from here and come and find you when we're done."

"Yes – yes, of course."

Margaret pulled the door shut behind her as she left. Kate waited until her footsteps had faded from hearing. Then she tossed a pair of gloves to Olbeck.

"Let's get some light in here, at least."

Olbeck let the blind roll up with a snap that sounded very loud in the silent room. Kate looked around. The room had an institutional look: grey carpet, patchy woodchip on the walls, a duvet cover in navy blue with a matching pillowcase on the one, thin pillow. Still, she imagined beggars couldn't be choosers: if it were a choice between this dull but functional room and the streets, Kate knew which she would chose.

Mandy Renkin had only had a few possessions, which was not unusual for someone who was shuttling between B&Bs, homeless hostels and other temporary accommodation. There were some clothes in the little chest of drawers by the window; it didn't take long for Kate to sort through them. Cheap and badly made, for the most part, although there was one obviously hand-knitted jumper that drew Kate's attention. She picked it up, noting the cable stitch, the good quality wool. Had Mandy's mother or grandmother made this for her? Or had she picked it up in a charity shop somewhere? Kate said as much to Olbeck.

"We need to find out about her family," said Olbeck. "Rav's digging into her records back at the station."

Kate nodded. She moved to the small bookcase that stood by the single bed. There were only five books contained therein. Four were romance novels in shabby pink and purple covers. One was an old copy of – Kate blinked and picked it up – Charles Dickens' *Great Expectations*. A strange juxtaposition with the other reading matter. Kate turned to the flyleaf of the book and saw the bookplate. *Awarded to Amanda Renkin for Excellence in English*. The date on the bookplate was twelve years ago. Kate stared unseeing for a moment, picturing the fourteen-year-old Mandy, smart in school uniform, accepting the pristine book from a school Governor, or perhaps the Headteacher. *Great Expectations*. Thinking of Mandy's eventual fate, the title was the cruellest possible cosmic joke. How had a smart schoolgirl gone from receiving a school prize at fourteen to dead on the streets at twenty six?

Kate replaced the book on the shelf, carefully. She had these moments in every case, where professional immunity failed. In every case, there were a few moments of pain, brief but excruciating, like a long silver pin being plunged into her heart. She'd told Olbeck that once and he'd said, unexpectedly, *I know, it hurts, but it's good that you feel that, Kate. You know you're in trouble if you ever stop feeling like that.*

Kate sighed, loud enough for Olbeck to look up from his own search. He opened his mouth to ask her what was wrong but shut it again as she shook her head, mutely.

There was a hesitant knock on the door, and Margaret Paling opened it and poked her head tentatively into the room.

"Father Michael is back," she said. "I've let him know you want to talk to him."

"Thanks," said Kate. "If you could ask him to come here, perhaps?"

"Yes, of course. One moment."

They heard the tap of her heels as she walked away back down the corridor. Kate turned her attention back to the small chest of drawers by the bed. There was nothing in the bottom drawer, a jumble of socks and underwear in the middle drawer, and in the top one, several packets of painkillers, crumpled tissues, a half-full cigarette packet and a framed photograph. Kate picked up up carefully. A woman – girl, really – who was clearly Mandy Renkin smiled out at her from the frame. Her cheek was pressed to the face of a baby boy, perhaps three months old or so, toothless mouth open in a drooling, gummy grin. Another of those pins pierced Kate's heart, and she blinked several times, swallowing hard.

There was another knock at the door.

"I heard you wanted to see me," said the tall, thin man who entered the room, obviously Father Michael. Olbeck and Kate heaved themselves to a standing position, pulled off their gloves and shook hands, introducing themselves.

Father Michael looked about the room and sighed.

"It's not much," he said apologetically. "We're always short of funds. It's getting worse now, with the benefit cuts of course. But we do what we can for these girls."

"I'm sure you do, sir," said Kate, sizing him up. He was probably younger than she'd first thought, late fifties perhaps, with a soft brown beard tinged with grey and narrow, sloping shoulders. His voice was unexpectedly deep and melodious – she could imagine he preached very well.

"We're trying to find out as much as we can about Mandy Renkin," said Olbeck. "Obviously, the more we know about her, the easier it is to find out who might have killed her. What can you tell us about her?"

Father Michael sat down on the edge of the bed and clasped his hands together.

"I hadn't known her for long," he said. "She'd not been here for more than a handful of weeks, only a month or so. Her social worker had passed the details of the Mission to Mandy at one of their meetings. Mandy had recently been released from prison, and I think she thought it might be a bit of a fresh start for her."

"What was she in prison for?"

"I'm not sure exactly. Soliciting or shoplifting or something fairly minor. It was only a short sentence, a matter of weeks."

"And when she was released she came straight here?"

Father Michael shook his head. "She was briefly in a hostel – a few days or so. I understood that Mandy had managed to complete a drug rehabilitation course in prison. That was why we were able to accept her here. We're very strict on there being no drugs and alcohol allowed on site and anyone found using or supplying them will be asked to leave."

Kate nodded. "Yes, Miss Paling said. She also mentioned that you and Mandy had had some sort of altercation recently. Can you tell us about that?"

Father Michael's rather thick eyebrows rose.

"An altercation?"

"Yes. An argument, a quarrel," said Kate, deliberately misunderstanding his repetition of the word. "Is that true?"

There was a moment's silence.

"Well, I suppose you could call it that," said Father Michael reluctantly. "I'm surprised at Margaret... There wasn't really much to tell."

Kate and Olbeck said nothing. They were skilled in letting the silence spool out for long enough that the person they were interviewing needed then to fill it.

"I found out that Mandy was using drugs again. Or, let me be accurate, I was informed she was using drugs again, and I wanted to hear what she had to say for herself."

"And what did she say?"

There was a moment's hesitation, so brief that Kate almost missed it.

"She told me it was a lie. That she wasn't using drugs again, and she didn't know who had told me that."

"Who had told you that?"

"One of the other women here. Claudia Smith."

Kate saw Olbeck scribble that name down in his notepad.

"Did you believe Mandy?"

Father Michael's narrow shoulders hunched for a moment. Then he shook his head slowly.

"I'm afraid I didn't believe her."

"You believed she was using drugs again?"

He nodded. "You get to know the signs. And I must say, I know very well when someone is lying to me."

"When did you have this argument?" asked Olbeck.

"Not long ago. Perhaps four or five days ago? I told her she couldn't stay here if she was using drugs, reminded her of the rules, you know."

"And how did Mandy react?"

Father Michael sighed.

"I'm afraid she became very foul-mouthed and abusive and ended up slamming the door to her room and locking herself in."

"I see," said Kate. "And what happened after that?"

"How do you mean?"

"I mean, how did you react?"

Father Michael half smiled.

"If you mean, was I upset by our argument, then of course I was, a little. But the most important thing about running a charity of this kind is that you have to, at some level, remain detached. Otherwise you just get carried away with the – well, the awfulness of some people's lives. So, I suppose I mentally shrugged my shoulders and went back to my office."

"What would have happened to Mandy if she'd left the Mission?" asked Olbeck.

"We would have tried to find her a place at a B&B or something. Perhaps another hostel. By evicting her from the Mission, we would have been making her effectively homeless, so the council would have had an obligation to house her."

"But that didn't happen?"

Father Michael stared at him.

"No, it didn't," he said. "Because she died before it came to that."

"Where you upset by her death, Father?"

The thick eyebrows jerked upwards.

"What a question, officer. The death of a young girl – of course I was upset. Of course I was. We were all devastated."

Kate stood up, thinking that they had enough to go on by now.

"Just one more thing, sir. Could you tell us your whereabouts on the night of the fourteenth of June?"

"That's when Mandy died?"

"Could you answer the question please, sir?"

Father Michael considered for a moment.

"Well – I'm afraid I was at home. I usually am in the evening."

"Can anyone confirm that, sir?"

Father Michael shook his head slowly.

"I'm afraid not," he said. He looked worried. "I live alone, you see. I didn't talk to anyone—"

"What's your address, Father?" asked Olbeck. He wrote down the answer as the priest answered him.

"Twenty six Lavender Street, Charlock."

"That's fine, sir," said Kate. "We'll leave our cards, and I'm sure we'll be back to ask you some more questions. If you think of anything at all that you think might be relevant, please don't hesitate to get in touch."

Father Michael nodded, his face serious. He stood back a little to allow them access to the door.

"Do you have any idea who might have done this dreadful thing?" he asked, just as they were leaving.

"Our enquiries are continuing, sir," said Kate, the usual response.

"I hope you catch him."

Kate and Olbeck said nothing, but smiled neutrally before saying goodbye.

J's Diary

I ORDERED THE FIRST GIRL ONLINE.

It's amazing if you think of it – how you can put in a request for a human being as easily as you might order a new television or even your week's shopping. Click a mouse and put something in your virtual basket: milk, sausages, chicken breasts, a woman. Just another type of commodity. Just another type of meat.

I purposely used a site I'd never used before or since, directing the responses to a new Hotmail address I'd set up specially. The credit card payment was more difficult. In the end, I used one of Mother's, thinking perhaps I could say it had been stolen if it were ever traced back to me. Of course, at that time, I wasn't foreseeing any of the kind of trouble that happened that night. I merely wanted to avoid any potential embarrassment. God forbid that anyone would recognise me. So, a strange agency and a strange girl was what I wanted.

I was very nervous before she arrived. It had only been a few weeks after Mother had died, and I still felt as if she were going to suddenly appear at any moment. Several times, I thought I heard her faltering footsteps in the bedrooms above me, and once, after a creak in the hallway, I was convinced that her head with its puff of white hair and her piercing steel-grey eyes would appear around the living room doorway momentarily. I even froze for an instant, clutching the arms of the chair, before realising how stupid I was being. There was no one there, of course. I kept telling myself, *She's dead. She's gone. She's dead. She's gone.*

So, the night the girl arrived, I was extremely jumpy. I prowled the rooms downstairs, glancing nervously at the clock as the hands inched around to 9:00 p.m. I'd gotten everything ready, and for the first time ever in my life, I actually felt like myself. I actually felt as if it *could* work. I regarded myself in the hallway mirror, pulling my tie straight. Yes. *It will work*, I told myself. *You can do it.*

The doorbell rang at that moment, shattering the silence in the house, and I'd actually jumped. Then I hurried to the door and opened it as quickly as possible. I'd taken the lightbulb out of the porch light socket, but I was still suddenly terrified that the neighbours would be looking out of their front window and wondering what a tart was doing ringing my doorbell.

I don't know why but I'd imagined a girl in heels, a leopard-skin coat, red lipstick. Stupid, really. The woman standing on the doorstep was short, thin, and dressed in a shabby blue fleece and skinny jeans and trainers. She looked a most unlikely prostitute, but as I hurried her into the house, I could see the fleece was unzipped slightly and a curve of damp cleavage visible beneath the zip. I felt a welcome surge of excitement.

I closed the door behind her.

"What's your name?" she asked, peering through the gloom at me.

"John."

Even in the dim light, I could see her lip curl. I think she knew it wasn't my real name.

"John, eh? Right you are, *John*. What d'you want to do?"

Funny, all this time I'd been frantically waiting for this moment, the moment of actually doing what it was I'd wanted to do for so long. And now that it was here and on the verge of happening, I found myself backpedalling.

"Do you want a drink or something?" I asked. My voice sounded tremulous – I despised myself. Why couldn't I sound forthright and authoritative? In my head, I could see Mother's sneer, the same sneer that had confronted me almost every day of my life.

I could feel my hands clench.

"Yeah, all right," said the tart, and I gestured towards the kitchen.

I'll come clean now and say I was already quite drunk. I was nervous – so nervous – and I had to have something to calm my nerves. I'd heard of alcohol having the wrong kind of effect, of course I had, but I was in such a state before she arrived that I thought I'd risk it. I'd already had about three large whiskies before the door went.

The tart strutted into the kitchen like she owned the place. I'd kept the strip light off and the only light came from a candle I'd placed on the kitchen windowsill. The girl stopped when she saw it and I could see she was momentarily disconcerted. Perhaps she was thinking that I only wanted to do the romance thing. I'd heard of men doing that – hiring tarts to pretend to be their girlfriends for the night.

I didn't want the romance thing. I wanted everything.

I poured her a whisky without asking her what she wanted. She sipped and made a face, as if it wasn't the best aged Laphroaig. After Mother died, almost the very day she died, I'd gone to the sacred drinks cabinet, where unopened bottles had stood ever since Father had left, and broken the seal on the first one I could find. There were only a few left now.

After her first sip, she knocked it back in one swallow, grimacing as if it were medicine.

"All right," she said. "I ain't got all night. Let's get going."

"R-right—" I began, but before I could say any more, the tart said something like "Fucking dark in here" and snapped on the light switch.

There was a moment of blinding dazzle after the strip light stuttered on. Both of us recoiled slightly, blinking. I had time for a second of outrage about the fact that she'd just taken it upon herself, in someone else's house, to dictate the light levels. It was *my* house. Who did she think she was?

I only had time for a second of thought because at that moment she saw me clearly. A moment later, a harsh disbelieving laugh rang out into the kitchen.

She was laughing at me.

For some reason I thought of Mother and her sneer that was half a smile. Before I could even open my mouth to tell her to shut up, I flinched backwards against the kitchen counter and suddenly the steak knife was in my hand.

"Shut up!" I hissed, and I thrust the knife forward.

Did I just mean to scare her? I don't know. All I wanted was for that mocking laughter to stop. The knife sank into her stomach, piercing the fleece. The tart said, "Oh," a sound of surprise rather than pain. We both looked down at the knife protruding from her belly, just to the right of the zip. I still had hold of the handle.

There was a moment of silence. Then she drew in her breath and screamed, shatteringly loud.

Panicked, I snatched my hand back and drove the knife forward again, not caring where I hit her. I just had to stop the noise. But the strangest thing happened. As the blade sank into her, again and again, I – well, I...

La petit mort, they call it. I was swept away, lost, carried away on a release so powerful that when it finally stopped, I believed for a second I had died too.

When I came back to reality, I was face down on the body of the tart, my hand still clenched around the handle of the steak knife that was buried deeply inside her. I was wet with blood and not just with blood. I rolled over onto my back, next to the body on the kitchen floor, gasping for breath and holding the knife against my chest like a talisman.

Chapter Four

"Don't forget we're training again tonight," said Olbeck as they got into the car.

Kate gritted her teeth.

"I hadn't," she said, after a moment. "That's all we do, every night. Every day and every night."

"You'll thank me," said Olbeck breezily. "Tell you what. How about we do our run and then you come over for dinner with me and Jeff?"

Kate was waiting to join the main road. She used the time spent gauging the oncoming traffic to think over Olbeck's suggestion. It was tempting. Jeff was Olbeck's partner – Kate kept thinking of him as Olbeck's 'new' partner, despite the fact they'd been together for just over a year. Jeff was thirty-eight, an academic specialising in sports sciences and a fitness fanatic. Kate knew who to blame for Olbeck's newfound fitness regime and his punishing insistence that Kate join in. Still, it was a minor niggle.

Jeff was warm, witty, nice-looking and a supportive and easy-going boyfriend to her friend. She'd spent many an enjoyable evening with the two of them: at dinner parties, at the theatre, at a barbeque with mutual colleagues and at lazy Sunday brunches at the local pubs. Kate and Jeff got on very well and she could see that he and Olbeck were a loving and committed couple. And yet... And yet...she felt guilty thinking it, but she couldn't deny it. Occasionally she wished it was just her and Olbeck again, as it had been when he was single. She felt terrible for even thinking that, but at the same time, she couldn't help it. *You're jealous*, she told herself again. Not jealous because she wanted Olbeck for a *boyfriend*, for God's sake. But jealous because before Jeff appeared, it was just the two of them and now there were three and now Kate was the odd one out.

It was funny; for years she'd been happy with her own company. She hadn't wanted a partner. Unlike those women who said they were happy being single because they thought if they said that sort of thing out loud, the universe would reward them with the perfect man, Kate really had been happy being single. She had enough friends and enough interests to fill those odd hours that weren't taken up with work. But now...she sighed inwardly. Now, she felt differently. *I'm lonely. I want someone of my own. Not just someone. One person – Anderton.*

Kate drove ruminatively, tapping her fingers on the steering wheel.

"Let's go and talk to Claudia Smith now," she suggested. "She sounds like she knew Mandy, even if just in a casual way."

Olbeck nodded.

"Sounds like a plan."

There were two branches of Boots the Chemist in Abbeyford: a small shop on the outskirts of the town and a much larger central store in the main shopping area. Kate and Olbeck made their way to the latter, reasoning that Claudia Smith would be more likely to be found here. They were correct. After enquiring at one of the make-up booths, they were directed to a small bank of tills at the rear of the store.

Claudia Smith was easily picked out by her nametag. She was a small, dark-haired woman. As Kate observed her as they waited in the queue, she could see that Claudia was an excellent example of a basically pretty girl whose thick make-up, hugely volumised hair and overload of cheap jewellery negated rather than enhanced her attractiveness. Kate looked at the thick foundation, the hard line of black eyeliner, the orange fake tan and the huge, cheap silver hoops which dragged down Claudia's earlobes. Why did women *do* this to themselves? Did they genuinely think they looked better? Kate supposed they must. She had a secondary thought that those kind of women probably looked at her and wondered why she wasn't making more of herself.

Claudia's till became free and Kate and Olbeck stepped forward.

Kate introduced herself and her partner and flashed her card. Claudia's heavily outlined eyes widened.

"Don't be alarmed, Miss Smith," said Kate, realising that Claudia was also casting anxious glances towards an older woman hovering nearby who was clearly her line manager. "We'd just like to talk to you about Mandy Renkin. Would you like us to wait until you finish your shift?"

Claudia looked as though she wanted to agree but perhaps realised that asking the police to wait – loitering in the aisles, with her work colleagues giving them curious glances – would be worse. She shook her head and said "I'll just ask if I can go" before scurrying off to her line manager. Kate and Olbeck shifted a little to allow some shoppers to pass them by. After a minute or two, Claudia Smith came back, minus her Boots tabard and with a much studded and fringed but obviously cheap leather handbag.

Kate's conscience gave her a little nudge.

"I hope we haven't got you into trouble with your boss, Miss Smith," she said. "We'll be happy to talk to her if necessary, explain how things are."

Claudia shook her head. She was walking quite quickly, with her head down.

"It's all right," she said in a small voice. "Is it okay if we talk as we go along? It's just I have to pick my daughter up from the childminder's."

She barely looked out of her teens herself. How old was her daughter? Kate asked her.

"Four." Claudia's make-up-caked face brightened a little. "Her name's Madison."

"Perhaps we can give you a lift," suggested Olbeck. "That might give us a little time to talk."

When they were parked a few metres away from the childminder's house in Arbuthon Green, Olbeck turned off the engine and turned in his seat to face Claudia and Kate, who was sitting next to her on the back seat.

"We're trying to find out something more about Mandy," he said. "Were you friends with her?"

Claudia nodded nervously.

"We were at school together."

"And you've been friends ever since? You kept in touch after you left school?"

"Sort of. We both – we kind of both got into bad situations." Claudia's eyes flickered downwards. "Mandy started seeing this guy, Mike Fenton. He was really cool, everyone wanted to be with him, and Mandy was the one who ended up with him. But he was really bad news, got her into drugs and all that. She kind of dropped off the scene for a bit, for a long while actually."

Kate had been listening closely. She suppressed a sigh at the usual sad story: schoolgirl promise squandered on a boy who was a bad lot, someone who dragged you down into the gutter. And once you were there, it was almost impossible to climb out.

"Did Mandy get back in contact with you? How did you both end up at the Mission?"

Claudia fiddled with her earrings.

"We kind of kept in touch, off and on," she said. Her gaze dropped again. "She was a good mate to me. She helped me out when – when I needed it. She'd got off the drugs then, left Mike and was kind of getting herself back together again."

"When was this, Claudia?"

"I dunno. About two years ago."

"Was Mandy working as a prostitute then?"

Claudia's orange-hued face went faintly pink.

"I dunno," she said, again. "We didn't really talk about stuff like that."

"But she was kind to you?"

Claudia nodded. "She was there for me when I need her. Gave me some money, helped me—" She stopped for a moment. "She helped me get out."

Olbeck shifted a little in his seat. "What happened, Claudia?"

The girl kept her eyes down and spoke haltingly. A sad tale of a relationship that seemed to start off well, an accidental pregnancy, an older man who, when his partner was at her most vulnerable, decided to begin abusing her.

"That's very sad," said Kate. "You left the relationship, though?"

"Yeah. I had to. I took Maddy one night and got - got out. Mandy helped me. She came and met us and took us to the hostel."

"Was that the Mission?"

Claudia shook her head. "No, a woman's refuge. We couldn't stay there for long, though. I used to take Maddy to a church toddler group, and I met Father Michael there. He told me there were mother and baby rooms at the Mission, and I managed to get one, after a while."

"How long have you been at the Mission?"

"Not long. Only a few months."

"But you like living there?"

Claudia shrugged. "Yeah, it's all right. I've got my name down for a council flat, but I dunno how long that's going to take."

Olbeck shifted again in his seat, easing the ache in his neck from twisting around to talk to Claudia.

"So Mandy was a kind girl, Claudia?"

"Yeah. Yeah, she was, as long as she weren't on the drugs. Then she were a right bitch." The girl coloured a little. "Sorry. It's just that - well - I knew she'd started using again just recently."

"How did you know?"

"I could tell. Also she started stealing again. She stole a silver locket that me mum had given me for Madison."

"That must have been very – hurtful," said Olbeck. "Were you angry with her?"

Claudia gave him the boldest look she'd managed so far.

"Yeah, of course."

"Did you argue?"

"Sort of. I didn't get a chance to say much. She just slammed out, and I didn't see her again."

Claudia's words seemed to strike her, and Kate saw her eyes become shiny with tears.

"I didn't see her again," repeated Claudia, softly.

"I'm sorry for your loss," said Kate, automatically. Claudia nodded silently, blinking.

"Did Mandy have a boyfriend that you know of, Claudia?"

Claudia shook her head.

"I don't think so. She never mentioned anyone."

"Did you ever see her with a man or – or a boy? Did anyone ever come to visit her that you know of?"

"No," said Claudia. She was shifting a little in her seat. Then she pulled out her phone and checked the time.

"I'm really sorry, but I've got to get Madison now."

"Right, that's fine," said Olbeck. As Claudia went to open the back door, he recalled something else.

"Claudia, one more quick thing. Did Mandy have a handbag that she used?"

"A *handbag*?" asked Claudia, and Kate was reminded of the line by Lady Bracknell in *The Importance of Being Ernest*. She tried not to grin. God knows, it wasn't funny in this context.

"What d'you mean?" asked Claudia. "Yeah, she had one, just one. She used it all the time."

"What did it look like?"

Claudia indicated her own bag.

"Like this. We got 'em together except Mandy's was white."

"Just like yours?" Kate checked. Claudia nodded. Kate quickly grabbed her phone and took a photo of Claudia's bag. Claudia didn't protest but looked a little startled.

"Thanks, Claudia. Here are our cards, if you think of anything else, please let us know."

Claudia didn't say goodbye. She ducked her head in shy, silent acknowledgement and got out of the car, closing the door quietly.

Chapter Five

During that evening's running session, Kate was forced, reluctantly, to admit to herself that it was getting easier. *Slightly* easier. Her face was still flushed a fetching shade of beetroot, and her t-shirt was still welded to her back with sweat, but even she couldn't deny that the actual running was getting easier. She was able to push herself a little further and run a little faster without feeling like her lungs were about to spontaneously combust inside her.

She didn't mention that to Olbeck. She'd never hear the end of it.

They finished their run along a section of the canal path, actually passing close to where Mandy Renkin had met her killer. Kate glanced at the derelict buildings as they jogged past.

"Why would she meet a punter here?" she asked, between puffs of breath. "It looks so dangerous. So dingy and dirty. Why go here?"

Olbeck was running along freely and easily.

"It's private," he said. "It's quiet, it's overlooked. Easy to do the business there if you didn't have anywhere else to go."

"Are you talking about Mandy or the perp?"

Olbeck eased down to a fast walk, and Kate followed him gratefully.

"I don't know," he said. "Surely that would apply to both of them."

"Well, exactly," said Kate, also noting that she was getting her breath back much more quickly these days. "We need to find out what Mandy's usual method of operation was. Did she normally work the streets? Had she been to this place before with punters?"

Olbeck nodded, swiping the sweatband strapped around his wrist across his glistening forehead.

"Why don't we try and track down some of her old associates? Find out whether she used to work with another girl, stuff like that."

Kate was walking normally now. She pushed some loose strands of hair off her hot face.

"Of course, there's another possibility," she said. She looked up at Olbeck and raised her eyebrows. "That she went there because she was with someone that she knew. Someone she didn't think would harm her."

Olbeck slowed. "Yes," he said slowly. "That's a possibility. That she went there with a friend or an old acquaintance."

"For sex?"

"I don't know. Who knows?"

"There didn't seem to have been any partner on the cards. Not according to Claudia."

"That's not to say there wasn't. Maybe Mandy was keeping it quiet."

"Why?"

They'd reached the end of Olbeck's street by now. Kate could see the golden lamplight shining out from the living room windows of his house, warm and friendly-looking. *I wish I had that at my place*, she thought wistfully. *Someone waiting for me at home.*

"Why would Mandy keep it quiet? I don't know. Maybe she was in a relationship with someone who was embarrassed or ashamed of her. Maybe she wasn't in a relationship at all. Oh, I don't know." Olbeck sounded irritated for a second. "We don't seem to be getting very far, do we?"

Kate shrugged.

"Let's leave it for now. We'll talk about it tomorrow."

"Kate!" exclaimed Jeff as he opened the front door. "Don't you look wonderful? Come in, darling."

"You're such a liar," said Kate, grinning and stepping forward into the hallway. "I look like a sweaty tomato."

"That's my *favourite* look," said Jeff.

"He's not lying, it actually is," said Olbeck, receiving a kiss from his partner, which made Kate slightly uncomfortable to witness. The awkwardness only lasted a moment. Jeff swept Kate into the kitchen, where the French doors were open to the garden and a table was laid for dinner outside.

"Why don't you grab a shower while I finish dinner?" suggested Jeff. "You know where the towels are."

"I don't have anything to change into."

"Borrow one of my t-shirts," said Olbeck. "Want a drink to take up with you?"

"Okay and yes," said Kate, accepting the cool glass of orange juice, beaded with condensation. She headed upstairs and locked the bathroom door, remembering that their shower was one that started off icy and rapidly became too hot without some judicious juggling of the controls. When she'd got it to an acceptable temperature, she stripped off her clothes and hopped in.

The bathroom was pretty clean and nicely decorated, but it had enough of a homely kind of clutter to feel very lived-in. *All they need is a couple of kids, and they'd be the perfect family,* Kate thought as she sluiced herself down. She was suddenly swamped with a wave of loneliness so severe that tears sprang to her eyes. She pinched the bridge of her nose hard, leaning back against the comforting spray of hot water.

Fifteen minutes later, she'd successfully washed the grime from her workout—and her emotions—down the drain.

"Better?" said Olbeck as she came back into the kitchen,

dressed in the old Rolling Stones t-shirt he'd left hanging on the doorknob of the bathroom door for her.

"Much," said Kate, emotions under control again. She accepted a refill of her glass and stretched her clean feet out on the decking. It was still very warm, the kind of warm night rarely experienced even at the height of a British summer. Olbeck lit a citronella candle to keep away the insects.

Jeff surpassed himself with the food. It was the typical fare: healthy, heavy on the vegetables and light on lean protein, but still intensely flavourful. The first course consisted of rice-paper spring rolls accompanied by little white bowls filled with soy sauce for dipping. When these were disposed of, Jeff brought out an Asian salad, bright with slivers of carrot, red pepper and spring onion, with thin ribbons of rare beef curled like moist, pink ribbons amongst the greenery.

"God, this is delicious," said Kate, trying to eat daintily although she felt like inhaling the plateful whole. "You're such a good cook, Jeff."

"I'm a man of many talents."

That remark resulted in a sly exchange of smiles between the two men. Kate, well-aware of the innuendo, kept her eyes on her plate, eating steadily. *What's the matter with me?* She never normally minded Olbeck and Jeff being all lovey-dovey. Despite the good food and the familiar company, despite the afterglow of the exercise and the beautiful night, Kate felt itchy and cross and miserable. She had to work hard not to show it. *Probably hormones*, she told herself. *Just my luck.*

When she got home that night, the house felt very big and empty. Kate walked around, checking the doors were locked and windows tightly shut. She watched television in a desultory manner for five minutes before pressing the off button on the remote irritably. Her mobile pinged and she read a casual, chatty text from her brother Jay which, somehow, she just didn't feel like answering right away. Kate picked up a book she'd been meaning to read for several weeks, opened the cover, scanned the first page and snapped it shut again. She switched on the kettle to boil the water for her camomile tea, waiting for it to steam itself to a stop while she looked out the back kitchen window onto the darkness of the back garden. Occasionally a neighbourhood fox trotted across the lawn, but he wasn't around tonight. Kate made her tea.

Balancing her delicate cup on its saucer – tea made in a big mug just tasted wrong to her – she stood for a moment at the big, bay window in the living room, having snapped off the overhead light. She watched the silent street outside, blinking through a veil of steam. *He's out there somewhere*, she thought, and turned abruptly away, wincing as she spilled a little hot tea over her thumb.

Safely tucked up in bed, she paged through the stored numbers in her phone, looking for the one right at the start of the list. Anderton's name glowed from the screen. Kate looked it for a moment, her thumb hovering over the call button. Then she sighed, put the phone down on her bedside table and turned out the light, lying down and drawing the duvet cover up to her chin.

J's diary

My most pressing problem was, of course, what to do with the body. I'm not one of these people who do what they do to have a corpse to play with. The thought makes me feel ill. What I seek is the moment of transformation – the sinking of the knife into warm, living flesh. Once that moment has passed, there's nothing left for me there. The body is just something cumbersome and unpleasant to be disposed of as quickly as possible.

After the first blind panic had passed, I realised that I had to get rid of the body. I may not have many visitors, but I do have *some,* and there was no way I could explain away the presence of a dead tart on my kitchen floor. Not for a moment! So something had to be done. Should I dump the body? Would I get away with it? I thought uneasily of DNA, of dropped hairs and clothing fibres all leading a trail back to me. If the body was found, then I would eventually be found out. Surely?

For a few hours, I thought of all kinds of ridiculous plans for disposing the body. Dropping it in front of a truck from a motorway bridge. Weighting it down and sinking it to the bottom of a deep lake. I knew that these fantasies were a way of getting through the horror of what I had to do. Of course in the end, I realised that the body had to stay here, in the house – or in the garden.

I thought for a while of dismembering it, but to be honest, that was beyond me, even if I had enough knowledge, dexterity and strength to actually do it. Just the thought of saws and axes chopping through bone and gristle actually made me retch. In the end, I wrapped the body up in several layers of thick plastic, taped it up and took it down to the cellar.

These old houses all have cellars. Those which have been renovated usually turn the dank, cobweb-hung, dark little rooms under the earth into modish studies, guest bedrooms, or perhaps a home cinema. Of course, Mother would never have countenanced anything like that.

Our cellar – my cellar – was as it probably had been when the house was built over a hundred years ago. The floor was brick, but right at the back, there was a boarded up aperture that was originally intended to house coal. The door in the planks at the front wasn't very big, but I was pretty sure I could get the body through intact. When I took a torch down to have a proper look, I could see the brick floor hadn't extended into the coal store – the ground was bare earth. *No wonder this house is so cold*, I thought to myself irrelevantly, before pushing myself through the little door of the coal store and gingerly standing up. I couldn't stand upright, and that presented a problem. How was I going to be able to wield a spade? I needed a deep hole.

One thing about me is that I won't give up. That used to be one of the insults flung at me by Mother, one of the many. *Stubborn as a mule, selfish, it's all about you, you, you...* Of course, the real root of the issue was that I was me and not Father, that for some reason, she'd been left with me instead of him. *Why can't you be more like your Father?* It was a constant refrain. In the end, I rather prided myself on being different to him, or I told myself that's what I felt.

So, even though burying the body in the coal store would be a tough and laborious task, it was one I set for myself and of course I completed it – eventually. I spent an hour or so every spare evening over the course of several weeks digging away with a short spade and hand trowel. Luckily, the cellar also contained a large chest freezer, and I was able to store the body in there while I prepared its final resting place.

Finally it was ready, and I levered the stiff corpse from its temporary icy tomb and transferred it to the hole dug beyond the coal store door. Once it was covered with a foot of earth, the coal door padlocked and the cellar door bolted, I toasted myself with the last of Father's whisky, raising a glass to a job well done.

For a good while after the killing, I was in what I now see as an exalted state. At first it was fuelled by the feverish grip of fear that I would be caught, but once this had abated, I felt something different but equally as intense. Everything about life seemed brighter. My usual dreary routine – work, household duties, watching television – all this seemed saturated with colour and emotion, sparkling with vivacity. I felt everything intensely. It was like being born anew, and it was an experience that I could never have anticipated. From the moment I thrust that knife into her stomach, everything had changed. I went about my day with a gladdened heart and a mind that was suddenly alive to the possibilities of the world.

And then, much as the fear had done, my acute euphoria began to ebb. Daily, little by little, this marvellous new feeling faded until the glitter and sparkle that had been mine was gone, the shine rubbed off by time and reality. I could feel the greyness gathering again, and my mood dipped and dipped and dipped until everything was back to how it had been before.

That was when I knew I had to do it again.

Chapter Six

THE NEXT MORNING, THE TEAM assembled in Anderton's office for a debrief. Kate had managed to grab a chair, but after seeing Theo hobble in on his crutches, she stood up again and made him take it. He collapsed onto it and stuck his plastered foot out carefully, giving her a grateful smile.

Anderton spun on his heel, realised how close he was to the wall and spun back again, thwarted.

"*When* do we move back?" he implored. "This is intolerable."

"Next Monday," said Jane, confidently. "I've just had an email from the Facilities Team. We're back in on Monday."

"Thank God for that. We'll have to have champagne. Now, where were we?"

"Stuffed into your office," said Olbeck with a grin.

"Very funny, Mark. How are we getting on with Mandy Renkin?"

Olbeck immediately became serious. "Kate and I have interviewed her friend, the priest who runs the Mission that provided her accommodation and one of the volunteers who works at the Mission."

"Get anything?"

Olbeck hesitated for a moment. Kate took up the baton.

"It seems quite likely that Mandy had gone back to using drugs. That could well be why she taken up prostitution again – to get the money."

Anderton nodded. "We'll have the tests back from the path lab this week. Should be easy enough to see whether that was the case. Now, it's a possibility that it's a drug-related crime, although I'm inclined to think that it's not. It's an angle worth investigating, though. Go through the records, see if we have any dealers we can lean on. Anyone with a record of violent crime, knife crime, that sort of thing. Rav, you do that."

He swung around, churning his hair with both hands. "What else? No one's mentioned a partner, a boyfriend. Was there one?"

There was silence from the team. Anderton lowered his hands and his gaze swept the room.

"You need to start doing some more questioning. Kate, Mark, go back to the Mission, talk to Father Whatshisname again. Get some more background."

"Fine," said Kate. "But we're interviewing the social worker today and the foster family."

Anderton raised his eyebrows.

"Okay, good stuff. Do a follow up at the Mission when you can. Okay team, unless anyone else has anything to add, let's get on."

No one had anything to add. They began to file slowly out. Kate, one of the last to leave except Theo, saw Anderton walk over to him and say something in a low tone, speaking too quietly for Kate to hear.

She lingered outside the office until Theo hobbled out on his crutches, and they walked back to the temporary office together.

"What did Anderton want?" asked Kate unblushingly.

Theo was by necessity looking at the floor as he swung himself along.

"What?"

"What did he say to you at the end?"

Theo looked up and grinned.

"Nosy. Nothing much. He just asked me to check the national databases for similar cases."

Kate frowned. "Similar?"

"Yeah. Similar weapon, similar MO." They reached the door

of the office, and Kate hurried to hold it open for Theo. "Thanks. Anyway, that's all he wanted. Why?"

"No reason," said Kate, rather absently. She was thinking.

"You can do it if you want. He's only getting me to do it 'cos I'm stuck behind a desk at the moment."

"I wouldn't want to deprive you," said Kate, grinning. "Let me know if you do find anything though, okay?"

They parted at the entrance to the office, and Kate went to sit down at her desk. The instant her backside made contact with the chair, she sprung up again and hurried back to Anderton's office. The door was shut, but she knocked anyway and was rewarded with an interrogative 'Yup?' from inside.

"Kate," said Anderton as she closed the door behind her. He looked surprised. "What's wrong?"

"Nothing's wrong," she answered. "I just wanted to ask you something."

"Uh-huh. What's that?"

"Why did you ask Theo to cross-check for similar cases?"

Anderton sat back in his chair. Slowly, he laced the fingers of both hands behind his neck and rocked back a little.

"Why do you ask?" he said after a moment.

Kate smiled.

"I asked first."

Anderton grinned. "There's no secret. I want to check whether there have been any other cases like this one."

"Why?"

His eyebrows rose. "Why? Why do you think? So we can find the person who did it, of course."

Kate shook her head, flustered.

"I didn't mean why, I meant—" She stopped herself for a moment. Then she took a deep breath and asked the question she really wanted the answer to.

"You don't think this is just a one off, do you, sir? I mean, you think there are going to be more."

Anderton took his hands down from behind his neck. He leaned forward, fixing Kate with his stare.

"Now, why would you say that?" he asked.

Kate kept her eyes on his but she shrugged.

"I don't know," she said after a moment. "Call it a feeling."

Anderton was silent for a moment.

"You scare me sometimes, Kate," he said. "I'll have to hide my thoughts from you from now on, God knows how."

Kate smiled.

"That depends on what they are."

She'd meant it to be a light-hearted response, but their eyes locked again, and she was shocked at the sudden rush of heat that went through her. She shifted a little in her chair, her gaze dropping.

Anderton cleared his throat.

"You're right," he said. "I have a bad feeling about this case. And *I* can't say how I know that. Call it a feeling."

There was a moment's silence. Anderton sat back in his seat again.

"Don't mention this to the rest of the team, okay? I could be wrong. I *hope* I'm wrong. Let's see how things – pan out."

Kate nodded. She had been intently focused on the case, but now her thoughts were swirling around something very different. She stood up and said goodbye, casually, just as if she wasn't thinking about jumping over the desk to throw herself into Anderton's arms.

Back at her desk, she stared blankly at the screen, barely aware of the bustle and activity going on around her. Then she closed her eyes. The intensity of her feelings shocked her. How was she going to keep her mind on the case? She suddenly became aware that Olbeck was stood behind her, repeating himself impatiently for what was obviously not the first time.

"What?"

"I said, what did you ask Anderton about?"

"Nothing," said Kate. Olbeck gave her an old-fashioned look.

"Seriously," she added. "I'll tell you later." She made a massive effort to stop thinking pornographic thoughts about her boss and turned her attention back to work. "What are we doing now?"

"Mandy Renkin's social worker," said Olbeck. "I've already made an appointment with her. Come on, you can drive, seeing as you're so keen on it."

Barbara Fee was a thin, harassed-looking woman, much wound about with scarves and with fine, flyaway hair messily pinned up in an unsuccessful chignon. Whole hanks of hair kept escaping, and Ms Fee would shove them back in with a distracted air. She received Kate and Olbeck in her chaotic office with the proviso that she 'really only had twenty minutes' before her next appointment.

"We'll be as quick as we can then," said Kate. "What can you tell us about Mandy Renkin?"

Barbara Fee pushed at a slipping hairslide.

"She was a nice girl," she said. "Had problems, obviously. Usual story: taken into care at an early age, in and out of the care system, drug problems, teen pregnancy, had her child taken away from her. What else did you want to know?"

"Was she ever fostered?" asked Kate. "I found a school prize that she must have received when she was about fourteen. She was obviously doing well at school then. That doesn't really tally with her later...life, shall we say."

Barbara Fee was hunting amongst the files of her messy desk.

"No, you're right," she said, rather absently. She found what she was looking for and offered it across the table to Olbeck, who took the thick manila folder. "That's her file. She *was* fostered, from the age of ten to the age of fifteen. Settled pretty nicely, actually. The family was one who tended to take on older children and teenagers, very experienced foster carers. Mandy did very well with them."

Olbeck was leafing through the file.

"So, what happened?" he asked. "Why did she go off the rails?"

Barbara tucked a loose strand of hair behind one ear.

"Teenage rebellion?" she said. "Unresolved issues with the breakdown of her family unit? She got in with the wrong crowd? Take your pick. You can only do so much for these kids, you know. At some point, you just have to take a step back and realise you're doing more harm than good."

"Could you give us the address of her foster parents?"

"Yes, of course. They're still fostering for us. Bernard and Adele Watkins." Barbara Fee handed over a scrap of paper with an address scribbled on it. "Terrible thing to happen to Mandy, but she wouldn't be the first. They live such dangerous lives, these girls. They're so vulnerable."

"Did you like Mandy?" asked Kate as they were ushered from the office.

Barbara stared at her.

"Like her? What do you mean? She was a nice girl, like I said."

"No, I meant did you *like* her?" asked Kate. "As a person?"

Barbara was rummaging in her bag for her keys. She withdrew a set that had to have had twenty keys on one inadequate key ring and locked her office door.

"Yes, of course," she said, vaguely. "Now, I really must go, if you'll excuse me."

They watched her walk away down the long corridor, the cork heels of her Birkenstock sandals slapping loudly against the tiled floor like ironic applause following her exit.

J's Diary

I'VE BEEN THINKING A LOT about Mother lately. It's annoying, because I thought I'd successfully managed to forget her, often for whole hours at a time. Oddly, it's not the old Mother that I think about, the white-haired, bespectacled, bent old lady who shuffled around the house. The weak one, the one who finally found out that a sharp tongue is no real defence. No, it's the Mother from a time I never knew that I find myself thinking about, the Mother of the photographs from the war and post-war: the dark-haired, slim and pretty Mother in her tea dresses and Victory rolls. The Mother who met my father.

My father has been a ghost in my life, always. Never physically here but always a shadowy presence in the house. He was never allowed to rest, never allowed to fade away into oblivion, like so many other of the men who never made it home from the war. Mother kept him alive, in her memory, in her conversation, in the photographs that littered the house. I think I was about thirteen when I realised the ratio of pictures of Father to me: one of me to every twenty of him. All of mine were baby pictures – I think the oldest one was of me as a three-year-old, dressed in muddy dungarees. In one of baby pictures, I'm sat on the hearth rug, waving a blurred object that I think is a rattle and wearing a blue-striped sailor suit.

The picture that takes pride of place in the living room is on the mantelpiece in an enormous gilt frame. It's a sepia-toned shot of my mother and father on their wedding day, 15th July 1940, my father in his uniform, my mother in blue silk. I know she wore blue because she told me – in the picture, her dress is a nothingy-brown colour. They were married two weeks before he was posted overseas, long enough for him to impregnate her with what turned out to be me. He never came back.

I don't know why I keep maundering on about the past. Perhaps it's because I'm getting older myself, and it necessarily preys more on my mind. It's the future I should be thinking of. The next girl, and the next one after that. If I am going to write about the past, I should write about the second girl and how it turned out to be as wonderful as the first.

Mother always accused me of being irrational, of having no self-control. She was wrong about that, just as she was about so many things. When I decide on a course of action, I always go through with it. I make my plans and set out my stall; step by careful step, I achieve what I want. When I decided I wanted to repeat what I'd done with the first girl, I spent weeks thinking about it, considering how to do it and get away with it, as I had so cleverly the first time. In some ways, the anticipation made things even better.

Much as it was convenient, having the tart come to my home, it just wasn't feasible or practical. For one thing, someone was bound to notice my visitor at some point, and for another, I couldn't continue to store the bodies at home. The coal hole would only hold one more at most, and there was no way I was going to start digging in the garden. I have never been a gardener, and since Mother died, all I have done is cut the lawn. If I started digging a huge trench in the back flowerbeds, someone would be bound to become suspicious.

But if I couldn't bring her here, where could I go? To visit a brothel was out of the question – I would be found out in a matter of minutes. I thought, momentarily, of hiring an anonymous room somewhere using a false name and paying with cash, but that was fraught with danger. I could be so easily traced.

I have to admit, I was stumped for several days. My predicament made me snappy and irritable, but luckily, people at work and the neighbours I met in the street put my bad temper down to grief over my recent bereavement. It was about the only time Mother was ever of use to me.

Eventually I decided I would go far away, to a small town with a thriving red light district. I would scope out possible sites where I would not be discovered, where I would be overlooked. Then I would find myself someone suitable, meet her at my chosen spot, and then...

I need to keep writing about the second girl but for some reason I find myself wanting to write about Mother. If I ever had to talk to someone about Mother – not that I ever would, or did – I think I would find it hard to explain exactly how she used to keep control of me, keep me cowed and shivering like a whipped dog. To this day, I don't know how she managed it.

There were only a few beatings, or perhaps it's more accurate to say that there were only a few that I can remember. One particularly painful one sticks in my memory because I remember focusing on the brooch she was wearing at the time. She had many brooches, and this one was in the shape of a butterfly, in a shade that recalled the summer sky at noon: a hard, pitiless blue. As the blows rained down, making my ears ring and my eyes squint down to slits, as I tried to absorb the jolts to my head and shoulders, all I could see was that butterfly shape. I think it was the last thing I remember seeing before I lost consciousness.

I think that was the last proper beating Mother gave me. I don't know, but I'm guessing that I was unconscious for a long time, and perhaps she thought she'd done some real damage. Perhaps she'd thought she'd killed me. Knowing her, it wouldn't have been anticipated grief for her dead child that stopped her doing it again. No, it would be the fact that everyone would find out, that everyone would finally realise the kind of person she really was.

It's no wonder, really, that I ended up the kind of person that I am. I learned it all from Mother: how to hide your real identity, how to put on a mask that fools the rest of the world. Only you know, deep inside, who you really are.

Chapter Seven

Kate went back to the Mission building the next morning, having rung ahead to check that Claudia was in residence. Margaret Paling was not in the reception booth this time; another woman, also grey-haired, also elderly, peered at Kate's warrant card suspiciously and let her through the security door to the lounge beyond.

Kate knocked on Claudia's door. A few moments later, it was flung wide by Claudia, who had a beaming smile on her face – a smile that cooled and died when she saw Kate.

"Good morning," said Kate, stepping forward across the threshold. "Were you expecting someone?"

Claudia muttered something, a possible negative, but Kate couldn't quite hear. The room was much larger than Mandy's, with two single beds against opposite walls, a large wardrobe, chest of drawers and, most significantly, a small girl with a mop of dark hair and large, dark eyes who was sat on the floor surrounded by toys and regarding Kate with a frown.

Kate cursed inwardly. Why hadn't she realised Claudia's daughter would be here? It was going to be almost impossible to talk about anything to do with the case in front of a small child. She thought quickly.

"I need to ask you a few more questions about Mandy, Claudia," she said. "Is there anyone who could look after Madison while we have a talk?"

Claudia shook her head, nervously.

"There's no one I'd leave her with here," she said. The little girl got up and pressed herself to the side of her mother, twining her thin little arms around Claudia's leg.

"No, okay," said Kate. "Why don't we all go for a walk? Madison, is there a playground near here you'd like to go to?"

There turned out to be a small patch of recreational ground with a couple of battered swings and a chipped and rusting climbing frame about five minutes' walk from the Mission. Madison clambered around the structure while her mother watched, and Kate tried to think of the questions she needed to ask. She was distracted by the thought that – given a different choice back in her teens – this could have been *her* life, trying to raise a child alone with no money and little support, trapped in a low-paying job if she was lucky and on benefits if she wasn't. *This could have been me.*

Kate suddenly and quite fervently knew that she *had* made the right choice back when she was seventeen. As hard as it had been at the time and for years afterwards. As hard as it sometimes still was. She'd made the right choice.

She made a massive effort to bring her mind back to the job. Claudia hadn't noticed her period of silence; she was watching Madison swinging herself back and forth with a proud, tender look on her face.

"Madison's a lovely little girl," said Kate, and she was rewarded by Claudia's pleased smile.

"She's a little monkey," said Claudia in the most animated tone Kate had yet heard from her.

"Mandy had a child, didn't she?"

Claudia's face clouded.

"Yeah," she said after a moment. "But he got took off of her by the social. She couldn't look after him properly. She was doing too many drugs at the time. It broke her heart when he went."

"I know I've asked you this before, Claudia, but are you sure that Mandy didn't have a boyfriend?"

Claudia still had her eyes fixed on Madison, who was trying to climb the frame of the swing and sliding down again. She shrugged.

"I told you, I dunno. I don't think so."

"Would she have told you if she had?"

"She might have. But I don't think she was seeing anyone. She always said men were bad news."

Kate nodded.

"How about you, Claudia?"

Startled, Claudia looked at her.

"What d'you mean?"

"Do you have someone? A boyfriend or partner? It must be hard raising a child by yourself."

Kate was only really making conversation, not really interested in the answer. A rising tide of blood suffused Claudia's face, and Kate regretted her casual words.

"No," said Claudia, after a moment. "I don't have no one."

Me neither, agreed Kate silently. *Me neither*.

"I FEEL LIKE I SHOULD be cutting a ribbon or something," said Anderton, one hand on the door to the renovated room. He flung it open with a flourish. "Ta-da!"

The team crowded in behind him, reacting with varying degrees of enthusiasm. Jane and Kate made appropriate 'oohs,' Olbeck, Theo and Rav nodded their cautious assent and Jerry lowered his brows and said something very similar to 'humph.'

"Well," said Anderton. "We're back in at least, thank God. I said something like this calls for champagne, didn't I?"

"You definitely said that," said Olbeck.

"Well, you'll find I'm a man of my word. We'll all have a little celebratory drink later."

This statement was met with a rather more enthusiastic response. The team sat down to their desks and applied themselves to their work with renewed energy. Kate rolled her chair back and forth over the new laminate and spun around a little, taking in the fresh new paint and the new skylights, which brought in the bright mid-summer sun.

She became aware that Theo was waving at her from the other side of the room.

"What's up?" she asked, making her way over to him.

He beckoned her down to his seated level.

"You know how you asked me about whether I'd found anything that resembled the MO? Similar murder weapon, situation, et cetera et cetera?"

"Yes," said Kate, alert now. She grabbed a spare chair and sat down next to Theo.

"Well, I've found one."

"Seriously?" Kate bent lower, looking at his computer screen. She lowered her voice. "Have you told Anderton yet?"

"Not yet."

"But you're telling me first?"

Theo grinned. "I'm nice like that. Also, you're subbing me in the run."

"Oh, that."

"Yeah, so I owe you. Anyway, look here." He tapped keys and brought up one of the database screens. "Murder of a prostitute in Brighton. Ingrid Davislova, age twenty-two years. Originally from Poland. She'd only been here a year or so, poor cow."

Kate read the rest of the details. The victim had been short, slim, dark-haired, and the murder weapon, which hadn't been found, was estimated to be some sort of serrated kitchen knife.

"This was just under eight months ago." She ran her eyes over the words and numbers on the screen once more. "It's good, Theo. It sounds like it could be our guy."

"I'm going to tell the boss. Give us a hand up, will you?"

Kate helped him up and balanced him while he tucked the crutches under his arms.

"Shall I tell him you know already?" asked Theo, stuffing the papers under one arm and wobbling a little as he attempted to turn around.

Kate shook her head.

"Not yet," she said. "Not just yet."

Kate's task for the afternoon was to interview Mandy Renkin's foster parents. Adele Watkins opened the front door of the Victorian-terraced house. She was a massive woman, not tall, but very overweight, with a fat, still-pretty face and short, curly grey hair. Clearly unembarrassed by her size, Adele wore loose trousers and a tunic in jewel-bright colours, and her chubby fingers sparkled with rings. Kate warmed to her immediately.

The house was very cluttered, the furniture was battered and the carpets were worn, but there was still an air of homely comfort throughout. A greyhound, as thin as its owner was fat, was curled in a dog basket in the messy kitchen, its sharp, bony muzzle resting on the side of the basket. Liquid brown eyes followed Kate as she walked past to the chair that Adele indicated at the table, and the dog's whip-like tail thumped. It whimpered softly.

"All right, you old softy," said Adele, and the dog jumped up immediately and came over to Kate, wiggling its bottom like a Caribbean dancer. Kate, charmed, stroked the head that had been laid in her lap as she listened to Adele talk about Mandy.

"Nice girl, lovely girl. Kind and intelligent. Too intelligent for her own good, I always thought. She had a tragic history. Well, my dear, they all do, to be honest."

"Have you fostered many children, Mrs Watkins?"

"Seems like hundreds. It's not, of course, but I've been doing this for – oh, twenty years now. I couldn't have any of my own. That's what got me started."

"I'm sorry to hear that," said Kate, automatically. She pulled the dog's silky ears gently, and it gave a whimper of pleasure.

"Well, perhaps it was for the best," said Adele. "I've been able to help a lot of children over the years, and if I'd had my own, well who knows whether I would have fostered any? No, I can't complain. I feel we've had a family, Bernard and I. It's very satisfying to know that you're able to give a child a stable home. There's so many kids out there who need one."

"Barbara Fee said as much. She said Mandy settled here really well."

"She did. She was a bit younger than the ones we usually have. We make a point of having the teenagers here if they need a place."

"Why is that?"

Adele pushed a plate of biscuits over to her. "Well, no one else wants them, my dear, you see? Most foster carers, most people who adopt – they want the babies, don't they? The littlies."

Kate flinched, unable to help herself. When would that ever stop hurting? She coughed, keeping her face as blank as she could.

Adele didn't seem to have noticed her momentary wince. She was looking out the kitchen window at a garden filled with a trampoline, a rusting swing and several bikes leaning up against the wall of a shed.

"Mandy had been in and out of care homes since she was five. She was desperate for a real home, somewhere where she could feel like she was in a family."

"Did she have any contact with her birth family at all?"

"No. No she didn't. Her mother was a chronic alcoholic. She's dead now, poor woman. I think she actually had Mandy put up for adoption, though. I mean, rather than Mandy being removed from her care."

Kate was careful to keep her voice steady when she asked the next question.

"How old was Mandy when that happened?"

Adele ran chubby fingers through her grey curls.

"I'm not sure, my dear, to be honest. It was such a long time ago now. I think she was two – two, maybe three?"

"And Mandy went into care? She wasn't adopted?"

"No, unfortunately not. No, they couldn't find a placement for her."

Kate scratched at the dog's ears, and it whined again with pleasure.

"That's sad," she murmured.

"Yes," said Adele, briefly. "It's amazing that she was as bright and as – well – normal as she could be by the time she came to us. Still, it took its toll though, those years in care. Yes, it took its toll."

"So Mandy came to you when she was ten?"

Adele nodded. "She settled immediately. Did well at school, made friends. We even thought she might go onto university."

"So what happened?"

Adele Watkins sighed. She eased her bulk a little in the slightly too-small kitchen chair.

"Oh, my dear," she said. "I could tell you that it was her boyfriend's fault. That would be the obvious explanation."

"Would this be Mike Fenton you're talking about?"

"Mike, yes – that was his name." Adele fell silent for a moment. Then she heaved herself off of her chair and went over to the kitchen dresser, crammed with crockery, cookery books, plastic toys, a child's sock, an empty beer bottle, a blackening banana and other assorted household detritus. From the chaos she extracted a small, framed photograph and handed it to Kate.

Kate looked at the picture. A teenage girl, bright-faced and smiling, dressed in her school uniform, with a slightly crooked fringe and freckles. Kate thought of that copy of *Great Expectations* in Mandy's room, the inscription on the flyer. Then she saw Mandy's dead face on Doctor Telling's examination table. She felt her fingers clench on the wooden frame.

"She was lovely," she said in a low voice.

Adele sat down again, heavily.

"She was. It's not—"

For a moment, her voice cracked. She turned her head sharply away from Kate to look again out of the window as if the view of the suburban garden fascinated her.

"It's not fair," said Adele after a moment. She cleared her throat. "Life's not fair though, is it, my dear?"

Kate said nothing but handed her back the picture, gently. Adele took it and propped it up against the vase of flowers that stood in the middle of the kitchen table.

"So, Mike Fenton is the one you blame?" asked Kate.

Adele looked at her with a gentle smile.

"No, I said that would be the obvious explanation. He was the one who introduced her to drugs after all. But no, I don't really blame him. Mandy made her own choices. She just made bad ones because she was missing something, you see."

"Missing something?"

Adele picked up the photograph again, regarding the bright, pretty face of the young girl trapped within the frame.

"I don't think you can conceive of the damage it does to a child when she has the kind of upbringing – or lack of it – that Mandy had," she explained. "When your mother doesn't want you – when you know your mother didn't want you – when you're rejected from that early an age, there's a part of you that doesn't ever recover. I think, somewhere deep down, you're always aware of the *lack*, you know. There's always a part of you that's missing."

There was a long moment of silence. Adele looked up at Kate.

"I'm sorry, my dear, are you all right?"

"I'm fine," said Kate with a clenched and frozen smile. "Thank you for seeing me, Mrs Watkins. You've been very helpful."

Adele looked a little surprised but heaved herself to her feet.

"Any time, my dear. I hope I've been of some help."

"Very much so," said Kate. She shook hands on the doorstep and handed over her card. "Thank you very much."

"Goodbye."

Kate made herself lift a hand in farewell as she reached the garden gate. Then she hurried around the corner, out of sight, and burst into tears.

Chapter Eight

"All right, all right," said Anderton. "I can see you're all eagerly eyeing up the booze behind me. Before we get stuck in, I want a quick rundown of where we're at. Who wants to start?"

They were all gathered in the once-pristine office, which was rapidly returning to its usual state of messiness. Behind Anderton's pacing figure stood a table with four bottles of champagne and a variety of glasses ranging from champagne flutes, a novelty shot glass from Ibiza and a beer mug. *Real* champagne too, not cheap fizz.

"Anybody?" asked Anderton.

Kate waved her hand.

"I interviewed Mandy's foster mother this afternoon. Mandy lived with the family for about five years until she left home to live with her boyfriend."

"Would this be the junkie one? Mark Fenton?"

"Mike Fenton, sir. Yes, that's the one."

Anderton propped himself against the table, causing the bottles to chink against one another.

"Whoops."

"Don't spill it," said Olbeck, grinning.

"God forbid. Anyway, what about this Mike Fenton? He's the one who introduced Mandy to drugs, got her on the downward spiral. I suppose we have eliminated him from our enquiries? Anyone checked on his whereabouts?"

Jane put her hand up.

"I did, sir. Did that as soon as I had the name from Kate and Mark's interview with Claudia Smith."

Anderton looked pleased.

"You did? Quick work Jane, well done." Jane smiled a bashful, modest smile. "So, what have we got?"

"Well sir, it definitely wasn't him."

"And why is that?"

"Because he's dead. Died about four years ago."

"Aha." Anderton eased himself from the edge of the table and began walking up and down again. "Let me guess. Drugs overdose?"

Jane shook her head. "Funnily enough, no. He was killed in a car crash."

"Well, there we go. He's still dead. Not our guy. Okay, what else?" He looked keenly across the room. "Theo?"

Theo was from necessity sitting down; his plastered leg stuck out in front of him.

He smiled rather self-consciously.

"There was a case, in Brighton, that strongly resembles our case here. Same sort of murder weapon. Same type of victim. The Brighton case was unsolved."

Anderton nodded. Kate, looking around at the other faces, saw a variety of expressions: uneasiness, excitement, scepticism, eagerness. Jerry was staring out of the window, his thoughts clearly far from this room.

Anderton raised his hand as if to quell a hubbub, although there was silence in the room.

"Now, I should mention that I asked Theo to look for cases with a similar MO," he said. "Don't go leaping to any enormous conclusions or anything. It's just something I thought should be looked into, that's all."

Olbeck asked the same question Kate had asked a few days ago.

"You think there will be more, sir? Are we talking another Ipswich, or something?"

Anderton had stopped pacing. He lifted his shoulders and dropped them.

"I don't know. I have no idea. I hope—" He was silent for a second. "We're planning for the worst, that's all. I hope I'm wrong."

There was another short period of silence, more loaded than the last. Then Anderton broke it.

"Now, don't go getting all panicky. I just want someone to follow up on the possible Brighton connection, that's all. Get a bit more info. Jerry!" Jerry almost jumped. "You've got contacts there, haven't you? Could you give one of them a ring, take a visit, that sort of thing?"

Jerry looked for a moment as if he were going to refuse. Then he shrugged.

"Okay, then. I'll go tomorrow."

"Good. Right then, if no one else has anything, I think we can call a halt to the official proceedings and prepare to declare this new office open." He turned to the table behind him and picked up the first bottle, ripping the gold foil from the top.

"Anyone got anything they want to say?"

"May God bless this new office and all who sail in her," said Olbeck, laughing.

"Quite right," said Anderton and the cork exploded from the bottle, ricocheting of the ceiling before a spume of froth shot out from the neck of the bottle, all over the new flooring. Jane shrieked and Rav whooped.

"Shit," said Anderton, grinning. "Don't just stand there, get me some glasses!"

Anderton began the slow journey around the room with a tray full of brimming glasses. He paused in front of Kate, Theo and Olbeck.

"Here you go," he said. The men took a glass each. Anderton went to leave.

"Wait," said Kate, suddenly reckless. "I'll have one."

All three men did a genuine double-take. Anderton was first to recover his composure.

"Right you are." He inclined the tray so that the biggest glass was nearest Kate's hand. "Why not? If you can't beat 'em, join 'em, eh, Kate?"

Kate took the glass and took a sip. Anderton moved on with the now-depleted tray.

Kate became aware of both Theo and Olbeck boggling at her.

"What?" she said, a little annoyed.

"Where is Kate Redman, and what have you done with her?" asked Olbeck.

"Check her pulse, she could be an alien imposter," said Theo, grinning.

"Oh, leave it out," said Kate. "I do have the odd drink, you know. I'm not *totally* teetotal. I've even got pissed with you both once."

"That was eight months ago," said Olbeck. "And you've not touched a drop since, at least that I'm aware of. What's the big occasion?"

Kate shrugged.

"Don't know. Just felt like it, I suppose."

"Well, damn it – cheers then." Olbeck clinked glasses with her, and after a second, Theo followed suit.

"You got any more on the Brighton case, Theo?" asked Kate after they'd all taken a drink. "Anything that you haven't told us?"

Theo was opening his mouth to answer when Olbeck cut across him.

"No, *no*," he said. "I absolutely forbid it. For once, we are not going to talk shop. Let's talk about something else. Anything."

"Wait while a deathly silence falls," said Kate. Then she relented. "All right, why not. Anyone seen any good films lately?"

Once the champagne ran out, the team decamped to the pub. Jane cried off, citing childcare arrangements, but everyone else headed for the battered old tavern three streets away that had almost become a second, unofficial office. Kate, Jerry and Olbeck sat down at the usual corner table next to the flashing fruit machines. Anderton and Rav headed for the bar, and Theo hobbled out to the garden for a cigarette.

Olbeck's phone rang. Answering the call, he waved an apology at Kate and Jerry and squeezed past them to take his phone call out in the relatively quiet street.

Kate and Jerry sat in an awkward silence, made somehow worse by the friendly tumult going on around them. Kate resisted the urge to check her own phone for messages. The unaccustomed champagne made her bold. Without stopping to think about whether it was a good idea or not, she turned to Jerry.

"So, why can't we be friends, Jerry? Why do we have this awkwardness between us? Is it something I've done?"

The smaller, sober part of her was aghast. Jerry was looking at her as if she'd just got up on the table and urinated in his pint glass.

"You what?" he said after a moment.

The tone of his voice should have warned Kate off, and if she hadn't drunk the best part of a half a bottle of champagne, she would have laughed and changed the subject and possibly ran out of the pub on the flimsiest of excuses. Instead, she repeated her question.

The long moment of silence that followed was lengthy enough for Kate to begin to feel rather unpleasantly sober. Then Jerry, not taking his eyes off hers, spoke.

"Yeah, you're right," he said. "I don't like you. Why would I?"

"Why would you?" Kate was aware she was blinking rapidly and shaking her head. "What do you mean? Why – why would you feel that way?"

Jerry scoffed. He turned to look back at the beer garden, the light dimming as the long summer twilight gradually gave way to night.

"Why wouldn't I?" he said. "Why? Why would I *like*, much less *respect*, someone who gets ahead by getting on her back?"

For a frozen moment, Kate thought she'd misheard him. Anderton was making his way back to the table with another tray full of drinks, Rav bringing up the rear.

"You what?" she asked, shock mangling her grammar.

"You heard me," said Jerry. "Slag," he added, almost as an afterthought.

Kate felt her hand go out without even thinking about it. Two seconds later, the remains of her glass of wine was running down Jerry's astonished face.

"Fuck!"

There was a confused scrimmage and a loud 'hey, hey' from Olbeck, who was making his way back to the table. Kate saw Jerry's hand clench into a fist, draw back. Time seemed to slow down. She was dimly aware that her lips were drawn back over her teeth, bared like an animal's.

"What the fuck? *Jerry—*"

Olbeck had his hand in front of Jerry's wine-drenched face, blocking his arm. Anderton and Rav were at the table, crashing down the drinks. There was a loud shout of "Oy! Take it outside!" from the bar. Kate and Jerry sat glaring at each other until Anderton clamped a hand about Kate's wrist and virtually dragged her outside into the street.

"*What* the *hell*?"

Kate said nothing, but stood rubbing her wrist. She thought of telling Anderton – of all people! – what Jerry had said, what he'd accused her of. Rage and shame mounted in her chest, flooded her throat and rose until it was pricking the back of her eyes. She turned away, shaking her head.

"Where are you going?"

"Home," Kate muttered. Olbeck appeared in the pub doorway with Rav close behind him. She mouthed a 'sorry' at them and turned, beginning to walk away, not wanting to see the surprise and shock on their faces.

"Kate, for God's sake—"

Anderton appeared at her side. She turned her head away and walked a little faster. She was aware she was behaving ridiculously, but her hurt pride didn't seem to be able to let her laugh it off and apologise.

"Kate Redman, would you stop behaving like a child and listen to me for a second?"

Kate came to a halt at the end of the road, finally stopped in her path by Anderton's tone. She'd heard that voice once or twice before in her career, never in the most cheerful of circumstances. She stared across the road, seeing the passing cars and the streetlights through a smear of salt water.

"What did Jerry say to you?" asked Anderton in a gentler tone.

Kate cleared her throat.

"It doesn't matter," she said. "I'm sorry about throwing the drink."

"Don't apologise to *me*."

Kate finally turned to stare at him. He was looking at her in a way she couldn't decipher.

"Well, I'm not apologising to him," she said through clenched teeth. There was a long, charged moment as their eyes met. Then Kate turned away.

"I'm going home," she muttered.

"I'll walk you home."

"Don't bother," she retorted and then immediately regretted her rudeness. Anderton took no notice. He put a hand under her arm and escorted her across the road during a gap in the traffic.

"I *will* walk you home, DS Redman," he said. "There's a man who kills women on the loose in this town. Do you think I'm going to have you walking about after dark in a tired and emotional state while he's still around?"

They had reached the opposite pavement by this time, and

Anderton removed his hand. Kate could still feel the warmth of where it had rested on the underside of her arm.

"Women?" she asked, after a moment.

"Well, a woman. Whatever the semantics are, I'm not having you walking home alone. Is that clear?"

"Yes, sir," murmured Kate. All of a sudden, she felt exhausted.

"Right, which way do we go?"

They walked in silence for several minutes. Kate could feel the alcohol wearing off, leaving a heaviness in her limbs, an incipient headache tapping at her temples. She rubbed her hands under her eyes. What an idiot she had been. But how much of a bastard was Jerry? Seriously, what *was* his problem? Why had he accused her of – of what he had?

"Why would he *say* that?"

"What's that?"

"Oh." Kate realised she'd spoken her thought aloud. "It doesn't matter."

"Okay."

They walked on a bit further.

"Why is Jerry such a pig?" Kate burst out, unable to keep it in any longer. "Why does he have such a problem with me?"

"I don't know," said Anderton, mildly. "He's never had much time for women."

"The ignorant, sexist, stupid *pig*."

"Now, Kate," said Anderton, stepping around the remains of someone's takeaway curry on the pavement. "Sexist pig he may be, but he's certainly not stupid."

"No?"

"He went to Cambridge, for a start."

Kate snorted, sure Anderton was joking. Then she looked at him more closely.

"You're joking, right?"

"Nope. Clare College, if I remember correctly."

"*Jerry?*" Kate struggled to keep her mouth shut as she thought, *Well, what the fuck is he doing in the police force?*

"It was a long time ago."

"No kidding." How old *was* Jerry, anyway? Surely he was coming up to retirement age. Kate said as much.

"Yes, that's right," said Anderton. They were approaching Kate's street. "That's another reason I would be – making allowances for his behaviour, shall we say? He's been on the force for years and that's all he knows. I can't imagine what he'll do with himself once he retires. It's making him snappy. Irritable. That's all. Not to mention the fact that he's had a bit of a hard year."

He didn't elaborate. Kate walked on in silence for a moment, picturing Jerry; trying to reconcile the abrupt, overweight, grey-haired, uptight policeman she knew with a Cambridge university student. The stereotypical image of one, at least: black-gowned, floppy hair, upper-class accent.

"Is this you?"

Kate realised they has stopped outside her garden gate. She looked up at her house, at the dark windows, the lack of light within. Then she looked at Anderton.

"See, this is why I don't drink."

"What do you mean?"

"I do stupid things."

They were standing very close to one another. Kate could feel his breath on her face, beer-scented.

"Is that what you call it?" Anderton said. He wasn't looking in her eyes, he was looking at her mouth.

Kate could feel the precipice beneath her feet. Down there was – what? Damnation? Or salvation?

"I don't know what else you'd call this," she said, and she stepped forward into his arms.

J's diary

After Brighton, I felt invincible. It had gone even better than I'd hoped. I'd spent a few days walking around the town, disguised as myself, disguised as a tourist. I stayed in a hotel, an anonymous chain hotel, because I wanted as low a profile as possible, particularly when it came to the actual night of the killing. I was pleasant to any of the fellow guests who spoke to me, although few did, as my usual disguise is such a boring, uninteresting one. I am totally forgettable. This is both a blessing and a curse.

I would find a nice restaurant and eat my evening meal there, companioned only by my book. I would have a modest glass of wine, eat my dinner and then go back to the hotel, murmuring a 'good night' to the receptionists behind the desk. I prepared myself in my room, excitement mounting with every minute that ticked by, fortifying myself with whisky and checking and rechecking that I had the knife tucked safely inside my jacket pocket. Then I would creep out, through the back entrance that I'd discovered on my first night there. Even if there were CCTV cameras about, my hat, scarf and glasses would provide enough camouflage.

It was on the third night that I found the perfect one: small, slim and dark-haired. I saw her emerge from a car at the side of the street that I'd already noted as a likely hunting ground. This is where the tarts worked, strutting for custom, taking their punters into the darkened wasteland that stood behind an abandoned factory. I watched from my vantage point and chose the right moment. She was looking about her as I came up to her and presented my request in a low voice. She was drunk or stoned or something; she was swaying on her feet, pupils dilated even further than they should be, even in the darkness surrounding us. There was no one else around.

She stumbled over the rough ground as we walked into the wasteland. I didn't touch her. She led me around a corner, where a breezeblock wall stood, and leant up against it. She almost fell against it. She pulled up her skirt in a bored manner, but by that time, I was trembling with excitement, and the knife was in my hand.

She didn't make a sound other than a small grunt as the blade sank in. It was me who made the noise: a groan muffled against the skin of her neck as the world swam away from me.

Chapter Nine

Something was wrong. Kate closed her eyes for a moment and then opened them again. She would normally open her eyes and find herself regarding her bedroom door. But, this morning, the spare bedside table was the first sight that met her eyes. Kate blinked. She had a few seconds of blissful ignorance, and then memory rushed back in to fill the gap. At the same moment, she became aware of Anderton's warm leg lying against hers beneath the covers. Kate shut her eyes tightly, cringing. *Oh God.* She'd ended up in bed with her boss. *Oh, God.*

She badly needed to pee, but she didn't want to wake him up. What the hell was she going to do?

After a few moments, she stealthily got up and crept from the room, bending double as if to hide her nakedness from the world.

In the bathroom, she took care of the pressing need of her bladder before checking her reflection. Tousled hair, flushed cheeks, the remnants of last night's make-up smeared under her eyes. Quickly, she swiped a flannel over her face and swished some mouthwash through her teeth.

"Morning," said the buried shape of Anderton as she got back into bed, wrapped in her dressing gown.

"Morning," said Kate, trying for casualness.

There was movement under the duvet, and then he turned to face her, smiling. Kate had a moment of disconnect: the surreal reality that was Anderton in her bed.

"What have you got that on for?" he asked, tugging at the dressing gown cord.

Kate mumbled something, a feeble protest that was rapidly lost as Anderton worked the cord loose and slid his hand underneath, pulling Kate towards him.

They were rapidly reaching a crucial point in the proceedings when a phone began to ring. For a few moments, they carried on until it became clear that the phone was going to keep ringing until someone answered it. Anderton cursed, rolled off Kate and snatched it up.

"Anderton," said Anderton, the gasp not quite gone from his voice. There was a moment when the voice on the other end spoke, and Kate saw his shoulders stiffen. She sat up in bed slowly, pulling the covers up and tucking them under her arms, suddenly self-conscious. Anderton still hadn't spoken.

"Where?" he asked eventually. Then nothing until the voice paused, and he said "I'll be right down. Just get everyone that you can down there and try and hold off the press."

He pressed a button to terminate the call and placed his phone very slowly and precisely back on Kate's bedside table, still facing away from her.

"What is it?" said Kate, already knowing and yet still dreading the answer.

Anderton didn't turn around for a moment. Then he rolled back on the pillow and looked at her, his face very serious.

"It's another girl, isn't it," said Kate. A statement, not a question.

Anderton nodded. He put out an arm as if he were about to draw her down next to him and then something stopped the movement. Kate hadn't taken her eyes from his face.

"Is it the same—"

Anderton nodded.

"Same weapon. At least it looks that way. Same type, small and dark-haired."

"Oh, God." Kate wanted to get up but she felt shy about revealing her nakedness, absurdly. The whole tempo of their connection had suddenly changed – from passionate and romantic to grimly purposeful. It felt wrong to be in bed with him, suddenly, as it hadn't done a moment before the phone call.

"Where was the body—"

Kate didn't seem to be able to finish a full sentence. Anderton understood her anyway.

"The same place. The warehouses, the rough ground."

Kate's eyes widened.

"But that's—"

"He's taking the *piss*!" said Anderton, cutting across her. He rolled violently out of bed and began to yank on his scattered clothes.

Kate watched, wanting to say something but not sure what, biting her lip. After he was dressed, Anderton looked as if he was about to head out of the bedroom door without even a goodbye. At the doorway, he stopped and then swung around and came back to the bed. He tipped Kate's chin up and kissed her, rather bruisingly.

"I need you there, Kate. Will you come?"

"Ye-yes," stuttered Kate, shaken a little by the violence of his kiss. Then she got a hold of herself.

"I'll come with you, shall I?"

Anderton shook his head.

"No, just get there when you can. Best we don't arrive together, eh?"

He gave her a rueful smile.

"Of course," said Kate bravely, to hide the quake in the pit of her stomach. Was he saying he regretted what had happened?

"Good. See you soon."

He was out the bedroom door without another word. Kate

waited until she heard the slam of the front door. Then she pushed back the covers and slowly swung her legs over the edge of the bed.

Under the streaming waters of the shower, she hung her head forward, letting the water roll over her face and closed eyes. There were too many emotions swirling around her head for Kate to even feel vaguely in control of herself. She made an effort, straightening up and trying to untangle how she felt.

Guilt. That was the main one. Guilt for having what could well turn out to be a one-night stand. She didn't *do* that sort of thing. No matter that she didn't *want* it to be a one-night stand. Sleeping with her boss – that was about the biggest no-no of them all. Okay, so she knew he was separated from his wife, but was he actually divorced? What about his children? Did he want a relationship with her, Kate, or was it going to be one of those dreadfully awkward working relationships where the fact that you'd once shagged meant you spent the rest of your career avoiding the subject with one another?

There was another, sharper layer of guilt too. Guilt that she'd been so distracted and so full of her own selfish inclinations that she'd not paid the attention to the case as she should have. And now another woman was dead. If Kate had been better at her job, worked harder, paid more attention – did that mean that they could have caught the man who was responsible already, caught him before he could kill again?

A small, reprehensible part of her wanted to relive the events of last night in detail, go over and over what had happened with a shiver of delight. And the juxtaposition of that feeling with the scene she now had to attend to was somehow the worst of all. What should have been a luxurious, sensual memory was now tainted.

For fuck's sake, Kate. Grow up and get a hold of yourself. You've got a job to do.

Kate dressed, pulling on sober clothes and brushing her hair back into its customary ponytail. The ache in unfamiliar places, the slight soreness when she moved was a constant reminder of what had happened last night.

There were other niggles as well, little jolts of uneasiness as memories surfaced. Kate hadn't had any condoms in the house – of course she hadn't, she hadn't had sex since 1995, or so it felt like – but Anderton had pulled a fresh packet from his jacket pocket. Why was he carrying them around? Of course, Kate knew there was only one reason that men carried condoms around. They were going to use them. And yes, she knew that it was the responsible thing to do but...but... He clearly wasn't celibate. Who was he seeing? One woman or many? Was he still sleeping with his wife? Oh *God*... Kate realised she was standing in the kitchen staring blankly at the hook on which her car keys hung. She shook herself back to reality and unhooked the keys.

As she started the car, her thoughts returned obsessively to Anderton's condom packet. Had he bought them at the pub before he walked her home? Did he plan to seduce her? Well, if he had, she'd made it pretty bloody easy for him, hadn't she? Where did she stand now, with him?

And why the bloody hell are you even worrying about this when you're about to visit a murder *scene?* She asked herself the question fiercely, gunning the accelerator.

It was a grey, nothing-y sort of morning, warm, humid and still. Kate parked the car a street away from the warehouses, wishing she'd eaten something or drunk a cup of coffee. She found a boiled sweet in her bag – where the hell had that come from? – and crunched it up. Blah, disgusting. What was wrong with her? Casual sex, drinking (albeit a fairly pathetic three glasses of champagne and half a glass of wine) and not bothering to eat breakfast? At least she was washed and dressed appropriately.

Kate dropped her head back against the back of the car seat for a moment. It was eight thirty eight in the morning and she was already exhausted. Then again, she hadn't exactly gotten much sleep last night. The thought provoked a guilty, half-gleeful smile, and she had to remind herself, yet again, that she was about to view a murder scene.

She was walking towards the waste ground when she realised she would be seeing Jerry for the first time since drenching him with wine. Her steps faltered before she remembered that he'd gone to Brighton for the day to check up on that similar case. Well, that was one thing to be thankful for. She could see the white plastic tent in the distance, the crime-scene tape girdling the scene, the various uniforms and plainclothes officers standing about. The flap of the tent was flung back and Anderton emerged, grim-faced. Kate's stomach flipped. She mentally shook herself. *There cannot be the slightest hint of what went on last night.* She took a deep breath and joined Olbeck and Jane and Rav where they were standing by the entrance to the tent.

"Morning."

Olbeck looked surprised to see her. He was opening his mouth to say something when Anderton shouted over.

"Kate! Over here, please."

"Talk to you in a sec," said Kate in an aside to Olbeck, not displeased at having to put off the inevitable questions. She walked over to where Anderton stood by the tent's entrance, trying to keep a blank face, trying not to smile inappropriately.

Anderton wasn't smiling. He nodded towards what lay inside the tent, and Kate, saying nothing, ducked inside.

The tent was close and hot already. Kate looked at the body on the floor, and any thought of smiling left her. She felt the shock of it as if she'd swallowed a pint of ice-water.

The dead woman was Claudia Smith.

Chapter Ten

Kate ducked back out into the open air. Despite the warmth of the day, her face felt cold and stiff.

"It's Claudia Smith," she said to Anderton, as if he wouldn't already know.

He nodded and indicated for her to walk ahead of him, towards the others.

They stood in a group, looking at one another. Kate could see her emotions reflected in the others' faces: anger, guilt, bewilderment.

"Well," said Anderton. "This takes things to a new level, as I'm sure you can imagine."

"Who found her?" asked Olbeck.

"A dog walker. He was walking along the tow path, and his dog hared off here and went straight to the body, wouldn't come when called, so his owner followed him. We've taken him down to the station already to take his statement."

Kate stood clutching her elbows, her eyes cast down. A memory recurred: Claudia's look of pride as she watched her daughter clambering about on the climbing frame. Kate winced. She would not think about Madison and how she was now, essentially, an orphan.

"Kate?"

Kate looked up. Anderton was looking at her, and there was something tender in his gaze that both warmed and, conversely, alarmed her.

"I'm all right," she said.

"That's two girls who lived at the Mission," said Rav. "That can't be a coincidence. Can it?"

"Unlikely," said Anderton. "Now, let SOCO and the docs do

their work here. Here's what we're going to do. Olbeck, Kate, you come with me to the Mission. Jane, go back to the office and dig up everything you can on our victim. Take Rav with you. Rav, pull all the CCTV footage from a mile-wide radius around this place. Go through it with a fine tooth comb. There must be *something* from last night."

Kate sat in the back of the car as usual, with Anderton driving and Olbeck riding shotgun. She looked at the back of the two men's heads, Olbeck's hair just a little too long, curling at the back of his neck, Anderton's grey mane neatly brushed. She remembered pushing her hands through his hair last night, bringing his face to hers. Kate jerked her gaze away, feeling her face heat up. She wondered what Anderton was thinking. Were his thoughts on the case or was he thinking about her? He met her gaze in the rear view mirror, and she snatched her glance away, knowing she was blushing and hating herself for it.

Margaret Paling met them at the door of the Mission, as if she'd been waiting for them to arrive. She was pale and wringing her hands.

"I'm so glad you're here," she said in a fervent whisper. "One of our girls is missing. She didn't turn up for work this morning and her bed's not been slept in—"

"Claudia Smith," said Anderton, sweeping past her.

"Yes, that's right," said Margaret, hurrying after him. "Has someone already told you? Oh. Oh no—"

She stopped, hands to her face. The police officers were already at the door of Father Michael's office. Through the glass door they could see that he was sat at his desk, staring unseeingly into space, his hands gripping the edge of the desk as if it were the only thing keeping him from falling.

He jumped up as the officers entered the room.

"You've found her? Please tell me you've found her?"

Anderton began to tell him of their grim discovery of the morning, speaking gently but inexorably. As he listened, Father

Michael's eyes filled with tears. He turned, stumbled, put his hands out to break his fall and ended up on his knees, grasping his office chair.

"No, no, it can't – it can't be true—"

Kate and Olbeck exchanged glances. Anderton let them raise the man up to his feet and gently turn him around to face them. Father Michael was blinded by tears, the face of a drowning man coming up for his last gasp of air. He groped for his desk, sat down and buried his head in his arms.

After a few moments, Anderton asked, quietly, if Father Michael would be prepared to identify the body. He had to repeat the question.

"What?"

"Would you be prepared to identify the body, sir? You knew Claudia well."

Father Michael burst into fresh tears. He managed to nod over the flood.

"I'll do it. I have to – I have to see for myself."

He continued to cry, more quietly now, in the back of the car sat next to Kate. She was surprised at the level of impatience she felt for him. He was acting more like a bereaved father than someone who ran the hostel that accommodated the victim. She met Anderton's eyes in the mirror again but this time, there was no embarrassment. It was a mutual expression of *'what is going on here?'*

Although it was unusual for Kate, she decided to duck out of the actual identification. She wasn't sure she was up to seeing the fresh theatrics that the sight of Claudia's body would produce in Father Michael. Sitting at her desk, she pulled herself up on that thought. Why *theatrics*? Why did that word come to mind?

Slowly she became aware that someone was speaking her name. With a jerk, she came back to reality to find Anderton at her shoulder.

"My office?"

Kate nodded, aware of Olbeck sitting down opposite her. He looked surprised to see her summoned by the boss. *If he only knew*, Kate thought as she followed Anderton to his office. Would he shut the door? For a moment, after she sat down, she thought he wouldn't, but he obviously changed his mind and shut it firmly.

There was a moment of tortuous silence.

"Kate—"

"Can I talk to you about Father Michael?" asked Kate, quickly.

Anderton blinked, sat back.

"Of course," he said, after a moment.

"What did you think?"

"Of his reaction?" Anderton watched her face, keeping her gaze. "I know what you mean."

"Do you think he could be bluffing?"

"It's possible."

"Don't you think it was over the top for someone who's supposed to have a fairly limited relationship with the victim?"

"Yes. It's not – not in character."

"Well, then..."

Silence fell. Kate tried desperately to think of something else to say. She could see Anderton gearing up to speak.

"Well, if that's everything," she said brightly, jumping up and making for the door.

"Wait. *Wait*."

Kate paused, her back to Anderton, her hand on the door handle. She was very aware of him walking up behind her, standing close enough for his breath to stir the hair on the back of her neck. Her hand slipped a little on the metal door handle.

"Aren't we even going to talk about it?" asked Anderton, speaking so softly she could barely hear him.

"Of course," muttered Kate. "It's just that—"

He leant forward and kissed the back of her neck, where the

skin was exposed and her hair swept up into a ponytail. She lost the power of speech entirely.

"Turn around."

She couldn't move, could only shake her head mutely. He gently turned her round and kissed her, pressing her back against the door. Kate, while glorying in the sensation, was very aware that only three inches of wood and metal kept her colleagues and superiors from discovering what was going on. As soon as the thought flashed across Kate's brain, there was a knock at the door and Kate and Anderton leapt apart as if propelled by an electric shock.

Kate, barely knowing what she was doing, went to sit back down at the desk. Anderton ran his hands through his hair and took a deep breath.

Rav barrelled in a moment later, waving a sheaf of papers.

"Sir," he said urgently, taking the spare chair by Kate. "CCTV from the night of the murder. You have to see this."

"What have we got?"

Anderton flung himself down in his chair and reached for the papers. Kate could almost admire the way he was acting, as if he and Kate had merely been talking about the case moments before, rather than pressed up against one another, panting and groping. It was very convincing. She then had the very unwelcome thought, *Perhaps he's done this before.*

She made an effort to concentrate on what Rav was saying.

"Look here. And here. The same car."

Anderton studied the print-outs alertly.

"This is last night?"

Rav shook his head.

"No. I've not been able to get that yet. But this is the night that Mandy Renkin was killed. This car was seen very close to the warehouses and look here—" He pointed to a blurry image of a dark-haired girl sat in the passenger seat of the car in question. "Doesn't that look very like her?"

Anderton brought the picture closer to his face.

"It does," he said quietly. "Now tell me you know who this car is registered to, Rav."

Rav was grinning.

"Of course. Address of the owner is Twenty six Lavender Street, Charlock."

Kate gasped. Anderton's fist curled, crumpling the paper.

"I *knew* it," he growled. "Father Michael. Is he still here?"

"No, Jane dropped him back at the Mission."

"Well, get him back here. Right now."

Rav was already heading towards the door. Kate got up, chewing her thumbnail. Her head was in a whirl: Anderton's kisses, Father Michael's car and the small, curled body of Claudia Smith all vied for her attention. She felt dizzy.

She was at the door when Anderton spoke her name, but this time she looked back, smiled and shook her head before she left the room.

Chapter Eleven

Father Michael took the chair falteringly. He looked around at the breezeblock walls painted an indifferent cream, the scuffed linoleum on the floor, the screwed down table with the air of man in a waking nightmare. He kept blinking, as if the harsh light from the strip light overhead hurt his eyes.

Anderton and Kate sat down opposite him and the duty solicitor.

Anderton began.

"Father Michael Brannigan, are you aware of why we've brought you in for questioning today?"

Father Michael was still looking about him. He folded his trembling hands in front of him on the table.

"Yes. Yes, you want to talk to me about Claudia." He looked directly at them both, his resonant voice suddenly gaining in strength and assurance. "I assure you that I did not kill her."

Anderton ignored his statement.

"How long have you known Claudia Smith?"

Father Michael blinked again.

"She's been at the Mission for a while. Perhaps six months? I would have to check the records."

"Did you know her before she came to live at the Mission?"

"Yes. Yes, well, very slightly. She used to attend a mother and baby group that the church ran at a local village hall, and I believe I first met her then, when she came along with her daughter."

Anderton nodded. His manner changed slightly, became more conspiratorial, more...matey.

"So you have known her some time, Father? Would you say you were friends?"

Father Michael smiled, rather tremulously.

"Friends? Well, I'm not sure that would be the right term. The disparity in our ages and circumstances... I liked her. I felt sorry for her and Madison. There was so much stacked against them."

"How so?"

Father Michael's smile vanished.

"She had a tragic past, you know. Not much family support, no real role model at home. She got into a relationship with a man who treated her appallingly."

"That was Madison's father?"

Father Michael nodded.

"Have you questioned *him*? He was a monster, violent, abusive. Has *he* been questioned about her death?"

"Enquiries are continuing," said Anderton smoothly, the usual response to that sort of question. He leant forward a little. "So you wouldn't say you were close friends with Claudia?"

"No – not as such, no."

Anderton sat back.

"What about Mandy Renkin?"

Kate was watching Father Michael's face closely. He didn't look shocked or guilty, merely blank.

"Mandy?"

"Would you say you were close friends?"

"No. Not at all. She was a young woman who lived at the Mission, that's all. I wished her well, I was concerned with her welfare but not – nothing much more."

Anderton brought his hand out from under the table. He was holding the print outs from the CCTV of Father Michael's car taken on the night of Mandy Renkin's death. He threw them onto the table in front of the priest and the slippery paper slid into a fan shape of dark images on the table top.

"So what was she doing in your car on the night of her death, Father?" he asked quietly.

Father Michael looked at the papers, seemingly uncomprehendingly.

"I – I don't—" he began.

"This is your car. Seen in the area of the crime, on the night of Mandy's death, with Mandy Renkin in the front seat."

"I—"

"What explanation do you have for this?"

Father Michael was silent for a long moment.

"I – it—"

Whatever excuse he had tried to come up with was discarded. Kate could see it in his face: the realisation that whatever reason he brought up just wouldn't wash.

"Is this your car?" continued Anderton, relentless.

After a moment, Father Michael nodded wordlessly.

"Speak up, please."

"I'm sorry, yes. Yes, it's my car."

"Can you explain what it was doing in the vicinity of the crime scene on the night Mandy Renkin died? Is that Mandy in the front seat?"

Again, that moment of wordlessness. Kate could see the man sat opposite her thinking hard. Was he working out his excuse or thinking up a plausible lie?

"That is my car," said Father Michael eventually. "But that's not Mandy."

Anderton narrowed his eyes. "It's not? Who is it then?"

"It's Claudia."

"Claudia Smith?" A nod from Father Michael. He clasped and unclasped his hands, suddenly an old man. "What was she doing in your car?"

Father Michael cleared his throat.

"I was just giving her a lift."

"Where?"

"To – to a friend's house."

"Who is this friend?"

"She didn't say. She just – just asked if I could give her a lift. It was a cold night, I didn't want her to walk, so – so I said I would."

"Where did you drop her off?"

Father Michael was staring at the CCTV printouts as if they fascinated him.

"I'm sorry?"

"Where did you drop Claudia off?" repeated Anderton.

"I – I don't remember."

"Whereabouts?"

"I'm sorry. I can't remember."

He was lying. Kate pressed the side of her foot against Anderton's shoe, the usual way she had of communicating with him. A second later, she realised, as she never had before, that she was essentially playing footsie with him and snatched her boot away as if his shoe had been red hot. It had done the trick though; he turned very slightly to her and she communicated her scepticism to him in a direct, wordless look. He nodded very slightly.

"I want to talk to my solicitor," said Father Michael, slightly too loudly. "Alone. That's allowed, isn't it?"

Left alone, Kate suddenly felt the awkwardness between Anderton and herself. Or she told herself she felt it. Did she really know what he was thinking? Would she ever?

Impulsively she turned to him and opened her mouth, but before she could say anything, he gave her a miniscule shake of the head, indicating with his finger the camera in the corner of the room. Chastened, Kate sat back in her chair.

Father Michael and his solicitor had only been away for five minutes, but in the silence that swamped the interview room during their departure, it felt more like five years to Kate. She'd never before been so pleased to see a suspect reappear.

Father Michael sat back down again in the same chair he'd had before. He folded his hands in front of him again, but they were steadier than they had been before.

"I've something to tell you," he announced with a glance at his solicitor, who gave him a slight nod.

"Yes?" Anderton sat up a little.

Father Michael cleared his throat.

"Claudia and I – Claudia and I were – we were in a relationship. Having a relationship."

He pressed his lips together as if he were unwilling to say more.

Anderton raised his eyebrows.

"Care to elaborate?"

The tone of Anderton's voice must have stung. Kate watched the blood rise in Father Michael's cheeks, visible even behind his beard.

"I – well, we – we were in a relationship, like I said."

"A sexual relationship?"

"Yes." Father Michael's face was fiery now, and for the first time, Kate felt a twinge of pity for him.

"How long had this been going on?"

Father Michael cleared his throat again.

"Not very long. Several months, I suppose. Perhaps six months."

"You can't remember exactly?"

"Well, I – no, not exactly." Father Michael pulled his folded hands under the table, away from their eyes. Kate knew it was because his hands were trembling again.

He went on, falteringly.

"We go – we used to go to a hotel near Arbuthon Green. That was where we were driving on the night of Mandy's death. That was why we were in the area and why Claudia was in my car."

Anderton kept his eyes on the man's hot face.

"What was the name of the hotel?"

"It was nowhere very expensive, nothing – nothing showy."

"That's not what I asked."

"Yes. Sorry. It's called The Pines.'"

"You stayed there how often?"

Father Michael's flush had been fading, but now it returned in a renewed, rosy hue.

"A few times a week. Sometimes on weekends. It depended on whether she could get anyone to look after her daughter."

"Anyone?"

"Well, her mother. She would only let her mother look after Madison. She was very protective of her."

His voice shook, and he looked down at his hidden hands. Despite herself, Kate was wrenched momentarily with pity. She tried not to think of Madison and her solemn little face, her big dark eyes. What would they have told her? How do you break something like that to a little child?

Anderton began the questioning again but Kate, drifting off a little, found herself picturing Father Michael and Claudia. Actually picturing them in bed together. Thirty years or more between them: education, class, even intelligence perhaps a chasm between them. Why had he pursued her? Or had it been the other way around? Had he been kind to her, poor Claudia, who had been so dreadfully treated by another man? Now Kate remembered going to interview her about Mandy Renkin, the way that Claudia had flung her bedroom door open in happy anticipation. She must have thought it was Father Michael who'd knocked.

What a risk he had taken, though, this priest who was supposed to be celibate, above the temptations of the flesh. No such thing, as Kate had good reason to know.

Her colleagues would be crawling all over the Mission now, checking computers and laptops and offices, digging into everything to try and prove a connection with the killings. Kate turned her attention back to Anderton, who was wrapping up this session of questioning.

"I think we'll take a break, there," he said, shuffling his papers into a rough stack. Father Michael sat back in his chair, raising his hands to his eyes. His solicitor bent forward and picked up her briefcase.

Kate was the first out in the corridor. She stood aside as Father Michael was escorted back to the cells; they would hold him for another twenty-four hours and then either charge him with the murders of Claudia Smith and Mandy Renkin or release him. She watched his thin figure disappear as the heavy door to the cells closed behind him. Was it possible that this stooped, bearded man was actually a serial killer?

"Got a minute?" asked Anderton, directly behind her, and Kate jumped.

They went to Anderton's office, but this time, he didn't close the door. Obviously there were to be no illicit kisses this time. Kate sat down at his desk, feeling a slow droop of her spirits.

Anderton flung himself into the opposite chair and began to flick through the paperwork.

"Can you get over to Brannigan's house tomorrow and start going through it?" he asked, his eyes scanning the papers before him. "Take Theo – oh wait, of course you can't. Take Rav and Jane and make a start."

Kate waited to see if he'd say anything else, something personal, something intimate. He didn't. He didn't even look at her.

"Yes, sir," she said, numbly, and got up to go. Unable to help herself, she looked back as she reached the doorway. Anderton still had his head down, intent on his work. Kate hesitated and then left, swallowing hard against the thickening in her throat.

Chapter Twelve

THE GOOD WEATHER TURNED THE next day; June's blue skies were obscured with thick grey clouds and spitting rain. Kate dug her summer raincoat out from beneath the pile of jackets and scarves that hung on the back of the downstairs toilet door and put it on. She sat on the bottom step of the staircase to lace up her trainers, caught sight of the time on her wristwatch and cursed. She was supposed to be picking Rav up at nine and he lived a good twenty minutes' drive from her place. It was already eight forty-five.

She sent him a quick text telling him she was running late, grabbed her car keys and locked up the house. She knew why she was late, which was most unlike her. She'd spent the night rolling from one side of the bed to another, trying to get comfortable, trying to ignore the gnawing in the pit of her stomach.

This is what happens when you get involved, *Kate,* she told herself. Months, no, *years* of happy equilibrium and celibacy and then one night of passion and it all goes to pot...

As was usual when one was in a hurry, the traffic was heavy, and every traffic light disobligingly went red as Kate approached it. She tapped her fingers on the steering wheel, gritting her teeth. Eventually, she drew into the driveway of the block of flats, drove into a parking space and beeped the horn. Kate raised her hand as Rav's flatmate, whom she knew very slightly, passed the car, obviously on his way to work. Then Rav knocked on her window, making her jump.

"Morning!"

"Hi," said Kate, smiling in spite of herself. Rav was the youngest member of the team, barely into his twenties. He'd joined the police force straight after sixth form college and barely looked any older than he had when he'd left school. Kate didn't have much in common with him, but they worked together well. She liked his energy and enthusiasm.

Whilst Rav strapped himself in, Kate tapped the postcode to Father Michael's house into the sat nav.

"Jane's meeting us there," she said. "Mind if we stop on the way and grab a coffee?"

"Nope, no problem." Rav looked slyly across at her and grinned. "As long as you don't throw it in my face."

Kate thought she'd misheard him for a moment. She looked over, eyebrows raised – and then she got it.

"Oh, ha bloody ha. Oh, my aching sides."

She snorted and put her foot down harder on the accelerator.

"What *happened* with you and Jerry?" asked Rav, clearly burning with curiosity, which Kate was not about to satisfy. She waved a hand in a dismissive manner.

"Not much," she said. "Storm in a tea-cup. Or a wine glass."

Rav giggled. "It was just so totally not like you. We couldn't believe it."

"Oh well," said Kate, uncomfortably. "Did you guys stay on much longer?"

"Yeah, 'til closing time. And *then* we went clubbing."

"Jerry went clubbing?"

"Yeah, I know, not like him, is it?" Rav pushed a hand through his thick, black hair. "Seriously, it was daylight by the time we all rolled out of the club. I'm still hungover now."

"Mmm-hmm," said Kate, having heard enough about Jerry. She wanted to forget that part of the night altogether if she could.

Rav checked his phone.

"We're still holding this priest, yeah?"

"That's right," said Kate. "Anderton wants us to go through this house with a fine-tooth comb."

They drove in silence for a minute. Then Rav spoke up.

"This is pretty bad, isn't it, Kate? This case, I mean."

Kate glanced over.

"Yes, it's bad. It's the worst I've dealt with since I started here."

Rav was looking out the window at the streets of Abbeyford as they rolled by.

"We don't get cases like this here," he said. "I mean, do we? Serial killings...that's something that happens to other towns, not here."

"Well," said Kate. "I suppose it doesn't happen here...until it happens here."

"What if—" said Rav, and then he hesitated. Kate looked at him enquiringly.

"What?"

"What if it's not a serial killing?"

Kate was drawing onto the street on which Michael Brannigan lived. She parked the car, switched off the engine and turned to face Rav more fully.

"What do you mean?"

"Well, it's only an idea," said Rav nervously. "And I'm not saying the murders aren't related, I mean, they are – they clearly are. But what if the girls died for some other reason? Something we haven't found yet."

Kate thought it through. It was an intriguing idea, and she said as much to Rav, earning a pleased smile.

"Maybe we'll have a clearer picture once we've done the search," she said. "But it's certainly an idea. We should bear it in mind."

"Will you tell the boss?"

"Me?" said Kate sharply. "Why would I need to tell him? Why me?"

Rav looked surprised at her tone, as well he might.

"Oh, no reason," he said, climbing out of the car. "I just thought you might mention it. It might sound better coming from you."

That remark followed Kate into the house. Why had Rav said that? Kate snapped on her gloves on auto-pilot. The forensic team would have already been over the house, taking their samples and fingerprints and photographs. Looking closely, Kate could see the faint dusting of fingerprint powder, the odd smear and scuff on the walls and windows. The room had that slightly ruffled look of a place that had been thoroughly searched by experts.

Kate moved carefully through the hallway and into the front room. Rav stayed by the front door, running his practised eyes over the hallway furniture, the pile of worn shoes and scuffed boots by the coat stand. Kate stood for a moment in the centre of the living room, trying to concentrate. *It might sound better coming from you.* What did Rav mean? Surely nobody could know. Could they? She felt suddenly feverish with anxiety. Surely Anderton wouldn't have told anyone? Would he?

Concentrate, Kate. She went to the bookcase, always a good place to start. There was a real jumble of books on the shelves, an assortment of classics, non-fiction and an unsurprising number of religious works. She ran her finger along the spines and then began to work methodically through the books, taking them out and shaking them. It was repetitive work, and her mind soon began to wander. To Anderton, inevitably. She took out her phone in the ridiculous hope that he had sent her a message. Of course he hadn't, although there was a text from Olbeck, which said, *training tonight ok? Pick u up @ 7pm x*

For the first time, Kate found she was actually looking forward to going running later. She wanted to be out in the fresh air, moving from one foot to the other, eyes fixed on the horizon and not thinking about anything to do with her boss, or murdered girls, or how she seemed to have messed up her life yet again. She texted Olbeck back an affirmative with a kiss on the end and then turned her attention back to the search.

Jane had arrived by now, and she waved to Kate before heading upstairs to the bedrooms. Kate could hear her footsteps creaking the floorboards above her. This was an old house, Victorian in age, and chilly despite the time of year. The carpet was clean, but threadbare; the sofa was an old Ikea model with a checked Welsh blanket tucked over it. It was obviously the home of a man with limited spare cash – on the face of it, the home of a man who was cultured and intelligent and thrifty. Could it also be the home of a man who had murdered two – perhaps even three – women?

Kate's phone rang, and when she saw Anderton's name on the little screen, her heart gave a thump that was almost painful. She made herself wait for three rings before she answered it.

"Sir?"

"Anything?"

"Sorry?"

"Found anything?"

Kate clenched her teeth for a moment. So this was how he was going to play it, was he? Pretend the whole thing never happened. Was it because she'd walked out of his office when he wanted to talk to her? Was he really that petty?

"Not yet, *sir*," she said.

"Okay, that's fine. I need you to get over to the PM – Mark and I are tied up here with questioning. Can you do that?"

"Of course," Kate said coldly.

"Good. See you later."

The line went dead.

Kate put the phone back in her pocket. Her throat was aching and for a moment she stared at the opposite wall through a mist of tears that she blinked rapidly away. Just as well, as Rav came through from the kitchen moments later.

In the car on her way to to the pathology lab, Kate found herself grinding her teeth in rage, both at herself and at Anderton. *You idiot, Kate. You know what happened in Bournemouth, you swore it wouldn't happen again, and yet here you are, making the same stupid mistakes. Don't you ever* learn? She repeated the last sentence out loud and then she yelled it. Unfortunately the car was stationary at the time, and she caught the gaze of an astonished elderly gentlemen, who was crossing the road in front of her and clearly perplexed at the sight of a red-faced women shouting at herself in the rear view mirror. Kate forced a smile as he shuffled away, staring back over his shoulder until mercifully the lights changed and she was able to accelerate out of his sightline.

Unwelcome memories assailed her as she drew into the car park of her destination. For the first time in a few days, she remembered Jerry's sneer and his accusatory words. "*Why would I like, much less respect someone who gets ahead by getting on her back?*" *There's no truth to that*, Kate told herself stoutly as she locked the car door. *No truth at all*. But, thinking back, she had to admit that it was possible Jerry might have gotten hold of the wrong end of the stick. There had been enough innuendo and rumour flying around for a while, after all. And hadn't he once been based in Brighton? It wasn't beyond the realms of possibility that he'd heard what had happened.

Nothing much *had* happened. Kate, like so many people, had had a short affair with one of her colleagues in Bournemouth. A ridiculous, disastrous affair that lasted all of six weeks. And yes, she admitted to herself as she went into the reception area of the labs, she'd fallen into bed with someone who was technically her superior. And yes, she admitted to herself as she flashed her warrant card and was directed up to one of the theatres on the first floor, she'd obtained her transfer and promotion quite soon after that affair had ended. But, and she was absolutely clear on this, her promotion had been gained entirely on her own merit. The way the affair had ended, she'd been lucky to get any kind of reference at all.

When she considered explaining this to Jerry, however, she was forced to give herself a mental slap in the face. *You made a mistake then, you made one now. Learn from it and move on, Kate. When you next see Anderton, be professional, be courteous and be distant.* She arrived outside the door she was seeking and smoothed back her hair.

The pathologist conducting the autopsy of Claudia Smith was Andrew Stanton, and if Kate hadn't been in such a neurotic and anxious state, the pleased expression when he saw who had come to act as a police presence might have both amused and irritated her. As it was, she barely noticed, automatically returning his greeting. Her gaze was drawn, inevitably, to the small body of Claudia Smith, which lay supine on the hard metal surface of the table.

For the first time in an hour, all thoughts of Kate's romantic troubles fled. She was struck, as she so often was at post mortems, by the intense vulnerability of the corpse. Claudia looked so young; of course, she had *been* young, but her body looked tiny, diminished in death. She had given birth to a child, but her shallow-breasted, narrow-hipped body looked too young and undeveloped to have done so. Stripped of that awful makeup, the fake tan washed away, her body had achieved a kind of morbid beauty; the purity of her profile suggested the blanched, sculpted face of a marble statue.

Andrew Stanton had a brusque, no-nonsense method of working; his hands were less gentle than the delicate fingers of Doctor Telling. Kate waited and watched, listening to the doctor commenting on his findings, trying not to wince. Occasionally she asked a question.

"When was she killed?"

Doctor Stanton was rinsing a scalpel and the knife clattered against the tap with a ringing metallic sound.

"Between 2:00 a.m. and 3:30 a.m., the night before last. I can't narrow it down much further than that, I'm afraid."

"That's fine," said Kate. "So she was killed in the hours of darkness? It starts to get light about four thirty at the moment, doesn't it?"

"Yep," said Stanton. "Summer solstice has just passed, I think."

Kate nodded.

"Any sign of sexual assault?"

"Not that I could find. She'd had a child, as I expect you know."

Kate nodded, thrusting the thought of Madison's lost little face away with an effort. Stanton, having finished the autopsy, pulled the green sheet up over the body, hiding Claudia's face away.

Kate rubbed her finger over her top lip, thinking.

"No sign of sexual assault at all?" she asked.

Stanton looked at her with surprise.

"No. Didn't I just say?"

"Yes. Yes, you did, sorry. I was just thinking..." She trailed off. No sign of sexual assault on Mandy's body either, although hadn't Doctor Telling found traces of lubricant? What did that mean? Had the killer raped or had sex with Mandy? Why not with Claudia? Was that significant?

It's probably nothing, thought Kate. Mandy was a prostitute. She'd probably had sex with another punter before she met the one who killed her.

She came to with a start, realising Doctor Stanton was speaking to her.

"So that's all sorted, right?"

"Sorry?" asked Kate.

"My report. I'll have it to you in the next couple of days, okay?"

"Right. Great," said Kate, still thinking.

Andrew Stanton took off his lab coat and threw it into the laundry basket by the sink. He switched from his professional manner to his usual semi-jokey, flirtatious banter.

"So," he said, "It's dinner on Friday, right?"

He always said that, and Kate normally treated it like a little joke they shared, refusing him in the same joshing manner. She opened her mouth to give her usual, humorous refusal. She suddenly thought of her last, clipped conversation with Anderton, felt a rush of misery and found her mouth saying to the good doctor, "Why not? I'd like to."

The look on Andrew Stanton's face made Kate wish she'd agreed before. He goggled for a moment before rallying quite magnificently.

"Seriously? I mean, great. Great! Seriously?" He looked at Kate's face. "Well, that's great. When shall I pick you up?"

Back in her car and driving back towards her house, Kate found herself giggling despite herself. Then she took herself in hand. *You shouldn't have done that, Kate. You don't feel like that* about him, you're giving him false hope. She slowed down for a junction, caught her own gaze in the mirror and found herself saying out loud, "Oh fuck *off*. I'm entitled to think of myself for once. It could be a nice evening."

She caught herself wondering how she could contrive to let Anderton know she'd gotten a date for Friday evening. Then the memory of poor Claudia on the autopsy table reoccurred, and she didn't think much about anything else for a time.

J's diary

IT'S FUNNY. THE FURTHER ALONG in my journey I get, the shorter the time I spend in my transformed state. By which I mean that glorious Technicolor feeling of really living after each time is getting shorter and shorter. Grey reality began to intrude mere days after I killed Claudia. It felt so unfair, as I'd had such a lovely time planning it. The anticipation was almost better than the actual event. Now it's over and done with, and the colour is draining back out of the world, the black clouds are gathering.

It would be wonderful if there could be some way of filming what I do so I could watch it over and over again. Of course, it wouldn't be the same as actually doing it, but it might tide me over for a few more weeks. I'm beginning to feel the urge again now, and there's no one suitable in sight. It makes me itchy and frustrated and I find myself pacing around the house in the evenings, drinking whisky and holding the knife in my hand. Plunging it into something soft, stabbing a pillow for example, brings a mere flicker of the real thing; it's not enough. And yet, how can I get the real thing when I haven't even found the next one yet?

It worries me because the worse the longing gets, the more likely it is that I'll succumb without having planned it all first. I simply cannot be caught. I *need* to go on doing this. It's the only thing that makes life worth living.

Chapter Thirteen

KATE WAS SO BUSY WORRYING about Claudia and Anderton and why they didn't seem to be getting anywhere with this case that she had completely forgotten that today was the day Jerry got back from Brighton. She walked quite confidently into the office, shoulders back, determined not to let Anderton know how she was feeling. Raising a hand to Rav at his desk, she swallowed hard when she saw Jerry sat opposite him. He looked up as if drawn by her gaze, gave her a blank stare for a moment and then turned his eyes back to his computer screen.

Kate fumbled her own chair out from under her desk and sat down shakily. Luckily, there were only a few people in the office to witness her discomfort. She sat it out for a few minutes, head bent down studiously, reading the same report over and over again without taking in a word of it, before deciding to head up to the viewing room. She wanted to see what was happening with the questioning of Michael Brannigan. And she wanted a coffee. That was it. No other reason.

She forced herself to go up to Rav and Jerry and ask them if they wanted a drink. Jerry ignored her, and Rav shook his head with an embarrassed smile. Kate smiled back brightly and wheeled around, marching from the room.

Up in the viewing room, she collapsed in front of the screens with a sigh. The sight of Anderton, even on CCTV footage, made a tide of longing rise up within her. She brought her coffee cup up to her lips, scalding her throat as she gulped.

"The receptionist at the Pines Hotel has made a tentative identification of you and Claudia Smith," Anderton was saying.

Father Michael leaned forward.

"That's good. Yes, we stayed there several times."

Anderton nodded slightly.

"The only trouble is," he went on. "Is that she is unable to confirm your presence there on the night of Mandy Renkin's death."

Kate saw Father Michael's knuckles whiten as his clasped hands clenched.

"Well, we were there," he said after a moment. "We were there all night."

"So you say. But the problem is that we have no way of confirming that fact. Did you sign the guest book?"

Kate reluctantly smiled. She knew damn well that the guest book would have been one of the first things he checked.

Brannigan shook his head.

"Well, why was that?" asked Anderton.

"I would have thought it was obvious."

"You didn't want anyone to know you were staying there. I see. The trouble is, Father, is that without a definite identification that night, with no record of your visit, we only have your word for it that you were ever there."

"Yes, I know—"

"When you were first asked your whereabouts on the night in question, you told our officers that you were at home alone, all night."

Father Michael's head dropped forward. He spoke so softly that Kate could barely hear his words.

"I lied."

"Yes," said Anderton, and he let the pause after his comment spool out for a few uncomfortable seconds. The implication was clear – that Father Michael was lying about everything.

Kate had seen enough. She dropped her empty coffee cup in the recycling bin and headed downstairs to her desk.

Rav had gone somewhere else when she got back to the office and only Jerry remained. Kate sighed inwardly. Then, mentally preparing herself, she walked up to Jerry.

"Hi."

He ignored her. Kate gritted her teeth.

"I'm sorry about the other night."

He still ignored her. *Fine, if that's the way you want to play it.*

"Can I borrow the file on Ingrid Davislova if you have it? Please?"

For a moment, Kate thought Jerry was going to continue to ignore her. Then, without raising his head or acknowledging her in any other way, he threw a cardboard folder across the desk at her.

"Thanks," muttered Kate. *You grumpy old fucker.* She took the file back to her desk and sat down.

Kate pulled the cardboard folder towards her and opened it. There was frighteningly little inside it. Just another case of a forgotten woman, someone who fell through the cracks, someone unimportant to those who have the power.

Was that what this killer was doing? Was he purposefully targeting the forgotten ones, the ones no one cared about? He wouldn't be the first. *There's a reason a lot of serial killers target prostitutes*, Kate remembered Anderton saying. *They're accessible and they're forgettable. And there's still a section of society who think that they deserve everything they get.* Kate remembered the serial killings in Ipswich in 2006, the headlines screaming, 'Prostitutes Killed' and the articles that referred to the victims as 'murdered prostitutes,' as if the fact that those woman had sold sex was the only thing that would ever define them – not the fact that they were mothers, daughters, sisters, aunts and friends.

Kate resettled her face from the frown than had emerged while she thought. She leafed slowly through the paperwork in the folder, looking for something, anything that might give her a clue to this killer.

She'd been reading for almost an hour when she spotted it. In the pathologist's report, he'd mentioned a small bruise on the victim's upper chest, just under her collarbone. In the usual medical jargon, the doctor had pointed out the unusual shape of the bruising, quite clearly the shape of a butterfly or moth. He speculated that it had been caused by a metal button, or badge, or brooch that was shaped like the insect, and suspected that it had pressed hard enough into Ingrid Davislova's flesh that the blood vessels beneath her skin were broken into the shape of the pattern. Kate stared at the pictures from the PM, the close-up shots of the mark, blotchy purple against pallid skin. She traced the shape with her finger nail. Why there? She touched the site of the bruise on her own skin. Surely that button or brooch or whatever it was had been pinned or sewn to the killer's jacket lapel. Ingrid had been stabbed from the front, facing her murderer – just like the others. Kate checked the medical report again. Ingrid had been one hundred and sixty seven centimetres tall, or about five feet and six inches, so if the bruise was at lapel height on her, then the killer must be much the same height. Was that right? Kate considered, chewing her thumb nail.

She found the pathologist reports from the autopsies of Mandy Renkin and Claudia Smith. There was nothing in them regarding a butterfly-shaped bruise. Was she just chasing shadows, looking for something that didn't exist? Kate rubbed her eyes. So – what about *these* women? They were all young, all small and slight, all with long, dark hair. They were all killed in out-of-the-way places: waste grounds, back alleys, places where most people didn't go, or if they did, not at night. Was that significant? Did they meet their killer there, and if so, *why*? Did they know their killer? Kate tapped her pen on her teeth. They must have done, surely? Why would you meet someone in what was essentially a rather sinister and dangerous place if you didn't trust them?

Which brought her back to Father Michael. He'd known both Abbeyford victims; he was in a position of authority. He was someone that they would trust. Kate found it hard to imagine the tall, thin man plunging a knife into anyone, but people were very often not how they appeared. Everyone had something hidden inside them: good or bad. For a moment, Kate remembered Anderton poised above her, his expression one she had never seen before. The strength of his hands, gripping her wrists.

She allowed herself a moment's luxurious remembrance and then dismissed the thought, turning her attention back to the files in front of her. Something nagged at her, something she'd recently noticed. Flipping the pages of the report in front of her, she remembered. The button-shaped bruise on Ingrid Davislova. If Father Michael had worn that on his lapel, then how could it have bruised Ingrid's chest? He was a foot taller than she was. Perhaps he'd pinned it lower down. But why would he?

Kate leaned forward, head in her hands, eyes scanning the words she'd looked at before. She had the feeling, growing for a while now, that she'd let these women down. No, the whole *team* had let these women down. They'd failed to catch the killer after Mandy Renkin's death, and now he'd killed again. She dug deep, forcing an acknowledgement. Was it because these women weren't important to anyone that no one had worked their hardest? That no one had really had the passion to see the case through to a successful conclusion? Or was there some other reason, some other reason why nothing seemed to be working?

Kate blew out her cheeks and stood up, fed up with it all. Olbeck looked up from his desk.

"What's up?"

"Nothing. I'm just frustrated, that's all. Thought I'd spotted something significant and now, I don't know..."

"What is it?"

Kate brought the files over to Olbeck's desk and told him about the butterfly bruise.

"Did it show up on any of the others?"

Kate shook her head.

"Well, then," said Olbeck, reasonably. "How does it help us?"

"Oh, I don't bloody know," said Kate. She got up again. "I'm going out for a bit."

Olbeck pushed back his chair.

"I'll come with you. I could murder a coffee. Whoops, bad phrasing. I could do with a caffeinated beverage, I mean."

They walked down to the local greasy spoon and found a wobbly table out on the grimy stretch of pavement at the front of the shop. Kate took care of the seats while Olbeck got the drinks.

Kate stirred her cappuccino and told Olbeck what she'd just been thinking.

"Seriously?" he asked. "You think we've all been – well, slacking a bit?"

"I didn't exactly mean that," said Kate, uncomfortably. "But it's just – why aren't we further forward in the case? It feels like whatever we do, something is – I don't know – *blocking* us from getting any further."

Olbeck was looking mystified.

"I'm not sure what you mean."

Kate shrugged. "I don't know exactly what I mean either. It's just a feeling, really."

"Feelings aren't evidence. If you're saying we should have caught him before he killed again then yes, of course I agree with you. But we're not superhuman, Kate. We can only go so far and so fast. You know that. We can't go hauling everyone who might even be vaguely guilty of something."

"Yes, I know." Kate drew a spiral in the foam of her coffee cup with the handle of a teaspoon. She gestured to it.

"That's us," she said. "Going round in ever decreasing circles."

"Listen," said Olbeck, leaning forward. "Maybe we are a bit out of our depth, I don't know. It's not like we get a lot of these cases in Abbeyford, thank God. Perhaps we ought to talk to Anderton. Perhaps we need more expert guidance."

Kate raised her eyebrows.

"Call in the Yard?"

"If necessary. It might happen anyway."

"Hmm."

Olbeck looked a little annoyed. "Well, what do you suggest then? You think we're not getting very far. For what it's worth, I agree. What do *you* think we should do?"

Kate stirred the dregs of her coffee moodily. She was starting to regret saying anything.

"What can we do? Just more of the same but more thoroughly. Talk to the people who knew the victims. Check alibis, check CCTV. Find something that connects them."

"We know what connects them. Father Michael."

"He's guilty of having an affair with Claudia Smith. We can't prove he's guilty of her murder."

Olbeck sat back in his chair, blowing out his cheeks.

"Maybe we're looking at this the complete wrong way. We're assuming it's a serial killer. What if it's not?"

Kate looked at him narrowly. "What do you mean?"

"Is it possible that these deaths are actually coincidental?"

"Oh, come on," scoffed Kate. "Same MO, same weapon, same victim type?"

Olbeck stared into the middle distance for a moment. Then he grimaced and threw up his hands.

"You're right. It's a stupid idea."

"Well, if it's ideas you're looking for, then I'm clean out."

The two of them were silent, regarding the empty, foam-caked cups before them. Kate, inevitably, felt her thoughts being drawn back to Anderton. For a mad moment, she opened her mouth to tell Olbeck, and then sanity returned and she shut it with a snap.

"Come on," said Olbeck. "Let's get back."

They walked the short distance back to the office in silence. Kate felt depressed, heavy with regrets and unspoken thoughts. She and Olbeck had never really had any secrets before. Now there was a big one between them. Now, there was distance.

J's diary

I CAN REMEMBER WHEN I FIRST found heard about John. I was seven years old – could I really have been only seven? – and it was an incredibly blustery rainy day, the water falling from the sky in rippling sheets. Mrs H, who'd popped round for her usual cup of tea and gossip session with Mother, had almost been blown in the front door, shrieking and dripping water all over the floor. I'd come to the doorway of the dining room and stood there, silently watching, until Mother and Mrs H had looked over and frowned to see me, their usual expression whenever they regarded me.

"Go to your room," Mother said sharply. I turned and trudged up the stairs as they went through into the kitchen. I heard Mother muttering something about my behaviour as they disappeared from view.

"...at the end of my tether, that child is so underhand. I sometimes think there's something really wrong with—"

Her voice faded out of my hearing, and I couldn't hear Mrs H's reply. I paused at the top of the stairs, my fists clenched. For some reason I thought of Mrs H's son, who was younger than me, although only by a few years. For a while, we'd been allowed to play together, but that had stopped suddenly. I wasn't that fussed about it, to be honest. He was a bit of a cry-baby and never wanted to play the games that I did.

I turned and crept back down the stairs. I wasn't going to be sent to my room like a baby. I was only seven, but already I was creeping around, listening at doors and overhearing things that perhaps I wasn't meant to hear. Looking back, I know now that it was the only way I could retain some power, the only way I could have something of my own that Mother didn't know about.

I tiptoed up to the kitchen door, which was slightly ajar. Mrs H and Mother were talking in low voices, and I could hear the thin stream of tea being poured from pot to cup and the chink of cup on saucer.

Why did they talk about it on that day? What made Mother suddenly open up to Mrs H about something that almost nobody else knew? I don't know. Perhaps Mrs H was gossiping about someone else who'd had twins, or a miscarriage, or a friend whose baby had died. I don't know, and all I have is conjecture. I couldn't hear proper sentences, just the odd word here. *Fraternal twins*, said Mother. *Died at birth*, said Mother. I could hear Mrs H expressing shock and sympathy, with just a tinge of greedy curiosity. *Terribly hard*, said Mother, and I could hear something in her voice that I had never heard before, a softness, a trembling.

There was silence for a moment in the kitchen. Then Mother said something else, whispering so I could barely hear. Then I heard Mrs H's loud repetition, the shock in her voice.

"*Strangled?*"

"Asphyxiated," said Mother, a big word that I didn't understand. "By the other cord."

"Oh my goodness, how terrible."

"*He* came out first," said Mother. "But by then it was too late."

Their voices sank again. I held my breath, straining my ears to try and hear more but the only thing that I heard clearly was the name *John*.

"His name was John," said Mother, and then I heard the shift and scrape of a chair as she pushed it back from the kitchen table, and I turned and fled.

Up in my room, I looked out of the window at the quiet street beyond, unseeing. Most of what had just passed was too big for me to grasp, but I must have retained the elements, the crux of it must have sunk deep into my psyche, because from that day forward, I often found myself thinking of John, of the brother I'd never known, the one who'd been with me when I was born.

For years I knew a part of me was missing. But there was something else too, something that grew and grew with me, a blackly blooming knowledge that lodged deep inside me and spread its dirty tentacles through my mind. I was born a killer, it seemed. There was no escape from that fact.

Chapter Fourteen

Kate slept with her mobile phone by her bedside, relying on the alarm clock function every morning to get her out of bed. The ringing woke her from a deep sleep, and she grabbed at the device, peering blearily at the screen. It was Anderton calling.

That woke her up. She sat up in bed and pressed the answer button.

"Kate," said Anderton. She could hear something in his voice, something that tightened her stomach, just from that one word. Something had happened.

"What's wrong?"

Anderton said nothing for a moment, but she could hear him breathing heavily. She found she was clutching the duvet cover in her free hand.

"What is it?"

"There's been another killing. Another girl."

Kate closed her eyes briefly. As the first wave of shock subsided, a thought struck her.

"But, Father Michael—"

"Is still in custody. Yes."

"Fuck," said Kate.

"Fuck indeed," said Anderton. "I need you down here right away. We're at Charlotte Street, the alley that runs along the back of it. Can you get here soon?"

"I'm on my way," said Kate, already scrambling out of bed.

The drive to Charlotte Street was a short one. Despite the warmth of the summer morning, Kate felt cold. She pressed herself back into the car seat, almost shivering. Another killing. *Another* one. And it had happened while they were questioning the wrong man. After a moment, she turned the heater on and adjusted the vent so that warm air blew onto her face.

She parked a few streets away from Charlotte Street. As Kate got out of the car, she could hear the choppy roar of a helicopter overhead. As she rounded the corner, the blue and white crime scene tape was almost invisible behind the seething mass of photographers, camera crews and journalists all vying for an interview – or better yet, a glimpse of the body, thankfully shrouded by a white tent. Kate set her features to neutral, took a deep breath and pushed through the tumult, ducking under the tape while a fusillade of camera flashes went off around her.

Anderton, Olbeck and Jerry were all in the tent, all looking at the body. Kate joined them without speaking. Looking at the small, curled shape on the dirty concrete, she was overcome with a sense of sick, sweeping déjà vu. The long, dark hair, the slender body...just like Mandy. Just like Claudia. Kate crossed her arms across her body, hugging herself. Who was this man who kept killing women? What was driving him on? How could they catch him, and what would happen if they couldn't? Kate felt something unusual, something almost akin to panic. How could they stop him? How many more women were going to die?

She wheeled around and went back out of the tent. Cameras flashed and she flinched, unable to help herself. Trapped between the tent and the phalanx of photographers, Kate hesitated, not even sure of where she wanted to go. She heard the flap of the tent entrance again and then Anderton was behind her, beside her. He put a hand under her elbow and steered her out of the view of the press pack, around and out of sight to where his car was parked. Gesturing for her to get in the front passenger seat, he closed the door after her and went around to the driver side door.

Once he was in the car with the doors closed, they sat in silence for a moment. Then Anderton reached over and took Kate's hand. Kate glanced around nervously, hoping no one could see them.

Then Anderton spoke.

"I'm lost, Kate. I don't know what to do."

There was something in his voice. It was barely perceptible but enough to make Kate's feelings of anxiety rise up a notch. He sounded – could it be possible? – as if he were close to tears.

"Three women have died, and I have absolutely no idea who killed them."

"I know," said Kate, helplessly. "I know what you mean."

Anderton raised his head and looked her in the eyes.

"What the hell do we do?"

So now it's 'we?' Kate forced the rogue thought down. This wasn't the time for recriminations. She shrugged.

"We keep digging. We keep questioning."

Anderton sighed and leant his head back against the headrest of the car seat, closing his eyes.

"The press is going to have a field day," he said, after a moment. "They'll rip us apart. I can see the headlines now."

"I know."

"The Chief Constable is going to have my balls on a stick."

"I know."

Anderton opened his eyes, gazing at the car roof.

"All right," he said. "Let's get back there. There must be *something*. Something we're missing."

They braved the photographers again and ducked back into the tent. Doctor Telling had arrived and was leaning over the body of the woman. Olbeck and Jerry were stood to one side, not speaking.

Kate realised she hadn't even asked who the victim was.

"We don't know," said Anderton. "No ID on the body, no handbag. Just like the others."

Kate moved around a little so she could see the girl's face, dreading the moment of recognition. But it never came; this woman was a stranger.

"I've not seen her before," she said.

"She's not from the Mission?"

"Not that I can remember."

Anderton looked at Olbeck, who shook his head.

"I can't remember seeing her there either."

Anderton brought one hand up to his temple, as if afflicted by a sudden headache.

"He's escalating," he said. "It's days since the last murder. *Days*, not weeks."

Nobody said anything for a moment.

Incredibly, Anderton smiled, a grim smile that was more like a grimace. He looked at his officers.

"This is good. It means he's getting careless. It means he'll make mistakes."

Jerry said nothing. Kate looked at him curiously. The white canvas of the tent gave everyone within it a pallid hue but, Kate suddenly realised, Jerry was worse than that. He was grey. He was staring fixedly at the body as Doctor Telling was beginning her examination. His hand crept up to his shoulder, squeezing his upper arm.

Kate was just about to ask him if he was all right when Anderton spoke his name, sharply.

"Jerry? Jerry!"

Jerry dropped like a stone. Kate gasped. Frozen to the spot for a moment, movement returned, and she leapt forward at the same time as Olbeck and Anderton. Jerry had fallen next to the body, the arm that had gripped his shoulder falling loose, as if pointing towards the dead girl. There was a moment of pure chaos, people shouting, pushing. Anderton got to Jerry first, calling his name in a voice ragged with panic, before Doctor Telling moved him aside with practised authority and laid her fingers on Jerry's neck. Then she put one slender, long-fingered hand under his neck, tipping his face upwards, and began mouth to mouth resuscitation.

"Call an ambulance," she gasped as she came up for air, but Olbeck was already doing just that.

Kate, barely knowing what she was doing, took Anderton's arm, drawing him away from where Doctor Telling was battling death before their eyes.

"He'll be okay," she whispered, just for something to say. She didn't believe it for a moment. Anderton took her hand, crushing it within his grip. They watched, helplessly, for what felt like endless hours before they heard the siren of the ambulance over the bay of the mob outside the tent.

Anderton went in the ambulance, with Kate and Olbeck following behind in Kate's car. Several photographers followed the ambulance, breaking away from the crime scene when they realised there was another element to the story breaking right there. Kate crawled through the mass of people blocking the road as she tried to keep the ambulance in sight. Hands thumped on the side of the car, making her flinch. Olbeck rolled down the passenger side window.

"Clear the road. Now!"

Kate put her hand on the horn and kept it there. Wincing, people began to fall back so she could pick up a little speed. She had to fight the urge to put her foot down hard on the accelerator and drive through, scattering paparazzi like confetti.

When they got to the Royal Abbeyford Hospital, Jerry had already been carted off somewhere. *The Intensive Care Unit*, thought Kate, hoping he had at least made it that far. Anderton was in a side room off the main reception area, pacing the small area of tiled floor like a man possessed. Kate came through the doorway first, and he came forward as if to throw his arms around her, bringing himself to a sudden halt as Olbeck followed her through the doorway.

"You all right?" said Olbeck.

"I'm fine," Anderton muttered.

Kate hugged her arms across her body. The three of them stood in a little huddle, not knowing what to do or what to say.

"Well, we can't all stay," said Anderton. "Christ, I've got a serial murder investigation to run."

"It's all right," said Olbeck. "I'll stay. I'll ring you later with a progress report and someone can come and take over."

"Doesn't he have any family?" asked Kate.

Anderton shook his head. "No immediate family. All right, Mark. Let's do that. Come on Kate. I'll drive."

They drove back in silence except for one outburst from Anderton while they were waiting at the traffic lights. He pounded the steering wheel with a fist, making Kate jump.

"I *told* him, the stupid idiot. I told him. 'You drink too much, you smoke like a chimney, you eat shit...' What did he think was going to happen?"

Kate knew it was a rhetorical question. She said nothing but shrugged and shook her head.

"Stupid *idiot*," said Anderton, and then the lights changed and they were off.

When they got back to the office, the atmosphere was palpable. Jane's eyelids were as red as her hair, and Rav and Theo were looking very sombre. As Anderton and Kate came into the room, everyone, bar Theo, leapt to their feet.

"He's still alive," said Anderton wearily. "That's about all we know for now. The doctors are doing all they can for him, and Mark will give us an update as soon as he hears."

"Was it a heart attack?" asked Jane, timidly.

Anderton nodded.

"We think so. Almost certainly."

He walked up to the notice boards and stood before then,

regarding the mess of scribbled notes, photographs, documents, connecting arrows and other information.

"Where to start?" was what Kate heard him say to himself, almost under his breath.

"We've got a tentative ID on the latest victim," said Rav and Anderton turned, his eyebrows raising.

"You have? Excellent."

"A Mrs Pauline Brennan reported her daughter Karen missing after she failed to return home last night. We spoke to her over the phone, and we're bringing her in to ID the body right now."

"Fits the description?"

Rav nodded.

"Small, long dark hair, young. She – Karen – went out clubbing with friends last night, she was supposed to get the last train home. Her friends say she left to catch it, but she never went home."

"And that alleyway is the shortcut home from the station. Sounds like it's her all right. Poor woman." Anderton sat down on the edge of a desk. "Let's get a positive ID before we do anything else. What else have we got? Anyone got any more information?"

Work went on that afternoon, but there was little sense of anything being accomplished. Jerry's desk stood horribly empty. At three o'clock, Kate texted Olbeck to see if there was any news, and he texted back, *still in ICU, no other news x*.

Mrs Pauline Brennan identified the body of her daughter, Karen Brennan, with the calmness of what Kate recognised as complete and total shock. The identification over, Mrs Brennan walked back out into the corridor and promptly collapsed, prompting another dramatic five minutes where officers swarmed, shouted and eventually ushered in the paramedics who, thankfully, advised after a few minutes' examination that the poor woman had merely fainted.

House to house enquiries were continuing along the alleyway

where the body of Karen Brennan had been found and in all the neighbouring streets. CCTV footage from the train station and along Charlotte Street was being examined. Kate sat at her desk and briefly imagined herself as the spider in the centre of an enormous web of information: words, pictures, data, number plates, descriptions, interviews, forensic examinations, post mortem reports... all of it flowing to her and over her while she drowned within the torrent, snatching vaguely with her hands at scraps of knowledge that took her no further.

And out there, hidden by the darkness of ignorance, was a man who killed women and who kept killing women, and she couldn't see how they would ever catch him.

J's diary

THE MASK IS SLIPPING. I can no longer rely on my disguise. No, that's not true. Of course I can rely on my disguise – no one can see through that – but at the same time, the real me, the one underneath the mask is beginning to surface. I am transforming. For months I could always chose who to be; it was me who decided which face to present to the world, but that is beginning to be the case no longer.

Now, when I look in the mirror, I'm no longer sure of who I will see looking back.

This scares me. The real me, the one who does these things to these girls, is the one who will not be accepted. They – and I don't need to say exactly who 'they' are – they will stop me, if they catch me. They cannot catch me. I cannot allow it.

But who do I mean when I say 'I'?

This last one scared me. I hadn't planned it, I wasn't even truly looking. I was merely walking back from the station, and I saw her walk into the alleyway, staggering a little. She was the right type: she was alone, she was drunk. All my objections fell away in an instant. Before I could tell myself that it was too dangerous, that someone would see, that she would call out or do something to call attention to what was happening…all of my internal objections counted for nothing. I was seized with the breathless, choking feeling that was beginning to come upon me more and more. I can no more conquer the urge than I could stop breathing.

My feet, seemingly of their own accord, turned to follow the girl into the alleyway.

There was no one else there – of course not, it was very late. I had taken a late train back to the town and of course, I was in my usual disguise. I entered the alleyway. I like to think that if someone else had been there to witness what was about to happen, I could have controlled myself.

I like to think that, but I'm not sure.

There was no one else there. I had the knife in my hand, and I was running before I could even acknowledge what I was doing. I fell upon her from behind – she gave one small choked cry of surprise – and then the knife was going in, again and again and again. I was frenzied, my cries muffled against her back.

When it was over, I got up and staggered home. I didn't even look behind me. It makes me shudder now, to think of all the evidence I left behind me. That's what scares me. I lost control and I know – I *know* that it will happen again. I can't be caught. But I can't stop.

I can't stop.

Chapter Fifteen

Kate pulled up outside her house at about twenty minutes to seven that night. She locked the car, pulled her bag onto her shoulder and wearily made her way indoors. The house seemed very silent. She threw her bag on the floor of the hallway, kicked off her shoes and slumped through to the living room where she flung herself down onto the sofa, fully intending not to move from that location for the rest of the evening, possibly even the rest of the night.

The doorbell rang five minutes later, and she swore so loudly she was surprised the person on the doorstep didn't hear it. Kate lay, eyes closed and muttering curses under her breath, before heaving herself up and stomping through to the front door.

She yanked it open to find Andrew Stanton on the doorstep, smartly dressed and carrying a bouquet of pink roses. To Kate's tired eyes, the unexpected nature of the sight was such that for a moment she thought she was seeing things…until memory came crashing back.

Andrew took in her dishevelled, clearly-not-dressed-for-a-date appearance, and the smile he'd been wearing when the door opened fell off his face so fast it would have been funny had it not been so embarrassing.

"You forgot," was all he said.

"I'm sorry. *God*, I'm sorry." Kate was hanging onto the door as if it were the only thing keeping her from collapse. After the horrors of the day, this added complication was about as much as she could bear.

"That's fine," said Andrew, stiffly. "Perhaps another night, Kate. Good night."

He turned away, flowers dangling from his hand.

"Wait!" Kate caught at his arm to stop him. "Wait, *please*, Andrew. I'm sorry, okay? Why don't you come in?"

Once he was inside the hallway, Kate shut the front door and leant on it.

"I'm really, really sorry," she said again. "I can guess you've seen what's been happening?"

"I have," admitted Andrew. "I guess I should have phoned ahead. My fault."

"No, *completely* mine," said Kate. She felt like hitting herself sharply on the forehead. Was there a single working relationship that she hadn't managed to fuck up completely? "I hope you haven't booked anywhere...?"

Andrew half-smiled. "Well—"

"Oh, God. Where?"

"Well – Bailey's."

"Oh, *God*." Bailey's was an extremely expensive restaurant located in a former stately home on the edge of Abbeyford. "That's lovely of you. Tell you what, wait here and give me ten minutes. *Literally* ten minutes."

She virtually pushed him through to the living room, ran through to the kitchen, poured him a glass of what she always thought of as 'Mark's wine,' kept exclusively for him, ran back through – carefully – with glass in hand, set it on the living room table, smiled brightly, said 'ten minutes!' and pelted for the stairs.

After a minute's shower, a frantic rub down, a squoosh of perfume and a slick of eyeliner, she grabbed her velvet jeans and silk shirt from the wardrobe, pulled them on, dragged a brush through her hair, plucked her one smart jacket from the hanger, yanked her strappy sandals from under the bed and pounded back down the stairs, arriving flushed but hopefully less dishevelled in the doorway of the living room.

Andrew was still clutching his bouquet of flowers. He didn't look like he'd had much wine. He looked up as Kate appeared, and his face softened.

"Wow. That's a transformation."

"I'm really sorry about forgetting," said Kate, making a mental note that she was no longer going to apologise.

It looked as though Andrew had forgiven her already. He stood up and handed her the flowers.

"That's lovely," said Kate. She couldn't imagine Anderton giving her flowers. The contrast made her clench her teeth for a millisecond before she put all thoughts of him far from her.

Andrew nodded.

"You look really lovely, Kate," he said and the warmth and sincerity of his tone made Kate smile with pleasure, despite her tiredness.

"Come on, then," she said. "Let's go."

OLBECK WALKED INTO THE OFFICE the next morning to catch Kate halfway through an enormous yawn.

"I know how you feel," he said, slinging himself into his seat opposite hers.

Kate shut her mouth with a snap. She looked at her colleague, noting the bruised half-circles beneath his eyes. Looking around the room, she thought, *We all look terrible. We're all running on empty.* It was no longer surprising that Jerry had suffered a heart attack; what was surprising was that the rest of the team was all somehow managing to keep going despite the unrelenting pressure and stress.

"I'm knackered," she said, rubbing her eyes. "How's Jerry?"

"No change. They kept telling me he was stable, but they wouldn't say much else." He gestured to a small plastic bag he'd put on his desk. "I've got his stuff here. Apparently someone needs to go and get him some night clothes or something like that."

Kate yawned again, barely listening. She was wondering whether to mention her date with Andrew Stanton. Normally of course, that would set her up for at least half an hour of teasing from Olbeck, but looking at him this morning, she didn't think he'd have the energy for even a mild joke.

Not that there was much to tell. The dinner had been pleasant enough, the food very good, and Andrew had been charming and attentive company. He'd dropped her off at home at about ten o'clock and given Kate a gentlemanly kiss on the cheek on the doorstep. At least Kate thought he had; her memories by then were somewhat hazy because she'd been almost hallucinating from tiredness.

She decided against mentioning it.

Olbeck was saying something to her.

"What?"

"I said, someone needs to go and get Jerry's things for him. Pyjamas and toothbrush and all that gubbins."

"Toothbrush? He's in intensive *care*, for God's sake, he's hardly going to care about tooth decay." Kate saw Olbeck's face and relented. "Okay, okay. I'll go if you like. I could do with getting out of here."

"Thanks. It won't take long. Just drop them off at the reception area, I think."

"Fine," said Kate, yawning yet again. She took Jerry's house keys from Olbeck, scribbled down his home address and picked up her bag.

Driving through the sunshine, negotiating the weekend traffic in Abbeyford, Kate found it hard to believe that somewhere out there in the town was a multiple murderer. Everyone on the streets looked so ordinary, so innocent, so untouched. Kate braked for a pedestrian crossing – a mother with a baby in a pushchair raised a hand in thanks and pushed the buggy across the road. For once, Kate didn't look at the baby; she looked at the woman pushing the pram, who was small and thin with long, dark hair. Was she a potential victim?

For a mad moment, Kate considered parking the car and following the woman home, just to make sure she was safe. Then she shook her head, bringing herself back to reality. *You have to catch this man*, she told herself. Because he's a killer...and because if you don't, you're going to end up in a mental hospital. We all will.

Despite the sat nav, she still got lost looking for Jerry's house, which was in a suburb of Abbeyford called Fenwick. The street was quite similar to the one on which Kate lived: rows of semi-detached Victorian houses with tiny front gardens, some of which had been paved or gravelled over to provide parking spaces. Kate had to shunt her car into a tiny space on the end of the row of back-to-back vehicles and then walk back to Number Twelve, which apparently was where Jerry lived.

Kate paused at the entrance to the front garden. The house had an uncared-for look: peeling paint on the window frames, a weed-choked patch of earth in front of the front bay window. There were yellowing net curtains hanging limply at the window of the downstairs rooms. Kate checked the scrap of paper on which she'd written the address, suddenly convinced she'd got the wrong house.

No, this was definitely Jerry's place. She found the house keys and walked up the little path to the porch and the front door, tripping over a loose paving slab, catching herself and looking around self-consciously in case anyone had been watching her. There was no one in sight. Kate tried the keys in the door and pushed it open, cautiously.

The house had the kind of dusty, stale, cooking-remnants aroma that Kate, rightly or wrongly, associated with elderly people's homes. The hallway was tiled in chipped red clay tiles, probably original, with the walls papered in a faded floral pattern. Kate stood for a moment, looking around, puzzled. Again, the feeling that she'd come to the wrong house resurfaced. This, surely, was not the home of a middle-aged man. She looked around again.

There, hanging on a coat rack of dark, polished wood, was a coat she recognised as one of Jerry's. Several pairs of black and brown men's brogues were tumbled carelessly in a corner by the door. Mentally shrugging, Kate walked through the doorway at the end of the hallway that led into a kitchen.

The kitchen was quite large but had clearly been refitted about thirty years ago, judging by the orange hue of the pine cabinets and the cheap, overly-shiny brass handles. The sink and counter were piled with dirty dishes. The floor was covered in drips of unidentifiable liquid, fluff, dust and scraps of tissue paper, while in the corner by the back door, empty beer cans and bottles were stacked in a collapsing cardboard box.

Another wooden door with an old-fashioned metal latch stood under the slope of the staircase, clearly leading to what had been the cellar. Kate observed the squalor, feeling something very much like pity rising up inside her. This was Jerry's house, his empty, lonely, dirty house. What a place to come back to after doing the job they did; it was cheerless, comfortless, without any company to render it more palatable.

Kate thought of what Anderton had said about Jerry. *He's had a hard year... No immediate family.* Poor Jerry. Now, his rudeness, grumpiness, abruptness – whatever you could call it – was more understandable. Kate thought of her own house, full of carefully chosen, beautiful things (nothing very expensive, but that wasn't the point); she'd made a home for herself with love and care and attention. Was this slightly queasy feeling of pity something more? Did Jerry and she have something in common? *You're both alone*, whispered a mean little voice.

She left the kitchen and looked quickly into the other rooms on the ground floor. She wasn't sure why she was bothering. *Just being nosy, Kate*. The living room was dim and musty, worn brown velvet curtains drawn against the sunlight, the net curtains between them and the window pane no cleaner when seen from this side of the window.

There was a silver-framed photograph on the mantelpiece of what was clearly a much younger Jerry, a quite startlingly handsome Jerry. Kate stared. She wouldn't have recognised the overweight, balding, angry middle-aged man in this picture of a dark-haired, dark-eyed young charmer, smiling at the camera. She picked it up to look more closely and then looked up at herself, framed in the dusty mirror over the mantelpiece. For a second, she seemed to see herself in twenty years' time: her skin wrinkled and blotched, her dark, shiny hair dulled and greyed. She put the photograph back, repressing a shudder.

She headed for the stairs, thinking that she'd already wasted too much time here. Why on Earth had she offered to come and do this? Jerry would hate to think of her poking around in his cupboards and drawers, finding his toiletries. Kate was uncomfortably aware that she'd offered to do this precisely so she could legitimately get out of having to visit the hospital to do her shift of waiting for news like an anxious relative. She reached the top landing and pushed open the door of what was obviously the master bedroom. "*Master*" bedroom, what a stupid, sexist term. Kate shook her head.

Again, the curtains were drawn against the sunlight, and the room had that stale, musty smell of a place uncleaned, unaired, and neglected. The smell of dust and something else, something ranker underneath it all. Kate wrinkled her nose. She hesitated for a second and crossed over to the window, pulling the curtains back enough to let a little light into the room. The bed was unmade, the duvet in its sombre navy blue cover tumbled in a heap at the foot of the mattress.

Kate opened the bedside cabinet, as it was the only piece

of furniture with drawers in the room. Working on the fairly reasonable assumption that Jerry might keep his nightwear next to the bed, she regarded the contents of the drawers with raised eyebrows. Each one was rammed to the top with porn: DVDs, videos, even the odd magazine. Kate grimaced and pushed them back with her foot. She straightened up and looked around the room. No chest of drawers, no tallboy. There was a cheap, flat-pack wardrobe over by the far wall. Kate opened one door, swept her gaze over the clothes hanging up and then opened the other door.

For a moment, she looked at what was contained within with no emotion. Later, when she was to replay this moment in her head, Kate realised it had reminded her of a case she'd been working on in Bournemouth, the murder of a homeless drug addict. The victim had been found in a derelict house, and when Kate had arrived on the scene and viewed the body, she had for a few seconds wondered why there were a pair of white gloves on the victim's chest. It had taken about twenty seconds of innocent perusal before she realised that the gloves were in fact his hands, cut off at the wrist and dropped contemptuously onto his body.

Looking at the interior of Jerry's wardrobe produced a similar response. A few moments of vague puzzlement before the thumping weight of reality crashed down.

There were two handbags in the wardrobe: one white, one black. Both, except for their colour, were identical. Fringed and tasselled, pockmarked with cheap metal studs. Kate could recall very clearly where she had last seen the black bag: over the slender shoulder of Claudia Smith.

Chapter Sixteen

KATE BREATHED IN SLOWLY. SHE felt hollow, as if a heavy weight was falling through the middle of her body, leaving empty space behind it. She closed her eyes for a moment, opened them, and looked again, as if what was in front of her could be transformed into something else by the passage of a few seconds. The bags were still there. Kate heard herself make a sound, a muffled groan or a gasp. She found herself backing away, slowly, moving backwards without looking until the backs of her legs hit the edge of the bed and she collapsed onto it into a sitting position. The old springs of the mattress creaked and groaned, echoing the sound of disbelief she'd made.

It can't be true. Not Jerry. Kate found she had her eyes squeezed tightly shut again. She must be mistaken, she *must* be. She lifted her head a little, looking again at the bags within the gloom of the wardrobe. Getting up, she groped in her pocket for a clean tissue. Wrapping it around her trembling fingers, she lifted the black handbag out from the wardrobe and put it on the bed, opening the top. She could feel from the weight of it in her hand that it wasn't empty, but it was still a shock to look inside and see a fluffy pink purse, a bunch of keys, a scratched lipstick, a balled-up tissue.

The keys had a plastic key ring attached, the kind that had an opening for a small photograph. Kate turned the blank side of it over with her tissue-clad fingers. The big dark eyes of Madison

Smith looked up at her from the depths of her mother's handbag. Kate heard herself again, a noise that was something between a gasp and a retch. She picked up the purse and opened it. A credit card in the name of Ms. C Smith. A debit card in the name of Claudia Smith. *No. No.*

Kate left Claudia's bag on the bed and went to fetch the white one. What had Claudia said about Mandy's bag? *"We got 'em together except Mandy's was white."* Kate ferried it across to the bed and put it by its negative twin. Inside was a red leather purse, pens, a notebook with a geometric flower print on the cover, tissues, baby wipes, cigarettes, a packet of condoms. Kate opened the purse. Amanda Renkin was printed on the one bank card contained within it.

There must be another explanation. There *must* be. Kate sat back down on the bed, the springs groaning beneath her, and pinched the bridge of her nose. *Think, Kate. Think.* Jerry had the handbags from two murdered girls in his wardrobe. Could he have taken them from the bodies? Of course he had, how ridiculous. Of course he had taken them – how else would they have gotten here? Kate realised her mistake. She meant, could he have taken them from the bodies without him necessarily being the killer? And if he had, *why* had he? Why tamper with the evidence?

Kate raised her head and stared at the open door of the wardrobe. A coldness was creeping through her body, as if an icy wave were moving slowly through her. If Jerry wasn't the killer and had tampered with evidence...well, the only explanation Kate could come up with was that Jerry had done it to shield someone else. Who?

You know who, whispered that small mean voice again.

Kate shook her head. This was ridiculous. Truly ridiculous. She stood up, wobbling a little, and walked to the window, staring out at the quiet suburban street outside. A woman walked past the house with bulging supermarket shopping bags in each hand, a little boy on a scooter following behind her. Could Jerry really be the killer? Kate thought back to the last crime scene, Jerry staring at the body, grey in the face, as within him his heart ruptured. What had Anderton said? *He's escalating. He will have made mistakes.*

Had Jerry seen something then and realised that he would be caught? Had he remembered something, some piece of evidence that would point the police to his guilt? *Was* he guilty? *He must be, Kate. How else can you explain finding these handbags?*

He might be shielding someone else.

Kate realised she was pacing the dusty carpet, arguing with herself. Who would Jerry shield? Who would he risk his career, his reputation, his freedom for? She turned on her heel and paced back. There was no one. Surely, no one. *It must be him*, Kate told herself, staring at her white face in the mirrored door of the wardrobe.

Oh fuck, what was she going to do? She probably shouldn't have even touched those bags, tissue or no tissue. She looked again into the wardrobe but there was nothing else there. No other bags or purses or anything suspicious.

She pulled out her phone and brought Anderton's number up on the screen. Her thumb hovered over the 'call' button for a moment and then she pressed it, listening to the ringing on the other end of the line.

He might be shielding someone else.

Kate jabbed the 'end call' button. Her chest felt tight. She told herself she was being ridiculous. Paranoid and ridiculous. She tried to think back over the times and dates, tried to tally them up with her own memories. *Anderton was with me the night Claudia Smith was killed. He was with me for the whole night.*

But had he been? Kate had slept for several hours. Was it conceivable that Anderton could have left her sleeping, crept out and... Surely not. It was impossible.

Other memories were creeping back. What had Anderton said when he walked her home? *There's a man who kills women on the loose in this town.* And Kate had queried the use of the plural. Why had he said 'women,' not woman? Only one woman had been killed then. She'd even said as much to him.

Kate groaned. What she was thinking was impossible. Surely it was impossible. There was no way that Anderton could have left her room, driven to the factory wastelands, somehow lured Claudia there and killed her, returning in time to be there, naked in bed, when Kate woke up. Surely not?

Kate was pacing again. She stopped dead, suddenly struck by a thought that was so devastating that she thought she might faint. She sat down hurriedly on the edge of the bed again.

What if it was both of them? Anderton *and* Jerry? Of course they would have rock solid alibis for some of the murders if the other one was committing them.

What you're thinking is madness.

Kate picked up her phone again and brought up Olbeck's number. On the verge of ringing it, she hesitated. Now that her imagination had begun working overtime, she saw News of the World headlines, tabloid fever. Was it possible that her phone was tapped? Had someone been leaking information to the media? She thought of the scrum of photographers that they'd driven through yesterday.

In the end, she sent him a text that read: *need to see you here at Jerry's URGENTLY. Can't talk over phone. COME HERE ASAP!*

After she put the phone back in her pocket, Kate stood for a moment in the middle of Jerry's fetid bedroom, hugging her arms across her body. Despite the dusty, prickling heat of the room, she felt cold. She could feel her lungs fluttering within her, her breath coming in short, tight bursts.

Realising she was three steps away from a panic attack, she forced herself to sit down again on the edge of the bed, drop her head forward and breathe deeply, in through her nose and out through her mouth. She kept this up until her hammering heart had slowed a little and she felt very slightly calmer. The buzzing in her ears receded.

The house seemed very quiet. Kate sat for a moment longer, trying to keep hold of the momentary calmness. Now that the thoughts in her head had settled a little, she became more aware of her surroundings, the dust flying in the shafts of sunlight that lanced through the gap in the dirty curtains. The smell of the room filled her nostrils. A thought struck her which made her heartbeat speed up again to alarming levels.

What if there were more bodies in the house?

Kate leapt up, her hand to her mouth. Her imagination was flying again, bringing up all sorts of hideous pictures. She thought again of tabloid headlines, pictures of erstwhile normal suburban houses that had concealed a raft of horrors. Would the paparazzi be camped outside this innocuous-looking Victorian terrace tomorrow morning? Of course they would. Perhaps they were already on their way. But how could they be?

Kate no longer knew what she actually knew or what she had conjectured. She felt dizzy with the enormity of what had happened. Where the hell was Olbeck? She breathed in sharply, and the room smelt even ranker than it had before. Kate backed away from the bed, eyeing the dark space beneath it. She stood for a moment, indecisively, wringing her sweaty hands. She knew she should look under the bed. She knew she should, but she quailed from the idea. Although it was unusual, she was afraid to look. *Come on, Kate. What could be as bad as what you're imagining?*

She took a deep breath, almost gagged and dropped to her knees with a thump, peering into the murk, sweating with fear. There was nothing under the bed but clumps of dust and hairs, an empty shoe box and a plastic biro. Nothing there. Kate sat back up, her in-held breath rushing out in one long sigh.

She checked her phone. Nothing from Olbeck. Nothing from Anderton. Her fevered speculation about her boss was beginning to die away. Surely it was too ludicrous a thought even to be entertained?

All of a sudden, Kate knew she had to get out of the house. Another minute here in this fetid, dusty atmosphere would see her lose the plot. She hurried downstairs, prickling with fear, terrified of what she might see in the corner of her eye. She closed and locked the front door behind her and stood for a moment on the porch, taking in great gulps of fresh air.

Her relief at being outside the house was so great that it took her a moment or two to realise that someone was talking to her, addressing her by name.

"—Redman?"

Kate blinked. The woman speaking to her from the pavement was vaguely familiar, but Kate's current emotional state was such that she couldn't place her. After a moment, thankfully, her memory returned.

"Hello, Miss Paling."

Margaret Paling was looking at her curiously.

"What brings you hear, dear?"

"Do you live near here?" asked Kate, countering with a question. Margaret waved a hand at the row of houses opposite.

"My house is over there. Number Fifteen. This is Jerry's Hindley's house, isn't it? Didn't he mention we were neighbours?"

Had he? Kate felt so battered by the revelations of the past hour that she couldn't remember.

Margaret was still looking at her with concern.

"Are you all right, dear? You're as white as a sheet. Quite as white as a sheet."

Kate opened her mouth to say 'I'm fine,' but somehow the words wouldn't come out properly.

"Why don't you come over and have a cup of tea?" asked Margaret. "Or a glass of water, or something. Seriously, dear, you look like you're about to faint."

Kate opened her mouth again to refuse politely and then

thought better of it. If this woman was Jerry's neighbour, it was possible she might have witnessed something. *At the very least*, Kate thought, *I'll be able to find out a little bit more about Jerry's background.*

"Yes, I will. Thank you."

Chapter Seventeen

Number Fifteen, Smithson Street, was almost a carbon-copy of Jerry's house in age, layout, décor and furnishing, except it was considerably cleaner and had none of the masculine accoutrements lying about. Margaret ushered Kate through the main hallway into a neat and tidy kitchen and sat her down at the table. She kept up a stream of inconsequential chatter as she prepared the tea, the words washing over Kate in a rather soothing stream that she barely heard. The kettle boiled and the water was poured into a fine china teapot to brew. Margaret handed Kate a plate of biscuits.

"I think you should have one of those, dear. Sugar's very good if you're feeling a bit shaky."

She hadn't yet asked what had so upset Kate. Kate wasn't sure what she was going to say if Margaret did ask the question.

The tea was hot and strong, and Kate drank it gratefully.

"Do you know Jerry well?" she asked.

"Not very well, I must say. We're neighbourly. Friendly but not *friends*, if you see what I mean." Margaret took a sip from her own cup. "How is he? We've all been rather worried about him."

"Oh, you know he's in hospital?"

"Yes, Mrs Culson at Number Nine told me yesterday. Poor man, he's not had a good year, what with his bereavement and everything else."

"Bereavement?"

"Yes, dear. His mother died, oh, it must be six months ago now. Terribly hard, isn't it, when you lose a family member? I lost my own mother last year, and it does take a while to get over it."

"I'm sorry," said Kate automatically. She was going to say "I didn't know" and then realised how callous and ridiculous that sounded. How could she not have known Jerry lost his mother? Why hadn't anyone told her?

The knowledge of what Jerry had done thumped her in the stomach again, and she put the remainder of her biscuit down on the little plate in front of her.

Margaret Paling chatted on.

"Of course, it's hard being on your own. I had Jerry over for dinner a few times, and I think it helped. He's always struck me as a bit of a lonely person. Very much keeps to himself."

The stuff of cliché: the quiet killer, the respectable murderer. Kate felt a hysterical giggle rise up inside her, and she coughed, a hand to her mouth. For a horrible second, she thought she wouldn't be able to control herself – she could feel raucous laughter rising up her throat – and she swallowed, crookedly, which hurt and helped to push the feeling down.

She wasn't sure Margaret had noticed. The other woman was engaged in pouring out the last drops of tea into Kate's cup.

Kate swallowed, and then swallowed again and cleared her throat.

"Have you lived here long?" she asked, once she could be sure of her voice.

Margaret set the empty pot back on the table.

"Around here? My whole life, dear. My mother and father bought this house before the war, I believe. I was actually born here."

"That's nice," said Kate, automatically. She wanted to check her phone to see if Olbeck or Anderton had tried to contact her, but she couldn't think of a way to do it without looking rude.

"Yes, I've seen a lot of changes in the town over the years. Not always for the better either. But never mind me. I'm just an old woman stuck in my ways."

Kate smiled again and did a sort of half shake of the head. What was there to say to a remark like that? An agreement was rude and a negation didn't sound right either.

"You're looking a wee bit better," said Margaret. "Now, would you like some more tea? Or I can make coffee, if you prefer?"

Kate managed a smile.

"You're very kind," she said, "But please don't worry. That cup did me good, and that's all I needed, thank you."

"That's no problem. Happy to help."

Margaret stood up.

"Now, would you excuse me for a moment, dear? I have to go to the little girl's room."

For some reason she giggled, a rather odd, girlish sound. Kate nodded and smiled automatically, her mind on something else.

When Margaret had left the room, Kate sat, trying to pin down what it was that was making her uneasy. Something that Margaret had said, just now. What was it? Something... something about *coffee*. That was it. What was it about coffee that was important?

Kate stared ahead, her fingers unconsciously tapping the table. Coffee and Rav – something Rav had said. What the hell was it? After a moment of blankness, the memory returned. Rav and she had been sitting in the car, and she'd wanted to stop for a coffee. That was it. Rav had joked about her throwing a drink in his face, because she'd done that to Jerry the night before. What an idiot she'd been.

Kate frowned, unsure of why her brain was telling her this was so important. Then comprehension dawned. After he'd joked about the coffee, Rav had said something about going clubbing: *that he and Jerry and the others had been at a club all night*. Hadn't he said something about it being daylight by the time they left? That was the night Claudia Smith was killed. How could Jerry have killed her when he was with the other officers at a nightclub for the entire night?

For a moment, Kate felt as if her brain had actually given way under the strain. If Jerry hadn't killed Claudia, then who had? Who had killed the other women? Who?

Kate came back to reality with a start, unsure of how long she'd been sitting at the table, staring into space and drumming her fingers on the edge. She looked around. The house seemed very silent. Where had Margaret gone?

Kate got up and stretched. It was time for her to go, but she should say goodbye first. She went out into the hallway and looked around, listening for sounds of movement. There was nothing. Kate hesitated. There was a tiny thread of uneasiness running through her, some almost subconscious sense of something not being quite right. Was it something else that Margaret had said?

Kate began to climb the stairs, thinking hard. Something about Margaret that rang another faint bell. What was it? For a moment, Kate feared she had actually gone mad, the fear and strain of the past few hours taking their toll. Was she being paranoid? She climbed further, treading softly, the old polished wood of the banister sliding smoothly under her palm.

Kate reached the top of the stairs. Through a half-open door to the right, she could see the edge of a bath, a sink, a tiled floor. That was the bathroom, but it looked empty. Where was Margaret? Had she actually come upstairs?

Kate shifted from foot to foot, standing at the top of the stairs. The old floorboards creaked under her feet. That sense of uneasiness was growing – in fact, it was almost fear. What was there to be afraid of? Was it the silent house, the disappearance of her hostess – or something else?

Beyond the bathroom door was another door. Kate tiptoed towards it and pushed it gently open. It opened into what was obviously the master bedroom. Kate hesitated in the doorway, unsure of what she was doing or what she would find. The room was empty, the double bed made neatly with a pink candlewick bedspread tucked across it. At the far wall was a small, wooden dressing table with an adjustable mirror on the top. On the surface of the dressing table, on a white lace doily, was a small, wooden jewellery box.

As soon as Kate saw it, she knew what she'd been thinking of. *Brooches.* Margaret's rhinestone brooch. Without stopping to think, Kate strode forward until she reached the dressing table and lifted the lid of the jewellery box.

A part of her had been expecting what she saw, but still she heard herself gasp. Again, she had that feeling of freefall, something heavy moving downwards through her body, leaving her weak and trembling. The dark interior of the jewellery box could not quite dim the blue shine of the butterfly brooch within it. Kate stared at it, seeing again the bruise on Ingrid Davislova's skin. She could hear the roar of her heartbeat in her ears, pounding like a bass drum, but even beyond that, she was suddenly aware of something, some other sound just on the edge of hearing: a whisper of a footstep in the corridor outside, the faint hiss of an indrawn breath.

Time stood still for a moment. Kate's horrified gaze rose slowly, from the jewellery box to the mirror. There was a flicker in the glass and a dark shape rushed at her from behind, growing larger with terrifying speed.

Already pumped full of adrenaline, Kate's body reacted before her mind did. She darted sideways just as the figure crashed into the dressing table, making the mirror rock back against the wall. As she turned to run, Kate caught sight of her attacker, dressed in an old-fashioned men's suit and hat that shadowed the face.

Despite her shock, Kate was thinking it must be an unknown relative of Margaret's: a son, a brother. Seconds later, the hat fell off as the person rushed forward, and Kate saw the face; it was Margaret's face but it had been distorted, teeth bared, eyes glaring. She was so shocked that she almost didn't register the knife before it came down in a sweeping rush that Kate, feinting right, barely escaped.

Sobbing with fear, Kate turned, scrambling for the door before slamming it shut in Margaret's maniacal face. Kate ran for her life, slipping a little at the turn of the corridor, stumbling down the stairs. Everything had happened so quickly that she was barely aware of anything else besides the overwhelming desire to run. She fell the last three steps, turning her ankle but hardly registering the flash of pain. Above her, she could hear the bedroom door thud back against the wall and Margaret's hissing breath as she ran after Kate. In three bounds, Kate reached the front door, scrabbled for the lock and handle, pulled.

The door was locked.

Kate had time to think about running for the back door, a second's vision of making her escape that way. Then the blow came, a hard punch to the base of her ribs, which drove the breath from her body for an instant. Margaret's body pressed up against hers from behind, pinning her to the door. There was an excruciating moment of pain as the knife went in, a shockingly intimate penetration, and then a dragging heaviness and a blooming dull heat.

Kate thought confusedly, *I'm okay, I'm okay, I've got my stab vest on*, but of course she wasn't on patrol anymore, was she? She wasn't wearing a vest. Margaret was panting loudly in her ear. Kate felt the knife pull back, leaving her body, and she thought, *She's going to stab me again*. Without thinking, she gasped for air and pushed herself backwards, bringing her head back sharply.

The back of her skull connected violently with Margaret's nose. There was a crunch and a muffled scream and then the pressure on Kate was relieved.

Margaret fell backwards, her nose gouting scarlet. Kate turned, feeling a great wash of blood from the wound in her back go flooding through her shirt, warm and wet. She staggered past Margaret, who was scrabbling to get up from the hallway floor, and limped into the first room off the hallway, the living room, before her legs gave way and she thumped down onto the carpet in front of the fire.

I'm going to die here, I'm going to die was the only thought going through her mind. Kate managed to turn over and face the doorway just in time to see Margaret, face streaked with blood, up on her feet and waving the knife. She saw Kate helpless and spread-eagled on the carpet and screamed triumphantly, running forward with the knife, ready to swoop down in the final, fatal blow.

It was Kate's legs that saved her. Strengthened and toned from weeks of training, they kicked not out, but up, catching Margaret on the run and pushing her towards the ceiling so that the momentum of her movement carried her up through the air, above Kate, to crash into the marble mantelpiece. The movement was too quick for her to cry out. Her head hit the mantelpiece, and she dropped like a stone, almost on top of Kate, who managed to roll away a little, screaming herself at the pain in her abdomen as the knife wound opened and the blood flowed.

Gasping, Kate propelled herself backwards on her elbows, pure adrenaline moving her muscles. Margaret lay, crumpled and silent, by the hearth. Kate reached the sofa, tried to pull herself up to a standing position. Was Margaret dead? Where was the knife?

Kate felt for her mobile phone in the back pocket. Every movement exploded with pain and brought with it a fresh flow of blood from the wound. She could feel her vision fogging; greyness began to creep into her line of sight. She managed to grasp the phone, brought it out, dropped it as it slithered through her bloody fingers. Breathing was becoming difficult now. Kate groaned, feeling the blood flowing like a river down her back, down her legs. Her shirt was sodden.

She took every last bit of energy, stood up and staggered to the mantelpiece. Her shaking fingers reached out to grasp the heaviest thing she could reach, a gold-framed black and white photograph. Kate gasped like a fish, took in what little breath she could and hurled the picture as hard as her fading strength would allow at the living room window.

Dimly she heard the crash of falling glass, but before the musical tinkle of the shards landing on the ground outside had faded, Kate felt herself slide forward, sinking to the blood-wet carpet as everything went black.

J's Diary

THE BUTTERFLY BROOCH IS BY my hand while I write. My eye keeps being drawn to it; this small piece of cheap, enamelled metal. I keep seeing portents in everything; the most random things become meaningful. Is this madness? There are those who would say that what I do is madness, but I don't *feel* mad. Quite the opposite. The more I kill, the more I feel in control. The cooler and calmer I get.

Perhaps that's what it's all about after all. Control.

Mother was always the one in control. There was only one time I saw her fearful. That was the day of my first transformation. The butterfly brooch had a part to play there as well; perhaps that's what reminded me.

It was last summer. For some reason, I had gone into Mother's bedroom, and the butterfly brooch was lying in the middle of her dressing table, quite alone. I stood there for several minutes, staring at it. I couldn't have said why.

There was a flicker in the glass of the dressing table mirror, and I looked up and into it to see the reflection of Mother standing in the doorway to her room, staring at me.

There was a moment's silence, oddly loaded. Our gazes met in the mirror. After a few seconds, she dropped her eyes to look at what I'd been staring at.

"Your father bought me that," she said, indicating the brooch with a nod of her white head. "On the day I found out I was pregnant with you and your brother."

I didn't say anything for a moment. John. It was the first time she'd ever acknowledged his existence to me. I was flummoxed, not only by the subject matter, but also by her tone. It was the first time in weeks she'd directed a normal, almost friendly word my way.

She walked up behind me, growing larger in the reflection. Seen side by side, our faces looked very similar despite the difference in our age. I had the strangest impression that she knew that I knew about John, about how he'd died. That she knew that I'd found the story out long before but she'd never mentioned it because she wanted me kept in suspense, in horror at what I'd done. She wanted me to be punished.

She leaned forward, smiling nastily.

"The wrong twin died," she said, almost whispering. I could feel her eyes on my face, greedy for my reaction to her words.

My face reflected nothing. After a moment, bored, she turned away and walked out of the room.

The strangest thing happened. It was as if someone else were standing behind me, as close as Mother had been. As if they stepped forward, into me. My vision blurred. All I could see before me was the hard, bright blue of the butterfly brooch. Rage flooded through me like a welcome fire.

I turned quickly and followed Mother, who was just taking a step downwards at the top of the stairs. My hands went out, but were they my hands, or John's hands? They connected with the small of Mother's back and pushed, just a quick little shove. I can still remember the feel of her birdlike ribcage under my palms for the brief second before she fell. It was the first time I'd touched her in years. She tumbled down, giving one short, sharp cry before she hit the hallway floor in a tangle of withered limbs.

I remained for a moment on the top step. Exhilaration swept

through my bloodstream like a drug; I felt drunk with power. I had killed Mother.

That wasn't quite true. She was still alive when I reached the hallway floor and bent over her. Her face was twisted awkwardly, her mouth opening and shutting like a baby bird's. One grey eye blinked at me.

I leant over, watching her pupil contract. Then I smiled slowly. I backed away towards the front door, step by slow step. She made a small sound of protest, something that wasn't quite a word. Was she trying to say my name? I hadn't heard the word *Margaret* cross her lips in months. I smiled again, smiled and waved a casual goodbye. Then I went outside and locked the front door behind me.

Walking away down the quiet street, I felt my soul grow wings. I knew then that I was able to transform, to become someone different. All it took was the courage to hold death in your hands and reach out and kill. I was trembling with the realisation that *that* was the secret I had looked for for so long.

Chapter Eighteen

THERE WERE VOICES RIGHT ON the edge of hearing, but no discernible words. Just the hum and babble of human speech, heard from some distance away. Then other sounds became recognisable: the rattle of curtain rings, the clank of something metallic, the ringing of a telephone. Kate heard them all without being able to think much about them, and after a time, the noises faded and darkness came back.

When she could hear the sounds again, they were louder and more intrusive. At the same time, she became aware of something else – a warm feeling of pressure on her right hand. She struggled for a moment to open her eyes, and after a few seconds, the blurry image of a ceiling and the top of a green curtain came into view. Kate blinked and her gaze dropped to see the welcome face of Olbeck smiling down at her. It was he who was holding her hand, she realised after another moment.

"Hi," croaked Kate.

"Hello, you." Olbeck leant forward a little, squeezing her hand. "How are you feeling?"

Kate considered.

"Crap."

Olbeck smiled.

"Geez, Kate, I knew you wanted to get out of running the half marathon, but you didn't have to go *this* far."

Kate laughed weakly and then gasped as pain shot through

her. She looked down at herself, fearful of what she would see. A mass of bandages was just visible under the hospital gown she was wearing.

"What happened?"

"Don't you remember?"

Kate blinked and the face of Margaret Paling swam back into view. The gleam of the knife as it came down, the warmth of the blood as it gushed out of her. Kate swallowed.

"I remember."

"That knife missed your lung by an *inch*, Kate. Someone was obviously looking out for you. You lost a lot of blood, but you'll be okay. You just need to rest and get better."

Kate felt the sudden hot surge of tears underneath her eyelids and blinked them away.

"I'll be okay?" she managed.

"You should be. You won't be running any marathons, half or otherwise, for a while."

"Silver lining," Kate said, trying to grin through her tears.

"Jay and Courtney have been here, but they had to go. I thought I'd sit with you for a while."

"Glad – glad you did." Kate was sorry she'd missed her brother and sister. She wanted to ask whether her mother had visited her but decided against it.

"What happened – afterwards?" she asked.

"After the attack?"

"Yes."

"Well, I got your text. I was in the middle of interviewing poor Karen's Brennan's mother, so I couldn't get back to you, and I couldn't leave immediately. I stopped the interview as soon as I decently could, and Anderton and I headed on over to Jerry's place. Of course, we couldn't find you anywhere, and we were starting to get a bit worried when this bloody great shower of glass explodes just down the street."

Kate smiled faintly, remembering hurling the photograph with all the remaining strength that she had. Thank God she had.

"What about Margaret?"

Olbeck looked serious.

"She's dead, Kate."

"I remember," whispered Kate. "She hit her head on the wall, on the fireplace, didn't she?"

"Well, yes. But she also fell on the knife. Talk about hoist by your own petard."

"It was – her though? The killings? She – she did them all?"

Olbeck squeezed her hand again.

"Oh, yes. We've found – well, I won't go into that now. Anderton will come and give you the run down when you're feeling a bit stronger."

"Okay." Kate could feel a heaviness dragging down her eyelids. She forced them open, fighting against a sudden great weariness.

"You're knackered," said Olbeck. "Get some rest. Me and Jeff will be back later."

He kissed her on the forehead, and Kate smiled weakly. She could still feel the warmth of his hand as she fell into unconsciousness.

Some time passed before she became aware of reality again. Like the last time, she heard the sounds of the ward before she opened her eyes, although there was no warmth of another human hand holding hers. Instead she heard her name, quite clearly.

"Kate. Kate."

Kate opened her eyes. Anderton was sitting where Olbeck had sat before.

"Welcome back," he said, smiling.

Kate tried to smile back. In truth, seeing him sat there without touching her, without holding her hand, hurt her almost as much as the healing knife wound.

"How are you feeling?"

"I've been better," said Kate, not wanting his pity.

"You did well."

"I'm just glad we caught hi—" She caught herself. "I mean, I'm glad we caught her. God, that sounds so weird, given the context."

"You're not wrong. The press are having a field day. Britain's first female serial killer and all that."

Kate rolled her eyes.

"What about Rose West? Myra Hindley?"

Anderton nodded.

"Well, there is a precedent, I suppose. But Margaret was killing on her own. Although—" He looked thoughtful. "We found her diaries. You'll have to read them when you're stronger. There's material in there that would keep a team of psychiatrists busy for decades."

He hesitated for moment.

"We found another body in the house. Searched the whole building – took it apart at the seams, obviously, after what happened. The body of a young girl, thin, dark-haired."

"Stabbed with the same knife?"

"That's right. Clearly her first victim. We know from reading her diaries that she killed her mother too. That's what started all this off."

Kate cleared her throat.

"Why did she do it?"

Anderton shrugged.

"Again, Kate, that's one for the psychiatrists. Repressed sexuality? Self-hate? Self-loathing so extreme she created a whole new persona for herself, someone who could kill women and in killing women, act out the rage and shame she had for herself? I don't know. I think it's fitting she went for victims who resembled her mother when she was young."

"Did they also resemble Margaret when she was young?"

Anderton looked startled.

"Now you mention it, that's true. Perhaps that was an element as well."

Kate was thinking.

"Why – why put the bags in Jerry's house?"

Anderton shrugged.

"She did a lot of things to throw us off the scent. Remember the condom lubricant found on Mandy's body? Nice little trick there to make us think it was a man. Well, of course we thought that anyway. Why wouldn't we?"

Kate closed her eyes momentarily. She remembered her frantic speculation on the identity of the killer after she'd found those bags. Jerry – and then Anderton. How *could* she have thought that? *That's something I'll never tell him,* she thought.

"How is Jerry?" she asked out loud.

"Better," said Anderton. Then he hesitated. "A bit better. They think he's going to pull through but…well, I don't think he'll be back at work again. But he is getting better."

"Good," said Kate and was glad she actually meant it. She wondered whether she and Jerry had been in Intensive Care together. Perhaps lying next to one another in beds side by side. What a thought…

"Their mothers were friends," Anderton was saying. "Margaret Paling's mother and Jerry's mother. That's his mother's house of course – he inherited it when she died, he's only been living there for a few months. Margaret had a key to his house which he probably didn't know about. She must have thought he'd make a good scapegoat."

Kate nodded, feeling the pillow rustle against her ears.

"She looked so harmless," she said. "I can't believe I sat across the table from her drinking tea and I had no idea. Not then. She just looked so ordinary."

"Well, that made it so easy for her, didn't it?" said Anderton. "Who on Earth would suspect a respectable elderly woman of these terrible crimes?"

"That's why it was easy for her to get her victims to the canal ground," Kate said, considering. "They trusted her. They wouldn't have been afraid of her."

"Exactly. We can't know what she told them, but I'd imagine it was quite convincing. They wouldn't have suspected her for a moment."

"Perfect disguise," said Kate.

"Exactly."

Kate sighed, thinking of the girls who had died. Could they have been saved? Could the team have done anything different? She had no doubt that there had been mistakes made that had possibly cost lives. She'd have to live with that. *I'm sorry*, she said to Mandy and Claudia and Karen inside her head.

"Thank God we caught her," she said, aloud.

"Indeed. Although, from the pace of the killings, it was likely we'd have caught her sooner rather than later anyway. She was becoming frantic."

"Right."

Anderton smiled faintly.

"That's not to do down your achievement, Kate."

"I didn't do much."

"Nonsense."

Kate couldn't be bothered to argue. She felt weak and ill. Talking about Margaret was bringing up memories of the attack.

Anderton noted her pallor.

"We'll talk about it later, Kate. It's all in hand."

"Thanks," she said, with difficulty.

"You just need to concentrate on getting better. It's not the same without you."

"Isn't it?" asked Kate. Their eyes met and for a second, she felt leap of something within her that lifted her temporarily out of her pain. It only lasted a moment before tiredness began to engulf her again.

"Get some rest," said Anderton, and the tone of his voice was such that Kate found herself smiling as she slid back into sleep. The last thing she was aware of as unconsciousness engulfed her was the warm faint pressure of his fingers as he took her hand.

THE END

ENJOYED THIS BOOK? AN HONEST review left at Amazon, Goodreads, Shelfari and LibraryThing is always welcome and *really* important for indie authors. The more reviews an independently published book has, the easier it is to market it and find new readers.

Sign up to Celina Grace's newsletter here at her website http://www.celinagrace.com for news of new releases, promotions and other goodies. You can unsubscribe at any time and won't be bombarded with emails, promise!

Want more Kate Redman? The new Kate Redman Mystery, **Snarl**, is now available on Amazon.

Snarl (A Kate Redman Mystery: Book 4)

A RESEARCH LABORATORY OPENS ON the outskirts of Abbeyford, bringing with it new people, jobs, prosperity and publicity to the area – as well as a mob of protestors and animal rights activists. The team at Abbeyford police station take this new level of civil disorder in their stride – until a fatal car bombing of one of the laboratory's head scientists means more drastic measures must be taken...

Detective Sergeant Kate Redman is struggling to come to terms with being back at work after long period of absence on sick leave; not to mention the fact that her erstwhile partner Olbeck has now been promoted above her. The stakes get even higher as a multiple murder scene is uncovered and a violent activist is implicated in the crime. Kate and the team must put their lives on the line to expose the murderer and untangle the snarl of accusations, suspicions and motives.

Snarl is the new Kate Redman Mystery from crime writer Celina Grace, author of Hushabye, Requiem and Imago. Available now.

ACKNOWLEDGEMENTS

MANY THANKS TO ALL THE following splendid souls:

Chris Howard for the brilliant cover designs; Brenda Errichiello for editing and proofreading; Kathy McConnell for extra proofreading; lifelong Schlockers and friends David Hall, Ben Robinson and Alberto Lopez; Ross McConnell for advice on police procedural and for also being a great brother; Kathleen and Pat McConnell, Anthony Alcock, Naomi White, Mo Argyle, Lee Benjamin, Bonnie Wede, Sherry and Amali Stoute, Cheryl Lucas, Georgia Lucas-Going, Steven Lucas, Loletha Stoute and Harry Lucas, Helen Parfect, Helen Watson, Emily Way, Sandy Hall, Kristýna Vosecká; and of course my patient and ever-loving Chris, Mabel, Jethro and Isaiah.

Printed in Great Britain
by Amazon

52663149R00288